PRAISE FOR VIKING VENGEANCE

"From one exciting event to the next, these characters really attract trouble! The one-legged race description is a hoot. And what hilarious competition-level names. The handling of a moral dilemma is admirable. I enjoyed all the adventure's details, most of which **I did not see coming**. This story was a trip I **thoroughly enjoyed**. Well done!" *Judge, 27th Annual Writer's Digest Self-Published Book Awards.*

"Pulls the readers into the story and keeps them engaged . . . **masterfully woven**." *Amazon Reader, Barbara B.*

"The books are **wonderful to read**! Keep them coming!" *Amazon Reader, Susan G.*

"**What a ride!** Filled with action and adventure and suspense, it's the characters who make this story. I care about what happens to these story people almost as much as I care what happens to my friends. **I'm hooked on the series!**" *Amazon Reader, Clio B.*

"A solid thriller filled with charismatic characters. A **FINALIST** and highly recommended." *2019 The Wishing Shelf Book Awards*

Would you risk losing everything for a chance at something better?

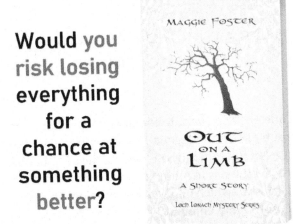

MAGGIE FOSTER

OUT ON A LIMB

A SHORT STORY

Loch Lonach Mystery Series

The Beverwyck Homestead inhabitants were used to harsh winter weather. Not so the visitors from Texas. When Jim Mackenzie and Ginny Forbes decide to take a Sunday afternoon stroll in the pristine wonderland outside their windows, they find their nerves and their wits tested. Lovely to look at, nature can't always be trusted and they find themselves literally out on limb, with death only an icy misstep away.

SIGN ME UP!

https://dl.bookfunnel.com/et9yw1y0qw

Click to join the Loch Lonach Community.

Get a **FREE** Short Story and access to insider news, Scottish lore, and entertaining details about life on the Loch Lonach Homestead.

Viking Vengeance

Loch Lonach
Book Three

DEDICATION

This work, the third in the series, is dedicated to the law enforcers of Texas and the wider world. Your courage, integrity, and dedication to justice inspire me daily.

In addition, I wish to thank:
- The Firewheel Fictionistas Writers' Group for their continued support and assistance
- Members of the Scottish community here and across the world, in particular, the cordial Nova Scotians I met while doing research for this volume
- My content experts and beta readers
- My long-suffering editor and brainstorming partner, Mary Foster Hutchinson, without whom none of these books would have been possible

ACKNOWLEDGMENTS

The Mackenzie Dress Clan Tartan is listed as WR1981 on the Scottish Tartans World Register.

Vengeance quote – "*The Lay of the Last Minstrel*" by Sir Walter Scott, Canto First, Verse IX, lines 7-10.

Vengeance definition – "A Dictionary of the English Language" published on 15 April 1755 and written by Samuel Johnson. Also found in the revised edition on page 800 of "Dictionary of the English Language" (1839) by Samuel Johnson.

The noble friend/enemy quote is from Chapter XIV, "*The Last Battle*" by C.S. Lewis (1956) NY: Macmillan

PR UNCIAL FONT

The Celtic font used on the covers, in the titles, and for the chapter headings in this series is PR Uncial, created by Peter Rempel. It has been a continuing source of delight throughout this endeavor and I am happy to have this opportunity to tell him so. It is free for personal use. You can download it here: https://www.dafont.com/pr-uncial.font

INSTALLING PR UNCIAL

Starting in 2018, Amazon released an update to its Kindle e-readers allowing the user to install custom fonts. Here is the link to the article with instructions on how to do that:
https://the-digital-reader.com/2019/01/02/how-to-use-kindles-new-custom-font-feature/

For Kobo e-readers, the instructions are here: https://goodereader.com/blog/e-book-news/how-to-add-custom-fonts-to-your-kobo-e-reader

DISCLAIMER:

Dear Readers:

This is a work of fiction. That means it is full of lies, half-truths, mistakes, and opinions. Any resemblance to any actual person, living or dead, is unintended and purely coincidental.

Similarly, the businesses, organizations, and political bodies are mere figments of the author's overactive imagination and are not in any way intended to represent any actual business, organization, group, etc.

Neither is this story intended as a travelogue. The locations mentioned in this book exist as of this writing, but the reader is warned that the author has re-shaped Heaven and Earth and all the mysteries of God to suit herself and begs the reader, for the sake of the story, to overlook any discrepancies in fact.

VIKING VENGEANCE

LOCH LONACH MYSTERIES
BOOK THREE

by Maggie Foster

"Vengeance, deep-brooding o'er the slain
Had lock'd the source of softer woe;
And burning pride, and high disdain,
Forbade the rising tear to flow"

The Lay of the Last Minstrel
by Sir Walter Scott

"Revenge is an act of passion; vengeance of justice. Injuries are revenged – crimes are avenged. This distinction is perhaps not always preserved."

Samuel Johnson

Cover design by M. Hollis Hutchinson

Foster, Maggie.
     Viking vengeance: Loch Lonach mysteries, book three / Maggie
     Foster

ISBN (pbk)
     ISBN-13: 978-0-9989858-2-4
     ISBN-10: 0-9989858-2-1

ISBN (epub)
     ISBN-13: 978-0-9989858-5-5

Fonts used by permission/license. For sources, please visit
lochlonach.com

EVERYONE KNOWS

Some laws are made to be broken.
The trick is knowing which – and when.

CAST OF CHARACTERS

Ginny Forbes	An ICU nurse
Sinia Forbes	Ginny's mother
Jim Mackenzie	An Emergency Room physician
Angus Mackenzie ("Himself")	The Laird of Loch Lonach, Jim's grandfather
Charles Monroe	A grieving husband and father
Hue Tran	A Dallas Police Crimes Against Persons Unit Detective
Gregory Gordon	The Laird of the Beverwyck Homestead, a psychiatrist

Loch Lonach is a Scottish community established before Texas became a Republic in the geographic region that would become Dallas. It has retained its culture and identity. Loch Lonach boasts its own schools, police force, churches, and other civic institutions. The head of the community is the Laird, currently Angus Mackenzie.

Chapter 1

Tuesday Night
Loch Lonach

Ginny Forbes threw her airsaid over her shoulder and hurried after the men. Period costume was not required for the Up-Helly-Aa, but a fair number of outsiders attended and it was permitted to show up in eighteenth century Scottish clothing. After all, the men got to wear their kilts. Why shouldn't the women have some fun?

The March of the Loch Lonach Men had begun at sunset, more than two hours earlier. It started on the outskirts of the community and had gone from house to house picking up the troops as it went. The participants had also indulged in a variety of pick-me-ups before, during, and after joining the parade and the atmosphere was most decidedly cheerful.

The skirl of pipes filled the darkening air between the land and the sky. It was deliciously intoxicating, causing the men to stride and the kilts to swing in a rhythm guaranteed to stir the blood. Each of the men bore a flaming torch, wore his claymore on his hip, and had a *sgian dubh* tucked into his sock. Three of them were also armed with bows and arrows.

Fire festivals in the dead of winter took many forms, some of them violent, all edged in fear, but this version was relatively modern and owed more to Hollywood than to Sol, the ancient

Norse goddess of light. All were invited to help build the Viking long ship that rode at anchor on Loch Lonach. The construction started in December and the crews worked hard to make sure the ship was finished by the last Tuesday in January. On that night the ship, anchored off shore to minimize the danger, was ceremoniously burned.

There was no special reason to light the fire using flaming arrows, other than it was really fun to watch. Those who held the bows had competed for the honor and would be roundly praised (and given drink to quench their thirsts) far into the night.

Ginny glanced at the sky, hoping the rain would hold off until they had retired to the Cooperative Hall for the singing, dancing, and celebrating that followed the burning. She found a vantage point on a small rise, and watched as the men ranged themselves along the shore.

The elegantly curved vessel could be seen intermittently, the moon emerging from the billowing clouds, and pouring colorless light on the loch, then slipping behind the veil and plunging the scene into torch-lit shadow once more.

Ginny watched as the three bowmen lit the rag-wrapped tips of their arrows and took aim. There was no signal. Each bowman let loose as he saw fit, aiming at the square sail, a piece of canvas soaked in something the fire marshal would have classified as an accelerant. The crowd held its breath, watching the fire catch hold, then begin to spread, the fabric dripping flame onto the deck of the ship.

The wind was rising and the sail flapped suddenly in the shifting air. Ginny could hear the crack of canvas, then a crackle as the deck caught fire.

"Oh!" The crowd sighed as the flames began to lick up the mast. As if the sound was a signal, the watchers erupted with excited chatter and laughter, then shrieks of joy from the children as the vessel became a bonfire.

Ginny stood watching, her mouth open, her eyes glued to the spectacle. She was vaguely aware of the dampness hitting her face, but the sensation was so *exactly* right that she ignored it. This was atavistic delight in its purest form, three of the classical elements (air, water, and fire) embracing the wooden sacrifice before them.

The flames roared, leaping higher, and now the crowd was having to look up to see the tops of the flames, and in that same moment, the heavens opened up and let loose a deluge.

Ginny shrieked and grabbed her airsaid. She threw the heavy wool over her head and held it up, using it to ward off the rain while she raced to her car. She slid into the driver's seat and slammed the door against the downpour.

Dripping, but out of the wind, she put the car in gear and drove across the park to the Cooperative Hall. The rain would not stop the party. Nor was there any danger of the fire getting loose, despite the rough wind. There was too much water both above and below the boat for it to do anything other than sink. Ditto the torches. She had heard them hissing out as she turned and ran.

She was not the first to reach the hall. The musicians had stayed behind, to warm up, and there were some who had chosen not to follow the procession. Ginny found the ceilidh already underway.

Ginny unbelted her airsaid and hung it over the coat rack. This left her momentarily tartanless, but still in shirt and skirt carefully designed for dancing. She helped herself to hot spiced something-or-other, then joined a swaying line of revelers singing loudly (on key and in surprisingly good voice), the words familiar and the martial sentiments stirring.

By the time the musicians had finished this set, the crowd had gathered from the soggy fields and the party was in full swing. By the time it broke up again, the rain had stopped and the moon could be seen, peeking out from behind the scudding clouds, washed and brilliant and silent in its ancient knowledge of the ways of man.

* * *

They had gone. All of them. The marchers, the women, the children, the old and the young, Scots and spectators. They had all gone. All except him.

The rain came down in torrents and lightning flashed, searing the image into his mind, and threatening to strike him dead. Not that he cared. The ship burned still, the flames abated, but not gone, not yet.

He watched as the vessel fell apart, the mast first, then amidships, then pieces of the decking. The wood roared and cracked and smelled of hot resin and dripping smoke. There was a faint odor of something else, too. Something unexpected.

The rain continued, settling in, a soaking rain, not as hard as the first barrage. The lightning went, too, leaving the loch in deep shadow beyond the flames. The darkness grew as the flames died, leaving him empty, spent.

When it was gone, when the last of the ship had slipped beneath the surface of the loch and the only disturbance was the sound of rain hitting the water, he turned his back and headed for the parking lot.

He saw no one, though he looked. Decent folk were indoors on a night like this. It was too cold for comfort, the cover of darkness cold comfort for a soul in torment.

* * *

CHAPTER 2

Wednesday
Loch Lonach

No one on the edge of the loch the next morning was moving very fast. Even those who had not stayed until they were thrown out last night had signs on them of the success of the party. They were cheerful, just somnolent, or sated, or simply conserving energy against future need, Ginny among them.

Loch Lonach and the park that surrounded it belonged to the city of Dallas. As a condition of being allowed to hold the Up-Helly-Aa there each year, the Scots promised to clean up promptly. More than thirty volunteers were therefore walking along the shoreline, pulling bits of half-burned Viking ship off the grass and depositing them either in plastic bags or a pickup truck that rolled along beside them. Ginny and her best friend, Caroline, walked side by side, eyes down, intent on the task.

"Too bad about the rain," Caroline said. "There's a whole lot more debris than usual and some of it isn't ours."

Ginny shrugged. "I don't mind. It was worth it." She smiled at the memory.

"Some of this must have come down river from the watershed."

"I'm sure you're right, but that piece is clearly ours." Ginny pointed to a curved section of hull rocking gently against the shore. The blackened timbers had come to rest in a spot where the current swirled, creating a heavily undercut span of bank.

They had to climb down to get to it. Caroline got there first. She put her hand under a plank and tried to lift it, then cried out, starting backwards, tripping over a root, and ending up in the water, her face white with shock.

"Caroline! What's wrong?"

She pointed a shaking finger at the wreckage.

Ginny turned to look. The fire must have been put out too soon to reach this part of the boat. There was superficial damage to the timbers, but they retained their shape and the joins were still in place.

Likewise, the thing that nestled in the curve of the bow retained its shape and distinctive features. The skull was black in places, where the skin had been charred, and white in others where the flesh had gone completely. Hair still clung to half of the scalp and the mandible on that side retained threads of sinew. The jaw swayed in the moving water, giving the unpleasant impression the skull was chewing. Ginny gulped, then turned and helped Caroline to her feet.

"Come on."

They climbed the bank and flagged down the pickup truck.

"What's up, ladies?"

Ginny took a breath to steady herself. "Can you tell me if the Laird is here?"

"I'll ask." The driver, one of the bowmen from the previous night, pulled out a phone. Caroline found a dry spot to sit down on and Ginny joined her. A moment later the driver approached them.

"Himself hasn't left yet, but he says his grandson is here and will that do?"

Ginny nodded. "Yes, he will do. Thank you."

The driver relayed the message and closed the connection.

He looked from them to the shore then back.

"What did you find?" he asked.

"Have a look."

He made his way down to the water's edge, stood for several minutes, then came back and sat down on the grass beside them.

"Deid afore?" he asked, dropping into the broad Scots that often accompanied times of stress within the community.

"I sincerely hope so."

They waited in silence until a car pulled up and Jim Mackenzie got out. He looked the group over, his eyes narrowing. "What's happened?"

The archer nodded in the direction of the shoreline. "We found something." He led the way down to the edge of the water, then stepped back.

Ginny's eyes followed Jim. He stared at the grisly discovery for a moment, then took out his phone and placed a call. She heard the driver asking, "What should we do?"

"Tell everyone just to stop and stay where they are until we get this sorted out."

"Right."

The driver climbed into his truck and drove off. Ginny could hear him calling to the next group of volunteers. The news would spread, and swiftly.

Jim settled down on the ground between Ginny and Caroline, putting an arm around each one.

"Come here."

It wasn't until she could feel his warmth beside her that Ginny realized how cold she was. She could hear him murmuring to Caroline, asking her questions, getting whispered responses, then, slowly, stronger ones. Ginny closed her eyes and relaxed against him, falling into a sort of limbo. Waiting. Until the police arrived.

The local police canceled the clean-up, saying they needed to examine every bit of evidence, then recanted and asked the volunteers to help them identify which pieces of flotsam were part of the Viking longboat.

Someone went out for lunch and brought back pizza. The truck driver set up a ferry service to the local facilities. Several searchers called for backup and the reinforcements arrived bringing jackets and hot coffee.

Himself showed up about forty minutes after Jim had. Ginny watched as he climbed out of his car, then surveyed the scene, noting Jim in conversation with a police officer, and the two women still sitting on the ground, now wrapped in blankets. He came over and spoke to them.

"How are ye lasses?"

"We're fine," Caroline said.

"Caroline needs dry clothes and something hot to drink and I could use a jacket." Ginny tended to think in terms of specifics when it came to first aid. She saw Jim's head swivel toward them as she spoke, then back to the policeman.

"Would you be willing to let me go get my car?" she asked. "I've got jackets and another blanket in my trunk."

Himself nodded. "I'll ask the officer for leave."

Ginny put her arm around Caroline's shoulders. "I don't care what that policeman says. You need to get out of those wet clothes before you catch a cold."

Caroline was shivering under the thin blanket and Ginny pulled her closer. Having come up with a plan, she was anxious to put it into action and was on the point of acting without permission when Jim suddenly broke free and came over, pulling them both to their feet.

"Come on. I am to escort you home to change, then to the police station to complete your statements."

By the time they were finished giving their statements, it

was late afternoon. Jim took Caroline home, then headed for Ginny's house. He glanced over at her. "Are you all right?"

She nodded. "It was a bit of a shock, but not the worst I've ever seen."

"Well, I'm sorry to hear *that*."

She caught his eye. "You realize what this means? Whoever put him there had access to the Viking long ship while it was being built."

"That had already occurred to me."

"Which means one of the Homesteaders is a murderer."

"Maybe not. Anyone can help build the ship and no one keeps records of who comes and goes. It could have been an outsider."

Ginny shook her head. "No one could stick something the size of a full grown man into the hull of the ship in broad daylight without being seen. It was someone who had access to the boat after dark."

"It's still possible the person who put the body in the boat didn't kill him. We don't know how he died."

Jim pulled the car to a stop in front of her house, then turned to face her, one eyebrow raised. "This makes three since October. You seem to be a corpse magnet."

Ginny gave him a dirty look. "I didn't find him, Caroline did. And allow me to point out that none of this started until *you* showed up."

"True. Well, at least it wasn't your ICU this time."

"Nor is it my responsibility."

"Maybe not, but I'll bet you end up investigating anyway."

Ginny opened the door and got out, then gave him an exceptionally bland look. "We'll see about that!"

* * *

Friday
Cooperative Hall

It was Friday night and Ginny sat alone at one of the many tables along the back portion of the hall, staring into her drink, thinking about the body in the Viking long ship.

He hung like Banquo's ghost over the community, demanding justice. The police had spent the rest of Wednesday sending divers to the bottom of the lake, finding the other pieces of the corpse. Someone had seen the autopsy, or knew someone who had. It said the aorta had been severed, cut all the way through in a single stroke.

The cause of death was listed as exsanguination, so he hadn't been alive when the archers let loose the flaming arrows. All three had been stoic, but all had been relieved to hear it.

The police had talked to everyone involved in building the ship. The Committee had supplied lists of volunteers. The Laird and the Parks Department had explained about access to the grounds and permits for building, launching, and sinking the ship. The space allocated to the actual construction had been carefully searched for clues. It was all very disturbing.

Sunk deep in her own thoughts, Ginny was slow to realize there was another person sitting in the back of the room, but he was no longer sober, and no longer silent. She lifted her eyes and looked over at him. Charles Monroe was having trouble steering his cup to his lips, spilling some down his front as she watched, brushing at it with a shaking hand, then trying to put the mug down and spilling that.

Ginny felt her heart twist as she looked at him. She knew his story. They all did. Only twenty-seven and a widower. His young wife and two small daughters had been killed by a drunk driver six months ago.

He normally wasn't this bad. She was trying to decide whether she should do something when another man approached. Geordie Hamilton took the mug away then put one of Charlie's arms around his shoulders and hoisted him to his feet. Ginny watched the two of them make their unsteady way across the room and out the door. When she turned back she saw Jim approaching.

"Was that Charles Monroe?"

She nodded. "He's getting worse."

"Himself was talking to the counsel about it last week."

Ginny sighed heavily. "Poor man. My heart goes out to him."

Jim nodded. "But crawling into a bottle is not the answer."

"I know that." Very well, in fact. She'd been tempted to do the same when the truth about her former boyfriend got out. She'd been stared at and whispered about and very nearly pushed over the edge by the solicitous busy-bodies in the Loch Lonach community.

She had taken to hiding from them for a while, even missing some of the ceilidhs. That had brought Himself to her doorstep and they'd had a talk about handling adversity. Not a very comfortable talk either.

"Come on," Jim said. "Himself requests the pleasure of your company." He held out his hand.

Such invitations could not be refused. Ginny rose and let Jim escort her into the presence of her Laird.

* * *

CHAPTER 3

Saturday
Loch Lonach Park

Saturday morning dawned fine so Ginny decided to go for a walk in the park. Typical for a weekend, there were numerous runners, walkers, and cyclists on the trail; a handful of preteens on the concrete tubes; a dozen tots, with accompanying parents, on the playground; and a lone man seated at the picnic table nearby. She realized with a start that she knew the man. It was Charles Monroe.

Well, the last thing she wanted to do was disturb Charlie. He would either be drunk again (or still) or hungover. Not good company either way. She started to turn away, but a movement caught her eye and she looked back in time to see him pull a gun out of his pocket and lay it on the table in front of him, his eyes on the playground.

Ginny felt her mouth go dry. He couldn't mean to hurt the children, surely? He was weeping, his shoulders shaking, his hands lifting, then lowering the gun.

She pulled out her phone and dialed 9-1-1, reported her suspicions, then turned the device off, and stowed it in her pocket. She needed no distractions for what she was planning to do.

She headed toward the picnic shelter, approaching him

from the side, making sure she was visible. She stopped at the edge of the concrete.

"Charlie?"

He glanced over at her, then looked back at the children.

"How are you, Charlie?" She stepped under the roof of the shelter and walked very slowly toward him. He didn't answer, but he did look up. His eyes followed her as she walked around to the other side of the table and slid into place across from him.

She held his gaze. "What's the gun for, Charlie?"

His eyes brimmed with tears. "For me."

Ginny sighed. "I cannot imagine how badly it must hurt to think of your family."

He shuddered with the grief, his face contorted. "Today is Annie's birthday. She would have been three."

Ginny reached across the table. "I'm so sorry!"

He picked up both of his hands, the gun still clutched in the right, and covered his face with them, sobbing. Ginny waited. He took a gasping breath and wiped his eyes with the back of his sleeve.

"I can't live without Mandy. I can't function anymore. I can't sleep. I can't work. I can't do anything. What's the point of trying?" He put the gun to his head.

Ginny kept her voice low. "You don't want to do that, Charlie."

He closed his eyes and his finger tightened on the trigger.

"Charlie." She softened her voice further, trying to stay calm, for him and for herself. "Those little children over there, some of them are the same age as Annie and Beth. Think. If you hurt yourself, they will look over here. Would you want Annie and Beth to see a man covered in blood? Would you want that for them?"

He opened his eyes and looked at her. "No."

"Put the gun back down on the table and let's talk. We can figure this out."

He shook his head. "No. We can't."

Something in the tone of his voice made Ginny pause. "Why not?" she asked.

"Because I killed him."

Ginny was momentarily disoriented. "Killed who?"

"The man in the boat. He killed my family so I killed him. There's no life for me here anymore."

Ginny felt her stomach knot as the image of the half-burned man rose in her mind's eye. Just yesterday she had told Jim this was not her responsibility. She didn't have to stay. She could leave, let Charlie shoot himself, or be taken by the police and dealt with however they saw fit.

Or she could try to help.

Charles Monroe was one of their own, the victim of both a heinous crime that took the lives of his wife and children, and a miscarriage of justice that released the culprit back onto the streets of Dallas with no punishment, and no way to prevent him from killing again. She could not condone Monroe's act, but she could understand it.

She heard sirens approaching and pulled herself together. It wasn't her place to judge. The Loch Lonach council could send him back to the police, if they decided that was the best solution, or deal with him themselves. They had the authority. She had none.

She leaned across the table and put her hand on Charlie's gun arm.

"Charlie! Can you hear me? LISTEN to me! Say nothing about the dead man. NOTHING. Do you hear me?"

He swallowed and nodded. "I hear you. Why?"

"I want to talk to Himself before the police find out. Can you keep your mouth shut for a little while?"

He nodded, lowering the gun and laying it back down on the table, the muzzle still pointed in Ginny's direction. She pulled her hand back. The police were already on their way up the hill, moving fast.

"Okay. Here's what you say. You tell them you were planning to kill yourself because of the grief. You couldn't stand it any longer. Got that?"

He nodded.

"They'll take you to the hospital. You cooperate with them."

He nodded again.

"Remember, Say NOTHING else. We'll find you."

"Put the gun down!" The police officer had his service weapon trained on Charlie's right ear.

"Let go of the weapon," Ginny said.

Charlie blinked, then did as she said, allowing the gun to slip from his fingers. The police officer moved in swiftly to secure it. As soon as that was done, others approached from the far side of the pavilion and took him into custody.

Ginny sat without moving, waiting for instructions from the police.

"Are you all right, miss?"

She nodded.

They marched Charlie off, locking him in the rear of the patrol car, then settled down to take her statement.

Ginny told them what she had decided they needed to hear. She had seen the gun, called for help, and intervened, talking him down until they arrived. He was here because this was where he would have been to celebrate the birthday of his dead daughter. Here he could feel the anguish of what he had lost and that pain would carry him through to his suicide. He needed mental health care. She was fine.

It was almost two hours before they were through and released her to go home. She hurried back to her car, pulled her phone out to tell her mother what was going on, and found a message waiting for her. She looked at it in surprise.

She got hold of her mother and let her know. "I've been summoned."

"When do you have to be there?"

"Ten minutes."

"Then you'd better go straight over. You can tell me all about it later."

"Yes ma'am." Ginny turned the car around. If she didn't get held up in traffic, she would just make it.

* * *

Saturday Afternoon
Cooperative Hall

Jim sat off to the side, here at the Laird's request, but sworn to silence. He'd gotten a call from Himself and been told what Ginny had done at the park. He'd come, of course, dropping everything and hurrying over.

He watched as Ginny walked the length of the hall and came to rest six feet in front of his grandfather.

"Virginia Forbes."

"Mackenzie."

Neither smiled.

Jim felt a tiny chill go down his spine. If this was an informal hearing, what was a formal one like?

Having established their respective places in the clan, the Laird sat down, his cane planted firmly between his knees, his hands resting on the knob.

"I hear things o' ye, Ginny, that I wish to ha'e clarified. I'm told ye sat down in front o' a loaded pistol at th' park this day."

"I did."

"Why was that?"

"To make sure, if it went off, it would not hit any of the children on the playground."

There was a longish silence as the Laird studied her face. Jim could see no evidence of remorse in her expression.

"Ye're a braw lass. Ye've nae need tae prove it tae anyone. But I ha'e tae wonder about yer judgment."

She said nothing, her eyes still on his, her face immobile.

"Why did ye no sit down at his side?"

"He needed to be able to see me and the only way I could be sure he would was to sit down in front of him."

"Did ye try to take th' gun frae him?"

She shook her head. "I'm not such a fool as that! We both know I could not have done it. He's faster, and stronger, and desperate."

"Ye told the police he didnae intend tae shoot the bairns."

"The gun might have gone off accidentally."

"So ye made th' deliberate decision tae substitute yerself."

Ginny stood up a bit straighter. "If I had to die to save even one of those children, it would have been worth it."

Jim felt his heart contract. 'Not to me, Ginny,' he thought.

The Laird's eyes narrowed, his expression stern.

"Virginia Ann Forbes. Y'er too valuable tae us tae tak' such chances. I forbid ye tae do so agin."

Jim watched the two of them stare at one another and held his breath. He knew just how stubborn Ginny could be. It was a full minute before she lowered her eyes.

"Aye, Mackenzie," she said, sinking into a graceful curtsy. When she rose, she stood in front of him, her head bowed, her eyes on the floor.

The Laird relaxed noticeably, his eyes still on his wayward child. "And now, lass, tell me what else Charlie Monroe said."

Her head came up swiftly. "What makes you think there

was more?"

A small smile appeared at the corner of the Laird's mouth. "I've known ye since ye were a wee bairn. Ye had something on yer mind when ye got here."

"Yes."

"Out wi' it, then."

"Charlie Monroe confessed to me that he killed the man we found in the Viking long boat."

Jim caught his breath.

"Auch, aye?"

"It's the man who killed his family." Ginny took a deep breath. "He shouldn't have done it. It was wrong to take vengeance into his own hands, but consider his provocation. The killer had been arrested, tried, convicted, then released onto the streets of Dallas without any controls or penalty. What self-respecting Scot wouldn't do what the criminal justice system failed to?"

She held her hand out toward the Laird. "I ask only that you bring him before you. Examine him. Decide what to do with him. He's one of ours. We owe him that much."

The Laird studied her face, his brow furrowed. "I'll gi'e it some thought. Ye may go."

She nodded then turned and left the hall.

Jim rose, crossed the space between himself and the Laird, then took a seat facing him.

"Ye ha'e questions, Jim?"

He nodded. "Several."

"Go on, then."

"First, did I see her curtsy to you?"

The old man laughed. "Aye, ye did, and a rare thing it may be, too, but she's well brought up."

Jim shook his head. "Why?"

"Why did she gi'e in tae me, ye mean?"

"Yes."

"Because she kens how much damage it would do tae th' clan for her tae throw awa' her life."

Jim felt a small stab in the region of his heart. "Will she keep her promise?"

"Aye, she will, but she'll reserve th' right tae decide. 'Tis in her nature."

Jim snorted. "If by that you mean she's stubborn, you're right. All she had to do was call 9-1-1 and wait. She didn't have to put herself in danger."

The Laird cocked his head to the side. "Th' lass puts herself in danger every time she reports tae work, does she no?"

Jim squirmed. "Well, yes, but it's not the same. That's her job."

"An' why do ye think she chose such a job?"

Jim met his grandfather's eyes. "The same reason I did, I suppose, to help people."

"Perhaps she thought tae help Charlie." His grandfather studied him for a moment. "Wha' would ye ha'e done, had ye been there?"

Jim sucked in a breath. "I wouldn't have let her use her body as a shield."

"Ye think ye could ha'e stopped her?"

He nodded. "If necessary, I would have slung her over my shoulder and dumped her in the sandbox."

He saw the corner of his grandfather's mouth twitch. "Force her tae obey ye? Ah weel."

"What do you mean by that?"

There was a definite twinkle in Angus Mackenzie's eye as he looked at Jim. "Ye'll find out, lad. Ye'll find out."

* * *

Chapter 4

Tuesday Afternoon
Cooperative Hall

The grapevine within the Homestead was a finely-tuned machine. By Monday evening, everyone knew the police had identified the body in the boat and, as a result, knew he was the man who had killed Charlie's family.

On Tuesday afternoon, Ginny slipped into the chair Jim had saved for her and looked around. The Cooperative Hall was full to bursting point.

Monroe had been released from the hospital that morning and brought here, in the custody and care of the clan. There was no doubt as to his guilt. He had confessed. The question was what to do with him. He now sat and waited. At the appointed time, he rose and faced the Laird.

"Have ye decided?" the Laird asked.

Monroe took a deep breath. "Aye."

"What will it be, then?"

"I choose exile."

A murmur swept through the crowd. Exile. As good as death to a Scot since there was no chance of reprieve.

"So be it."

Charlie was led from the room.

Jim leaned over and spoke in Ginny's ear. "Himself asked us

to stay."

When the others had gone, the Laird came over and sat down facing them.

"Halifax ha' agreed tae tak' him." He shook his head. "There's nae been a man choose exile in o'er fifty years and there's nane among us knows how tae manage it. Th' council is o' th' opinion tha' Monroe should disappear. Tha' means no air or train or boat." He looked straight at Jim. "Ye'll ha'e tae drive him, lad, and I have it in my mind tha' Ginny should accompany ye. The twa o' ye can pass fer a young couple on vacation." He looked from Jim to Ginny. They both nodded.

"Ye'll stay at th' Homesteads on th' way. Ginny. I'll ask ye tae plan th' trip. Ye've a good head fer details. Clothing, food, money. Whatever is wanted. Ask fer what ye will.

"Jim. Having chosen exile, he should cooperate wi' ye, but, ye'll need tae be prepared fer trouble. If Monroe flees, ye ha' the choice o' tryin' tae recapture him or let him go. 'Tis winter and he may fall prey tae the weather or beasts. He's no a stupid man. He'll stay close as long as he's able."

"How soon?" Jim asked.

"Twill depend on how lang it takes tae prepare. We'll talk agin when I know more."

As they walked out to the parking lot, Ginny looked over at Jim. "Will he cooperate, do you think?"

"I know nothing about the man."

"Well, we'll have plenty of time to get to know him. It's over two thousand miles to Nova Scotia from here."

* * *

Forty-eight hours later, Jim and Ginny were poring over the maps laid out on her mother's dining room table.

"How long is this trip going to take us?" Ginny asked.

"Five ten-hour days on the road. Each way. Grandfather wants to know which of the Homesteads to contact. He needs to arrange payment."

"Here's what I suggest." She traced the path on the map. "Nashville, Pittsburgh, Albany, Bangor, cross into Canada at Calais, then drive on to Halifax."

Jim frowned. "The border runs right down the middle of the St. Croix River at that point and I don't know what we'll find. It could be frozen solid, or broken ice, or open water. I think we need a land crossing."

"Couldn't Charlie use a fake ID and cross with us?"

"I don't think we can take that chance. It's too easy to transmit images electronically and the Dallas police are not stupid."

"He could wear a disguise."

"Facial recognition software can see past anything we could come up with. What's more, they've got a new procedure. It started with bomb-sniffing dogs and ended with mechanical sniffers that can collect samples of DNA from the skin cells our bodies slough off."

Ginny sighed. "Okay. Your turn to suggest something."

It took them an hour, but eventually Jim was satisfied. He pointed to a spot just south of Houlton, Maine.

"We can drop Monroe here and he can walk to this point." He put his finger on the end of a long dirt road on the Canadian side. "You and I will cross lawfully at Houlton, then pick him up on the other side." He stood up and stretched. "I'll show this to

Himself and see what he has to say. Now, what about those clothes you said you wanted me to try on?"

Ginny and her mother had searched the area thrift stores for heavy winter clothing and Ginny spent the next thirty minutes giggling at the sight of Jim struggling into turtlenecks that turned out to be too small and a white camouflage parka that hung on him like a badly formed polar bear costume.

"Very useful." He smiled at her. "Lots of room for extra sweaters."

"What about the pants? Can you wear them?"

"The length's good and the waistband draws up so I think it will be fine."

Ginny picked up the rejected turtlenecks. "I think these will fit Charlie. We'll take them over tomorrow and find out. You'll need to supply gloves, shoes, boots, turtlenecks, and at least one heavy sweater. Let me know if any of your things need washing or mending."

Jim caught her as she turned and drew her into his arms, smiling down at her. "No one has offered to do that for me since my mother died."

Her brow furrowed. "Am I being too bossy?"

"No. I like the thought of you taking care of me. Are you worried, Ginny, about being alone on this trip with two men, neither of whom is your husband and one of whom is a murderer?"

Ginny felt a chill go down her spine. "Should I be?"

"No. I will protect you."

She closed the front door on him feeling more than a little apprehensive. She hadn't even considered what it might mean to be alone with two big, strong, potentially lethal men. She had better consider what type of protection *she* should take.

* * *

CHAPTER 5

Friday Morning
Jim's Apartment

Jim was packing. They were scheduled to leave on Tuesday and he would have preferred sooner, but there had been problems getting coverage at the hospital, so he had to work. Which left only two days to finish getting ready.

He pulled out his duffle bag and began throwing items into it. He'd been taken aback when he saw the list of things Ginny was planning to bring, but he'd looked over her choices and found them both reasonable and efficient.

He and Ginny would both need their passports to prove citizenship on re-entry, and their U.S. driver's licenses would be honored in Canada, as long as the insurance was in place. He tucked photocopies of his documents into his duffle, then glanced at the time. The rest would have to wait.

Himself had arranged a conference with one of the more unusual members of the clan. A transplant from upstate New York who'd grown tired of bitterly cold winters, he brought a different skill set and some novel attitudes to the Loch Lonach Homestead. Jim was looking forward to meeting him.

* * *

Friday Morning
Brochaber

"Reggie, ye'll no have met my grandson, I think?"

Reginald MacDonald held out his hand. "Hi!"

Reggie turned out to be neither old nor young, incorrigibly cheerful, and permanently in top gear. Jim listened in growing amazement as Reggie told Himself where they were on the preparations.

"He'll need to have an accident, of course, and in this part of the world that means a boating accident. Actually, I think fishing, night fishing, would work best. He can go overboard and not be found and we can find his wallet and phone in the boat and he can either rent the boat or use a friend's, which might work better, actually, since then we can control access. Can he swim? Let's hope so. He can flounder a bit, in case anyone is watching, then go under and swim to shore or just quietly slip away, depending on the phase of the moon and where he is on the lake and the actual weather conditions and whether he can actually swim. We'll cross that bridge when I get my hands on him. Then once ashore, he'll go underground until departure." Reggie paused for a moment to grab a breath and Himself seized the opportunity to insert a comment.

"He can swim and fish."

"Oh, good. That makes it easier. Has anyone told him he has to walk out of the house just as if he's coming back in a few hours, take nothing, leave everything? Because if he takes anything with him, the experts will spot it. We've had people found because they couldn't leave a favorite record album. No clothes he wouldn't wear to go fishing in, no mementoes. Actually, it might be a good idea to stage a break-in. That way, if anything is missing, it can be attributed to the thieves. That makes it more complicated, of course, and more suspicious, but it might be worth the risk. I'll have to think about that. Actually, I think I'd rather he went over with a splash. That way it will look more like he tripped and maybe hit his head on something. Can we put some of his blood on the side of the boat, I wonder? That sort of thing gets investigated. On the other hand, if it's his blood, that lends credibility to an accident. How about blood and hair? We could smear it on the boards, or something of the sort. Then he went over and maybe he couldn't swim, oh, no, wait. He can swim. Got to factor that in. The cold water will make it harder to breathe, shock when he hits the water, you know, but it also prolongs life, so a cold water drowning will have them searching for longer than usual. Not that it's cold in Texas. Not like New York. We'll need to tear his jacket, I think, as well as smear the hair and blood. The divers will have wet suits, so I don't think it will require a special crew, just the usual suspects. How about we find a nice witness that can see him go into the water? I might be able to use that, as long as it's not anyone who knows him because we don't want them connecting the drunk driver to him, much less the Up-Helly-Aa. Anyway, you leave that part of it to me. I'll pick him up on the shore and take him underground until time to leave. You can pick him up on the other end."

And on that note Reggie seemed to have finished. He closed his mouth with a snap and turned to Jim, his face glowing with enthusiasm.

Jim glanced uncertainly over at Himself, then nodded to Reggie. "Yes, we can pick him up wherever you say."

"You understand you may need to go off-the-grid if the police figure out what we're up to, which will mean no GPS and no Internet access, which is going to feel weird since we're all born with a silver phone in our mouths these days. You'll need paper maps, just like the olden days. I can supply those. Can you read one? Of course, you can. I'll get you a full set once you've decided on a route. We can get topos, too, but I don't think you'll need that. You'll want to stay on the highways, not set off cross-country. Do you know how to turn off the GPS in your phone? It isn't enough to just turn the phone off, you know. Not if someone really wants to find you. For that, you'll have to take the battery out. I'll show you how and give you some suggestions for how to avoid the satellites and I think it would be a good thing to take some burner phones with you. I'll set those up as well."

"Ye'll need a car, Jim. Have ye an idea what sort?"

Jim nodded. "An all-wheel drive with snow tires and chains, to make sure we can keep going on ice and snow and over poorly maintained roads. Ginny wants to take camping gear so it will need to be big enough to handle that and the luggage."

"She kens ye'll be staying at the Homesteads?"

"She does. She said she wanted to be prepared for the worst so it wouldn't happen."

Himself chuckled. "Aye. She'll make a good job o' it, too. Have ye' a route picked oot?"

Jim opened the paper map he'd brought with him and laid it on the table in front of the other two.

"I'd like to get as far as possible as quickly as possible so the first stop should be here." He pointed to the Nashville area.

The Laird nodded. "Cumberland, aye, and then?"

"Pittsburgh, Albany, and Bangor, in that order. That's assuming they can and will take us in."

Himself nodded. "Ye've no need tae worry about tha'. I'll mak' some calls. What about th' crossing?"

"The last leg takes us through Houlton, Maine, into New Brunswick, then down to Halifax. Ginny and I will cross at the official border. I plan to drop Monroe here." Jim put his finger down on the map. "There's dense forest at that point, on both sides of the Slash. If he can avoid the camera traps and intruder alarms, we can pick him up here."

Himself nodded. "We'll see wha' we can do tae help wi' that." He turned to Reggie. "If 'tis nae trouble, I'd like Jim tae see the caverns afore he leaves us. They'll expect him tae know what's here."

Reggie nodded. "I've got time now." The two of them turned to look at Jim.

"What?" he asked.

"We've no talked much about the Homestead, Jim. I think it's time ye had a look at it."

"You mean the living history exhibits?"

"Nae, lad. There's a great deal more tae th' Homestead than that." Himself pulled on his Inverness cape, then led the way out to where Reggie's car was waiting.

"Is it all right if I go through the drive-through on the way over?" Reggie asked. "It's likely to be a while before we surface again and it's lunch time."

"Aye. 'Tis a guid thought."

Jim sat in the back of the car, mystified. Likely to be a while before they surfaced again? They needed to eat first? Just what was he getting into?

* * *

CHAPTER 6

Friday Afternoon
Homestead Grounds

They left Reggie's car in the parking lot and walked across the grounds toward the central compound. It lay at the heart of the site, surrounded by a privacy fence, and screened by bushes.

Jim had been inside the compound before. Ginny had taken him in and shown him how the clan arranged the living history exhibits for the paying public.

The trio walked past the numerous storerooms and staging areas, and what felt like a mile of bulletin and display boards before they reached the security room. It was manned by a pair of peace officers, both members of the clan.

All three of them were biometrically identified before being issued ID badges and allowed access to the inner office areas. Jim noted with interest that Reggie was wearing a shoulder holster, gun in place, and neither of the guards seemed the slightest bit disturbed by it.

"This way." Himself gestured down a short hall. He stopped in front of an elevator, pushed a button, then caught Jim's eye.

"Ye may ha' noticed th' Loch Lonach Homestead has its ain distillery."

Jim grinned. "Yes. I bought a bottle the first time I came out here. Not bad. It needs aging, but not bad otherwise."

The doors opened and the three men entered the elevator. Reggie reached over and pushed the single button on the panel. It was labeled, 'Entrance.'

Jim left his stomach topside, but it caught up with him before they reached their destination. When the elevator doors opened, Reggie led the way out. As soon as Jim was clear, Reggie closed a metal gate across the elevator entrance, the latch snapping into place with a well-oiled click.

Jim stepped forward into a semigloom broken by warehouse style lamps strung along a roof that seemed too far away to be feasible. It took him a minute to realize that the ceiling was actually the roof of an underground cavern.

"Wow!" Jim turned slowly, taking in the size of the cavern.

"Aye. It's that all right."

"I'll go get a cart," Reggie said.

Himself moved off down one of the paths, angling to the right and following the gentle decline around a stalagmite as big as a hundred-year oak. He turned to face Jim.

"Th' public disnae get tae come doon here."

Jim's head was still swiveling from side to side, trying to take in what he was seeing. "Why not? Lots of people would pay to come see this."

Himself nodded. "Tis no a tourist trap. 'Tis a refuge."

Jim focused suddenly on the old man's face. "A refuge?"

"Aye. Fer the clan." He gestured toward a bench set along the edge of the path. "Sit, lad."

His grandfather stood in front of him, eyeing the vast space.

"Th' first settlers found th' caves and used them tae store food and cattle. The temperature is a constant sixty Fahrenheit, gi'e or take a degree or twa. O'er time they explored deeper and found this place. The laird and council realized what could be done here. They surveyed th' land above and filed claims, then built farms and ranches, all wi'oot revealing th' secret.

O'er the years, successive lairds ha'e added tae th' design. They constructed the community above and secured th' access tae the caverns below." Himself paused, then turned to face Jim.

"When th' fightin' breaks oot, the clan will come doon here. We've space fer fifty thousand souls."

Jim stared at his grandfather. There was no hint of a smile. Jim swallowed. "What fighting?"

"Th' world changes, lad, and trouble's comin'. We mean tae be ready." He fixed Jim with a hard eye. "There are nae sae many as know o' this place. Ye hold th' fate o' fifty thousand o' yer people in yer hand. Will ye keep th' secret?"

Jim nodded, feeling foolish, and a little afraid. What *had* he gotten himself into?

* * *

By this time, Reggie had returned with a golf cart.

"We'll spend some time doon here, lad, you an' I, but no today." Himself climbed aboard and indicated that Jim should do the same. "There's nowt tae do this day but show ye th' way oot. Ye'll need tae know where tae pick up Monroe."

Jim nodded, then grabbed one of the bars as the vehicle moved off. He was having trouble wrapping his head around the implications of what he was seeing.

"Am I allowed to ask questions?"

"Ask away."

"How big is this place?"

"Nobody kens fer sure. 'Tis aboot twenty miles tae th' exit we'll be using, but we've mapped upwards o' two hundred miles o' trails and passages."

Jim whistled silently. "How tall, inside, I mean?"

"Th' equivalent o' a ten-story building straight up here and in th' other large rooms, wi' two hundred feet above that tae ground level. Did ye no wonder at th' length o' th' ride down?"

Jim nodded. "I did, but I had no idea what it meant." They were passing a wide variety of—he didn't know what to call them. Stations? Compartments? Sections? "I assume there's fresh water somewhere."

"Aye, and a sanitation system in place. Also air shafts and ventilation."

They rounded a corner and Jim suddenly recognized the shapes they had been passing in the deep shadows. "Casks!"

Himself chuckled. "Aye! Whisky in sherry casks. Just as ye suggested."

The corner of Jim's mouth twitched. Not actually a smile. He hadn't smiled since setting foot down here, but he was starting to recover from the shock.

As they rode on, he began to notice signage indicating there were other areas of the complex. One caught his eye.

"You have a hospital down here?"

"Tis nae a hospital. More a medical clinic, but 'tis set up fer surgery as weel as illness. And 'tis well stocked."

Jim leaned forward. "How well stocked?"

His grandfather looked back at him over his shoulder. "What do ye need, lad?"

"Morphine, for the trip to Nova Scotia."

Reggie nodded. "Not a problem."

Jim lifted an eyebrow. Access to narcotics was heavily regulated. Did this place have the necessary licenses?

"Here, lad. Look here." Himself was pointing something out. "That way lies th' living quarters, wi' th' kitchens and food storage. In th' other direction is th' mill. We raise th' sheep and goats topside, then bring th' wool down here fer preparation, spinning, and weaving. Cotton, too. Nae silk worms, yet, though I would like tae include them. Natural fibers only. We're unlikely tae ha' access tae petroleum products after th' war starts. Th' oil fields are high-profile targets."

Jim peered off to the side and could just make out lights in the next cavern over, and a sound like bumblebees in the distance.

"And o'er here is th' soap manufacturing."

"Soap."

Himself chuckled. "Good Scottish soap. Ye canna save civilization wi' oot soap."

Cloth and soap and food and whisky. What else?

"O'er here is th' pharmacy."

Jim turned his head quickly, but couldn't get a good look at the area indicated. "Where do you get your drugs?"

Reggie answered that one. "We make them."

"*Make* them?"

"We have pharmaceutical manufacturing for all the botanicals, minerals, and animal extracts. We grow the plants and raise the animals. The minerals have to be purchased in bulk, but we've got enough stockpiled for ten years of manufacturing. The lab grown drugs, not so much. We have some, but not all. On the other hand, the newest—the stem cell and DNA based targeted therapies—are state of the art. We have some of the best minds in the country working here. In addition, we have labs set up to make all the basic chemicals we've gotten used to: rubbing alcohol, iodine, hydrogen peroxide, bleach, ammonia. That sort of thing. The pharmacy also makes hand lotion, toothpaste, and deodorant. The machine shops can make any tool you can think of. We use computers to design, 3-D printers to manufacture, and a wireless net for internal communications. That ID badge you're wearing includes GPS and biometric monitoring as well as voice interface."

Jim was having trouble taking it all in, especially at the speed Reggie was dishing it out. He grasped at something more manageable.

"Will my phone work down here?"

"Normally, no, but we have antennas and solar collectors topside and relays throughout which we can control from a variety of locations. That way we can turn them off if we need to, but otherwise they're left on, so, yes, your phone will work down here at the moment. Also ham radio for when the cell towers come down. And satellite phones for as long as the birds are up there, and we can reach them. Electricity is produced by solar panels and wind turbines set up on the farms and throughout the community. We generate enough for all our needs and sell the rest back to the power company, but we also stockpile power, mostly in the form of batteries, though we're still using combustion engines for some of the tasks."

They turned a corner and Jim could see daylight ahead.

"There's th' entrance." Himself waited until the cart came to a full stop, then climbed out.

He led Jim along a steadily widening ramp. It curved upward, out from under the rock face and into the sunshine. Jim found himself standing on the edge of a farm, a dirt road stretching off in both directions under the vast Texas sky.

"We'll make sure you have directions to this spot," Reggie told him. "We wouldn't want you to get lost."

Jim turned and looked back at the cavern entrance. It was there, but almost invisible, the rock and dirt covered in scrub brush and hardy Mesquite trees. He could just see the edges of the opening and the metal rails that indicated a gate that could be lowered at need. The path would not admit any but the most compact of cars, no trucks or SUVs. It was a very private, not very impressive hole in the ground. He turned to his grandfather.

"Are the Homesteads all like this?"

"Aye. All strongholds intended to shelter th' clans, though nae all ha'e caverns in which tae stash them."

"How many are there?"

"Five hundred and twelve on th' North American continent."

Jim blinked. If each Homestead could handle even just 20,000 people, they could save ten million Scots. Enough to start afresh after the cataclysm. "Wow."

"Aye. Ye needed tae know afore ye headed north, sae ye'd ha' some idea what tae expect. I'll also need tae gi' ye some names and other information, but 'tis enough fer one day."

Jim turned and followed the other two down into the cavern. He said nothing on the ride back, listening to the conversation between Himself and Reggie as they discussed additional plans for Monroe's disappearance.

Jim had had private reservations when he first heard Reggie explaining what he wanted to do. Those had vanished as the day unfolded. It was abundantly clear that Reginald McDonald was capable of anything. It was equally clear that Jim's relatively quiet life as an ER junkie was behind him.

* * *

CHAPTER 7

Friday Afternoon
Monroe Residence

Ginny had spent the day with Charlie Monroe hustling him from shop to shop, selecting clothing, luggage, and personal care items. He'd been cooperative, but silent. They were settled now in his kitchen with hot drinks in hand and Good Brown Stew on the stove. Ginny looked at him. He was much too thin, pale, with dark circles under his eyes, and a dull look to his skin and hair.

"How are you, Charlie?"

He shrugged.

"Are you sleeping?"

He nodded, then shrugged again.

Ginny sighed. "Are you having second thoughts?"

He shook his head. "There's nothing for me here. At least this way I can make a fresh start."

"Has Reggie talked to you, yet?"

"He gave me something to read. Couldn't concentrate, though." He shifted in his chair. "When do we leave?"

"Tuesday morning."

"What am I supposed to do in the meantime?"

"Act normal. Which, in your case, means show everyone you are doing as told. Take your medications, sleep, bathe, wash your clothes, cook, eat, throw out the trash, pay the bills, and be sure to keep your follow-up appointment with the psychiatrist on Monday."

Ginny's phone buzzed and she pulled it out of her pocket.

"Where are you?" Jim's voice.

"Charlie Monroe's house."

"Alone? Is that safe?"

"I hope so."

"It's Friday night. Are we going to the ceilidh?"

"Of course! I've just been telling Charlie that we all have to act normal." She met Charlie's eye. "I tell you what. Come on over and have some stew. There's plenty. Then the three of us can go to the dancing together."

"Okay. I'll be there in twenty minutes."

Charlie had his eyes on her. "I don't feel real sociable."

"You need to be seen in public. We'll need witnesses."

"Oh."

Ginny set the table and laid out drinks and condiments, watching as Charlie helped himself to a pickle, then a sniff of the stew. He was young and essentially healthy. With care, he should recover.

* * *

Friday Evening
Dallas Police Substation

Detective Tran looked over her list of things to do, assigning priorities. She had cleared most of her cases this week and could now focus on the body in the boat.

It had been more than a week since the discovery. The police had interviewed everyone involved in the building, transporting, and destruction of that boat, also all of the people involved in picking up the debris afterwards.

The Medical Examiner's office had been prompt and efficient, producing a completed autopsy within forty-eight hours of the discovery. The DNA records had come back on Monday afternoon, which allowed the police to start canvassing the neighborhood. The victim was a Mexican national with a string of priors, so he was in the system.

So was one of the Scots.

The Scot was the surviving spouse in the latest of the drunk driving incidents the dead Mexican had caused. It might mean nothing, of course, but it was interesting.

According to her sources, Charles Monroe had not been involved in the boat burning ritual this year. He *had* been picked up in the park last Saturday, waving a gun around, and threatening to shoot himself. He'd been charged with a Class C misdemeanor, and been referred to the inpatient psychiatric unit for a mandatory three day evaluation. According to the accompanying notes, he'd been released back into the community, with supervision, on Tuesday.

Detective Tran had a history with the Scots. She had investigated an attack on Ginny Forbes last October, then enlisted her help to investigate a murder at the hospital in December. An interesting young woman, with a guileless face that made her transparent to questioning. She and another young woman had discovered the latest corpse.

Even more interesting, Miss Forbes had been on site when Mr. Monroe was waving that gun around. Her statement to the police had indicated Mr. Monroe was so disturbed by his loss that he was no longer able to care for himself.

Detective Tran's eyes narrowed slightly as she considered the possibility. He had motive and he had access to the boat, but he might not have had the physical coordination necessary to deliver that death blow. That had taken skill and control. The degree of alcoholic impairment would be critical. She should pull Mr. Monroe's medical record and see what the admitting physician and psychiatrist had to say on the subject.

* * *

Friday Evening
Cooperative Hall

Ginny slipped out of the cheerful throng just getting ready to start the next dance and made her way across the hall to where Himself and Jim were standing. There had been something wrong with Jim during dinner.

She kept her voice down, a non-committal smile on her face. "Am I interrupting?"

Both men turned to face her. Himself looked just the tiniest bit ruffled, a first in her book. Jim looked angry.

"I see that I am." Ginny turned on her heel and started to retreat, but Jim caught her arm.

"No, Ginny. Please come back."

She did as asked, waiting for him to explain.

"We were just discussing honesty." Jim's eyes slid toward his grandfather.

Himself clarified. "Jim got his first look at th' caverns today."

"Ah." Ginny looked at Jim, wondering what it must have been like for him, not having been brought up in the community, to have seen the extent of the preparations going on below their feet.

"You didn't tell me about that when you suggested I abandon all the plans I had for my life and come here instead."

"I had nae authority tae do so, until ye came."

"Did my father know about this?"

"Aye."

"Is that why he left?"

"We ha' a difference o' opinion, but not o'er this."

"Are there other things you haven't told me yet?"

"Many."

The older man regarded his grandson with a look that Ginny classified as speculative. Jim was glaring, but in control, aware he was being watched.

"Will you tell me?"

"In guid time."

Jim nodded curtly, then turned and strode off in the direction of the door. Ginny gave Himself a quick look, got a short nod in reply, then hurried after Jim.

She spotted him moving in the direction of the loch and followed. His legs were longer than hers and he was clearly burning through a head of steam. It was all she could do to keep him in sight for the first quarter hour. When he reached a rise that served as a lookout point, he climbed the rocks and came to rest at last, staring off across the water.

She climbed up behind him, making sure he could hear her ascent. As she reached the crest, he looked at her, then turned his eyes back to the loch. She walked over and took up a position beside him.

In a city the size of Dallas, few places were ever really dark; man-made light reflected off every surface. She could see him easily. He had his arms crossed on his chest, his legs planted firmly on the rock, his face full of thunder.

She slipped her arm around his waist. He uncrossed his arms and pulled her closer.

"Talk to me," she said.

It took him a minute to get started. "I feel as if I've been lied to," he said. "As if I was lured here under false pretenses."

"Would you have come, if you had known what the Homesteads were?"

"I don't know. I had plans, and they didn't include preparing for war."

She looked up at him. "You fight every day, to save lives."

"That's different. I don't have to fight another human being, just disease and decay, and I don't have to be responsible for 50,000 people, just the ones that come through my ER."

Ginny sighed. "I'm told that being responsible for other people is what makes us human rather than animals."

"Most animals care for their young and some have family groups. Some mate for life." He looked down at her and she felt his arm tighten around her.

"And most of those family groups have an alpha male. Right now, that's your grandfather."

Jim snorted. "You've got that right!"

"It could be you. It will be, if you choose."

"Maybe I don't want the job."

She shrugged. "You don't have to take it. Young males have been known to leave the herd and strike out on their own."

"Or be driven out."

She shook her head. "You're too valuable for that." She felt him stiffen.

"Now I feel like a commodity."

"We all are."

He looked down at her and she shrugged.

"Each of the Homesteads maintains a list of resources they possess. That includes human resources. We are occasionally loaned and sometimes traded, with our consent, of course. If one of the Homesteads needs an engineer, for instance, they recruit from among the others. The idea is that, at any given moment, each Homestead will have all the resources it needs to survive. We're unlikely to get much warning and we need to be ready."

Jim looked down at her for a long moment. "You believe it's

coming?"

She nodded. "History is full of examples of militant peoples conquering their peaceful neighbors. The mistake the neighbors make, each time, is believing the militants will live and let live."

She took a deep breath. "We already know we can't win this war, but we can survive it, and preserve the better parts of civilization in the hope peace will come again."

She looked up at him. "The question for you, Jim, is whether you want to be the hammer or the anvil."

"Are those my only choices?"

"You can be the one giving the orders or one of the ones taking them."

"Or I can refuse to do either."

She sighed. "Yes. In which case, you will be asked to keep the secret, but nothing else."

He let go of her, frowning, and stood looking out over the water. "Maybe it would have been better to stay in Virginia."

She nodded slowly. "Perhaps, for you, but if you had, I would quite likely be dead, so I have to be glad you came."

He turned suddenly and pulled her into his arms. "Oh, Ginny! I didn't mean it that way." He put his cheek down on the top of her head, holding her close. "I just meant I'm not sure I'm up to it."

"You're not alone, Jim. We all feel that way."

He sighed deeply. "You've been living with this your whole life."

She nodded.

He looked down at her. "Well, I'm still mad at my grandfather for not leveling with me, but I guess I can see his point. It's an awfully big secret."

"It's not just you. Most of the clan don't know the whole truth. All they know is that there's a shelter that might or might not be needed at some point in the future."

"And in the meantime, we just go about our lives as usual."

She shook her head. "Not you. As the heir to Loch Lonach, the responsibility for the clan falls on your shoulders. There's a lot to be done to get you ready."

He frowned, then looked down at her. "And you? What responsibility to do you have in all of this?"

She sighed. "That remains to be seen."

* * *

CHAPTER 8

Friday Evening
Cooperative Hall

Himself put away the phone and looked around, hunting for Reggie MacDonald. He found him at the punch bowl, flask out, adding a bit of the *water of life* to the water in his glass. Himself made his way across the room, touched Reggie's arm, and steered him to a quiet corner.

"Tak' Monroe out the-nicht."

"Tonight?" Reggie's eyebrows rose. "Why the hurry?"

"Th' police are lookin' fer him. I want him oot o' the way."

Reggie nodded. "Give me half an hour. I'll call you and tell you where to find the boat. Then he's to go home, get his fishing gear, and drive to the dock, just as if he were planning fresh fish for breakfast. Remind him that the house must not look suspicious. The police will go over it with a fine-toothed comb. They'll notice if something is missing."

"Aye. I'll tell him." Angus Mackenzie surveyed the room. No Monroe. He checked the assembly rooms, but he wasn't there, either. A search of the restroom, grounds, and kitchens all turned up nothing. Himself frowned. He caught Jim and Ginny just coming in.

"Ha'e ye seen Monroe?"

Jim nodded. "He was sitting on the edge of the lake, on a

bench near the water fountain."

"I ken th' place." He wrapped his cape around his shoulders and let himself out onto the grounds.

The Cooperative Hall had been built adjacent to the loch, abutting it, but private. The Laird sauntered along the path, spotted Monroe without trouble, and wandered up to the bench, sitting down on it and greeting the young man pleasantly.

"A bonnie nicht."

"It is."

"A canny man might be thinkin' o' going oot fishing."

Monroe blinked at the Laird, then turned his eyes to the sky, then back to the surface of the water. "Not much moon."

"True. E'en a guid fisherman might trip and fall o'er board on a nicht wi' nae moon. Could be lost. Ye'd need tae be careful, but the catch might be worth th' risk."

Monroe's eyes narrowed. "It would be a good place to do some thinking."

"Aye. Ye'd ha' th' loch tae yerself. Nane tae disturb ye."

Monroe nodded slowly. "Do you know a good place to go night fishing?"

"Reggie does. He was plannin' tae go oot this nicht. Loch Lavon, I think. Ye know it?"

"Yup."

"Tis mild fer a February nicht. Ye could make do wi' just yer tackle and a flask maybe, and yer coat, though ye could leave that on the seat o' the boat if ye wanted tae ha'e yer hands free tae cast."

Monroe nodded.

"Ha'e ye one o' the floating key bobs?"

"No."

The Laird climbed to his feet. "Come wi' me, then. I've one I can let ye ha'e."

Monroe rose and followed him to the parking lot. The Laird opened the trunk of his car and pulled his tackle box to the edge, making sure it could be seen by anyone watching. He dipped into his supplies, fished out the device Reggie had given him earlier that day, and turned to Monroe.

"Here, lad. This will see ye hame." He dropped his voice as Monroe leaned in to inspect the contents of the tackle box.

"There's a homing beacon in the bob, already activated. Swim ashore away frae th' lights then walk tae th' edge of the pavement. Reggie will pick ye up and take ye tae th' Homestead. I'm tae remind ye tae take nothing but th' fishing gear."

Monroe nodded, dropping the beacon into his pocket. "Where do I go after I pick up my tackle?"

"Reggie should be callin' any minute noo."

The phone went off and Himself answered it, leaning against the trunk of the car while Monroe pulled a lure out and held it up to the light.

"Ye're nae able tae go, then? Ah weel. Ye and Charlie will ha'e tae go another time." He hung up the phone, then turned and leaned into the trunk.

"Lavon, Little Ridge Park." He stood up and handed a lure to Monroe. "Ye can borrow this one fer when ye do get tae go and let me know how it does fer ye."

Monroe nodded. "I'll do that."

* * *

Friday Night
Lake Lavon

Charlie Monroe stood in the bass boat and looked out over the dark water. He had taken a moment to pull Lake Lavon up on his computer and had seen a power plant warm water outlet next to Little Ridge Park. It made an excellent place to go overboard. He would be wet, but not frozen.

He baited his line by the light of the electric lantern, then cast it out over the water, watching the lure sink. He wondered what kind of fishing there might be in Canada.

He'd been trying not to think about what he was doing, but now the reality swam up to him from the depths, surfacing and disturbing the waters of his mind. He'd never much cared for cold weather. Well, that had better change, and fast.

He would never see any of his friends again. Or his family. He had a brother, five years older than he was, and a sister-in-law. Both were dentists and seemed to be perpetually abroad, caring for the needy somewhere in Africa. He hadn't seen them in years, might not even recognize them if he did.

He'd visited his in-laws and given them a few things he thought they might like to have, to remember their daughter and grandchildren by. That had been a hard visit. He'd been careful not to tell them what he planned to do. No need to distress them further. He'd liked Mandy's parents and they had liked him.

His own parents were dead, killed in an airplane crash, along with his maternal grandparents, when he was seven. He would never visit their graves again. Or Mandy's. He put his hand to his eyes, pressing hard, trying not to weep.

He'd left the Navy when his paternal grandfather died of a heart attack, to come home and care for his remaining grandmother. She had Alzheimer's and was in a facility run by the Homestead. She hadn't recognized him the last time he went to visit.

He pulled back on the rod and cast again, not caring where the lure fell.

He didn't have to go. He could stay and take his

punishment. He had killed a man. He deserved to be punished. If he confessed, and didn't get sent to the looney bin, that meant time in prison, in the company of hardened criminals. They would become his new family. It was that thought, as much as anything, that had made up his mind for him.

He watched the lights of a car move along the edge of the lake and wondered if it was Reggie MacDonald, coming to get him. He'd met the man, once, when he'd been sent down into the caverns to work on a covert communications project.

He'd had a promising future until last August, until that monster had taken everything from him. He found a lump in his throat and swallowed it with difficulty, his vision blurring.

What was he doing out here on the lake, planning to fake his own death, to escape into the night? Why had he let Ginny Forbes talk him out of shooting himself?

Had he been afraid? Afraid to die, to be with Mandy and the girls? Maybe he believed that suicides didn't get to go to heaven. Maybe he'd just been unable to pull the trigger.

He didn't understand that. He should have been able to kill himself without a second thought. He'd gone to the park and tried to make himself feel how bad it hurt, how his heart stopped beating when he thought of his girls. Annie's birthday present was still in the closet, wrapped, ready to give to her. He'd been close. Why had Ginny stopped him? Why had he let her stop him?

He reeled in the line and cast again, his eyes on the ripple it caused on the surface of the lake.

The psychiatrist had talked to him at length. He'd been sympathetic, had said what he was feeling was normal. He'd also said the pain would fade, that he'd be able to face life again, in time. What if he didn't want to feel good again?

If the psychiatrist was right, then starting over made sense. Mandy would want that. She was always supporting him, encouraging him. Charlie felt a tear trickle down his cheek and brushed it away.

He'd done as told, except that he could NOT leave without a picture of his girls. He'd put the flash drive inside three layers of plastic baggies, then duct-taped it to his skin, inside his clothes. It would be safe there. Eventually he'd find a computer he could use. He'd have his girls back.

He tugged gently on the line, trying to imagine the fish at the bottom of the lake. The fish was hungry and would take the bait thinking it was safe to eat.

Charlie, too, was facing a lure, only, unlike the fish, he knew there was a hook inside. He could give himself up and endure whatever came. Or he could kill himself. Or he could leave everything he had ever loved behind and start over. Which of those was the honorable choice? Was there any way to tell?

His ancestors believed the Norse gods sent omens, messages to mortals, to guide them. What he needed was a sign. 'Mandy,' he pleaded, 'give me a sign. Tell me what to do.'

The line he was holding tugged suddenly as a fish took the bait. Charlie jerked back on the pole to set the hook. He let out some line and tugged again, feeling the fish pull, then slide to the side. Charlie followed it in the dark.

The fish was pulling hard. Must be a big one and probably a bottom-feeder. Catfish, most likely. Charlie pulled too, trying to get the fish off the bottom, then gave him some slack and pulled again. This time the fish seemed to be coming toward him, rising. Charlie leaned back, keeping the tension on the line, but he couldn't see what he was doing. He stumbled over the bench and tripped, then, with a startled cry, went over the side and into the water.

He had sense enough to drop the line and let himself sink, then drift. The water was murky and for a moment he wasn't sure which way was up, then his head broke the surface and he could see the shore. He had lost one of his shoes. He kicked off the other, took a breath and submerged, heading for the edge of the lake.

He had already identified a landing spot. He surfaced, then pulled himself onto the rocks as quietly as possible. The key fob was still there, clipped to a belt loop. After a bit he rose and started to walk along the shore, carefully, since he could not see the ground and he was shoeless. Ten minutes effort brought him to the edge of the picnic area. A careful look around showed him one car, lights out, visible against the backdrop of the city. As he watched, a thin shadow detached itself from the side of the car and came over.

"You all right, then? Not drowned?"

Charlie swallowed hard. "Not drowned." He followed Reggie MacDonald over to the car.

"Here." Reggie handed him a blanket.

He climbed into the passenger side of the car and drew the blanket around him as Reggie put the car in gear and drove off.

Charlie found himself responding to the vibration of the car, the warmth of the heater, and the aftermath of the immersion. His gaze rested on the lights of Dallas, his home no longer, then he took a deep breath and closed his eyes. An image of his dead wife rose before him. He could see her, smiling at him, nodding to him. He smiled back.

* * *

CHAPTER 9

Saturday
Forbes Residence

It was their last prep day and Jim was on the phone with the Laird. Ginny could hear his end of the conversation.

"I understand that." There was a pause. "I agree it's a good choice for the first leg of the trip, but we're still going to need something that can handle ice and snow." Jim looked over at her and made a face. "Okay. I'll wait to hear from you." He put the phone away and shook his head.

"Himself says they've got a small commercial truck that will hold all the gear and both of us and Monroe. The windows are tinted and hard to see through and the second row of seating is moveable so we can put him on the floor, completely out of sight." He sighed. "He's right about wanting to make sure no one sees a third head in the car as we drive off into the sunset."

"We're going east."

"Sunrise, then." Jim added his trauma bag to the pile of items to be packed.

Ginny pulled out a small black velvet bag and emptied the contents onto the table. She watched as Jim's eye widened.

"What's this?"

"Four thousand dollars' worth of small gemstones, suitable

for turning into cash or barter on either side of the border. It was your grandfather's idea. In case we get into a liquid assets pinch."

She tucked the gems carefully back into the bag and tied it shut, securing it in her purse, then caught Jim's eye. "I just wanted you to know I was carrying them."

* * *

Saturday Midmorning
Monroe Residence

On Saturday, Detective Tran drove to Monroe's house, parked on the street, and waited for the patrol car to pull up behind her. She rang the doorbell, then knocked. When no one answered, she moved around the side of the house and let herself into the back yard.

There were toys scattered about the yard, the brightly colored bits of plastic splattered with mud. Nothing had been picked up. Nothing had been cleaned. The implication was clear. The children were gone and nothing mattered any more.

Detective Tran moved to the back windows and looked in. There was no evidence of life inside. She pounded on the back door and called out.

"Charles Monroe?"

Still no answer. She moved across to the other side of the yard. The garage was closed, but had windows set in the doors. She stretched up and looked inside. No car.

"Gone fishing."

Detective Tran turned and found an old man leaning on a fence across the alley. "I beg your pardon?"

"He went fishing. Last night. I saw him drive out."

Detective Tran pulled out the small book she carried with

her at all times. "What time did you see him leave?"

"'Bout eleven."

"You are sure he went fishing?"

"Put his tackle in the car. Drove off. Didn't see him come back."

Detective Tran asked a few more questions, but it was clear her informant had told her everything he knew. She thanked him and made her way back to the front of the house.

He might be at the lake, of course. Or spending the night with a friend. It was too soon to put out a missing person's report. It was a nuisance not to have found Monroe at home, but no more than that. Not yet.

* * *

Sunday Morning
Hillcrest Regional Medical Center

Ginny yawned as she made her way to the parking garage elevators. It was seven-thirty on Sunday morning and she was thinking about nothing but bed.

"Miss Forbes?"

She looked up to see a petite Vietnamese woman standing in front of the door leading to the ambulance bays. "Detective Tran!" Ginny smiled. "To what do I owe the pleasure of this visit?"

"I am sorry to have to catch you coming off shift, but I would like to ask a few questions, if I may, before I have to speak to someone else."

Ginny tried to express pleased puzzlement. "Yes, of course! What may I do for you Detective?"

"I would like to know if you've seen Charles Monroe since that incident on the playground."

Truth was always best, where possible. "Yes, of course."

"When, please?"

Ginny wrinkled her forehead. "I was with him most of Friday."

"The day before yesterday."

"Yes."

"Did he say anything to you?"

"Not much. He's still pretty depressed. We talked about how important it was for him to take his medication and keep his appointment with the psychiatrist on Monday."

"Was he drinking?"

"Alcohol? Not while he was with me."

"Did he say anything to you that made you think he was planning something?"

"No, nothing." Ginny frowned. "Is there a problem?"

"He may be missing."

Ginny's frown deepened. "Missing! Have you spoken to Himself, Angus Mackenzie, I mean?"

"That is my next stop. I was hoping you could tell me a little bit about Mr. Monroe."

Ginny outlined the story for the detective, seeing her nod. "He was released on condition that someone stay with him and we've been taking it in turns. Oh, dear. I hope nothing has happened to him." Ginny firmly kept her mind off the plans for the trip.

"You are concerned for him?"

Ginny kept her frown in place. "Yes. He was suicidal on Saturday. Last Saturday, I mean. He might have had an accident, I suppose, but yes, I would rather know he's safe."

"We'll be checking into both possibilities. In the meantime, if you hear from him, or of him, would you please let me know?"

"Yes, of course."

"Thank you, Miss Forbes. Good day."

Ginny waited for the elevator, worrying about what the detective might have read on her face. She hoped nothing. She had told the exact truth, except that she had no intention of calling in when Charlie did appear, if he did, that is.

She rode up to the fourth floor, let herself into her car, locked the door, then pulled out her phone. She tapped out a carefully worded message to Himself.

Detective Tran caught up with me at the hospital this morning, looking for Charlie. I couldn't help her, since I haven't seen him since Friday night so I referred her to you. He seemed depressed when I talked to him. I hope he hasn't done something stupid, poor man. Will you let me know when you find him?

With any luck, Himself would see it before he had to face the detective, but whether he did or not, it would be clear to everyone that Ginny believed Charlie was in town, possibly in danger, and that the Scots were actively looking for him. It had all the appearance of innocence. Which was all she could hope for at the moment.

* * *

CHAPTER 10

Sunday Midmorning
Auld Kirk

Angus Mackenzie spotted the detective before she spotted him. She was scrutinizing each face as it left the church, clearly looking for someone. He glanced at Ginny's note again, then started across the grass.

"Was it me ye were lookin' fer?" he asked.

She turned round. "Good morning Mr. Mackenzie. I am hoping Charles Monroe is here."

"Charlie?" Himself gave a start. "What's amiss wi' Charlie? He's no been threatening tae shoot hisself agin'?"

"Not that we know of. We would like to have a word with him, though." The detective's eyes continued to examine the faces of the people as they streamed onto the lawn. Angus waited beside her, his brow furrowed.

The working relationship between the clan and the local police was distant, but cordial. There was no reason for the police to suspect collusion, but there was always a chance someone had let something slip. The fact that they had sent a homicide detective, rather than a regular police officer, was ominous.

When the last worshipper had left the building, the detective stepped inside and looked around, then turned to

Himself.

"Did Mr. Monroe come to church this morning?" she asked.

Himself shook his head. "I didnae see him."

"Miss Forbes said you were taking it in turns to keep an eye on him. Is that correct?"

"Aye."

"Whose turn would it be today?"

Himself blinked. There had been no need to assign anyone after Reggie collected Charlie from the lake on Friday night. He wrinkled his brow. "Let me see." The entire council had been present when Charlie had chosen exile, and most of the clan. Who among them could be trusted to help fabricate a careful half-truth?

"Jean Pollack ha' yesterday, I'm thinkin', and Geordie Hamilton t'day. If ye've a wee minute I'll ca' them fer ye."

"Yes, please." Detective Tran waited while Angus pulled out his phone and peered at it. Text messages could be tracked. Voice was safer. He just hoped Geordie was paying attention.

"Can you put it on speaker phone, please?"

He nodded. No flies on this woman. "Geordie? Yer on speaker and I've a wee question fer ye from a detective whose lookin' fer Charlie Monroe. Hae ye seen him t'day?"

"Nae. Not a swatch."

"Was it you 'twas tae check on him this day? Did ye go o'er tae his hoose?"

There was a tiny pause. "Auch, was it my turn, then? I'll go noo."

Himself looked over at the detective, who nodded.

"Hae ye a key, Geordie?"

"Aye. Is there something ye be wantin', other than Charlie?"

"Nae, jus' th' man hisself."

"Ask him to wait for me," she said.

"Geordie, the detective wants ye tae wait fer her."

"I'll be oot front."

"Thank ye!" Himself hung up the phone. "Tha' reminds me. Charlie an' Reggie were goin' fishin' Friday nicht. But they had tae cancel because Reggie couldna go."

Detective Tran took out a notepad. "Do you know where?"

Himself nodded. "Loch Lavon."

"We'll check that out. Is there anything else you can tell me?"

Himself shook his head.

"All right. Thank you for your help."

Angus watched the detective get into her car and drive off. He made his way to his own car, got in, and drove over to the Homestead, checking frequently to see if he was being followed. Once inside the shelter, no one could eavesdrop on them. The walls were too thick and the caverns too deep. With the communications net in privacy mode they would be able to talk freely.

* * *

Sunday Afternoon
Caverns beneath the Loch Lonach Homestead

The three of them sat in one of the meeting rooms, steaming cups of coffee in front of them, the remainder of the table covered in notes.

Himself looked over at Charlie. "Jim and Ginny canna leave 'til Tuesday morn, but we can get ye awa afore that and maybe should."

Reggie looked dubious. "The plan is for them to drive to the entrance and pick him up there."

"I'm thinkin' th' police may ha' decided tae follow Miss Ginny. They spoke tae her this morn at th' hospital."

"Damn." Reggie was silent for a full minute. "Okay. Here's the thing. If the police are actually tracking us, any of us, that implies they think we know where Charlie is, that we're hiding him, and that we can lead them to him, which means that we have to make sure they can follow any one of us and we lead them exactly nowhere. It also means we have to find a way to get Charlie out of here and to a rendezvous of some sort that won't attract their attention and isn't overlooked by any of the electronic devices they have access to, which includes all the traffic and security cameras. What's more, whatever we come up with will have to be communicated to Jim and Ginny and if any of us go talk to them or phone them or use the e-mail or text systems it can be tracked. The police will have warrants ready as soon as they have enough to convince a judge there's reason to suspect a conspiracy to obstruct justice." He drummed his fingers on the table.

"Getting Charlie out just means making sure there's no surveillance going on at the moment and that could include satellite and helicopters, though I can't believe anyone thinks he's worth the kind of money we're talking about since he's not a terror threat, just a murderer. There's no reason to think the feds are interested in him, is there?" Reggie looked from Himself to Charlie, then back. They both shook their heads.

"Okay. So what we have to do is take Charlie out in something that looks like it could not possibly have a human being hidden inside it, especially not one his size. I've got just the thing, too. It's a modified motorcycle. The saddlebags have a very nice hideyhole and, if opened, are full of clothing and sundry other useful camouflage. You won't be comfortable and there's a limit to how long you can stay in there, but it's enough to get you past a cordon. We just have to figure out how far we have to go and in which direction and then we have to identify where to decant you that's safe to wait and then we have to figure out how to get Jim and Ginny to the right place without alerting the police to the pickup spot. Do you have their route?"

"Aye." Himself pulled a map from the pile of papers and handed it over. Reggie studied it.

"We need something that's far enough out of town that it makes a convincing place to stop, but not so far that Charlie can't be unpretzelized." He traced the route on the map, then studied the images of the area.

"Here. See this? The super center has a covered area, garden department, probably, and it's on the back side of the building and it abuts this residential area and the residents obviously don't like the super center because they've planted shrubs all along this edge; close enough so they screen the houses from the store. We can park Charlie in the store and he can get into the car while it's under the awning."

Reggie chewed on his lip. "We need to make sure Charlie can't be seen entering the car or suddenly appearing inside of it. No chance of someone noticing two heads going behind the building and three coming out."

"I've already thought o' that. Jim wasnae happy aboot using th' van, but he'll make do."

"Okay. How about this? They need to purchase something biggish at the superstore and they will need to have help loading it into the van so they go around to the loading dock and open the doors and the men hoist it inside and during the distraction Charlie slips into the van with his head down and no one the wiser."

"Can ye get Charlie into the store wi'oot th' cameras noticing him?"

"We can disguise him as one of the workers—cap, vest, work gloves, that sort of thing."

Himself nodded. "Th' Gunns live o'er that way. They can tak' him tae the supercenter and let him slip oot o' their car intae th' shadows."

"I'll set it up." Reggie nodded vigorously. "I like it. Now we just need to let Jim know what he needs to do. Will he come to you before he leaves town? Do you have any kind of meeting planned? How about you have him over to dinner? How about you have both of them over and feed them, or you could go to Ginny's house. No, better they should come to you so you can control the access. I've got some nice little toys that will let you know if anyone is listening in. You don't want to disable them, you understand, just be aware they are there so you don't say anything you don't want overheard. Make sure you meet in an inside room with no windows, and no computers. They can turn those webcams on remotely, you know."

"I didnae know that."

"True. You can have a cordial farewell dinner conversation and be passing notes at the same time. I'll write the whole thing up right now so you can take it with you. Once we get Charlie in the car, he'll need to stay out of sight until we can be reasonably sure the police are no longer following them, which may be over the state line. I'll get back to you on that."

The Laird rode up in the elevator, thinking about the creativity and complexity of the new plan. Things could go wrong with something like that. He had to hope that Jim could pull it off, and Monroe, too, otherwise there was no telling what sort of trouble they might get into. He sighed and headed home.

* * *

Chapter 11

Jim set the remainder of his hospital-approved burger aside and picked up his coffee. "Grandfather wants us to dine with him tonight, a sort of last supper before we take off."

Ginny was poking away at a tuna casserole, picking out bits of unidentified material. She lifted an eyebrow in his direction. "I'll look forward to it. I can always trust his cooking."

Jim laughed. "Who would have thought? He's really quite good. I suppose it was either learn to feed himself or go hungry."

Ginny risked another bite of the casserole. "When did your grandmother die?"

"I was fourteen. I think he misses her."

Ginny nodded. "I remember her. She was always kind to me. She would give me milk and ginger snaps."

Jim smiled. "She was stern with me. I remember being scolded for bringing wildlife into the house."

"What kind of wildlife?"

"Garter snakes and horny toads and an assortment of insects."

"Not those horrible big roaches?!"

"No. Beetles. Also fireflies and grasshoppers."

Ginny shook her head at him. "Boys!"

He leaned toward her. "You can't tell me you didn't catch fireflies. I won't believe you."

She smiled. "I did, but I didn't bring them into the house. I just chased them around the yard, trapping them in my hands, then letting them go."

Jim had a sudden vision of Ginny at age five, eyes alight as she watched the firefly's glow escape between her fingers. He was still smiling at the image when she spoke again.

"Detective Tran was waiting for me when I got out of work yesterday morning."

Jim came back to the present with a thud. "Detective Tran?"

"She wanted to know if I'd seen Charlie."

"What did you tell her?"

"The truth."

Jim's brow furrowed. "All of it?"

She dimpled. "No. She very obligingly asked me nothing I could not answer honestly. I did see Charlie, on Friday, at his house, and at the ceilidh. Has she approached you?"

Jim shook his head. "No. Come to think of it, I haven't seen him either. Where was he on Saturday?"

Ginny shook her head. "I have no idea, thank goodness." She caught his eye. "But I think I can guess who does."

Jim's eyebrows rose. "And we've been summoned to dinner."

* * *

Monday Afternoon
Police Substation

Detective Tran sat at her desk on Monday afternoon, a small frown on her face. The office was old, even by Dallas standards, and had seen battle somewhere along the way; there were scars on the linoleum tile. They did not bother her.

She had arranged the room to suit her needs. The whiteboards on the wall hung in perfect alignment, both to plumb and to one another. Markers lay in the same location in each of the trays. The papers on the desk were sorted and labeled and did not move in the breeze from the central heating.

So far, the only viable suspect was Charles Monroe, and he was proving hard to pin down. A background check had revealed that he, Monroe, had trained as a Navy Special Warfare Operator. He'd served a total of eight years, then left with an honorable discharge, giving family medical issues as a reason. His SEAL training had included using a knife to kill quickly and silently in exactly this manner, but there was no physical evidence to tie Monroe to this death.

She set down the report, rose, and walked over to the first of the three whiteboards. This one was the calendar.

The time line was unclear. The coroner hadn't been able to do better than 'killed two or three days before he was found'. His blood alcohol level indicated he was quite seriously drunk at the time of his demise, but no one remembered seeing him either in a bar or one of the local liquor stores prior to that time.

Without knowing where the homicide occurred, it was hard to narrow down the geographic search area. They had started in the more heavily Hispanic areas of town and sent in officers who both spoke the language and understood the culture, but had discovered nothing useful.

Most likely the victim had gone into hiding when he escaped police custody last November. That hadn't been one of Detective Tran's cases so she was having to catch up.

There were three vehicular homicides on his record (in

addition to the one that killed Mr. Monroe's family), two in Houston and one in San Antonio. In each case, the offender had done time in the county jail, then been deported back to Mexico, only to surface again in Texas when he killed someone else. In each case, he'd had a blood alcohol level well above the legal limit, and no driver's license.

Two of the incidents had been side swipes on the highway. In one of those the deceased's vehicle had spun out, then flipped over, crushing the occupant. In the other, the vehicle went off the overpass and landed on the highway below. The third incident was a grandmother struck while waiting for assistance on the side of the road.

In the two side swipes, the other drivers had been speeding and there was some discussion about who was actually at fault. The grandmother was another matter. She'd been inside the car, with her flashers on when he rear-ended her. The impact had snapped her neck.

The collision that killed the Monroe family was similar. It was one of those days when the Texas sky opened up and dropped an astounding amount of water in an even more astounding amount of time. Visibility had been close to zero. Evidence from the scene indicated Mrs. Monroe had pulled over to the right hand side of the road, turned on the flashers, and prepared to wait it out.

The car had been struck from behind and knocked off the roadway into a normally dry culvert. It rolled, landing on its roof, smashing the front and back windshields and two of the four side windows. Someone saw the wreck and called 9-1-1. By the time the police got there, ten minutes later, the culvert was full of water. All three bodies were found still strapped in their seats. All three were pronounced dead at the scene, and the autopsies showed impact injuries and water in their lungs.

Detective Tran had looked closely at the survivors from the

other three known incidents. All had motive, but none had the training required to wield a knife in that particular way. There could be other victims, of course. If the drunk driver had done the same in Mexico, he might have powerful enemies on both sides of the border.

Detective Tran eyed her calendar. The culprit was last seen in Dallas on the day he missed the deportation bus. That day was marked in purple on the calendar, as was the day his body had been found, and the time frame within which he probably died.

Her brow furrowed. Many people could have done the killing, but not many could have arranged to dispose of the body in that spectacular manner.

A more experienced murderer would have left the body where it fell. The fact that it was moved indicated a strong need to do so. The place it was found seemed to implicate the Scots. It was their ship and their people. But they had seemed genuinely shocked at the discovery.

Detective Tran approved the tight-knit Scottish clan structure, and the deference shown by the young to their elders. It mirrored her own upbringing. Furthermore, when she researched the Up-Helly-Aa, she found another connection. Fire festivals were a tradition in both cultures.

The Scots had been instructed by the Laird to cooperate, and there was no reason to think they had not answered every question completely and truthfully. She had several witnesses willing to swear Charles Monroe was not involved in building the Viking ship. He had done so in the past, but not this year. They had been discreet, but the consensus was that the death of his family had resulted in his taking to drink, and that the liquor had incapacitated him. He had not been seen on the grounds at any time during the construction, or while moving the vessel to the water in preparation for the burning, or during the ceremony and subsequent celebration.

But that did not cover every possibility. She would very much like to ask Mr. Monroe where he was during those crucial hours between the completion of the building and the destruction of the ship. Unfortunately, no one had seen Charles Monroe since he left the Cooperative Hall on Friday night. Detective Tran picked up the green marker and made a note on the calendar, then moved to the second board.

The body in the boat had been identified from DNA collected at the times of his multiple arrests. There was no trace evidence to lead them to the scene of the killing. What the fire hadn't destroyed (and it had taken all of the victim's clothing and most of his skin), the water had washed away, or the fish had gotten to. All they had was the autopsy.

The circumstances of Mr. Monroe's skill set and his connection to the Scots made him a 'person of interest', but neither exonerated nor condemned him. Detective Tran made a new note, in red this time, indicating that Mr. Monroe's whereabouts were unknown for more than a week surrounding the presumed time of death.

She'd done some discreet digging. He'd lost his job in late November. Everyone was terribly sympathetic, but he was not showing up for work, and when he did he was often drunk. They couldn't have that. They were sorry. They hadn't seen him in two months.

He had dropped out of school at about the same time. He'd been studying communications technology, and making good grades. The school had provided attendance records, and interviews with his teachers had produced regretful reports of a promising future lost.

The Scots had been more useful. He was one of theirs and they'd been keeping an eye on him, before as well as after that incident in the park. A rather careless eye, as it turned out.

There had been no formal arrangement until a week after the ship burning, the day he'd been released from the hospital. After that, they'd had someone assigned to him.

But they had dropped the ball and let him go off fishing on his own. Not on purpose. A witness had been found who had overheard a conversation between Angus Mackenzie and Charles Monroe, discussing the need to cancel the fishing trip since his companion was unable to go, which corroborated what the Laird had told her. Apparently Mr. Monroe had decided to go anyway.

The Sheriff's Office had found the drifting boat, and one of his shoes, and his pole, a fish still attached, but no body. They had sent divers down and dredged the bottom without results. Most bodies that went missing in Texas lakes were found inside cars, trapped and drowned, but all the lake bottoms had refuse in them, and much of it could catch and hold a man. He could still be down there. It was just that the accident was so convenient.

She and the man, Geordie Hamilton, had looked through Mr. Monroe's house on Sunday. It would have to be done again, with a warrant and evidence collection team, but she had seen no indication of a hasty retreat.

There had been only one thing, a pamphlet on the subject of creating a new identity. It was face down on the bedroom floor and half hidden under the bed. She had been careful not to disturb it, and it might not mean anything, given Mr. Monroe's mental state, but, then again, it might.

Which brought her reluctantly back to her alternate theory. It was at least possible he had faked his death and left town. The only people who did that, in her experience, were those with something to hide.

* * *

Chapter 12

The Laird met them with a typewritten sheet that started, *"The police are probably listening in. Say nothing about Charlie."*

Jim could see Reggie's hand in this. His grandfather was shrewd, but Reggie struck him as twisty as an eel.

As the dinner progressed, Himself passed around detailed instructions on when and where to pick up Charlie. They included an elaborate set of stage directions that had Ginny grinning and Jim wondering if any of this was really necessary. He took a pen out of his pocket and wrote on the latest piece of paper. *Why?*

Himself offered coffee or something stronger and borrowed the pen. *The police think he killed the man in the Viking ship.*

Jim felt his blood run cold. For the first time, he realized he was planning to help a murderer escape justice. That was a crime and, if caught, he could lose everything, his license to practice medicine, his job, maybe even his freedom.

He looked up and found his grandfather's eyes on him.

The Laird rose, went over to the sideboard, and poured three fingers of whisky into a glass, handing it to Jim.

"Ye were suggesting we age th' whisky a mite longer. See

wha' ye think o' this."

Jim took a sip. "Very nice. How old is it?"

"Tha's th' twenty year old. We've got some hundred year stashed awa' waitin' fer a suitable occasion."

Ginny rose and came around to stand beside Jim. She reached for the glass. "May I?" He handed it to her and she took a tiny sip. "Oooo, that is nice." She handed the glass back and put her head down beside his ear. "We need to talk." He nodded and reached for his pen.

Is there anywhere safe to talk?

Himself nodded, writing. *The caverns.*

"I don't suppose you have a bottle of this twenty year old stuff you could let me have?"

"Auch. Aye, but 'tis o'er tae th' Homestead. Would ye be wantin' it tonight?"

"Yes, please. I'd like to take it with me on this trip." Jim turned to Ginny. "Tell me again why we have to drive north in the dead of winter?"

She laughed. "Because if I don't use up my accumulated vacation days, I'll lose them. Also, the schools are in session, which means the reference librarians will be available. And the tourists won't be there so we'll have the archives to ourselves. I love traveling in winter! Besides," she teased, "if you take enough of that twenty year old antifreeze, you won't even notice the cold."

Jim nodded. "All right. Let's go get it."

* * *

Monday Evening
The Caverns

Himself steered the golf cart along a series of passages, none of them marked, and Jim was soon lost.

"We keep th' good stuff awa' frae th' masses, ye ken."

Jim nodded. "Of course."

They pulled up beside a rack bearing labels with years and lot numbers. His grandfather handed Jim three of the bottles. "One fer each o' ye and more when ye get back. Gi'e th' third tae Charlie when ye say, 'Goodbye'."

Himself picked out two more bottles, tucking them carefully into the golf cart, then drove to a lighted space furnished with couches, coffee tables, and rugs. It was a genuine room with a ceiling, walls, floor, a door with a lock, and soundproofing.

"Ha'e a seat, Jim."

Himself handed one of the bottles to Ginny, who took glasses from the cabinet and poured each of them a drink, then retired to a spot just out of Jim's line of sight.

Himself sat down facing Jim. "Now, lad. Y'er wonderin' whether ye should be mixed up in this criminal activity, am I right?"

Jim swallowed hard, then nodded.

"Ye're no required to do sae. 'Tis yer choice."

Jim licked dry lips. "If I get caught, I could lose everything I've worked so hard for."

Himself nodded. "Yer takin' a risk, aye."

"Why are you willing to break the law for this man?"

"Had ye been here, Jim, ye would ha' already heard all o' this. As 'tis, I'll gi'e ye th' short version." He took a sip of his drink, then licked his lips and began.

"Th' rot set in after th' end o' World War II. Politicians reshapin' th' world tae their own ends. Killin' unborn babes and destroyin' families wi' easy divorce. Th' welfare state makin' it cost effective tae be idle. Bullies trying tae strip us o' our right tae feed our families and defend our homes. Freedom ha' been stolen, bit by bit, in th' name o' safety, but nane o' us is safer now." He shook his head.

"We're photographed and listened in on and chronicled and it does nae good. They open th' borders tae all comers, but th' foreigners are no required tae obey th' rules, nor be gainfully employed. Whatever problem they create, th' government raises taxes on the law-abiding and th' number of those is dwindling." He took a breath.

"Criminals get protection, their victims nane. Schools canna teach for fear o' th' distrust it breeds. The truth is murdered in th' name o' political correctness. In th' land o' th' free, it's as much as yer life is worth tae speak yer mind in public, or attend church, or go about yer own business wi'oot government interference.

"I'm no talkin' about illegal activity, ye ken. No drug runnin' or bank robbery. I'm talkin' about farmin' and buildin' houses, and selling bread ye baked in yer own oven. We're nae longer a free country, Jim." He sighed.

"There's still good in it, but th' government is nae longer on our side. Wee Charlie is a fine example. Th' police want him caught and tossed in prison for th' crime o' killin' th' man who killed his family. Had th' perp been in prison, Charlie would no be in this pickle. Th' justice system fails and blames th' wronged man." The Laird took another pull on his drink.

"Charlie is nae killer, nae more than his ancestors were. Put him in prison and he'll either die or be changed for th' worse. Send him into exile and he'll ha' a chance to turn his life aroon'd, tae start agin. He'll be punished, ye ken. 'Tis th' lesser o' two evils, but still an evil."

Himself shifted in his seat. "Th' council sat on it and voted and Charlie was gi'en th' choice. We ha'e a duty tae him and tae th' clan, tae deliver him safely. But you ha'e nae duty to do th' deliverin'. Some other man can do tha'."

Jim sat quite still, his drink in his hands, trying to sort out what he was feeling. Charlie had certainly gotten the raw end of the deal. Why should a law-abiding citizen (bar the murder, of course) be imprisoned when an illegal alien (also a murderer) who has gate-crashed a country and thumbed his nose at the law, get off with no punishment at all?

His grandfather was also correct in pointing out that, had the justice system delivered justice, Charlie would not have been obliged to kill anyone (except possibly himself, but that was another discussion).

The clan had judged Charlie. He had submitted to the council and accepted his fate, stoically, Jim had thought. He would not have wanted to face that choice himself. So what was his role in all of this? He took a sip of his drink.

Among the things Jim had studied in school was how to resolve an ethical dilemma. They came up fairly regularly in health care.

Jim recognized this one as a *Locus of Authority* dilemma. There were two authorities, both of whom were claiming jurisdiction over Charles Monroe. Jim understood the clan system and recognized the chain of command. He knew that the clan dealt with its own offenders and that a laird could stand *in loco parentis* for any of its members. In theory, at least, he recognized the authority his grandfather was claiming.

If he conceded that the council had the right to try and condemn one of its own, did it follow that all the members of the clan had a duty to help make that judgment happen?

There was more than DNA involved. Being a clansman meant being a member of a culture, a rather unusual one. The trappings didn't matter. You could still be a Scot even if you never put on a kilt.

But there were certain things that were required. These he had learned from his parents: the work ethic that made it possible to get into medical school and graduate with a respectable ranking, the self-reliance that allowed even the poorest member of the clan to hold his head up in public, the mandated hospitality that meant no one, clansman or not, would ever be denied food and shelter when in need.

Jim was, by blood, by breeding, and by conscious choice, a Scot, and the Scots had a long history of fighting for what they believed in.

He rose to his feet and looked around. Ginny sat on the end of one of the sofas, silent, her eyes on him. He turned on his grandfather.

"Is what you're doing here education or indoctrination?"

"Some would say one, some th' other. We teach th' bairns history, all of it, not just wha' gets inta th' local school books, then we teach them how tae think. They're given opportunities tae build strength o' character, and tae practice virtue. 'Tis a community tha' prides itself on givin' its young th' tools tae function, then getting oot o' the way and lettin' them find their own ground."

Find his own ground. The clan would expect its next laird to be a true leader, in deeds as well as words. If Jim declined the honor of accompanying Charlie to Canada, it would prove he was unfit for the job. He turned and looked at Ginny.

"What about you? Are you willing to risk your career and freedom for this man?"

She nodded. "In the cause of justice. Yes."

Jim believed in justice. He had to, for he also believed in mercy and without justice there could be no mercy. He also believed that a man was responsible for himself and his family and that the obligation could not be handed off to a government, no matter how benign. What's more, he believed that self-respect required making the right choice, even if that came with a price.

If he was a member of this clan, if he wanted to lead them, he needed to decide right here, right now, how he was going to handle difficult choices. The risk to himself was not the issue. Courage was not the issue. Obedience to the Laird was not the issue. The issue was which course of action would an honorable man choose? Framed that way, he had his answer.

Quite unconsciously, he squared his shoulders, drew himself up to his full height, and pulled in a deep breath. Ginny rose to her feet, her face calm, her eyes on his.

"I'll go," he said, to her.

She smiled and nodded, then walked over, bringing her glass up to touch his. "And I will go with you."

* * *

CHAPTER 13

Tuesday Morning
Forbes Residence

Ginny pulled her eyes open again to find Jim laughing at her.

"Wake up, sleepyhead! It's time to go."

They had finished packing last night and agreed that Jim should have breakfast at her house before they took off. Her mother had cooked and Ginny was grateful, but Ginny was not a morning person. She spooned another bite of eggs into her mouth, finished off the juice, poured the coffee into a travel cup, and shook her head, trying to clear it of the cobwebs.

"Okay. I'm ready."

"You are not!" He was laughing again.

"What?"

He pointed at her feet. No shoes.

"Oh." She put the cup back down, then hurried upstairs to finish dressing. Her mother followed her up.

"Are you all right, darling?"

She nodded through the toothpaste. "I'll be fine. What about you? Will you be all right without me?"

"Of course. Himself will take good care of me."

"We'll call when we get in tonight, but it may be late."

"Call anyway."

Ginny slipped on her shoes, hurried down the staircase,

handed Jim the coffee thermos, then gave her mother a hug.

"Have a safe trip," Mrs. Forbes said.

"I'll take good care of her," Jim promised.

Ginny climbed up into the passenger side of the van. Jim closed the door on her, then took his place behind the wheel. He grinned at her as they turned the corner.

"Alone at last!"

"Don't get any ideas," she warned. "Remember, this is just a cover story, not a honeymoon."

She saw his eyes light up at the word, but he said nothing, just continued to smile to himself.

* * *

Tuesday Morning
Dallas, TX

Jim steered the van northeast to the suburb Reggie had chosen as a rendezvous point. He still wasn't happy about the choice of vehicle, but it handled okay and he had to admit that it made a very unlikely get-away car. No one would give them a second glance.

Ginny pointed out the store. "There it is."

"What's our excuse for pulling off the road so soon?" Jim asked.

"I need Texas souvenirs to use as hostess gifts and they have to be purchased before we leave the state."

They located the Texas knick-knacks and selected amusing items for each of the Homesteads they would be visiting, then made their way to the camping section.

Reggie had been specific. They were to purchase something large enough to require the loading dock.

They settled on a generator. It was small enough to fit easily in the back of the van, but heavy. It would require male muscle to get it in. They paid for their purchases, then drove around to the back of the store.

Jim examined the set-up and silently approved Reggie's choice. The area had a recessed dock with an overhanging roof that protected customers and staff from the rain, and poor lighting. He looked for, but did not see any cameras.

He parked, then got out and went around to open the back. Ginny did the same on the passenger side, opening the side door. Two workers in safety vests approached, the generator perched on a dolly between them.

Jim stepped out of the way and let them hoist the box into the space he had cleared for it, then closed up and walked back to the driver's side door. He glanced up in time to see one of the workers re-enter the store with the dolly. The other had vanished.

He waited until Ginny was settled, then put the car in gear and backed out, looking over his shoulder to make sure he didn't run into anything.

"You all right back there?" he asked.

"Fine. Thanks for the lift."

"You're welcome. Keep your head down."

Jim maneuvered back out onto the highway. In ten minutes they were beyond the immediate metropolitan area and on their way.

* * *

Tuesday Midmorning
Forbes Residence

Detective Tran pulled up in front of the Forbes' house and got out. The door was opened by Mrs. Forbes.

"I would like to speak to Miss Forbes, please."

"I'm afraid you've just missed her. She and Jim, Dr. Mackenzie, left this morning. Is there something I can help you with?"

"She is gone?"

Mrs. Forbes nodded. "For two weeks, maybe a bit more."

"May I ask why? I mean, why now?"

"She said finding the body upset her. She had some vacation time available and decided to use it."

"I see. Thank you very much." Tran took her leave and headed back to her car, thinking hard.

It could be true. It could be that the artless Miss Forbes who had been visibly distressed by the discovery of the body had truly needed a vacation to recover from the shock. The smitten Dr. Mackenzie would leap at a chance to take her away and spend some quality time with her, just the two of them. No surprise there. Why drive, though? Winter vacations usually meant an airplane ride and lift tickets.

Mr. Monroe had been missing now for four days. There was no reason to think he had waited around, then hitched a ride with the young couple. He would just be in their way. Nor was there any reason to think that either Miss Forbes or Dr. Mackenzie would knowingly engage in criminal behavior. Both had too much to lose. And yet—

Detective Tran put the car in gear and drove back to the office. She had some thinking to do.

* * *

CHAPTER 14

Tuesday Afternoon
Little Rock, AR

Ginny was stretching her legs at a road side park just outside Little Rock, Arkansas. The winter sun was already low on the horizon and they had another hour to go before they would reach Memphis, then three to Nashville and thirty minutes, minimum, to locate their destination. She zipped up her jacket, smoothing the collar and feeling for the chain that should have been around her neck, the one that held her talisman. It wasn't there. She hurried back to the van.

"Jim! I've forgotten my talisman!" She grabbed her phone. Ten minutes later her mother had confirmed the talisman had been left behind, and promised to send it on by Homestead courier to Settler's Cabin in Pittsburgh, their second stop.

"That's a relief! It should be there before we arrive."

Jim was looking at her, one eyebrow raised, a half-mocking smile on his face. "Can you manage without it?" he asked.

She sniffed, adjusted the driver's side seat and mirrors to suit herself, then pulled out of the parking lot. Jim craned his head over his shoulder, watching for obstructions, but refrained from backseat driving, for which she was grateful. When they were safely on the highway, he relaxed, leaning against the passenger side door. Ginny thought he was going to sleep, but found him watching her instead.

It made her nervous at first, but the van's controls were familiar, and the road was clear. Charlie, apparently unconcerned, had curled up on the air mattress in the back, and could be heard snoring.

Ginny actually liked driving. In her native Texas, she especially liked to go west, to the vast flat regions where the roads went on forever. On a clear night she had been known to turn off the car headlamps and drive by moonlight, not hurrying, windows down, the night breeze caressing her soul.

The sun set behind them, turning the clouds ahead deep gold, then rose, then pale blue before fading into night. She heard Jim sigh and glanced over.

"I wish it was our honeymoon," he said.

"With Charlie along?" she whispered.

He laughed. "Well, no. Just the two of us. I want to take you home with me, to set up housekeeping, and start making little Mackenzies. Himself would like that."

"Hush! Charlie might hear you, poor man."

She could see Jim shrug. "He should find a nice Canadian woman and marry her."

Ginny frowned. Jim might be right, but it sounded cold-hearted to say so. Charlie and Mandy had been very much in love.

* * *

Tuesday Evening
Memphis, TN

They stopped on the other side of Memphis for dinner and ate in silence, each occupied with his own thoughts. Jim was thinking about family.

An only child, he had never felt alone. Why was that? Was it an inherently male trait, to be sure of one's self and one's place in the world? Or had his parents given him that?

Neither had he felt any urgency to settle down and reproduce. He'd heard women talking about a biologic clock and just assumed men didn't have one. During medical school he'd had any number of women express interest in him, but he'd been too busy to pay much attention.

Ginny was another matter. He'd been making a fool of himself over her from day one. Well, day two. Or day one, if you were using a twenty-four hour clock. He'd told practically everyone that he wanted to marry her, including her, and today he'd told her he wanted children by her. Without thinking it through, just blurted it out.

Here was the urgency he'd never felt before. He wanted to swoop in on his white horse and carry her off, to settle down in a little house with a picket fence and big oak tree and a monkey swing. His imagination peopled the yard with tiny redheads, shrieking as he chased them across the lawn, then caught them and tossed them into the air, to catch them again, and cover them with kisses. Her, too.

He paid the tab (Charlie paying cash for his own, to foil anyone who might want to track their movements through the credit cards), then herded his charges back to the car.

"It's your turn to drive, Charlie."

They were moving into a part of the country where they might see snow. The prudent thing was to let both of the others get a feel for the van before then. Ginny, at least, had driven in Colorado in the winter time. As far as he knew, Charlie had not.

* * *

Tuesday Evening
I-40, headed east

During the drive from Memphis to Nashville, Ginny entertained them with miscellany about the area, all gathered during her genealogical trips.

"The Natchez Trace stretches for more than 400 miles and is approximately 10,000 years old. As bison moved up the river, they broke through the forest growth and trampled out a path to the Nashville salt licks. The Chickasaw and Choctaw Indians used the Trace as a trade route and the white man followed.

"Franklin, TX is named for Franklin, TN, because many of the early settlers in Texas came from Nashville. Robertson Colony was founded by the Nashville Company and stretched all the way from modern Austin to the Red River.

"One of Nashville's curiosities is the full-sized replica of the Parthenon located in the middle of town. The structure and decorations are believed to be very close to the way the original Parthenon would have appeared. The statue of Athena is terrifying."

"How do you remember all this stuff?" Jim wanted to know.

"I've visited and it helps to have family connections. You might be surprised at how many Scots made American history."

"Don't bet on that. My parents went to a lot of trouble to make sure I knew what the Scots have done for the world."

Charlie peered out at the approaching city. "Do you have directions to the Homestead? We're getting close."

Jim pulled out the instructions. "From I-40, take exit 188, turn left, under the highway. Follow the signs to TN-249 then turn right on E. Kingston Springs Rd toward the Cheatham Wildlife Management Area, then follow the signs to the Homestead. Three miles."

Ten minutes later Ginny sang out. "There."

Charlie turned north on a paved road that was suddenly only one lane in each direction, without lights or shoulders. It took another twenty minutes to find the turn off to the Homestead, then ten minutes to the front gate.

The guard admitted them and pointed out a series of picturesque cottages along the front drive that turned out to be Bed & Breakfast establishments, with all the amenities necessary for tourists. They pulled up as instructed and the three of them got out, realizing it was close to eleven p.m. The door opened as they approached.

"Come in! Come in! We've been expecting you. Hard day was it?" The well-upholstered woman who greeted them gave them no chance to linger, hustling them into the front room, plying them with hot milk, seeing their luggage taken to their rooms, arranging for a breakfast wake-up call, and in general tucking them in for the night as fast as possible. Jim was not sorry. He made sure the car was locked, brushed his teeth, then fell into bed, and was asleep before his head hit the pillow.

* * *

CHAPTER 15

Wednesday Morning
Nashville, TN

Early the next morning, Jim hoisted his bag over his shoulder and went to collect Ginny. "If you aren't downstairs in ten minutes I'm coming to get you," he threatened. "Charlie and I will meet you in the dining room."

The two men settled down to enjoy the breakfast buffet and Jim took the time to get coffee for Ginny, then, when she still hadn't surfaced, a plate with eggs, bacon, and slices of tomato (the state fruit).

He had his eye on his watch and was just deciding he would have to carry her bodily out to the car when she slipped into the room. The Matron approached their table with a fresh pot of hot coffee and Jim rose to greet her.

"I haven't had a chance to thank you for your hospitality last night. I'm afraid we were dead on our feet."

She smiled at him, cocking her head to one side. "You'll be the Mackenzie's boy."

Jim blinked in surprise. "I am. How did you know?"

"Angus was best man at our wedding. Angus, Jr., I mean."

Jim smiled. He was the fourth of that name.

"You look like him."

"So I'm told."

"Is there anything else I can get you? I know you want to hit the road as quickly as possible."

"Could we get some of your excellent coffee to go?"

"Of course. I'll be right back."

Jim turned to the table to find Ginny's eyes on him, a Texas souvenir in her hand.

"Give her this, please."

The Matron returned promptly with three paper coffee cups. "You can add the sugar and cream here, then put the lids on and take them with you in the car."

"God bless you, ma'am!" Jim produced the gift and watched her eyes light up. "We would be so pleased if you would accept this small token of our gratitude for your kindness." He handed over the Texas-sized shot glass, a tumbler designed to hold sixteen ounces. "I wish I could fill it, but I know you make excellent whisky in Tennessee and will not have a problem finding something to put in it."

She laughed, delighted with the joke. "Thank you! Please give Angus my love when you see him."

Jim found himself suddenly at a loss. He didn't know the woman's name. Ginny came to the rescue, holding out her hand.

"This has been delightful, Mrs. Montgomery. Thank you, for everything."

"You're very welcome, my dear. I hope we have the pleasure of seeing you again some time."

"I hope so, too."

They took their leave, fixed the coffees, gathered up their belongings, and made their way out onto the street.

Jim was fiddling with the car remote, his head down against the cold wind and did not see Charlie pull open the side door on the van, then freeze. He walked right into him.

"Hey!" He looked up, starting to protest, then saw what the

problem was. Ginny stepped up beside him, reaching for the passenger side front door, but Jim put his arm out to stop her, then pushed her behind him.

"Get in. Quietly."

The stranger held what looked like a .45 automatic, trained on Charlie's chest, his eyes darting between the two men. "Let the lady get in first."

Jim swallowed hard. "Let her get up front."

"No. She rides with me, to make sure you two behave."

Jim could feel Ginny pressed up against his back. She peeked around his shoulder, took in the situation, then stepped out from behind him without a word, moving toward the back seat.

"Good girl. Now come sit beside me."

The muzzle of the gun wavered between Jim's chest and Charlie's, the stranger unsure which of them was the more important target for his purposes. Ginny climbed in and settled down where he indicated.

"May I drink my coffee?" she asked.

"Got some for me?" She handed the cup over and he tasted it. "Perfect."

He focused his eyes on the two men. "Get in. You look conspicuous standing there."

Charlie handed his bag to Ginny. "I'm going to get into the driver's seat," he said.

The stranger nodded. "And you," he indicated Jim, "can get into the suicide seat. Just you remember, the both of you, if you try anything, she's the first to die." He waved them toward the front of the car, then placed the gun to Ginny's temple.

Jim felt his blood turn to ice. He moved carefully to comply with the demand, climbing into the passenger side seat and closing the door.

"You." The stranger indicated Ginny. "Close the door. Then

come back over here."

She did as told.

"All right. We're going to drive out of here just like nothing is wrong. Got it?"

Jim nodded to Charlie, who started the engine and pulled away from the curb. They drove out of the Homestead without being stopped, just waved through by the guard on the gate.

"Where are we headed?" Jim asked.

"Highway 40, east."

If the hijacker took them too far out of their way, they'd have to find someplace else to stay tonight, always assuming they were still alive when night fell, but there was no reason to share their plans with him. Ginny had checked in with her mother last night. They could be dead and dumped long before anyone had the slightest idea they were in trouble.

Jim surreptitiously studied their extra passenger. His clothes were nondescript: dark blue sweats, running shoes, a black jacket appropriate to the weather. He was wearing a knitted cap that said 'Virginia is for Lovers' on it. No glasses, no jewelry. At least one tattoo, partially visible on the left side of his neck. Nothing, other than the gun, to indicate this was not just another law-abiding citizen.

He had lowered the gun to chest level. It was no longer pushed up against the side of Ginny's head. That was good. But it was still aimed at her. Jim licked dry lips, then half-turned in his seat so he could talk to the hijacker.

"How can we help you?" he asked.

The stranger met his eyes. "Just do what I tell you to and no one will get hurt."

Jim wished he could believe that. It had been decades since someone willing to take hostages had also been willing to let them go.

Jim took a slow, deep breath. They could not go to the

police. Not with Charlie in the car.

"How did you get in?" he asked.

"Over the fence."

"And into the van?"

Ginny answered that one. "He slid a wire inside the insulation and pushed the unlock button."

The hijacker nodded, grinning. "Smart girl."

"Why didn't you just steal the van?" she asked.

"I was going to, but by the time I got in, the guard had locked the gates."

"Why this vehicle?" Jim asked.

"Covered windows and Texas plates. The sleeping bag was a nice surprise."

"I take it you don't want us stopping in Nashville for gas." Jim's voice sounded a lot calmer than he felt.

"No. How much have you got in the tank?"

Jim looked over at Charlie, who glanced down at the gauge. "About half a tank." He looked over at Jim. "It will probably get us to Knoxville, but no farther."

"Okay." The stranger stretched his legs out on the air mattress, his eyes settling on Ginny.

Jim followed his gaze. She was sitting with her eyes on the floor, her jacket pulled tight across her chest, her chin buried in her muffler.

"Are you cold, darlin'?" the stranger asked her.

She nodded without looking at him.

"I could warm you up."

Jim felt his whole body tense. There was no way he was going to let this bastard touch Ginny.

She shifted slightly, turning to face the intruder. "No, thank you."

Jim was thinking furiously. Both he and Ginny were armed, but the weapons had been secured before they left the car last night, to make sure Charlie didn't have access to them. Jim had carried the pistol cases in with him, then into his room. They were in the overnight bag under his feet, unloaded, useless.

There was a rifle, too, but it was even more useless, secured in the locked and tethered traveling case required by law. The handgun licenses he and Ginny carried were civilian version, not law enforcement, so the guns were there to deal with any marauding predator they might expect to encounter in the winter wilderness. It hadn't occurred to Jim that the predator might have two legs.

Charlie glanced up at the sky, then over at Jim. "Did you get a weather report before we left? Looks like there's a front moving in."

Jim looked back at the hijacker. "Is it all right if I look up the weather?"

He frowned. "No phones. Hand them over, all of them."

Jim and Ginny did as instructed.

"Where's the other?"

"I don't have one," Charlie volunteered.

"I don't believe you. Hand it over."

"It's true. I ditched it."

The stranger's eyebrows rose. "Ditched?"

Charlie nodded. "I'm a fugitive, running from the law."

The stranger's eyebrows rose all the way to his hairline. "You shittin' me?" He looked at Jim.

Jim shook his head. "It's true."

"What did you do, man?"

"I killed someone."

"Why?"

"He killed my family."

"Wow. Good job, man!"

"What about the radio? Can we use that to pick up a weather report?" Charlie glanced in the rearview mirror.

The stranger peered out the window, looking up at the gathering clouds. "Okay."

Charlie reached over and the radio sprang to life. Country and Western music. Well, it was Tennessee. Charlie twisted the knob. A sermon, a fairly common occurrence in the Bible Belt. He tried again.

"—accident at the 24/41 interchange. Traffic is backed up for five miles. Weather report for this February Hump Day includes a cold front barreling down from Canada. This one may bring us up to two inches of snow. Temperatures are expected to stay at or just above the freezing mark so be careful on bridges and overpasses.

"BREAKING NEWS: The incident last night at the Riverbend Maximum Security Prison has detractors calling for the warden's resignation. Sheriffs' deputies have mounted a massive manhunt for the three escaped convicts. Citizens are reminded to use caution if approached by a stranger and not to give lifts to anyone who appears to be stranded on the highway. The three convicts are identified as—"

"Shut that off!"

There was sudden silence in the car. Jim saw Charlie glance in the rearview mirror, then put his eyes back on the road. Ginny's head had snapped around to look at the stranger, but as Jim watched, she dropped her eyes to the floor again, carefully showing no interest. Jim, on the other hand, met the stranger's gaze. He shrugged.

"We don't care. We'll take you anywhere you want to go, then forget we ever saw you, as long as you agree to do the same."

* * *

Chapter 16

Wednesday Morning
I-40, headed east

The trip from Nashville to Knoxville was nerve wracking. Jim spent the entire time with his eyes on the intruder, his brain in overdrive.

Charlie and the convict had struck up a desultory conversation on the subject of murder. Charlie explained how he had brought a body onto the grounds of the loch and hidden it in the Viking ship. He'd had to take up some of the floorboards, tuck the body underneath, move ballast to compensate, then put the boards back in place. It was the first time Jim had heard the story and, by the look on her face, the same was true for Ginny.

Jim was increasingly impressed with Charlie Monroe. He hadn't had a drink since entering the hospital. His mind was clear and Jim wasn't at all sure Charlie wasn't controlling the conversation, in spite of his laid back manner. He let the intruder brag and expressed appropriate respect for the professional's expertise.

It would have been better if the intruder hadn't been confessing, of course. It increased their chances of being killed to shut their mouths, but establishing rapport was always the first step in any hostage situation and Charlie had managed to find common ground.

Jim applied himself to figuring out how to end the siege. Knoxville was less than two hours southwest of the Virginia border. If they stayed on this highway, he would be back in home territory by early afternoon. Who could he call on? What resources did he have access to?

Approaching the situation logically, the first goal was to get the gun away from the hijacker. If—when—they disarmed him (three to one, after all) they could use the duct tape to restrain him. So, how to manage that, without getting shot?

Jim's eyes drifted over to Ginny. She was moving restlessly, shifting her position, and glancing out the window. She looked up and their eyes met.

"I need a rest stop," she said.

Jim nodded. "How much farther to Knoxville?" he asked.

"Twenty minutes," Charlie answered. "Shall I find a place to pull off?"

Jim looked at the intruder, who nodded.

"Okay, but we do it my way."

Jim nodded. When Ginny left the car, she could run. That would leave the other two at the mercy of an angry felon, who might shoot them, but at least she would be safe.

Charlie could drive off and leave her behind. If Jim lunged at the intruder at the same moment, would that be enough to surprise him?

If the intruder left the vehicle, they could drive off without him. Well, not if the reason was to escort Ginny to the restroom and back. They couldn't leave while she was being held hostage.

Jim shifted slightly in his seat and saw the hijacker's eyes turn in his direction. No movement had gone unnoticed. Not so far. Jim rolled his shoulders, carefully, wishing he didn't have to keep his neck craned over his left shoulder. His muscles were protesting. He blinked. The hijacker must be in the same condition.

It took effort to hold a gun trained on anything for two hours straight. If asked, Jim would have said it couldn't be done. At the very least, the hijacker's control over the weapon must be impaired. What's more, he probably knew it.

Jim let his eyes roam, trying to see the problem from the hijacker's point of view. Most likely he planned to shoot them and take the car. Charlie was trapped behind the wheel, which made it impossible for him to move quickly. Jim was the greater menace, restrained only by the threat to Ginny and his seat belt, so with Ginny out of the car, the gun would be aimed at Jim. What else?

How big was this hijacker's bladder? Healthy human kidneys produced an average of two ounces of fluid every hour, more in the hour after drinking coffee since caffeine was a diuretic.

It was just barely possible that the hijacker would let Ginny take her purse with her to the bathroom. Women sometimes need things they keep in their purses and he would know that. Was there anything in the purse that could be used as a weapon? Fingernail file? Cuticle scissors? Spray perfume?

Jim's eyes lingered on Ginny, fighting down the image of a bullet ripping through her flesh. Assuming it didn't kill her instantly, he didn't have much in the way of first aid for an injury of that sort, just pressure dressings and morphine.

Morphine.

If he could figure out some way to get morphine into the hijacker, he could incapacitate him. He didn't have to give him enough to kill him, just make him so groggy he couldn't hold the gun anymore. Then they could overpower him without fear of being shot.

Maybe Ginny could sneak up on the hijacker and slap him on the back, injecting the morphine into a muscle as she did so.

Except, she would have to open the vial and a syringe package and draw up the dose (maybe in the bathroom?), then get the needle into him, then get him to hold still while she pushed the plunger down. Too many steps. If only there were a faster way to deliver the medication. Like an auto injector. *A lightning fast auto injector!*

Jim had two. One had epinephrine in it. All that would do is make a wide awake crazy man out of the currently calm escaped criminal. The other would knock him out.

Jim did some rapid calculations in his head. The second auto injector held a ten milligram dose of midazolam, twice the recommended amount for a healthy, adult male. Onset was typically fifteen minutes, with a half-life on average of three hours. The double dose could easily put the hijacker into respiratory arrest. The duration meant they would have to hold onto him for several hours, to make sure he didn't suffocate.

Ginny could get the auto injector out of the medical kit and hit the hijacker with it. That was do-able, assuming the hijacker thought she was no threat to him. The real problem was the fifteen minute onset time. How were they to keep him from shooting them while they waited for the drug to kick in?

Divide and conquer? Give him three moving targets and hope he couldn't shoot straight? Charlie could go out the driver's side door and drop to the ground. Ginny could be in the baggage compartment, ready to leap out the back. Jim?

Well, on the assumption that the hijacker would keep Jim in his sights while Ginny was in the back, Jim was the most likely of the three to take a bullet. The car seat would not stop it. The intruder would be firing from a seated position, which was awkward, but he was very close and it would be hard to miss a mass the size of Jim at that range.

What would happen if Jim leaned forward, as if he was trying to get something off the floor of the car? What about the seatbelt? If he loosened it, would the alarm kick in? Once the car was stopped, of course, it probably wouldn't care.

So, if he and Charlie could both dive for the floor at the same moment, release the seatbelts, open the doors, and jump out, all in smooth, coordinated effort, there would just be the fact that Jim might not be faster than a speeding bullet.

Jim frowned. What else? They were rapidly approaching the city limits. Charlie was watching for a place to pull off the highway.

The first thing to do was get Ginny out of the car. She might be able to get help, but even if she didn't risk it, the hijacker couldn't, realistically, follow her into the ladies room. His best bet was to use the gun trained on Jim to control her. So she would behave and come right back.

At that point, Jim could direct her to the back of the car, to get the auto injector out of the medical kit. Assuming she understood what he was getting at.

Jim crossed his fingers. They could communicate in medical-ese and probably not be understood by either Charlie or the intruder. She would have to find a way to get close enough to the hijacker to inject the medication, though, and Jim could not help with that. What he could supply was a distraction.

What kind of distraction? Could he spill something? Or throw something? There was a thought! If he could empty his bladder into something, he could throw the urine onto the hijacker. His (now empty) coffee cup was sitting in the holder. He could fill it up and toss it at the hijacker.

Then what? The gun might go off at the shock of being doused with urine. Jim needed something to throw the hijacker's aim off. If he couldn't see, he couldn't aim, not as well, anyway. What about knocking the gun away? Was there anything he could use for that and if he did so, where would the bullet go?

Jim was suddenly aware that the car was slowing down. Charlie had found a gas station he liked the looks of.

Jim glanced at the items in the front of the car with him. His coffee cup and Charlie's. Maps. His overnight bag. The jacket he'd shed about halfway between Memphis and here.

"Is it okay if I pick my jacket up off the floor?" He waited for the hijacker to nod. "Thanks." Jim bent down and retrieved the garment, draping it across his lap.

He watched the gas station appear on the side of the highway and waited as Charlie pulled up to the tank. Charlie looked over at him as he shut off the engine.

"We're here." Jim turned around in his seat and looked at the hijacker. "Okay. Tell us what to do."

The hijacker motioned to Ginny with the gun.

"You go take care of business, but come right back. No shopping and don't speak to anyone. If I see anything suspicious, anything that looks the slightest like you told someone what was going on, he gets a bullet through the brain. Understand?" He raised the gun and pointed it at Jim.

She nodded, then let herself out, shutting the door behind her.

Jim swallowed, then put his plan into action.

"I need to pee, too."

"You stay here."

"What about me?" Charlie asked.

"You, too."

"It's kind of urgent," Jim said.

The hijacker's eyes narrowed. "You stay right where you are."

Jim squirmed, in a good imitation of physical discomfort. "Okay. How about I pee in the cup?"

"What cup?"

Jim held up the large coffee cup he'd been given at the

Cumberland Homestead.

The hijacker nodded slowly. "Okay, but no funny business."

Jim nodded, released his seatbelt, then carefully undid his zipper and positioned the cup. In truth, it was a big relief to empty his bladder and the cup was almost full before the stream started to taper off.

"Lord! Me, too." Charlie said.

"All right, you wimps."

Charlie followed suit, filling his own coffee cup. He looked over at Jim, who had put the cup back in the holder while he closed his pants. "Where are we going to dump these?"

"Wherever the man says," Jim replied.

The sound of bladders being emptied had produced an effect on the hijacker. He was looking distinctly uncomfortable. He located the coffee cup that had been Ginny's and placed it near at hand, but did not undo his fly.

Ginny was back almost before the men had finished their business. Jim was grimly amused. Is that what it took to get a woman to hurry? The threat of a bullet through the brain? She opened the side door and started to climb in.

Jim gasped, his eyes opening wide.

She looked up at him. "What?"

"I completely forgot to remind you. Did you take your midazolam today?"

She blinked, but that was all. "Oh, Christ! I forgot all about it!" She looked over at the intruder then back at Jim, her brow furrowing. "Where did you put it last night?"

"In my medical bag. In the back."

The hijacker was looking at her, his eyes narrowed, his expression suspicious. "What is that?"

Ginny looked at him, frowning heavily. "I have to give myself injections every day, in the morning."

"What are you? A diabetic?"

"She needs it for her autoimmune disorder," Jim volunteered.

"And I'm late. Is it okay if I do it now?" she asked.

He looked at her for a very long moment and Jim held his breath. This was one of the weak links in his plan. Would the hijacker believe her?

At length he nodded. "Get the bag and bring it up here so I can watch you. Don't forget. I've got my finger on the trigger so —"

She nodded. "No funny business. I know."

She climbed back out onto the pavement, leaving the side door open behind her, and moved around to the back of the car, opening the rear doors. She made a convincing show of trying to get hold of the bag, being unable to reach it, then climbing into the van, pushing obstacles aside, making noises and talking to herself. Jim watched the hijacker, waiting for an opening, one hand on the coffee cup, the other on his jacket. He could feel Charlie's eyes on him.

Ginny swore loudly and the hijacker glanced in her direction, just for a second, but it was enough.

Jim threw the urine at him, hitting him in the face, followed in almost the same motion by the jacket, which landed on his outstretched gun hand. The jacket was leather, and heavy. It knocked the gun to the steel floor and the gun went off.

Jim heard another splash. By that time he had gotten his feet under him and launched himself into the back of the van, knocking the hijacker over and landing on top of him. He pinned the gun arm to the floor.

"NOW, Ginny!"

She climbed over the cargo, then over Jim, and jammed the auto injector into the hijacker's thigh.

There was a steady stream of cursing coming from their captive, but Charlie had added his weight to the other two holding him down and there was nothing he could do to dislodge them. Charlie had also taken the trouble to stamp on the hijacker's hand, forcing him to release the weapon.

"We've got this," Jim told Ginny. "Go fill the tank so we can move the van."

She slid off the still bucking hijacker and climbed out, closing the doors as she went.

To Jim, worried someone would notice the commotion and come to investigate, the next few minutes were excruciating. In reality, Ginny had the tank filled and was back behind the wheel, moving the car away from the pump and parking it around the side of the station in less than ten minutes.

Jim and Charlie sat on the hijacker until he stopped struggling.

"Twelve minutes." Jim had been keeping an eye on his watch. He examined his patient. "Still breathing."

Jim was kneeling on the intruder's abdomen, Charlie on his arms. Jim smiled at him.

"Thanks for the help."

"Any time."

Ginny wrinkled her nose. "Do I smell what I think I smell?"

"Yes."

"Did he wet himself?"

"No. We did that for him, though, considering the circumstances—" Jim glanced down and was not surprised to see a large wet spot on the hijacker's pants.

The hijacker was now flaccid. Jim showed Charlie how to hold his chin up so the airway stayed open. "I'll be right back." He retrieved his ambu bag and fitted it over the hijacker's nose and mouth, squeezing air into his lungs.

Ginny watched for a minute, then took off in the direction of the restrooms.

"Where's she going?" Charlie asked.

"Probably to get soap and water. This car suddenly got a lot less environmentally friendly."

He was right. She was back in a few minutes with gloves, paper towels, and a spray cleaner. She set to work wiping out the puddles and trying to disinfect the surfaces.

"What can I do?" Charlie asked.

"Find that bullet."

It took Charlie ten minutes to decide the slug must have exited through the side door. "I found the casing, but that's all."

Jim glanced out the window. He didn't see the frantic activity he would expect if someone had been shot or even heard a shot. Perhaps the sound had been mistaken for a backfire.

"Okay. I guess we got lucky." Without his coat and with the adrenaline beginning to wear off Jim was getting cold.

"Ginny, can you take over here?"

She slipped into Jim's place, making sure air was still getting into the hijacker's lungs. Jim picked up his jacket and looked at it, then decided it needed to be cleaned before he would be willing to put it on again.

"Look!" He put his finger through a hole in the heavy leather.

"Better your jacket than you," Ginny said, and Jim had to agree.

* * *

CHAPTER 17

Wednesday Noon
Knoxville, TN

It was twenty minutes before their patient began breathing on his own again. They turned him on his side and bound his elbows, wrists, knees, and ankles with duct tape.

While they waited, they ate lunch, threw out the trash, and re-arranged the gear. At one point, Jim glanced over to see Charlie pick up the discarded pistol, clear the chamber and remove the magazine, then stow the parts in his overnight bag. Jim approved the safe handling of the weapon and made a mental note to retrieve the gun the first chance he got.

"We have to dump him somewhere he can be found," Jim said.

"Today?" Charlie asked.

Jim looked out the window. "Well, if not today, then somewhere the weather won't kill him overnight." He looked back down at their charge. "No sooner than four hours from now."

"Which means we might as well be driving as sitting here."

"I suppose so."

"Which way do we go?"

They could not make it to Pittsburgh tonight. The storm was rotating over that area and the roads had already started to close.

Jim hauled out his phone. Interstate 40 turned into I-81 just beyond Knoxville. I-81 would take them through Virginia and Maryland, then into Pennsylvania where they could pick up I-87 and follow it into New York, which would get them back on route. So the detour wasn't disastrous, just inconvenient.

He outlined his plan and the other two nodded.

"Sounds good," Charlie said.

Jim glanced at his watch then picked up the phone and dialed his grandfather.

"Jim! 'Tis good tae hear yer voice lad."

"Grandfather, we've had a bit of a problem come up." Jim explained about the change of route without explaining the cause. "Is there a way you can cancel the Pittsburgh arrangements and get us something else? We're going to be on I-81 for the rest of today."

"Auch, aye, lad. Let me call ye back."

Jim set the phone aside, his mind going back to their unwanted cargo. Where were they going to be in four hours? Roanoke. There was snow predicted in the area before nightfall. Where could he stash the hijacker that he'd be protected from the weather, warm enough overnight, if that was how long it took to find him, and guaranteed to be found?

Jim considered the possibilities. Police stations, fire stations, and hospitals were all places of refuge, but it would be hard to drive up, toss their charge out the door and drive off without attracting attention. What he needed was a place routinely open to the public.

It took him thirty minutes to find a likely prospect, a mall that boasted twenty-four hour entertainment. The entrance was in an alcove, protected by an overhanging roof and sheltered from the lights in the parking lot. If they tucked the hijacker up against the doors, someone would find him.

Dressed in white and driving a white van, with the snow blowing around them, he and Charlie could drop their unwanted passenger and drive off with minimal chance of someone noticing. They might be no more than a ghost on the security camera footage, even if someone looked.

It was a risk, of course, but Jim could not lug this escaped convict all over the northeast. He had to dump him.

What would the police do when they found him? Assume the dropper-offers didn't want to speak to them. Assume they knew more than they should. Assume they were on the wrong side of the law. But it wasn't a crime to capture an escaped felon and leave him, trussed like a Thanksgiving turkey, to be found by someone else. Assuming he was alive, of course.

Best case scenario (for the hijacker), the mall cops were paying attention and found him on their next circuit of the facility. It would take Jim and Charlie less than ten minutes to unload their burden and maybe they could move faster. As soon as they were gone, security could move in, rescue the convict, and read the note Jim was planning to write.

Worst case scenario, no one noticed him until tomorrow when the sun came up. If he was properly padded and his airway was clear, he should be cold, but not injured. The pavement would hold some of the heat, the building would provide more.

Jim's phone buzzed.

"Jim, th' Charlottesville Homestead can tak' ye. They prefer ye arrive afore midnight. Can ye do that?"

"Hang on a minute." Jim put his hand over the mouthpiece. "How far are we from Charlottesville?"

"Five hours minimum, maybe more. It will depend on the weather."

Jim glanced at his watch. Twelve-thirty. No, wait. The phone said one-thirty. They had crossed over into the Eastern time zone and lost an hour in the process. Still reasonable, even with dropping the convict off, and weather delays. Probably.

"Yes. We can do that."

"I'll arrange it, then. Call when ye get in."

"Thank you."

Jim put the phone away and checked on their prisoner, then moved forward to tell the others.

"That just leaves the weather," Ginny said.

"Assuming they haven't set up a road block," Charlie added.

"We are a very long way from Nashville. Maybe they won't think he can have come this far."

"But if they have?" Charlie asked.

Jim set his mouth in a grim line. "Then we dump him on the side of the road and pray he doesn't die and you will have to walk from Tennessee to Virginia."

* * *

Wednesday Afternoon
Bristol, VA

There was no road block. They paused in Bristol, on the Virginia side of the border, but did not linger. They needed to make tracks if they were going to get to Charlottesville before midnight.

Jim was keeping an eye on the heavens. According to the weather reports, they were driving into a developing nor'easter. What they were seeing was the outlying edge of a slowly rotating storm that would intensify.

By the time they reached Roanoke, thick, low-level clouds blocked what remained of the late afternoon sun. The temperature had dropped twenty degrees and the wind was rising. The snow had begun, too, not very heavy, but wet, making the highway surface slushy. The roads would stay passable as long as the heat lasted, then begin to ice over.

Roanoke was battening down the hatches, the inhabitants scurrying for home. Ginny had pulled over in an unlighted parking lot to allow the men to get into their white outerwear and to cover the license plates with white trash bags. They manhandled their still snoring prisoner into one of the sleeping bags, in preparation for the drop.

They had no trouble locating the shopping mall and no trouble spotting the mall cops. They had to wait fifteen minutes before the two patrol cars moved off in opposite directions. The snow was definitely coming down now.

Jim watched a handful of shoppers hurry out of the entrance, all eyes on the ground and faces bundled against the weather. When the coast was clear, Ginny drove up to the door. Jim and Charlie jumped out, seizing the soiled air mattress, with the sleeping bag and its occupant upon it, hauled it out of the car and deposited it in the space between the outer and inner mall entrance doors. Jim made sure the convict was on his side and breathing easily, the explanatory note pinned to the outside of the cocoon, then headed back to the van.

"I'm driving from here," he told Ginny. She moved over to the passenger seat and Charlie got into the back. The whole thing had taken just over seven minutes.

"Let's go."

The first chance he got, Jim pulled off the road into a deep black spot and climbed out, removing the trash bags and restoring the license plates to view.

"We don't want to attract any attention, especially in this storm. The authorities will be preparing for trouble. I suggest dinner and a bathroom break before we leave Roanoke, then no more stops until Charlottesville."

They were on their way by six, the storm warnings now making regular appearances on the radio. Jim listened carefully then settled in for what was likely to be a difficult drive.

* * *

Wednesday Evening
Dallas, TX

Detective Tran tapped the hard copies on the desk, to bring them into alignment, then stapled them together and tucked them into her growing file on the Monroe case. She had requested the warrants be expedited, carefully explaining her suspicions, but was aware it might be days before she heard back.

It might not work, either. All she had was circumstantial evidence.

It was possible that neither Miss Forbes nor Dr. Mackenzie was colluding in Mr. Monroe's escape, that the disappearances were nothing more than a coincidence. It was possible they were cooperating under duress, Mr. Monroe having threatened them in some way, but she didn't believe it. If they were in danger, someone in the Loch Lonach community would know of it. The Laird would be asking for help, not being sympathetically unhelpful.

She tucked her notebook in her pocket, gathered up her coat and headed out. No. Either she would find Mr. Monroe in Dallas, or she would find him with those two love birds, and if that happened, it was going to be most interesting to hear what they had to say about it.

* * *

CHAPTER 18

Jim watched the road disappear under the accumulating snow. The wind buffeted the van, pushing it across the icy road and into the path of oncoming traffic, very slow moving traffic. He fought to keep the vehicle on the road and in the right lane.

They had turned east onto I-64, cleared Waynesboro, and were approaching the outskirts of Charlottesville. The instructions called for them to turn south onto US-29, then take the second exit, Shepard's Hill road.

It was inevitable that the tailored-for-Texas van would be unable to handle the snow and ice. Jim made the exit from 64 to 29, following the sharply curving roadway down the incline, missed the even sharper turn at the bottom, plowed into the already damaged guard rail, knocked it the rest of the way down, then slid off the roadway and into the ditch. The van came to a stop, nose tipped down at a six degree angle, the rear wheels still on the pavement, but only just.

For a moment nobody moved.

Jim had been concentrating so hard on getting down the ramp that he'd had no thought for his passengers. He pried his fingers off the wheel and turned around. "Is everyone all right?"

The only light inside the van came from the dashboard, giving their faces a sickly green cast.

"Yeah," Charlie said.

Ginny nodded. "I'm fine."

Jim sucked air into his lungs. "Okay. I'm going to get out and look at the damage. You two stay still."

Jim put on the emergency blinkers, grabbed a flashlight, zipped up his polar bear parka, and got out. He walked all the way around the vehicle, watching for traffic and making sure he didn't step in front of the van, just in case it decided to slide further into the ditch.

All four tires were still inflated and three were on some version of solid ground. The fourth hung out over a drop of about three feet, with the guard rail caught in the undercarriage. The left front fender was crumpled, but they hadn't hit the rail hard enough to trigger the air bags.

It was not possible to tell if the van would slip further forward, but there wasn't really anywhere for it to go if it did. They had reached the bottom of the slope and the ground on the other side of the guard rail was relatively flat and covered in fully grown trees. The real danger was if the van slid sideways off the roadway, tipped over, and rolled.

Jim approached the vehicle from the passenger side. He opened the door and motioned for Ginny to get out. Once she was on the ground, he did the same for Charlie. He positioned them away from the vehicle, assigning Charlie the task of looking for traffic coming down the ramp and handing Ginny a pair of glow sticks with which to signal.

Once safety had been established, he pulled out his phone. It was not easy to be heard over the wind and with the snow flying in his face, but he managed. Ten minutes of effort told him everything he needed to know. He joined the other two in a huddle.

"The tow trucks are all in use by the police, who are coordinating rescue efforts. There are no taxis or cabs running until the storm abates. The homestead crews are out helping the first responders."

"Should we stay in the car?" Ginny asked.

Jim shook his head. "If it were stable and visible, that might be best, but it's on a curve, half off the road, in danger of rolling over, and it's white. I don't like our odds."

"So what do we do?" Charlie asked. His jacket had turned out to be inadequate and he was jumping up and down, trying to keep warm. "We can't ask the police for help. It's too risky."

Jim looked at Ginny and swallowed hard. "I know someone I can call. She might be able to come get us and take us the rest of the way to the Homestead."

"She?" Ginny asked.

"Sarah Sumner. My former girlfriend."

"Oh."

"Go ahead," Charlie said. "Though I wouldn't blame her if she didn't want to get out in this."

Jim found himself very nervous about this idea. He would rather not have called on Sarah. He hadn't been especially nice to her about his move to Texas. But, if her number still worked, and she still lived here, and she still had the Jeep that used to be his, she would come. He dialed the number.

"Sarah? Can you hear me?"

"Yes. Who is this, please?"

"It's Jim Mackenzie."

"Jim! I haven't heard from you since you left Virginia. To what do I owe this honor?" She sounded almost as cold as the snow falling on his cheeks.

"Sarah, I have a huge favor to ask. I'm stranded and I need to be rescued."

"Where are you?"

"At the junction of 46 and 29, headed south, in the ditch."

"You're here? In Charlottesville?"

Jim heard the excitement in the question. "Yes."

"The police have asked everyone to stay indoors." Was there an accusatory note in that statement? Or was she just leaving herself an out?

"I know. I said it was a huge favor."

"Never mind. I'll be there as fast as I can manage. See you soon."

Jim spent the time until she arrived making sure they had everything stuffed into the backpacks Ginny had thrown in at the last minute saying she would feel naked without them. Jim blessed her over-packing instinct. It was something he would never have thought of, but the packs would be a lot easier to handle than the wheeled bags.

He watched as a pair of headlights loomed out of the storm, made their way up US-29, then came to a stop on the shoulder. A slight figure in a yellow parka got out and approached them on foot. Jim went to meet her.

"Jim! It is you!" She threw her arms around his neck and kissed him. Jim was required to return the salute.

"It's good to see you, Sarah. Thank you so much for helping us out!"

"Us?" She turned at Jim's gesture, seeing the other two standing on the road. "Three of you?"

"Yes, and backpacks. Can you manage?"

"Of course." She gestured to Ginny and Charlie. "Come on you two, climb in!"

They settled into the back of the Jeep, then Sarah got behind the wheel and Jim, with an uncomfortable sensation of duplicity, climbed into the passenger seat beside her.

"Will the car be all right there?" she asked Jim.

"We don't have a choice. It's stuck."

"Okay. Where to?"

"Do you remember the year we went out to the Homestead?"

"That living history place? Yes."

"That's where we're going. Follow 29, then right on Shepard's Hill Road. They're expecting us."

Sarah glanced over at Jim, then back at Ginny, seated behind him.

"I have a feeling there's a story here." She put the Jeep in gear and drove carefully back up onto US-29.

They followed the signs and were outside the Homestead gates by eleven thirty. The guard admitted them promptly, directing them to the main building where they were met and escorted inside.

"What a miserable night!" the Matron exclaimed. "I'm Mrs. Lauder." Jim made introductions all around. She looked at the group, then back at him. "I understood there would be three of you?"

Jim nodded. "There are. Sarah here, lives in Charlottesville and has just rescued us off the side of the road. We will need a tow truck to get the van back, but that can wait until tomorrow."

"I'm afraid it will have to." She turned to Sarah. "Would you like to stay the night so you don't have to go back out into that storm?"

"Thank you, no. I would like a cup of coffee, though, if that's possible?"

"Of course!" Mrs. Lauder had helpers. She sent the youngest, a girl, to the kitchen and directed the two boys, both high school age, to escort the party to their rooms. "But do come back down and meet us in the den so we can welcome you properly. The fire's going so nicely. It almost makes up for the cold."

Jim set his backpack down in the room assigned him, peeled off his coat and hung it up to dry, then shucked his urine-stained clothing, jumped in the shower, sluiced off, wrapped a towel around his hips, and went to get clean clothes out of the pack. He found Sarah had followed him in. She was leaning against the closed door.

"God, you look good!"

He eyed her, then collected the clean clothes and went back into the bathroom to dress. He continued the conversation through the locked door. "So do you."

"How's Texas treating you?"

"I've got a good job at a local ER and the promise of more if I keep my nose clean." He tucked in his shirt, unlocked the bathroom door then sat down in the bedside chair and pulled on dry socks and shoes.

She nodded. "I'm glad of that, anyway."

"Sarah, we need to go down."

She let out a long breath. "You call me up and tell me you're in town and my heart does flip-flops. Then I find you're not alone, but there's no ring on your finger."

Jim stiffened his resolve. It had to be faced. "I asked you to come with me and you chose not to."

"Can I change my mind?"

"No."

"So, there is someone."

"Yes."

He saw her face harden. "Is it that pale scarecrow?"

"Would it matter?"

"Yes!" she exploded. "She's not woman enough for you." Sarah came towards him and Jim felt his mouth go dry. He had been very much afraid of this. "You need someone with fire in her belly."

"We need to go down."

"We need to talk."

Jim let out a breath. "Yes, we do, but not tonight. Come on." He took her arm and steered her out into the hall.

Once in the den, Jim helped himself to a scone and a hot toddy, then sat down on the couch. He would have sat next to Ginny, but she had selected a recliner and there was no room for him in it.

Sarah sat down beside him, sipping her coffee and answering polite questions from the Matron about how she knew Jim and what she did in Charlottesville.

Jim listened for a bit, then excused himself. "I'm sorry. I've just remembered. I have to call my grandfather." He stepped out into the hall and dialed Texas. It was a good thing it was an hour earlier there.

"We're here." Jim explained about the car trouble. "We'll need to stay at least two nights. I doubt if we can get the car fixed any sooner."

"I'll see tae it on th' morrow." There was a pause on the line. "Are ye all right, Jim?"

Jim considered what he might say to that, then decided on a shortened version of the truth. "It's been a long, harrowing day, and I'm tired."

"All right. We'll speak agin tomorrow."

Jim went back to find Ginny making her escape from what had to be an awkward situation for her.

"Sleep as late as you want, dear. Come down to the kitchen when you're ready for breakfast and we'll fix something up."

"Thank you. Good night." She smiled at Charlie, then turned to Sarah and held out her hand. "I'm very sorry we inconvenienced you, Ms. Sumner, and very glad you were willing to rescue us. Thank you so much."

Sarah had risen in surprise. "You're welcome."

Ginny brushed past Jim, headed for the staircase. He caught

her wrist. "Are you all right?"

She nodded. "Of course."

He followed her up the stairs with his eyes, then turned back to the den and found Charlie also leaving.

Mrs. Lauder turned to Sarah with a charming smile. "Are you sure you wouldn't prefer to stay overnight?"

Sarah hesitated, then shook her head. "Thank you, but I think I'd better not."

"They'll be closing the gates in ten minutes. Perhaps you'd like to come back tomorrow for lunch?"

Sarah turned from looking at Jim to looking at Mrs. Lauder. She smiled. "Yes, thank you. I'd like that very much."

"Good! We start around eleven a.m. and it runs to two p.m. You're very welcome to join us."

"I'll be here. See you tomorrow." She waved to the room in general, then allowed herself to be escorted out.

* * *

Wednesday Night
Blue Ridge Homestead

Jim climbed the stairs, located Ginny's room, and tapped on the door.

"Come in."

He closed the door and came over, sitting down on the edge of the bed. She set her book aside.

"What do you want to know?" he asked.

"Nothing."

"Nothing?"

Ginny shook her head. "I knew you'd had experience of women before you met me. I don't need particulars."

Jim frowned. "That is an exceptionally gracious and mature

attitude."

"I am exceptional. Perhaps you had noticed."

"I had." He bit his lower lip. "And now, having proven how mature we both are, tell me the truth. Are you all right?"

He watched the corner of her mouth twist.

"Do I have a choice? You didn't plan this. I doubt if you would have told me about her, if the hijacker hadn't forced your hand."

"You have no need to be jealous, Ginny. She had her chance and we've both moved on."

"I'm not jealous."

He was taken aback at that. "You're not? Then why do you look so unhappy?"

"Don't you understand? She's still in love with you."

He nodded. "Yes. That much I got."

"If you want—" She stopped, then swallowed, then continued. "If you decide to go back to her, or someone else, I won't try to stop you."

"Oh, Ginny!" He felt his heart constrict. He'd seen this coming, of course. He'd promised she could trust him, and here she was, faced with a woman he'd failed to mention, a woman he'd known well and had left behind. How was he to prove he wouldn't do that to her?

Jim moved up beside her and gathered her into his arms. "Ginny, I'm going to tell you again and I'm going to repeat myself as many times as it takes. I love you. I want to marry you and to spend the rest of my life with you and no one else." He took a deep breath.

"I'm guilty of being young and inexperienced and wanting to have a college girlfriend. I probably said things to her I shouldn't have."

"Jim, you don't have to explain."

"I want to. I should have told you about Sarah long ago. I'm sorry."

She sighed and put her head down on his shoulder. Her hair was thick, luxuriant, and smelled faintly of shampoo. He closed his eyes and breathed in the fragrance. He couldn't remember ever doing that with Sarah.

"You'll have to face her," she said.

"I know."

There was a period of silence during which Jim thought about all the things he and Sarah had said to one another before he left for Texas, then Ginny spoke.

"Thank you, for rescuing us from the hijacker."

"Thank you for your help."

"You're lucky I understood you."

"I knew you would."

Another silence, then, "Jim, I need to sleep."

"I know." He kissed the top of her head, then climbed off the bed. What he wanted to do was crawl in with her, to hold her while she slept, but that wasn't going to happen. Not tonight. He turned out the light, and made his way back to his own room, got into bed, tucked his hands behind his head, and stared into the darkness.

If he'd had any lingering doubts about Sarah, this emergency had given him a chance to put them to rest. It would be easier to remember her now, without remorse. It was a very lucky thing that, when he asked, she had said, "No."

Now, if only he could figure out how to get Ginny to say, "Yes."

* * *

CHAPTER 19

Thursday Morning
Blue Ridge Homestead

Ginny slept late the next day and woke feeling better. She called the Pittsburgh Homestead to ask about her talisman only to hear that the storm had grounded all deliveries and the talisman had not arrived. She asked them to call her when it did, then hung up, pushing her disappointment aside.

She made her way to the kitchen and found Mrs. Lauder had hot eggs, sausage, potatoes, coffee, sourdough bread, oatmeal, and cinnamon rolls ready to go.

"This is absolutely delicious." She smiled at the Matron. "Where are the men this morning?"

"Both of yours are helping to dig the van out of the mud." Mrs. Lauder glanced at the clock. "They've been at it for two hours. I'm expecting them back any minute now."

Ginny started to say that she didn't have any claim to Charlie, then decided against it.

The storm had passed, moving further up the eastern seaboard, and was currently dumping rain and snow on New York and Boston. Here, the clouds had cleared, leaving behind a pale blue sky and a foot of fresh snow. The sun was out, too, anemic by Texas standards, but enough to make the pristine snow too white to look at.

"We're very grateful for your help," Ginny said.

"Heavens, child! That's what we're here for." She fixed Ginny with a sharp eye. "But you know that."

Ginny smiled. "I do."

Mrs. Lauder took a sip of her coffee, then set it down. "Tell me about that other woman, Sarah."

"I didn't know she existed until last night."

"I thought as much. Men!"

Ginny laughed. "He might have gotten around to telling me, eventually, and she *was* willing to rescue us, for his sake."

"Humph." Mrs. Lauder cocked her head sideways. "Well what about Jim, then? He's your laird's grandson, I gather?"

"Yes."

Mrs. Lauder gave Ginny a look that made it clear she was expected to pay for the mouthwatering breakfast in equally juicy gossip. She obliged with a summary of Jim's background, his professional credentials, and his arrival in Texas leaving his Virginia connections behind.

Mrs. Lauder sat up suddenly. "Wait a minute! He's Jamie and Tibbie's son? I thought he looked familiar! That was such a sad thing, both of them dying like that. I haven't seen their boy in years. I understood he was in school at UVA."

Ginny was startled, then scolded herself. Of course the Virginia Homesteaders would know all of their number. Hadn't Jim said he'd gone to the dances here?

"I thought he grew up in Richmond?"

Mrs. Lauder nodded. "We all get together for the Games and Tartan Balls so there's a lot of mixing." She smiled. "He's turned out rather nicely."

Ginny smiled back. "Yes. He has."

They were interrupted at that moment by the sound of arrival. Mrs. Lauder jumped up. "They'll be wanting coffee."

Ginny rose and lent a hand getting the half dozen cold, wet

men dried off and warmed up. Jim cornered her in the kitchen, putting his arms around her and giving her a big hug.

"Ummm! What did I do to deserve that?" she asked.

"It's on account."

"On account of what?"

"On account of the fact that Sarah's coming to lunch and I will have to pay attention to her."

"You be nice to that poor girl, Jim."

"I will. I promise. Up to, but not including proposing marriage and/or agreeing to name one of our children after her."

"I plan to make myself scarce so you can have a heart to heart with her, but if she's still here at dinner—" Ginny left the sentence unfinished.

Jim sighed. "I sincerely hope it doesn't take that long." He held her close for a moment, then steered her over to the table and sat beside her, talking about the car.

"There's damage to the undercarriage, and it needs a new front panel. Nothing that can't be repaired here, but it will take time. And a thorough cleaning, of course."

"So what's the plan?"

"Leave it here and take another car north. We can come back this way, swap them out and take this one back to Dallas with us. Apparently we can have our choice. I've already seen the stables."

"Horses?" Ginny grinned. "I'm not sure I can handle a stagecoach."

He snorted. "No. A sweet collection of four wheel drive vehicles, all with snow tires and chains. If I had known, I could have called here last night, rather than bothering Sarah."

"Oh! But then I wouldn't have gotten to meet her! This way, I have something to use against you if you step out of line."

Jim responded to this threat by throwing an arm around her

waist and pulling her onto his lap, then kissing her thoroughly. Ginny was pretty sure he would have done it again, had not Mrs. Lauder entered at that moment, advanced upon him with determination, extricated Ginny, then put Jim to work on the lunch preparations while she interrogated him about life in Texas. Ginny made her escape upstairs, feeling flustered, but not altogether unhappy. He was a very good kisser.

* * *

Thursday Morning
Dallas, TX

It was gone. Detective Tran didn't have to check twice. The flyer she had seen, the one about establishing a new identity, was no longer under the bed. Someone had removed it. She would not even be able to refer to it in her report, as it was *fruit of the poisonous tree*, obtained during an unlawful search. It would not matter. There would be more evidence. She was sure of it.

She walked back out into the main living area, watching the crime lab go over the house, collecting items, bagging them, leaving receipts on the kitchen table.

"Last thing he did was look up the lake. Before that, he copied some files onto a removable drive. We'll know more when we get the computer back to the lab."

Tran nodded.

"Detective."

She turned to the speaker, one of the trainees.

"No evidence of flight. All his clothes are here. So are all the things you'd expect to see: toothbrush in the holder, pictures of his kids on the table, suitcases in the closet, nothing missing from the walls. The only weird thing is this." He held up the device. "He left his phone."

"Bag it."

In addition to the house, they had his car, and keys, and wallet, one of his shoes, and the fishing gear. Everything except the man himself.

He might still be here, dead in a ditch, or wandering the streets, concussed and confused. It was possible, she supposed. They would know more when the lab finished going over his things.

* * *

Thursday Afternoon
Blue Ridge Homestead

Ginny was curled up on the den sofa, staring into the fire. They made a handsome couple, Jim and Sarah. What's more, Sarah was intelligent and genuine and they had a history together. If he decided to go back to her, Ginny couldn't complain. A man needs encouragement and she'd been afraid to commit, afraid of making a fool of herself again. She heard a step behind her and looked up. It was Charlie Monroe.

"Am I interrupting?"

Ginny forced a smile into place. "Not at all. Please join me."

He sat down on the sofa. "I haven't had a chance to thank you, for all you've done for me."

It had been almost two weeks since the incident at the playground. Clean living and something positive to do had worked wonders on him. He looked better than he had in months. He brought his hands up and rubbed his face with them, pushing his hair back and ending with an impromptu cockscomb. It was clear he had something on his mind.

"What is it, Charlie?"

He licked his lips, then swallowed. "Am I supposed to repent? Are they going to make that a condition? Because I'm not sorry for what I've done. He had it coming."

Ginny sat and looked at him for several minutes, trying to decide what she could say. Eventually, she took a breath and tried to answer him.

"Who lives and who dies is supposed to be something we leave to God."

He frowned. "That's what the preacher says, but that's not how the world works."

"No, it's not." Her brow furrowed. "You know Jim and I both work in a hospital."

He nodded.

"If we left everything to God, no one would get medical care. There'd be no research, no surgery, not even pain killers. You could take the position we're interfering in God's will."

He nodded.

Ginny continued. "You could argue the same for the law. Left to ourselves, humans are pretty brutal creatures. Over time we've developed codes of behavior, so we can coexist, but different cultures value different things, and there are always some who don't play by the rules." She took a breath.

"In your case the judicial system failed to control the drunk driver, so you reverted to an earlier version of the law, one in which the evil was eradicated, rather than incarcerated."

Charlie nodded vigorously.

"The problem is, you acted without authority. That put you in the same category as the other lawbreaker. The Scots believe—still—that it's more virtuous to do your own dirty work. It's not politically correct to say so, but it's a part of our history, especially in Texas. Which brings us back to your question." Charlie's eyes were on her, a clear intelligence in them that gave her hope for his future.

"Repenting is between you and God. The Halifax Homesteaders aren't going to make you wear a scarlet letter, but neither will they tolerate an abuse of their generosity. And they're going to be watching. I won't ask you to go against your conscience. You must do what you think is right. But you might consider this. You may be the only Texan they ever meet. It will be a chance to show them what we're made of."

He took a deep breath. "I'm gonna miss being a Texan."

She smiled at him. "You're never going to stop being a Texan, Charlie. You're just going to have to stop bragging about it."

* * *

Chapter 20

Thursday Afternoon
Blue Ridge Homestead

Jim paused at the door to the den, catching the tail end of
Ginny and Charlie's conversation. He coughed loudly, then
entered the room and located the remote control for the
television.

"Has either of you seen the news?"

"No. What's up?" Ginny asked.

"Take a look."

"—convict had escaped from a maximum security facility in
Nashville, Tennessee. The other two convicts are still at large
and with the discovery of this one, more than four hundred
miles from Nashville, the search has been extended to include
the states of Kentucky, West Virginia, Virginia, and North
Carolina. The public is cautioned to avoid giving rides to
strangers on the highway. Chet, you said they have footage
showing the body dump?"

"Yes, Marsha, though it isn't technically a body dump, since
the man was found alive."

Ginny and Charlie were both glued to the television. Jim sat
down next to Ginny and watched the film clip again. It was
difficult to see exactly what was going on. The lighting was
poor and the snow kept getting in the way, but he could see

enough.

"The footage shows two men getting out of a white van and carrying something into the shelter of the store front, then they both get into the van and drive off. Police were unable to read the license plate and the public is encouraged to call if they saw a vehicle matching this description in the vicinity of the Roanoke mall around five p.m. yesterday."

"I understand the felon was restrained with duct tape, right Chet?"

"That's right, Marsha. Apparently, someone didn't want him getting loose. The police are examining the tape and the other materials found on the scene for forensic evidence in the hope of getting a lead on the men in the white van."

"Looks like someone did the police a favor, Chet."

"It certainly looks like it, Marsha, but the question on everyone's mind is why didn't these men just turn him over to the police? Why dump him at the mall?"

"That's a very good question, Chet. We'll look forward to hearing more about this bizarre development as soon as it becomes available. In other news—"

Jim turned off the sound.

"In their place," he said, "I would wonder if the two men on the tape were the other two escaped felons. Which means they may be looking for us."

"Jesus!" Ginny had whispered, but the force of the exclamation hit them all.

"If we keep Charlie out of sight, what they will see is a man and a woman, not two men. All they have to go on is what we left at the scene."

"No fingerprints," Charlie said. "I was wearing gloves. So were you. The blankets, sleeping bag, air mattress, and duct tape could have come from anywhere."

"What they have is our DNA."

"What? The urine?"

"Yes."

"But it's all mixed up: yours, mine, and his."

Jim shook his head. "What they will look at is the cells floating in the urine. Those come from the lining of the bladder and will be both complete and different for each of us."

"They won't match the other convicts' DNA," Ginny pointed out.

"No, they won't. As soon as they finish those tests, they'll know we're not their remaining two escapees." His brow furrowed. "The danger is exactly what those two on the television mentioned. People with nothing to hide would have taken him to the police station, probably bragged about capturing him. They would have wanted their fifteen minutes of fame, not dumped him and run off. The police will be wondering what we've done."

"We're the victims here!" Ginny exclaimed.

Jim shrugged. "We told the hijacker we were running from the law. If I were in his position, I'd be sure to share that information with the police."

He took a breath, then let it out. "As far as I know, the police do not have a DNA profile on me, just my fingerprints." He looked at Charlie. "What about you?"

"It won't be hard to get a sample on me." Charlie shrugged. "Hair, nails, blood. They'll be all over my house."

"I'm beginning to understand why so many criminals kill their victims." Ginny frowned.

"Yes, but we couldn't do that. We're the good guys, remember?" Jim ran his hand through his hair. "We just have to hope they don't make the connection soon enough to keep us from getting Charlie over the border. There's no way we can make it to Albany tonight. It's eight hours on good roads and the storm is still in full blow north of here, so there's no advantage to leaving before tomorrow." He stood up. "Get your gear and stack it in the front hall. I'll get us a loaner. We can pack this evening and leave first thing in the morning."

* * *

Thursday Evening
Blue Ridge Homestead

The SUV's middle seats had been removed, which left space for Charlie to sit comfortably on the floor, and the Blue Ridge Homestead had loaned them a thick pad and some additional blankets to take the place of the air mattress and sleeping bag. The larger items were already stowed and Ginny was exercising her talent for efficient packing, Charlie handing stuff to Jim who handed it in to her.

"Everything all right with Sarah?" she asked.

"She was very angry with me. Look what she did." Jim stepped up to the car and showed her the left side of his neck. There were several fresh scratches on it.

"Oh, Jim!" Ginny couldn't help laughing. "Have you put anything on that?"

"I cleaned it, but I can't see it very well."

"When we get inside, let me put some antiseptic ointment on it for you."

"Deal."

Ginny's smile faded. "She's going to wash her hands, isn't she?"

Jim had climbed back out onto the pavement and was collecting the next item for packing from Charlie. He looked up at her in surprise.

"I assume so. Why?"

"She has your DNA under her nails. If she feels vindictive

enough, she could accuse you of attacking her and use that as evidence she had to fight to get away."

They finished packing the car in silence.

"I think I'd better talk to her," Ginny said.

Jim nodded. "I'll drive you over."

They made arrangements with Mrs. Lauder to eat late, then, leaving Charlie with instructions to keep an eye on the news, drove off to deal with Sarah Sumner.

* * *

Thursday Evening
Sumner Residence

Ginny had Jim drop her, then drive off. She went up and rang the bell.

Sarah opened the door enough to see who it was, her eyes narrowing suspiciously.

"What do you want?"

"I want to tell you about Jim."

"Why should I listen to you?"

"Because you love him."

Sarah frowned, then opened the door and let her in.

Ginny sat down on the sofa and waited until Sarah took a seat facing her.

"I don't think Jim told you why he left Virginia."

"He said it was a family obligation."

Ginny nodded. "He is heir to a responsibility his father left to him. He's in the process of finding out what that means and deciding if he wants to do it."

"You mean like a prince, in line for the throne?"

"More like a son inheriting his father's business."

Sarah's eyes narrowed. "Where do you fit in?"

"I'm one of his teachers."

"Not his girlfriend?"

Ginny sighed. "I'm no one's girlfriend right now." She swallowed, then told Sarah about last October. When she got to the part about Jim, she saw Sarah's face blanch. "He almost died?"

Ginny nodded.

"But he's all right now?"

"Yes."

Sarah stood up suddenly and walked over to the window. She lifted the curtain and looked out. "He's waiting for you."

"We're on assignment. He's responsible for me and for the other man you met."

She looked over at Ginny. "It was a shock, when he left, and again yesterday, when he called. I hadn't really expected to see him again." She looked back out the window and Ginny could see a tear running down her cheek. "I still love him and I can't have him."

Ginny rose and came over, putting her arm around Sarah's shoulders. "You have a very special place in his heart. One that no one can take from you." She fished a tissue out of her pocket and dabbed at the tear, then handed it to Sarah. "I think he'd like to stay friends, if you're willing."

Sarah turned toward her, the floodgates opening, and Ginny put her arms around her. Ginny found herself crying, too, her own shattered dreams mirrored in Sarah's. Eventually Sarah broke away, blotting her face with the tissue.

"You'll take good care of him?"

"Yes."

"I do want to stay friends. I'd like to be friends with you, too."

Ginny blew her nose, then gave Sarah a hug. "I'd like that very much. We're coming back this way, to pick up the car.

Maybe we can get together then?"

Sarah smiled and nodded. The two women clung to each other for a minute longer, then Ginny broke the embrace.

"Wish us luck."

"I do."

She opened the door and let Ginny out, then waved at Jim, smiling, tears still rolling down her cheeks. Ginny gave her a final hug, then hurried down to the car. She climbed in and closed the door behind her, wiping the tears from her face and blowing her nose.

"Did she hurt you?" Jim asked in alarm.

"Oh, no! I've promised we'll all get together when you and I come back to pick up the car."

Jim stared at her.

"Drive, please."

He put the car in gear and drove off, headed back to the Homestead.

"I don't understand."

"I told you, she's still in love with you."

"And?"

"And real love wants what's best for the other person."

Jim was frowning hard. "So you manipulated her feelings?"

"No. I just told her what you were up against and she chose to support you. She wants to be a friend to you. Lifelong, if the two of you can manage it."

Jim shook his head. "I will never understand women. She was trying to claw my eyes out this afternoon."

Ginny sighed. "All she wanted was assurance that she is an important part of your life and always will be. The college girlfriend. Irreplaceable."

Jim looked over at Ginny, comprehension dawning on his face. "A place that is hers and hers alone."

"Yes."

He reached over and took Ginny's hand, then nodded. "I know just how she feels."

* * *

Thursday Night
Blue Ridge Homestead

Jim closed the door to his bedroom, kicked off his shoes, and settled down to call home. He wasn't looking forward to it, but he had to let Himself know what was in the wind.

"Grandfather, it's Jim."

"Aye. I've been expecting yer call, lad. Tell me what's amiss."

Jim took a deep breath then summarized the events of the day before.

"Hijacked! But ye were able tae capture him?"

Jim could hear the pleased tone of voice coming over the line.

"Yes. Well, it was three against one and we had resources."

"I'm verra glad tae hear it."

"But there's a problem." Jim outlined the method of overcoming the hijacker and the DNA trail they had left for the police. "So, it seems reasonable they will put two and two together and send someone after us."

"Auch, lad! This will tak' a wee bit o' thinking aboot."

"I know. I'm sorry."

"Dinna be sorry ye were able tae solve yer problem and escape wi' all yer skins intact."

"The car will stay here and be fixed. The Homestead has given me a loaner."

"Tis just as well. Detective Tran ha' been granted a warrant tae use th' GPS in th' van tae find oot where ye are."

Jim's mouth dropped. "That can't be legal!"

"Tis legal enough. Th' judge signed off on't on th' grounds neither you nor Ginny were th' legal owners and I had gi'en th' detective verbal permission tae search where she wanted. I suggest ye ask the lads at Blue Ridge Homestead tae disable th' van's GPS afore she gets a chance tae execute her warrant."

Jim's mouth twitched in grim satisfaction. "Not necessary. Reggie did that before we left Dallas."

"Weel, th' joke's on her, then! But ye need tae know, tha's no all she asked for. She also requested warrants fer yer phone and Ginny's fer th' same reason."

Jim felt his stomach clench. "And you're just now mentioning it?"

"Calm yerself, lad. She were denied, on th' grounds tha' neither you nor Miss Ginny ha' done enough tae support probable cause."

"Well, thank God for that." He should take the threat seriously, though. If—when—Tran got wind of the hijacker, the rules might change. "How do you know all this?"

"Do ye remember Alison Gorrie?"

"Wasn't she Grandmother's best friend?"

"Aye, she was. She works at th' police substation. She lets me know when there's aught tae do wi' th' clan."

"Very useful."

"Aye. She's a harmless auld grandmither and nae a one o' them gi'es her a second glance. Tha' makes her verra useful indeed. Ye'll find such o' th' clan placed strategically throughout th' community."

Jim blinked. Here was another example of the careful organization behind the Homestead system.

There was a pause on the other end of the line. "Wha' else is troublin' ye, lad?"

Jim was startled, then realized his grandfather must have

heard something in the tone of his voice. He took a breath.

"I hadn't expected to be back in Charlottesville so soon."

"Homesick, are ye?"

"It's not that. It's the people. I ran into my—well, I had to call my old girlfriend up, and ask her to rescue us."

There was what sounded like a stifled laugh on the other end of the line. "Ye had nae told Ginny aboot her, aye?"

Jim shook his head at the memory. "She was gracious and generous, but I'm afraid it didn't put me in a very good light."

"She'll come aroond, lad, if ye behave yerself frae now on."

"I'll do my best."

"Tha's all any man can do. Weel, I'll get back tae ye as soon as I've a notion how tae handle th' police and th' DNA."

"We're leaving first thing in the morning."

"Then I'll let ye get tae bed. We'll talk agin tomorrow."

Jim hung up the phone, but couldn't go to bed, yet. He opened the map app and pulled up Charlottesville.

At a conservative estimate, there were two weather-related highway incidents for each hour of road surface between them and Albany. With the further complication of a police dragnet, he needed to come up with a backup plan.

He'd brought in the paper maps, to supplement the electronic ones, and laid them out in front of him, folded to show the routes he and Ginny had discussed, and the changes made necessary by the hijacker. He sighed, then took a deep breath and settled down to figure out a viable route from Charlottesville to Albany.

* * *

CHAPTER 21

Friday, one a.m.
Blue Ridge Homestead

Ginny sat up suddenly, the scream still ringing in her ears. She looked around the darkened room, wondering if she had actually cried out. All was still. All except her heart.

She dropped her head into her hands and tried to pull her shattered nerves together. The images were beginning to blur. There was the cliff edge and the fall. She'd been over that cliff many times, almost nightly in the weeks following Hal's death.

This night there had been additions. The hijacker with a gun to her head, the gun going off. The police closing in, a dark prison cell, no light, no air, and a very large, very ugly man bearing down on her. Jim standing on the far side of the abyss, looking at her, then turning and walking away.

She hadn't realized she was weeping until he pulled her into his arms.

"Ginny? What's wrong, darling? I heard you cry out."

She swallowed then shook her head. "It was just a dream."

He brushed her face with his hand, wiping the tears off and looking around for tissues.

"Hold on a minute."

He left her and she had a sudden, terrifying moment of déjà vu, but he was back again almost immediately. He grabbed the extra blanket off the end of the bed and wrapped her in it, then settled the two of them against the head of her bed, his arms around her.

"Now, tell me about the dream." His voice was a rich baritone and he was using it now in his professional capacity. He had dropped the pitch and slowed the pace, letting the sound roll over her in waves. "Is it the same nightmare you've been having?"

She nodded. "But it's all right. I'll be all right."

He sighed. "I absolutely hate the thought that you don't need me. I want to be essential to your health and happiness."

Ginny felt the corner of her mouth curve up.

"But," he continued, "since you don't, I have to throw myself on your mercy. Please, take pity on me. Let me help. Try to, anyway."

She looked up at him and their eyes met. This was one of the things they shared, this instinct to fix whatever was broken. But this trip wasn't about her.

"Go back to bed, Jim. You need your sleep."

"I will, as soon as you've answered my question."

He didn't look angry, or upset, or even worried, just gently concerned. He waited and Ginny sighed to herself. If she refused, he might think it worse than it actually was. Perhaps the time had come to level with him.

She took a deep breath, then leaned against him and closed her eyes.

"Death by being pushed off a cliff. Death by gunshot to the head. Death by prison guard rape. Death by—" She stopped. Her fear of losing him wasn't in the same category. She hadn't agreed to marry him. He was free to walk away at any time.

"What was that last one?"

"It doesn't matter. The theme is death and for some reason I'm terrified of dying."

"Well, that seems perfectly reasonable to me."

"I thought I'd gotten over this."

"Your conscious mind has, it's your subconscious that's still struggling."

"Do you have bad dreams about—you know?"

He hesitated for a moment. "My latest scan showed no markers of any kind. I'm clean, Ginny, but, yes, I do."

"How do you handle them?"

"I get dressed and go for a walk in the park." He gave her a hug. "I remind myself that he is dead and I am alive." He bent down and kissed the top of her head.

"Dreams are the way our brains handle the things that happen to us," he said. "They try to make sense of it, to organize and file it away. We can help by calling up the images and assigning meanings to them."

She could smell his skin, not fresh and scented as if he had just stepped out of the shower, the man himself. It surrounded her, warm and earthy and subtly sweet.

"The gunman is obvious. The threat was real and you know exactly what a bullet can do. You also know he is back in prison. Let's try a little experiment. Shall we?"

Ginny nodded.

"Take a deep breath for me and hold it. Now visualize his face behind bars and let the breath out all the way. Feel satisfaction." Jim's voice was warm in her ear. "He's no further threat. File it away."

"Okay. Done."

She closed her eyes and turned her head so she could rest her cheek on his chest. In this position she could hear his heart beating, calmly, steadily.

His voice was still warm, but softer, almost as if it was coming from farther away, but she could feel his breath on her cheek as he spoke.

"The chasm is a symbol. You must cross it to get on with your life, but you have no idea what will happen if you try."

Ginny tensed. "I fall."

"All humans dream of falling. It goes back to the time when we lived in trees. The symbol, the chasm, is using your survival instinct to keep you where you are. You must learn to ignore the symbol and concentrate on what's on the other side."

Jim was on the other side.

"Close your eyes. Now look at the cliff edge. You cannot fall because it isn't real. Turn your back on it and walk away."

Ginny pulled up the image of the cliff in her mind. She tried to turn away, but couldn't. She suddenly felt as if she was plummeting into the darkness and started to shake.

"Stop." Jim's voice was warm in her ear, the command gentle and persuasive. "It's not real. You're standing on solid ground. Feel the earth beneath your feet."

She was struggling, but the sensation of his arms around her was strong.

"I can feel you."

"I'm holding you. We're both standing on solid ground. You are not falling."

She sucked in a ragged breath. "I am not falling."

"Turn your back on the cliff. We'll walk away together."

Ginny felt a shiver go through her body, but she was able to hang onto the image. She turned away from the cliff.

"I'm doing it! I'm walking away!" She opened her eyes and smiled up at him. "Thank you!"

He bent down and kissed her swiftly. "You're welcome! Now, get some sleep. Tomorrow is going to be a long day."

He turned off the light and closed the door behind him. This time there was no sensation of being deserted.

* * *

Chapter 22

Jim stashed his overnight bag in the SUV while Ginny climbed into the passenger side seat. Charlie had settled into the back, his eyes alert, his expression relaxed. He almost looked as if he was enjoying himself.

"What did she say?" Ginny asked.

"She loved it."

Their hostess gift this time had been a large box of pecan pralines and an assortment of jalapeno suckers for the youngsters. Jim handed Ginny another cup of coffee then climbed behind the wheel of the SUV.

The highway department had had a full day to plow and the conditions were passable. The sun was out and the temperature already above freezing.

The shorter route, I-95, would dump them smack into D.C. traffic, so Jim had decided to use Interstate 81, which took them first into Staunton, Virginia, a picturesque little town on the edge of the George Washington National Forests He found a gas station and pulled in to top off the tank and give everyone a chance to stock up on edibles before starting the long drive north.

He'd been thinking quite a bit about the possibility of being pulled over by the police, either on the Virginia border, as part of a search for the escaped convicts, or as a result of the investigation into Charlie's movements.

Jim had no idea how they were going to avoid an eventual charge of aiding and abetting a fugitive from justice, but he needed to be ready to hide Charlie and make sure the car could be searched. That meant disposing of the hijacker's weapon.

He pulled the car around to the side of the station, then slipped on a pair of gloves and reached into Charlie's overnight bag to retrieve the weapon. It was clearly not a gun he would want. The serial number had been filed off and there were spots of rust on the contact surfaces. So he wouldn't feel any regret at what he planned to do.

He disassembled the weapon, dropping each piece in a separate baggie, then did the same with the magazine and ammunition. That left him with six baggies of gun parts.

He located Ginny's cleaning solution and poured some of the ammonia-based liquid into each bag and finished by scooping a handful of snow in on top of that. It made a blue slush that felt oddly toxic in his hand. He carefully closed each baggie and stashed them in the storage compartment between the two front seats. He planned to drop them in six different garbage cans between here and the border. The first should be in Staunton, but not at the same place where his credit card would show they stopped for gas.

When the other two got back to the car, Jim explained his plan. Charlie's face took on a hard edge when he heard.

"You don't trust me with a gun."

"I don't trust the state police to believe it's not your gun if it's found in your possession. We don't want them to think you and I are the other two escaped convicts, remember?"

Charlie relaxed. "Right. Okay. So what do we do?"

"I want you to drive until we get almost to the Virginia

border, then Ginny."

"What's gonna happen at the border?"

"Nothing, I hope, but if they've set up a road block, that's where it will be."

"How are we going to find out?" Ginny asked.

"The phone. We can use the traffic app to see if there are stopped vehicles on the roadway."

She nodded. "Okay. There must be a low rent district in this town. Let's go find a dumpster."

They did, then repeated this plan in Harrisonburg, New Market, Mount Jackson, and Woodstock, being careful not to leave fingerprints on any of the deposits.

Winchester was the last town in Virginia on Highway 81. They disposed of their last baggie of contraband, then found a comfortable café and had lunch. They checked the image of the state line just north of Winchester and found a string of cars stopped on I-81.

"We'll have to find another way."

The three of them bent their heads over the device.

"How about over here?" Charlie pointed to a series of back roads that wound along a creek bed. "They won't have plowed this section."

Jim nodded, zooming in for a closer look. "They may have barriers in place."

"We can go around those. The SUV can handle off road."

"Okay. We'll have to move over to 11, then pick up the backroad, then take our chances on running into someone who wants to know why we're off the highway."

"I need a fishing pole," Charlie said.

"What?"

"No one questions a man with a fishing pole. It's obvious what he's doing and that nice little creek probably has good eating in it."

Ginny nodded. "We need to get you a better coat, anyway. Let's find a sporting goods store."

As it turned out, they had no trouble outfitting Charlie in waders, a winter weight jacket, and a pole and gear suitable for fishing an icy stream along the Virginia/West Virginia line. They loaded their gear in the car and headed off.

* * *

Friday Morning
Waco, TX

Detective Tran looked around the restaurant and approved Mr. Gibson's choice. It had taken her the full two hours to drive to Waco for this meeting, and would take her two more to drive back to Dallas, but she had decided it would be worth it. Failing an opportunity to ask Mr. Monroe himself where he had been while the man who destroyed his family had ceased to be a serial killer and become a body in a boat, she needed to speak with anyone who might be able to fill in the gaps.

The warrants on Mr. Monroe had come back promptly, allowing her to search his house, and financial and phone records. The credit cards indicated a trip to Waco that covered the time in question and the call records showed him contacting his former in-laws. She could have questioned them via phone or computer link, but if what she suspected was true, and he had visited them before he skipped town, they might know something they didn't know they knew. She wanted to see their faces.

"Mr. and Mrs. Gibson." She held out her hand then took the seat indicated. "First, please accept my condolences on the loss of your daughter and granddaughters. It is a terrible tragedy."

Mrs. Gibson nodded, unable to answer, but Mr. Gibson did.

"Thank you. We're still trying to wrap our heads around it." He reached over and took his wife's hand.

"Was she your only child?"

"No, there's another girl, Patsy. She's in Houston."

"I am so sorry to bring up the subject, but I need your help finding Mr. Monroe—Charlie."

Mr. Gibson nodded. "When the police called, they told us he was missing. That's why we're here. That's a very nice young man. I would really hate it if something happened to him, too."

"They told you it looks like a boating accident?"

Mr. Gibson nodded.

"What we are trying to do is reconstruct his movements up until the time he disappeared." Tran pulled out her notebook and opened it to a fresh page. "His records indicate he came to visit you three weeks ago."

Mrs. Gibson nodded. "That's right. He brought us some things that belonged to Mandy, and pictures of the girls."

"Please forgive me, but I have to ask. Did he seem depressed to you?"

They both nodded.

"He was saying things. It was as if he didn't expect to ever see us again." Mrs. Gibson put her hand on her husband's arm, then looked over at Tran. "We told him how we felt about him, like a son. We loved him that much. We asked him to stay with us, and he did, for a few days."

"He was at your house?"

"Yes. We talked almost the whole weekend, late into the night. I made up the couch for him, but I don't think he actually slept. He had breakfast with us on Monday morning, then excused himself, saying he was going to try to catch some shut eye at the hotel."

"You did not spend Monday together?"

"I had to go back to work," Mr. Gibson said.

"Yes," Mrs. Gibson said. "But he came to dinner that night and we spent Tuesday together, going through—"

Mr. Gibson finished for her. "Going through Mandy's things. He picked out a few to take back with him."

"Was he still here Tuesday night?"

Mrs. Gibson nodded. "Yes. He was planning to leave, but I had called Patsy and arranged for her to have dinner with us on Wednesday. She especially wanted to see him and we talked him into staying one more night."

Mr. Gibson nodded. "I'm off on Wednesday. No classes. So I could come and be with him and Martha. I wanted to be there on Tuesday, but I couldn't break away."

"When did he arrive in Waco, can you recall?"

"Saturday, wasn't it?" Mrs. Gibson looked at her husband.

He nodded. "Yes. We had dinner that night at the club, then took him to church with us the following morning."

"That's right." Mrs. Gibson's expression cleared, then clouded again. "That was hard on him." She looked over at Tran. "They were married in that church."

Tran set her notepad down and folded her hands, softening her body language. "We think there is a possibility it was not an accident."

Mrs. Gibson looked Tran in the face, unsurprised. "Suicide, you mean."

Tran nodded. She described the scene in the park.

"Oh! How horrible! Annie's birthday, of course!"

"But someone stopped him. They put him in the hospital?" Mr. Gibson asked.

Tran nodded. "He was evaluated and released on medication."

"He shouldn't have been left alone," Mr. Gibson said.

"Are you familiar with the Scottish community in Dallas?"

"Loch Lonach? Yes, of course." Mrs. Gibson nodded.

"Angus Mackenzie accepted responsibility for Monroe's safety. We think Monroe—Charlie—slipped away from his escort the night he went fishing."

"You think he might have drowned himself." Mr. Gibson's face was grave with the implications.

"Except, we have not found his body, or a suicide note. It is also possible he hit his head and has wandered off. Or there may be another explanation."

"You'll tell us, if you hear anything?"

"I will."

"Send him to us," Mr. Gibson said. "We'll make sure he gets the care he needs. If you find him."

"When," Mrs. Gibson corrected.

Mrs. Gibson stood up and the other two followed suit. "We'll be praying for his safe return. You let us know if there's anything we can do."

"Thank you very much for your time. I will be in touch."

Detective Tran settled down behind the wheel and headed back toward Dallas, turning the interview over in her mind.

The credit card records indicated four nights in the hotel, Saturday afternoon through Wednesday morning, which corroborated what the Gibsons had told her. There were also receipts for restaurant meals. She would compare those to the notes she had taken about the meals supplied by Mrs. Gibson. She should also check purchases of gas and cross-reference them with date/time stamps and mileage on the car, also any calls he may have made.

If there was no discrepancy, she could probably accept the story as true. Which would leave her with a very big question. If Charlie Monroe wasn't responsible for that man's death, who was?

* * *

Friday Afternoon
I-81, headed north

Jim took over the driving, happy to find the SUV had better traction than the van. As expected, the roads were covered in ice and snow, the conditions muddy and treacherous, and warnings had been posted, along with a few barriers, suggesting that reasonable caution included turning around and going home.

They slid their way through all of these, arriving on the West Virginia side without encountering a living soul. At that point 671 turned into West Virginia Route 28, though the road conditions did not improve, and they were able to follow 28 into Inwood, WV, then get back on I-81, headed north. All three breathed a sigh of relief.

An hour and a half later they were in Harrisburg, PA. They paused long enough to fill the gas tank and pick up some drinks, then got back on the highway.

The plan was still to make Albany before the gates closed. They pushed through the long hours, sharing the driving, and keeping a close eye on the weather. The day had gone surprisingly well and Jim was beginning to get his hopes up.

They were only twenty minutes south of Albany when they got stuck. The snow wasn't the problem this time. This time it was the wind.

* * *

CHAPTER 23

Friday Night
New York state

The night had settled around them soon after leaving Harrisburg. In Scranton, they topped off the tank again and grabbed burgers to go. Charlie had curled up in the back and gone to sleep. Ginny had done the same in the front passenger seat, leaving Jim alone with the cold night air.

Snow was still falling. New Yorkers were used to this sort of thing in February, but Jim was not. His shoulders ached from the constant tension and his eyes burned from too little sleep.

By ten p.m., Jim was wondering if he should give up trying to get to the Homestead and find a hotel instead. But, the traffic was still getting through and the best strategy seemed to be to keep going.

He had planned to turn east on the Berkshire Connector to cross the Hudson River south of Albany, then head north, which would put them on the correct side of the river as they approached the Albany Homestead.

He made the exit and headed toward the Castleton-on-Hudson Bridge, noticing there were cars on the side of the road and people walking toward him along the verge. He was stopped before he could see what the problem was. A man in uniform approached, indicating he should roll down his window.

Ginny had waked when Jim put on the brakes. She looked at him, then climbed into the back, quietly woke Charlie, covered him with one of the blankets, then sat down on the seat and propped her feet on him.

"Yes officer?" Jim leaned out the window.

"The bridge is closed."

"Oh. Okay. Where do I go to get across?"

"You can't. They're all closed."

"*All* of them?" Jim could hear the dismay in his voice. He tried to dial it down.

"Structural damage. Some of the barges got loose and rammed the supports. We can't open the bridges until the engineers say it's safe."

"How long will that take?"

"Forty-eight hours, if the storm holds off."

Jim took a breath and thought for a moment. "Is there somewhere we can get a room for the night?"

The officer looked dubious. "I doubt it. We have passengers stranded all up and down the state."

Jim gritted his teeth. "Then can you help me get turned around?"

"Sure. Just follow me."

The officer stepped out into the roadway and stopped the foot traffic, then indicated to Jim to pull forward, then backup, then forward again, until he was facing west.

"Thank you, Officer."

"My pleasure."

When they were rolling again, Ginny moved forward, took her seat and looked over at Jim.

"Now what?"

"Is there any way we can tell where the bridges *aren't* out on this river?"

Ginny called up a traffic information site. "Barricades in place from Port Edward to Poughkeepsie."

"What's our best bet?"

"Not north. The storm is still causing trouble up there."

"South, then. How far?"

Ginny studied her phone. "Newburgh."

Jim growled. "I wish I'd known that when we were there earlier."

Ginny looked over. "I'm sorry, Jim. I was supposed to be navigating. I should have caught this."

Jim pressed his lips together. She was right. Her assigned job was to keep an eye on the road conditions and weather reports and to communicate problems to him.

"This is going to add another four hours to the trip, assuming we can get across and find our way to I-90. I don't suppose you can tell me how to do that?"

Jim could hear the sarcasm in his voice. He was mad at Charlie for being the reason they were in this mess, mad at Ginny for having overlooked the closures, and mad at himself for not having done a better job of planning, even though he'd lost half a night's sleep trying to prevent just this sort of delay.

She was silent for a moment, consulting her device.

"I-84 across the river, then north on either US 9 or the Taconic State Parkway. US 9 goes through all the urban areas along the east side of the Hudson. The Taconic is scenic, twice as wide and mostly divided. Your choice." Her mouth snapped shut. Jim could hear it.

He hadn't meant to take it out on her. The bridge closures were not her fault and none of the three of them had enough experience driving in the northeast to anticipate this problem. About the only thing any of them had done wrong was not listen to the radio. He should have thought of that.

"Ginny, I'm sorry. I was just looking forward to getting to

bed tonight."

Charlie had crawled out from under the blankets and was listening to this exchange.

"Why don't you let me drive for a while? You can take a nap. It's very comfortable back here."

Jim considered this for a moment, then pulled over to the side of the road and let Charlie take his place.

"Wake me when we get to Newburgh."

"Okay."

Jim settled down on the bedding finding the space wide enough for his shoulders, but not long enough to accommodate his legs. He had to lie on his side with his knees bent. This further aggravated his temper. He struggled with his bad mood for a little longer, then closed his eyes and let himself relax.

The trip had been a success so far, in spite of the challenges. They'd managed to slip out of Texas without being stopped; to be hijacked by, then capture and dispose of, an escaped convict; to survive a wreck in a nor'easter; and to turn a hostile ex-girlfriend into an ally, all in the space of four days. No wonder he was tired. The motion of the car was very soothing and the next thing he knew they had stopped.

"Newburgh," Charlie announced. He pulled into a gas station and threw open the door, letting the frigid air stream in. Jim grabbed his coat and credit card, gassed up the SUV, then moved it into a parking place. Rest stop and food taken care of, they piled back into the SUV and headed for the other side of the Hudson.

They'd agreed the Taconic would probably be faster. Jim finished his sandwich, watched as Charlie negotiated the turn onto the Parkway, then decided he might as well catch another hour's worth of sleep. Scenic as the road might be in daylight, he wouldn't be able to enjoy it in the frozen darkness.

He settled down on the floor of the car and tried to fall asleep, but couldn't get comfortable. He dozed, then woke suddenly when a foot descended on him.

"Hey!"

"Sorry," Ginny said. "I was trying to reach the cooler."

Jim moved his leg aside, allowing her a foothold in the space between the seats. She sat down on the seat, looking down at him.

"What?" he demanded.

"Nothing."

"Fine." He closed his eyes and tried to ignore her. She had stretched out on the seat. He opened one eye halfway and peered up at her. Her face hung above his, just inches away, draped in deep shadow, but the dashboard lights shone on her arm, reaching down to touch him. She brushed his hair, very, very gently, then sighed.

He opened both eyes, reached up, and caught her around the waist, pulling her off the seat and down onto his chest.

"I'm sorry, Ginny," he whispered. "I'm sorry I lost my temper. Please forgive me."

"I'm not mad, just sorry I let you down." She snuggled into his arms and he moved over, making room for her on the bedding, then curled up around her and covered them both with the blanket. There was no further conversation, just a warm feeling of ease. With her in his arms, he found he could sleep.

He let the motion of the car lull him, trusting he would wake when the car made the transition to the Interstate. When he opened his eyes again to find Ginny asleep in his arms, the sun was up and Charlie was gone.

* * *

Chapter 24

Charlie peered into the gloom, confused by the shifting lights on the snow. They made it hard to estimate distance. Even as good as he was at hunting, and he was, the unfamiliar terrain had him at a disadvantage. He kept missing his footing, slipping on the wet forest floor, and walking into overhanging branches. He was cold, wet, tired, and he was dismayed.

He hadn't planned any of this. He hadn't planned to kill that monster, or to confess, or to be a fugitive from justice. The last time he'd been out in the forest at night was that camping trip two years ago, with Mandy and the girls.

Mandy! Dear God! Mandy and Beth and Annie, all dead. How was he to bear it? The pain overflowed, running down his cheeks, hot, then freezing, the ice crusting his lashes.

He brushed at his eyes, stumbling forward. What had made him think he could escape? Did he really believe running off to Canada would work?

The wind had died down and the night was filled with small noises, recognizable as rodents or birds or snow falling off the branches. Nothing to fear. No reason to fear anything, anyway, even death. Would he get credit in heaven if he died out here?

He was fighting for credit. He'd left the other two asleep in the car with the idea that he would draw his guilt away from them. What had they done to deserve being imprisoned for helping him? Why had he allowed them to put themselves at risk? The memory of the two of them, curled up together, his arms around her, brought a fresh wave of tears.

He struggled to the top of a small rise, then paused for a moment to look around. Amazing how deep the snow was. It would be easy to freeze out here. He'd heard it was a painless death, hypothermia. You got tired, then sleepy, then died without noticing.

He didn't deserve an easy death, though. That was what he'd been thinking when he chose exile, a long life full of exquisite pain. Fitting for him, for his crime. For not being able to protect his girls.

He covered his face with his hands, his shoulders shaking and in his mind he heard Mandy's voice. She was singing to him. *Oh, Charlie is my darling, my darling, my darling.*

She had sung it to him first on their honeymoon, when he lay half asleep and she thought he wasn't listening. Later, she had sung it as a lullaby. He'd been ill and fretful. Then, one day, on a picnic, she had turned to him and sung it, laughing, running, teasing, beckoning him to follow her.

He lifted his head and tried to locate the sound. It was coming from that clump of trees, ahead and on the left. He pricked his ears to catch the tune again. Yes! There it was! He stumbled down the rise and started up the ridge.

Charlie is my darling. She'd meant it that time. He could still see her face: high cheekbones and wide set blue eyes, freckles across her nose, laughing rosebud lips. He struggled to the top of the ridge and looked around. There! He'd seen something white whisk around behind the tree. He hurried to follow.

He plunged into a snow drift. It was a lot deeper then he'd realized, but he couldn't let that stop him. He had to catch up to her. He struggled forward, fighting his way through the heavy, wet snow. The backpack was slowing him down. He shrugged it off.

Charlie!

Over to the right. He'd missed her somehow. He turned right and pushed on, deeper into the forest, out of the heavy snow and into a clearing. There was moonlight here and forest floor and shifting shadows. She had to be here.

Charlie!

He jerked his head up, trying to see where the sound came from and lost his balance. His left foot slid out from under him and he fell, landing with a sickening sound of breaking bone on a sharp outcrop of rock beside a swollen stream.

The next three hours seemed even more dream-like than chasing Mandy across the snow. There had been pain, followed by numbness and bitter cold, then the awareness that he was lying in a puddle, one that was growing deeper. He had roused himself enough to crawl to higher ground, but now lay listening to the sound of the rising water and another, much more cautious, sound. Something moving through the snow, breaking through the crust, then pausing to look with eyes that shone in the night, then disappeared, then shone again. It was with a sense of deep regret that Charlie remembered the gun was in the backpack he had discarded.

He scanned the immediate area, looking for anything that could be used as a weapon, and found a number of small rocks. Before he'd been allowed to use a rifle, he'd used a slingshot to bring down the squirrels from the trees. Not the rubber band variety, a sling as described in the Bible, the David and Goliath kind. He had a good eye and a good arm. All he needed was some sort of strap.

He pulled his belt off, then dug out his wallet and his *sgian dubh*. He cut the wallet apart, then cut slits the width of the belt into one flap.

He loaded a stone into the makeshift sling and climbed to his feet, all his weight on the uninjured leg. He looked around, estimating how much space he would need for a clean throw, then selected a tree in the vicinity of the glowing eyes. He whirled the sling around his head, then let fly. He missed the tree he was aiming at, but hit another. A second attempt landed right where he wanted.

He spent the next twenty minutes stockpiling stones, then sat down on a small hummock to wait for dawn. If he was to have any chance of getting himself back to the highway, it would have to be in daylight.

Perhaps they wouldn't attack. Perhaps they would think him too difficult a target. He loosed a stone anytime he saw those flashing eyes, but was pretty sure it was a hopeless endeavor. Wolves were pack animals. It was February, and he'd seen more than one. They looked hungry.

He fought the urge to give up, to settle down in the snow and go to sleep. He set his mouth in grim determination. If they wanted to eat him, they would have to kill him first, and he was going to go down fighting.

* * *

Saturday Dawn
Taconic Parkway, NY

The first thing Jim noticed when he woke was how cold his nose felt, then the condition of his bladder, then the soft warmth nestled up against him shifted, and he realized it was alive. This brought a smile to his face even before he opened his eyes. He considered going back to sleep, but, realistically, he couldn't do that.

He pulled his arm out from under Ginny's head and eased the blanket free, then had to figure out how to rise from the confined space without waking her. He ended with a modified pushup that allowed him to roll over and put his weight on his toes, then rock back on his knees and ankles.

He zipped up his parka, shivering in the cold, then stretched, looking out the side window and seeing dense forest covered in heavy snow. Most of the area still lay in shadow, a few thin shafts of early sun managing to make their way through the canopy to turn dim shapes into dazzling displays of white ice.

They were not moving and it was cold. The whole car was cold. How long had the heater been off?

He peered out the windshield between patches of frost. They were in a small parking lot. There were no buildings, no signs of civilization. What possible reason could Charlie have had for stopping here?

Even as he formed the question in his mind, Jim had his answer. He threw open the door and jumped out. No Charlie. No tent, no fire, no evidence of a campsite. He hurried around the back of the SUV and opened the doors, checking the items stored there. Charlie's pack was gone. So was Jim's pistol.

He closed the doors and leaned against them, thinking furiously. Car trouble? Jim walked all the way around the vehicle. Nothing obvious. All four tires inflated, no evidence of a collision. No gas?

Jim hurried up to the front and let himself into the driver's side of the car. He turned the motor on. Gas tank half full. He turned the heater up full blast.

By this time Ginny was rousing.

"What's going on," she asked. "Why have we stopped?"

"Charlie's gone."

Ginny blinked, then frowned. "Gone where?"

"How should I know?" Jim felt a wave of fury, tainted by guilt. If this was his idea of being responsible for a murderer, he should be sent back to kindergarten.

Ginny said nothing for a full minute, then, "He's on foot. He can't have gone far. We'll find him."

Jim narrowed his eyes. "I don't recall making the decision to go after him."

"You will." She zipped up her coat then went around to the back of the car. Jim found her pulling out tea bags.

"What are you doing?"

"First things first. I can't function without caffeine."

Jim turned off the motor and closed himself up in the now warm interior. He dug out a protein bar and settled down to a reasonable facsimile of breakfast. Ginny did the same, then sat down next to him and handed him a pill bottle.

"What's this?"

"His antidepressants. I found them in my bag. He hasn't been taking them."

"Hell."

"They have some pretty unpleasant side effects."

"So does blowing your brains out."

"Is that why he took the gun?"

"Either that or protection, but he only took one magazine. He knows he'll need more ammo, unless he knows he won't."

"Then we'd better find him before he does something rash. We need a map."

She pulled out her phone and tried to power on the device, then frowned down at it. "It's dead."

Jim located his and looked at it. "Mine, too."

"Not to worry, I brought a battery backup. Or I can use my laptop, or we can tap into the car's battery or the generator we bought."

Jim blinked. "You packed four different ways to recharge a

cell phone?"

"Five. I have the power cable and an assortment of converters. Let me have your phone."

"Wait a minute." Jim dove into his own luggage and pulled out a twelve-volt battery, with attachments.

"What's that?"

"A signal booster. At least, that's why I bought it, but I think it will also recharge phones." He peered at it for a moment, then his expression cleared. "I was right!" He attached his phone to the device and set it on the floor of the car, then turned back to her, smiling.

"Plus I have a solar panel and an MEC."

"A what?"

"A muscle energy converter. You wear it and it turns the energy you produce by moving into electricity." He grinned at her. "You're not the only one who came prepared. Eagle Scout, remember?"

"I remember." She smiled at him and he felt the tension in his shoulders easing.

"We still have to decide what to do about Charlie," he said. He ran his hand through his hair, looking around at the apparently endless forest. "I wish I knew where we were."

"We're on the Taconic Parkway at a place called Roeliff Jansen Kill State Multiple Use Area in Dutchess County, NY."

He stared at her. "How did you find that out without Internet access or GPS?"

"It's on the sign that marks the entrance to this parking area. I went out and looked around."

Jim stared at her, unsure whether he was annoyed or impressed. It might get old in a hurry if she made a habit of one-upping him. As he watched, her smile faltered, then disappeared.

"All right," he said. "When we get the phones back, we'll

see if they can tell us how far from Albany we are."

"Albany!"

Her cry startled him. "What?"

"I didn't call Mother last night. With both the phones dead, she can't reach us. And we didn't show up at the Homestead as expected. There's no telling what she may be thinking."

Jim frowned. Himself would wait as long as possible before sending out a search party, but it had been more than eight hours since they were supposed to arrive. Even his grandfather would be getting worried by now.

"Can you turn your phone on yet?" he asked.

She picked it up and tried. "Yes."

"Any reception?"

"No."

He took her phone, set up the signal booster, and scanned the skies.

"Got it!" Two bars. He dialed Texas. "Grandfather? It's Jim."

"Auch, aye! Are ye all right, lad?"

"We're fine. We're having phone trouble. I'll tell you all about it later. I just wanted to let you know we're safe."

"Th' Homestead said ye dinna arrive."

"True. We're still headed that way, but I can't talk, the phone's about to die again. I'll call you later."

"All right, lad."

"Please let Mrs. Forbes know."

"I will."

Jim hung up and looked at Ginny. "Okay, Charlie next."

She nodded. "He'll be hungry and thirsty." She reached for her backpack, added snack bars and water, then opened the door, climbed out, and headed for her overnight bag.

It took Jim a minute to catch on, but when he saw her pull out her weapon, then throw the backpack over her shoulder, he understood. He hurried to get in front of her.

"This is my job." He saw her mouth open in protest. "No." He cut her off. "You stay here."

"Don't be a fool, Jim. You need my help."

"I need for you to do as I say."

He watched her eyes ignite, then cool to freezing point. She closed her mouth, turned her back on him, and stalked off.

Jim frowned. Well, he was sorry if he'd offended her, but the last thing he needed was for Charlie to take a shot at her. She could be as angry as she wanted, as long as she stayed here, out of danger. He pulled out the rifle and slung it over his shoulder, took a last look at her rigid back, set his jaw, then strode off into the woods.

* * *

Saturday Morning
Taconic Parkway, NY

Ginny waited until she could no longer hear the sound of Jim's retreating footsteps, then turned and looked at the empty forest. She was struggling with her conscience, furious with him for refusing her help, furious with herself as well. She very deliberately made herself another cup of tea and sat down to drink it.

She had made a mistake. She had shifted into problem solving mode on finding Charlie gone, and assumed Jim would welcome her assistance. She should have remembered her instructions.

Angus had been very clear. "Let the lad try. He needs tae prove himself." Her job was to support him, to guide him, if necessary, but not to supplant him. She finished the tea, then cleaned the cup and put the stove away.

Jim would find Charlie and the two would talk. Then either

Charlie would come back of his own volition or he would leave and that would be that. Unless Jim decided to force the issue.

She walked to the edge of the forest, peering into the green gloom. There was a lot about Jim she still didn't know. What would he do if frustrated? Would he lash out? She should have asked Sarah that one.

She turned and found herself pacing, frowning hard. Sarah. She'd been invited to come to Texas, but had declined. Why? Had Jim condescended to *her*? Dismissed *her*?

When Angus died, Jim would become Laird. A laird needed to be willing to accept help, from women as well as men. Jim's tendency was to patronize her. What he needed was a good dose of humility, something that—

Ginny whirled at the sound. Unless it was a stranger, Jim had fired the rifle. Not at Charlie, surely? At something else. Someone else? If he was firing at an animal, it was unlikely to be for food. If he was firing at a human, Charlie included, that meant trouble.

Ginny felt her nurse's training kick in. Bullets cause bleeding. She was already moving when she heard the second shot. She grabbed her backpack and swung it over her shoulder.

She had no idea what she would find. He might not need her help. If he didn't and saw her, he would be angry with her for disobeying. Maybe she could sneak up on him, assess the situation, then slip away.

One thing was clear. Whatever was going on, there was no way she could just sit quietly drinking tea and wait to see what might or might not emerge from the shrubbery. She took a deep breath and plunged into the woods.

* * *

CHAPTER 25

Saturday Morning
Taconic Parkway

Jim looked around at the forest, cursing under his breath. He felt attacked on all sides. Here he was, clawing his way through the snow, following the (admittedly easy to see) trail of a fool, risking his livelihood and maybe his life for someone who didn't care enough to stay put and do as told.

Ginny, too. Up to this point, Jim had had the much more comfortable position of being the man in charge, in charge of her medical care, in charge of their relationship, in charge of this expedition.

But today she had calmly and correctly analyzed the emergency, made a plan, and started to implement it. So what did he do? Nothing he was proud of. Instead of rejoicing to see her confidence returning, he resented her interference.

Jim was thoroughly male and had been raised in a household where the male and female role models made it clear there were differences between the two. His mother had deferred to his father on every occasion—that he knew of. It suddenly occurred to him to wonder if they'd had discussions outside his hearing.

Come to think of it, there'd been a few times when he'd wondered at the strained silence. But he'd never suspected anything. They worked together as a team. He was never able to play one parent off against the other.

Jim paused for a moment to catch his breath and make sure he was still following the broken twigs and scuffed snow that marked Charlie's passing.

His mother had stayed home and baked cookies. In a world where everyone had a paying job, she was an aberration. But she was not idle. There were times when Jim had been away on a sleepover and had come home to find she wasn't back yet. He'd learned, after he left for college, what she'd been doing. Lecturing. On subjects like epigenetics and neuroplasticity and telomere reconstruction.

The forest noises had been changing, but Jim had been too preoccupied to notice. He was suddenly aware of water, not very far off. Charlie's trail headed in that direction. Jim picked up his pace. In another ten minutes he could see the stream.

Jim had no trouble following the mud slide that indicated Charlie's descent into the snow bank, nor locating the discarded backpack. He took a moment to look through the pack, found his pistol, checked it carefully, then unzipped his parka and tucked the gun into his belt. He pushed on, leaving Charlie's pack where it could be picked up on the way back.

Now he could hear sounds other than water—a voice, and animals snarling. He paused, feeling the goosebumps rise on his arms, then moved closer. He sank to the ground, easing the emergency medical kit off his back, and drawing the pistol.

Jim was not a hunter. The only animal he'd ever killed was a squirrel he'd accidentally hit with the car. His mouth went dry at the sight that met his eyes.

Charlie stood, one leg clearly out of commission, his eyes on the woods and his belt in his hands. As Jim watched, Charlie swung the belt, then loosed a missile. It hit something that yelped, then growled.

Jim could see four animals on their feet and one on the ground. Gray wolves, gaunt, their ribs showing even through the thick winter fur. Two had blood on their jaws. Jim watched as one of the animals reached down and pulled another hunk of flesh from the recumbent wolf.

Two feeding, two waiting to feed. How many more were lurking in the bushes?

Jim knew he had eleven rounds in the pistol. What he didn't know was whether he could bring down a wolf with a single slug, whether the others would flee or attack when he started firing, and where, exactly, a wolf's heart lay. He tucked the .45 back in his belt and pulled the rifle out of its case.

He put his eye to the scope, and had a sudden flashback to a day three months ago, the day he'd started his living history training. He'd been taken out to the range and presented with two weapons. One was a rifle. The other was a musket. He'd never handled either before.

He had shouldered the rifle and looked through the scope and seen a coyote in the hills beyond the range. His instructor had carefully lowered the barrel and pointed him at the target.

"Focus on center mass," he'd said. "Never look at your target's eyes."

He hadn't been too bad, for a first try with a long gun, managing to hit the target twice. The musket had been another matter entirely, both difficult to load and difficult to aim. "With both weapons," his instructor had told him, "in spite of the difference in sophistication, do it right the first time. You won't get another chance."

Jim was lying on his stomach at the edge of the ravine. He settled the rifle along the ridge, took careful aim at the larger of the two wolves standing over the carcass, exhaled, and squeezed the trigger. The animal yelped, jerking sideways, then snapped at its companion. It staggered a few paces off, then fell.

The wolf Charlie had hit with the rock and the one Jim had seen in the bushes both looked at the newly injured animal. The nearer one rose from its crouch and stalked slowly in that direction, circling the area. The smaller wolf of the feeding pair turned on the newcomer, growling and snapping. The one closing in skirted the female and began making its careful way toward the dying animal.

Two down.

The fifth wolf held preternaturally still, his head coming slowly back around. He lifted his nose and sniffed the air and Jim suddenly wondered if he was up or down wind of the animal. When its eyes turned and looked directly at him, he had his answer.

Charlie had also turned and was looking at him. He raised a hand, and crooked a finger.

Jim licked his lips. He'd heard about Charlie's background. He knew he could handle a rifle, and a dozen other weapons, and he'd seen what he could do with a belt and a rock. He could be counted on to kill wolves, but could he be counted on *not* to kill Jim?

Jim went back to the scope. He lined up on the animal eyeing him and fired again. This time he missed. He swore to himself. That first shot had been nothing but luck. Well, not entirely. He *had* been practicing. It was just that he didn't have years of hunting experience and that wolf seemed to know it. It rose, ignoring the two men, and approached the downed alpha male.

The wolves circled, growling, then each seized a limb and began to tear their fallen leader apart. Jim watched them rip open the thorax and drag the vital organs out onto the snow, the fresh blood making startling splashes of crimson on the pristine white.

Jim lowered his weapon, picked up his medical bag, and began to make his way over to where Charlie stood.

"God, I'm glad to see you," Charlie said. "I think I broke my leg."

Jim looked at the other man, his eyes narrowing. "Why did you run?"

Charlie looked sheepish. "I was feelin' sorry for myself. I thought maybe it would be better for you, for the two of you, if I just disappeared."

"And now?"

Charlie sucked in a breath. "I don't deserve it, but I'd be very grateful if you'd take me back. I won't give you any more trouble."

Jim nodded slowly, then handed him the rifle. "Keep them off my back while I look at your leg."

"What have you got in this?"

".308."

Charlie nodded. "That'll do. Four rounds or five?"

Jim blinked. He had no idea how many rounds of ammunition the magazine held. Reggie had supplied the weapon and magazine. "In case of bears," he had said.

"I don't know."

Charlie released the magazine, took a look, reinserted it, and chambered a round. "Three."

Jim helped Charlie sit, then pulled out his shears and cut the fabric away from the leg, noting the misaligned bone and surface abrasions. Not a compound fracture, but it would need more than a simple pull to reduce it. He needed to get Charlie to the Homestead for treatment.

"Anything else?"

"Some scrapes and bruises. So far."

"So far?"

Charlie pointed at the brush to his left. "There's one over on this side, beneath that spruce, and at least one more, over there." He pointed in the opposite direction. "They'll attack from both sides, at the same time."

Jim felt his skin crawl, but turned back to his work. The sooner he was done, the sooner they could leave.

"I need to immobilize this leg." He pulled the bandages and splints out of his bag, then glanced up at Charlie's face. He was clearly in pain and applying the splint was going to hurt.

Jim slipped his fingers over Charlie's pulse, finding it rapid, but strong enough, and his respiratory rate was okay. He pulled out the morphine, made a slit in Charlie's pants, grabbed a handful of muscle, and injected the medication.

Jim sat back for a minute, giving the medicine a chance to start working and looking around at the situation. The three visible wolves were concentrating on the two dead ones, but he had an uncomfortable sensation of eyes on the back of his neck.

Charlie suddenly snapped up the rifle and fired at something over Jim's shoulder. Jim started and twisted hard, finding a smaller animal standing at the top of the rise, hair bristling, teeth bared, an ugly growling noise coming from its throat.

"Sorry," Charlie said. "Hold still." He took aim and dispatched the animal. Jim watched it fall, then turned back in time to see the three he had been watching all standing still and silent, their eyes on the pair of men in the hollow.

Jim said nothing, but went to work stabilizing the limb. He didn't like the idea of having to get all the way back to the car with a drugged cripple, and hungry wolves on his heels. He could see how much it hurt Charlie as he applied the stabilizer and wrapped it carefully with elastic bandages. How much worse was it going to be to try to walk on that leg?

The morphine wouldn't help, not for that. It would lower

Charlie's blood pressure and respiratory rate, countering the adrenaline that must be sustaining him at the moment.

He had finished applying the bandages and was trying to make sure Charlie still had a pulse in that foot when Charlie raised the rifle again. In the same instant that Jim heard it go off, he turned and found himself under attack.

He tried to pull his pistol, but couldn't get to it before the wolf was on him. He felt the animal's teeth close on his arm and could smell fresh blood superimposed on the worst case of dog breath he'd ever encountered. Snarls and growling filled his ears and the gray fur blocked his view in every direction.

There was a pistol report, then another, then a third, followed by the animal falling heavily on him, no longer fighting. Jim shoved it off and put his hand on his arm, applying pressure to the wound.

He looked around, expecting to find Charlie had somehow gotten hold of his pistol. Instead he found Ginny standing above them, her eyes on the wolves.

She fired again, hitting an animal in the process of springing for Charlie's throat. This one looked younger, a juvenile, which might explain why it hadn't attacked in the same instant that the larger animal had attacked Jim.

It yelped, then turned and staggered off in the direction of the adults. Ginny took aim and finished it off with another round.

She raised her pistol and fired again, at the half-fed trio, hitting each with a single round, wounding them, causing them to run into the woods. Jim watched as the trees shook with movement, then heard howling as the wolves regrouped.

Ginny lowered her weapon, cleared and holstered it, then pulled something out from her backpack. Without a word, she unfolded a blue tarp and slid it under Charlie, pulling him onto it, folding it over him, making an envelope of it, and securing him in it with duct tape. Jim was surprised to see how efficient her movements were.

She threw her gear back into her bag, picked up the rifle, checked to make sure it was empty, then stowed the weapon in its carrying case. After which, she turned her attention to Jim, inspecting his arm, padding it with gauze, and wrapping a bandage around it.

Jim unclenched his teeth with difficulty. She shouldn't be here. What if Charlie hadn't abandoned the pistol, had turned it on her? How was he supposed to keep her safe if she refused to obey him?

"I believe I told you to stay with the car." He could hear his voice shake.

She met his eyes. "You did." She packed up the medical gear. "Can you stand?"

He nodded and allowed her to help him to his feet, finding his legs rubbery from the adrenaline. She handed him the medical bag.

"Let's get going," she said, "before the rest of them decide they prefer human flesh to wolf à la carte."

She threaded a rope through the grommets in two corners of the tarp and fashioned loops long enough to go around a torso. She slipped one over her own shoulder and settled the rest of the gear in place, then waited for Jim to do the same. When they were both in harness, they started the long, arduous task of hauling Charlie and all the gear back to the SUV.

* * *

CHAPTER 26

Saturday Morning
I-90 to Albany

Jim's arm hurt and he kept bumping it as he hauled. He wanted to abandon the gear, and maybe Charlie as well, but the sight of Ginny, grim-mouthed and dogged, kept him going. It took them an hour to get back to the SUV.

Back out on the Parkway, he had an opportunity to look around. Each of the bridges was labeled with someone's name, then the word 'kill'.

He was certainly in the mood to kill something. Charlie had precipitated this whole mess. If he'd driven straight on to Albany, or waked Jim when he was unsure what to do next, Jim's arm wouldn't be throbbing.

He deserved the pain, of course. Charlie wasn't the only one at fault. Sleeping in the back while the confessed murderer ran off into the night!

And what about Ginny? What if one of the wolves had attacked her? Or she had fallen and hurt herself? Didn't she understand the danger? What was Jim supposed to do then?

It took a while, but he finally calmed down enough to pay attention to something other than his anger. When he did, he found himself watching Ginny drive. It was yet another moment of disconnect.

Here was the ICU nurse turned marksman, calmly killing, and yet, not calm. Her eyes had an intensity in them that reminded him of a patient he'd had years ago, a woman so desperate to save her child that she'd thrown herself in front of a speeding car. Both mother and child had died that day.

They followed I-90 north until it intersected US 20, then northeast on NY Hwy 4 until they spotted the first sign for the Albany Homestead. Jim was glad to see the gates. Both he and Charlie needed a doctor.

* * *

Saturday Noon
Beverwyck Homestead

"Oh my dears! Come right in. We heard you'd had some trouble on the road. I'm so glad to see you safely here. They call me Mother Gordon."

Ginny looked at the trim woman with the elegant hands and eloquent dark eyes and felt the label out of place.

"I'm so sorry to trouble you, Mrs. Gordon, but we need emergency medical care."

The Matron picked up the phone and in less than ten minutes they found themselves in an elevator very similar to the one back home, then an underground medical facility. The staff had apparently just arrived. Some were still wearing coats, others were turning on lights and equipment.

Ginny watched as the triage nurse looked first at Jim's arm, sending him off to have the wound cleaned by a very efficient looking woman with an iodine scrub brush, then at Charlie's leg.

Ginny stayed with Charlie. They stripped him and went over him carefully, deciding the fracture would have to be reduced under conscious sedation and could not be casted until the swelling went down. The good news was that he had all his pulses and no evidence of frostbite. Ginny answered questions as well as she could, then sat still for an examination of herself.

When they were done with her, she asked and was shown to a room and found her overnight bag there. She showered and changed clothes, then put together a collection of soiled clothing and located the laundry. She had all of Charlie's things and her own, but Jim was still wearing some of his. She had his outerwear, though, and got to work on it.

It was the same over-sized parka she had found for him in Dallas. There was blood on it. Most of it had to be the wolf's, but some of it was Jim's.

Blood was always hard to get out, especially if it had been allowed to set, but she knew a trick or two and managed to remove most of the stains. All the damaged clothing was due to be discarded in Halifax anyway. When they got there, if they did, he could buy another jacket.

The next step was mending. She had to ask again, but the Matron was fully prepared both for the task and for Ginny's need to do it herself. She worked swiftly, focusing on the needle, trying not to think. It should not have been necessary to stitch up either his sleeve or his arm.

She was seated in front of the fireplace, a bright table lamp illuminating her work, when Jim found her.

"I have a favor to ask," he said.

She didn't raise her eyes from her sewing. "How may I assist you?"

"I want to wash my hair."

Ginny nodded, gathered up her sewing, and followed him upstairs.

She wrapped his bandaged arm in plastic, to keep it dry, then helped him wash the blood, mud, and forest debris away,

They had exchanged hardly a word during this process and only those that were necessary to get the job done. She left him toweling his head, picked up the sewing and dirty laundry, and turned to leave.

"Ginny, wait, please."

He took the dirty clothes out of her arms and dropped them on the floor then steered her over to the sofa and sat down next to her. Ginny fixed her eyes on the carpet, determined to stay calm.

He took a deep breath. "I have been behaving like a prize fool. First I got my ego bruised because you have a head on your shoulders, which I already knew. Then I told you to stay behind when we both knew I would need your help. Then I couldn't bring myself to say 'thank you' for dealing with that wolf. Can you forgive me?"

"Of course." She said the words easily. They meant nothing. Well, she meant she forgave him, but it didn't fix the underlying problem. She waited for the other shoe to drop.

"But you and I need to talk about following orders."

And there it was.

"I had a good reason for telling you to stay behind. Charlie had my pistol and I had no idea how desperate he might be. If he was going to shoot at me, I didn't want there to be a chance he might hit you."

Ginny understood. He didn't want the distraction of having to worry about her, where she was, what she was doing. The solution for that, though, was to trust her.

"My job is to protect you. I can't do that if you won't cooperate."

A part of her wanted to argue. He had been in no condition to protect himself, much less her. Another part admitted he might have been able to save himself. His own weapon was in his belt. All he had to do was get to it. *While fighting off the wolf with his bare hands?*

"I need for you to trust me, Ginny."

Trust him? What she ought to do was wash her hands of him. If he was too proud to accept her help, why should she offer it? Let him make his own mistakes. *Even if they killed him? Angus wouldn't appreciate that.*

The moment she saw that wolf, its teeth in Jim's arm, she'd known what she had to do. It would have been easier on Jim if she could have fired from cover, but she couldn't hide and be sure of killing the wolf.

She'd had no choice, but he had. He could accept her help without rancor, or he could consider her actions a challenge to his authority. He'd chosen the latter. She rose to go.

"Wait, Ginny. You understand, don't you?" He reached for her, but she took a step back.

"I understand perfectly." She met his eyes. "May I go?"

He nodded. She picked up the laundry and left.

* * * ·

Saturday Afternoon
Dallas, TX

"Ma'am? I was asked to give you this." The officer handed over a sheaf of papers.

"Thank you, Sergeant."

Detective Tran glanced through the new reports. The weekend had been quiet, so far, for which she was grateful. The visit with Monroe's in-laws had shaken her faith and she wanted to go over the evidence again. Not that you could call it evidence, really. It was more an absence of evidence.

The credit card receipts and phone records had all corroborated the assertion that Mr. Monroe was in Waco from Saturday through Wednesday evening. He'd gassed up his car in Waco, then driven home, where he was seen with two of the Scots, who had been found and questioned.

They reported bringing food and finding Mr. Monroe sitting alone in the house with no lights on, the food in the refrigerator spoiled, and messages on the phone unanswered.

Tran flipped to the relevant section in her folder. She scanned the medical record. Monroe had told the psychiatrist he'd gone to see his in-laws to say goodbye.

He'd been booked into a local hotel and it was those records she had been going over today. Summarized, Monroe appeared on security cameras in the hallway at the hotel for the times he was alleged to have been there. The new reports dealt with the room access, which was via computer card. There was nothing to suggest he had done anything other than come and go as expected.

No alibi was unbreakable, but this one seemed pretty solid. She reached for her computer and modified the search area to include hospitals and morgues within a two hundred mile radius of Dallas. She should also send officers to all of the homeless shelters, especially in the neighborhood of Lake Lavon. Someone might have seen something.

If he hadn't actually drowned (and they might still find his body), he might have taken himself off somewhere, trusting the carrion to dispose of his remains. Texas could be a vast and lonely place.

She sighed to herself, put the files back together, then headed home. As much as she hated to admit it, the truth was they might never find out what happened to Charles Monroe.

* * *

CHAPTER 27

Saturday Evening
Beverwyck Homestead

Jim watched Ginny go, then stretched out on the bed to think. She had submitted, hadn't argued with him or challenged him, or in any way tried to defend her actions. So why wasn't he happy? Because she wasn't.

He shifted restlessly on the bedclothes. This was not a vacation. He'd been given a job to do. She needed to listen to him, so he could deliver Charlie safely to Halifax. He couldn't do that if she kept ignoring him, defying him.

Jim frowned to himself. She should *not* have assumed she was included in the search party. Why had she done that? Did she know something Jim didn't? About Charlie, maybe?

Jim stared at the far wall suffering misgivings. It was at least possible.

She had said she hadn't known Charlie before his family was killed. Except, she'd danced with him every Friday night for over a year. Jim had seen how the dancers worked together, had tried to emulate their easy partnerships, had hoped he and Ginny would be such a pair, faultlessly in synch with one another, one day.

She had sat down across the picnic table from Charlie, in his line of fire, in spite of his emotional state, and gambled her life that he wouldn't shoot her. He hadn't pulled the trigger then. Maybe she believed he wouldn't pull the trigger now.

That still left accident, of course. Charlie might have been aiming for Jim and hit Ginny by mistake. Jim wasn't wrong about the danger. Except, Charlie left the .45 in the backpack. That didn't look like a man bent on shooting his way out of custody, or committing suicide, either.

Ginny had gone to the Laird and pleaded for Charlie and Charlie knew it. Maybe she had counted on his feeling an obligation to her, enough of one to allow them to finish the journey.

She had shopped for him, cooked for him, and talked privately with him in Dallas and Charlottesville, and Jim didn't know what they had discussed on those occasions.

He stared at his analysis. It made a cogent argument for Ginny going after Charlie, to see if she could find out why he ran, and try to talk him into coming back. Ginny, not Jim.

He grew very still. She could have pointed that out to him, but hadn't. She had held her tongue and let him work it out for himself, which argued a subtly of mind he hadn't expected from her. More like something Angus would do.

Which reminded him, he owed Himself a call. He reached for the phone and dialed his grandfather's number.

"Jim! I was beginnin' tae wonder."

"I apologize for not getting back to you sooner. We've had a lot going on here."

"Tell me, lad."

Jim took a deep breath then dove in. He left out nothing, telling his grandfather about Charlie's escape and recapture, about having to be rescued by Ginny, about his mishandling of the whole affair. When he was through, there was a silence on the other end of the line, then his grandfather's voice.

"What does th' doctor say aboot the wolf bite?"

"That it should heal cleanly. He put in a couple of stitches and put me on antibiotics and pain killers."

"And Charlie?"

"He's in traction. They want to reduce the swelling before they put the cast on."

"And Ginny?"

Jim hesitated. "She's unhappy with me."

"Aye? Why is that?"

"I was a bit sharp with her about not following my instructions."

"Tis a guid thing she ignored ye."

Jim threw his undamaged arm out in exasperation. "She put herself in harm's way. Didn't you tell her not to do that again?"

"Aye, I did, but I dinna forbid her tae rescue my grandson frae hisself, if needed."

"I didn't need rescuing!"

"Are ye sure aboot that?"

Jim took a deep breath. "No. I'm not sure, and I'm not sure it wouldn't have been better if she'd gone after Charlie by herself, but he had my gun and a reason to shoot anyone who came looking for him."

"Ye've no forgotten she's a qualified marksman?"

"I haven't forgotten. I just wasn't sure she'd shoot Charlie, even if she needed to."

"Th' lass'll do what she must. Ye can trust her common sense."

Jim snorted. "If she had any common sense, she'd have stayed home."

"She's followin' my instructions."

Jim caught his breath. "What instructions?"

"I couldna come wi' ye myself so I sent her."

Jim's jaw dropped. "You planted a spy on me?"

"Nay, lad. She's there tae help ye, if ye'll let her."

"Let her? I can't stop her!"

"Dinna underrate th' lass, Jim. I've kent her fra her birth. She's more capable than most men I've known. A true Viking throwback, like yer mither was."

Jim was caught off guard. "Wait, whose mother?"

"Yours, lad. She's brave and strong and clever, like Tibbie. 'Tis a shame they never met."

Jim found himself speechless.

"And now, if ye've nothin' further tae complain o' where Ginny is concerned, there's th' other matter tae discuss."

Jim pulled himself together. "The police."

"Detective Tran ha' been busy. She talk'd wi' th' staff at th' hospital, then interviewed Ginny's mither, and a neighbor who saw ye packin' and described th' van."

"Okay. What else?"

"She ha' searched Charlie's hoose an' seized all manner o' stuff an' sent it tae th' crime lab."

Jim nodded. They had expected that.

"She went tae interview Charlie's in-laws."

Jim's brow furrowed. "Why'd she do that?"

"Because Charlie's credit card receipts show a visit tae Waco startin' on Saturday and finishing on Wednesday, which covers th' time th' drunk was killed and stashed in th' boat."

Jim let that sink in. "He has an alibi."

"Aye! And she's tryin' tae break it."

"Does she know about the Homesteads, that we're staying at them?"

"Sinia Forbes told Detective Tran ye hadna made hotel reservations as ye didna know where or how far ye were going each day."

"So she doesn't know where to look."

"No yet, but tha' woman is nae fool."

Jim nodded. "I'm hoping we can get back on the road

tomorrow. With luck we'll be on the border by midmorning the day after."

"Call me frae Bangor."

"I will."

"And ye might just consider givin' Miss Ginny th' benefit o' th' doubt afore ye go handin' doon orders and expectin' tae be obeyed."

Jim put the phone away feeling chastened. It wasn't that he didn't know what Ginny could do. It was just that he couldn't bear the thought of seeing her hurt again. So, in his haste to protect her, he'd made it clear he didn't think she was smart enough to stay out of the line of fire. Put that way, he could understand her anger.

He sighed heavily. He'd better go apologize again, and mean it this time. He crossed the hall and tapped on her door.

"Ginny?"

When he got no answer, he turned the knob. The door was unlocked and the room empty.

She could be anywhere, of course, but his mind immediately flew to the worst case scenario. She had run out into the snow and would die of cold. She had gone for a walk and met with an accident or a wild animal or human predators. She had left him.

Jim felt his heart racing and tried to talk himself down. Her coat was gone. She wouldn't freeze. If she had her pistol with her, it was the wild animals and human predators who should be on guard. As for abandoning the trip, she had promised Himself she would see Charlie safely to Halifax. She might be unwilling to follow Jim's instructions, but she would keep her promise to the Laird.

He pulled his phone out and dialed her number. The buzzing that reached his ears showed him her phone, abandoned on the desk.

Jim did a quick search of the room. The only thing missing was her coat, so she was on the grounds somewhere. But if he was going to find her in the snow-covered woods, dressed as she was in a white parka, he was going to need help.

* * *

Saturday Evening
Beverwyck Homestead

Ginny dropped the laundry on the floor of her room, closed the door behind her and leaned against it. All he wanted to do was keep her safe. Safe and out of danger. Safe at home, with the bairns, and the kine, and the cooking pots.

Why did the thought of that life make her crazy? All *she* wanted was to be useful. She could be useful as someone's wife, someone's mother. Why did she want more?

She pulled out her phone and dialed home. Her mother answered immediately.

"Ginny, darling! Are you all right?"

"I'm fine."

"Himself said there was trouble with Charlie, that you spent the night on the side of the road."

"Both true, but Charlie is safe and we are all three at the Albany Homestead."

"The news is full of the storm."

Ginny listened to her mother's description of the damage and wondered how they had managed to miss the downed power lines and tree trunks.

"How are you and Jim getting along?"

Ginny almost smiled. Her mother had an uncanny knack for reading her moods.

"We've had a fight."

"What about?"

"It's the same old thing. No man likes to be shown up by a woman." She explained about the wolf.

Her mother sighed. "I don't see that you had any choice."

"I know."

"How's he taking it?"

"He apologized for his bad mood."

"Oh? That sounds hopeful."

"Mother, you didn't see his face! He looked like he wanted to scrape me off the bottom of his shoe. He's very well brought up, but he couldn't hide his true feelings." And, in all honesty, it was better to know.

"Maybe his feelings will change."

"And maybe pigs will fly. I'm not going to hold my breath."

"I wish I could give you a hug."

"Me, too."

"You know I love you very much."

"I know."

"And I'm very proud of you."

"I know."

"And Himself is counting on you to keep Jim in line, discreetly, of course."

"Of course."

Ginny hung up the phone feeling homesick and depressed. She had asked her mother, once, how she had managed to find and marry Ginny's father. She'd been told they were introduced by their parents, both sets having decided it would be a good match. They'd been right. Too bad that hadn't been an option for her.

She scrolled through her messages, finding a text from Pittsburgh, dated yesterday morning. The package had arrived. What were her instructions? Too late to ask them to send the talisman to Albany. She instructed them to send it on to

Bangor.

She set the phone down on the desk, pulled on her coat, and opened the door. The hallway was empty. She slipped out and made her way down the staircase as quietly as she could, hurrying past the great rooms to the back entrance and out onto the grounds, glad she hadn't run into anyone, hadn't had to speak to anyone. She struck out for the quickest way into the woods.

She walked hard for twenty minutes, struggling to understand herself. She didn't want to be a man. She didn't even want to compete with men. The firing range was a good example. She took no pride in beating other shooters. She compared herself only to the numbers on the target and how well she had performed last time out.

Was she sorry she was a good shot? No. Was she sorry she'd had to use that skill? That was more difficult to answer. She'd worked very hard to get that good. Why? So she could save a life? Maybe. Her own, maybe. Someone weaker than herself, maybe. A child, an elderly person. Someone who actually needed to be rescued.

He'd been on the ground with the wolf on top of him, its teeth clamped on his gun arm. What, exactly, was the definition of 'needed to be rescued'? Even if Jim had managed to get his gun out and shoot the wolf dead—with his weak hand and at close quarters—he could not have gotten Charlie back to the car unaided. Could he?

Ginny found her imagination working overtime. Jim had pulled his gun from his waistband, fired into the face of the wolf (splattering gore everywhere), avoided the death spasm that was said to prevent prying the animal's teeth apart, risen to his feet, picked up Charlie with his good arm, and the two of them had hobbled out to the car on Charlie's broken leg, carrying all the gear, Jim losing blood at every step, the wolves following, waiting for one or both to fall so they could attack again. Right.

The image of his face, the expression on his face as she knelt to inspect his wound, rose before her eyes. His opinion of her at that moment had been clear.

She blinked hard, scolding herself for being foolish. It didn't matter what she felt. He was the one who mattered. He would be Laird of Loch Lonach. Male. A physician. A good choice.

She had thought, for a while, she might be useful, but it didn't have to be her. Anyone would do. In Jim's eyes she was superfluous. Worse, a liability. He shouldn't be wasting his time talking her down off the ledge. He had better things to do. It made sense to let someone else teach him. She would go home and let someone else take over.

Ginny was fighting hard to be rational, to banish emotion, but she was human and the feelings would not be denied. She found herself ankle-deep in snow, staring at the trunk of a fine, old oak. She balled up her fist, her soul aching to lash out.

How dare he despise her? How many times did she have to prove her worth to him? How many ways? She hauled back and hit the tree, feeling the shock run up her arm and across her shoulders. It hurt, but it was a good hurt. Physical pain was so much easier to bear than psychological pain. She did it again.

There was a low sound coming from deep inside, forced out between clenched teeth, an elemental cry of protest at her own helplessness. She had saved his LIFE. And he hated her for it.

She hit the tree again, harder, trying to make the anger and frustration and disappointment go away. WHY couldn't he appreciate her for who she was? WHY did he have to be such an arrogant, self-righteous, STUPID male? AND WHY DID SHE CARE?

She was pounding the tree with both fists now, grinding her

teeth, shrieking with anger and impotence and completely unaware that she was no longer alone. A hand came around from behind her head, caught her wrist in mid punch, and held it, turning her away from the tree, pulling her into his arms, holding her tightly.

"Stop, lass! Ye'll hurt yerself."

Ginny struggled to break free, pulling back and trying to twist out of his grip. She couldn't speak. It was all she could do to breathe.

"Easy, lass. I'll not hurt ye."

She looked up to find a tall man with bushy white eyebrows. He was surprisingly strong for someone clearly no longer young. She stopped struggling, knowing he would let go sooner if she cooperated.

"That's better."

He was looking at her, studying her and she blushed at the realization that she had been caught making a fool of herself.

"Come wi' me, lass."

"No!" Ginny tugged again, this time succeeding in pulling free, and backed away. She hadn't meant to sound so rude. It had just come out that way.

He crossed his arms, and she saw the eyebrows come together. He was clearly trying to decide what to do with her and the intensity of his gaze made her take another step back.

She saw him blink, then his expression softened.

"Dinna be afraid, lass. I'll no hurt ye. I'm Gordon."

Mrs. Gordon's husband. All right. Fine. But she was in no mood for company. She took another step back, intending to run.

He made no move to stop her, instead reaching into his pocket and pulling out a phone. She watched him select a number then lift the phone to his ear.

"Angus? I've Ginny Forbes here. She's a wee bit upset and I

thought ye might wish tae speak wi' her." He held the phone out toward her. "Yer laird, lass."

She swallowed, then stepped closer, reaching for the device. She tried to lift it to her ear, but her shaking hands wouldn't cooperate.

"Let me." He took the thing back and pushed a button. "Angus? Yer on speaker."

"Ginny?"

She swallowed hard. "I'm here."

"I see ye've met Dr. Gordon."

Doctor? "Yes, sir."

"Are ye all right, lass?"

"Yes."

With Gordon holding the phone, Ginny could not walk away. She had to stay close enough to be heard. He was watching her and Ginny felt as if he was eavesdropping.

"Yer mither tells me ye and Jim had a wee fallin' oot."

"Yes."

"Tell me, lass."

Ginny drew in a shuddering breath. She didn't want to talk about Jim. "There's nothing to tell. I did what I had to. He wasn't happy about it. End of story."

"Weel, tha' doesnae sound sae bad. Ye'll be makin' it up afore long."

Ginny felt the cold seeping into her bones and started to shiver. She needed to bring this conversation to a close. She would be polite, she decided, but firm. Instead she found herself blurting out what she really wanted to say.

"I want permission to come home."

There was a short pause on the other end of the line.

"Ye've no forgotten why I sent ye on this journey?"

"I have not. He doesn't want my help. Nor does he need it."

"And wha' makes ye say that?"

"I'm just getting in his way. Let me go back where I belong, where I can do some good."

She heard another pause.

"I'm thinkin' my reasons fer sending ye still hold. Yer there tae keep him oot o' trouble. Where would he ha'e been if ye'd no' been there tae deal wi' th' wolf?"

Ginny drew in a ragged breath and tried again.

"Your grandson is a good man. He's strong and brave and capable. Please let me come home."

"What did he do, lass? What did he say tae ye?"

Ginny felt her heart constrict. "Nothing!"

"It must ha'e been something, tae bring ye tae this pass."

Ginny put her face in her hands and tried not to disintegrate. She could hear Gordon's voice, close to her ear, speaking into the phone.

"Gi'e me a chance tae talk tae them, Angus. I'll call ye back."

She was shivering, hard, her face still in her hands, her eyes closed. How had she managed to screw this up so badly? Instead of a quiet hour or two exorcising her frustration in solitude, she had two powerful men hovering over her while she tried to escape a third.

"Here, lass." Gordon slipped the phone into his pocket, then put his arm around her shoulders and steered her down the path. Ginny had just enough self-control left to stay on her feet and keep moving.

He took her back toward the main complex, then veered off to what had to be his house. He let her in the front door, sat her down in the kitchen, and put the kettle on. While the water boiled, he cleaned and bandaged her torn knuckles, then applied ice packs to control the swelling.

He put the first aid kit away and came back with a bottle, adding some of the liquid and a thick syrup to the hot tea. Honey and whisky. Ginny sipped the hot toddy and felt all the comfort of that mixture sliding through her veins. By the time he had settled down, his own drink in front of him, she had stopped shivering.

He regarded her across the table, then pulled out his phone again. Ginny listened to his end of the conversation.

"Mother? Aye, I've got th' lass here, wi' me." He listened to the reply, then shook his head. "I think no. Tell him she's safe, but naught else." He listened for a minute longer. "Aye. I'll do that."

He hung up and put the phone away, then his eyes settled on her.

"Now, lass. Tell me the truth. Why are ye running away from Jim Mackenzie?"

* * *

CHAPTER 28

Saturday Evening
Beverwyck Homestead

Jim sat in the dining room with Mrs. Gordon. She had carefully explained that Ginny was with the Laird of Beverwyck and the Laird was a psychiatrist. She was safe, but Jim could not see her until they were finished talking.

Through the haze of his fear, he heard those words, over and over again. She had been found, taken in, was being cared for. Over and over, he saw her face during their last conversation, heard his grandfather's rebuke, heard his own words to her. Selfish. Self-centered. He suffered flashes of chagrin, then anger alternating with raw fear. She was safe, but that might not be enough if she was also through with him.

"Tell me about her."

"What?"

"Tell me about Ginny. How did you meet?"

An image of that evening rose before his eyes. Ginny in full bloom, dressed in velvet, her thick braid curled on her head like a crown. Hard on its heels was the vision of her the next day, the day he started to love her.

"What's she like, as a person?"

Jim thought for a moment before answering. "Curious, tenacious. She wants to understand things. She can think clearly. She can dance and sing and—" He had been going to say, "shoot," but felt it would open up a subject he wasn't prepared to discuss. "—cook. And she's very good at organizing things."

"A useful talent. What does she want to do with her life?"

"Do?" Jim stared at the woman across from him.

"Does she want to continue bedside nursing, or move into management? If she's good at organizing, she'd make a good Director of Nurses."

Jim found himself at a loss. He'd never considered what would happen to Ginny after he married her. Had he expected her to give up her career? To devote her life to him? He licked dry lips, then nodded. "Yes, she would."

"Or maybe we could use her in one of the Homesteads. Is she good with numbers?"

"Numbers?" He was beginning to sound half-witted.

"You know, budgets, bookkeeping, managing money."

"I don't know."

"Does she want children?"

Jim tried to remember if she'd ever said. All he could hear was his own voice, telling her what *he* wanted. "I think so."

"Not all women do, especially those with successful careers."

Was it Jim's imagination, or was there a barb in that comment? Mrs. Gordon took a sip of her coffee, her eyes still on him. "She was engaged to that other man, I think you said."

"No, thank God! He asked, but she turned him down."

"Smart girl."

"Yes." Everyone said so. Everyone but him.

Jim wasn't sure he could handle much more of this. He looked at his watch, again. "Will it be much longer?" he asked.

"I shouldn't think so. Are you hungry?"

Jim shook his head. Nauseated was more accurate. Sick with

fear. He'd never fully understood that phrase before. He did now.

* * *

Saturday Afternoon
Beverwyck Homestead

Ginny met Dr. Gordon's eyes.

"How did you know I was there?"

"Th' cameras are motion activated. When ye left th' complex, my wife was notified and she alerted me."

"You spy on your guests?"

"'Tis a dangerous place and we've needed th' surveillance tae help us find missing bairns. Why were ye hittin' the tree?"

Ginny looked down at her hands. "I was frustrated."

"And ye needed tae hit something?"

"Yes." She lifted her eyes. "I thought I was alone."

"Yer never alone, lass. Not as long as ye belong tae a Homestead." He took a sip of his toddy. "I took th' liberty o' calling yer laird this afternoon when th' three o' ye came in."

Ginny waited.

"Angus and I go way back, ye ken."

Of course.

"Here's wha' he told me. Yer headed fer Halifax. Yer traveling wi' two men, one o' whom is the young Mackenzie. An' yer boyfriend recently proved tae be no friend."

Ginny knew Angus Mackenzie well enough to know he would have a motive for telling Gordon about her. Not just gossip, either. Angus never did anything without a reason. He wanted something from Gordon. Something to do with her. She looked across the table at him.

"Are you the Laird here, sir?"

"Aye, lass."

That made him her host. As such, she owed him a certain amount of obedience. Also thanks for taking them in, and for the medical care. In lieu of a curtsy, she bobbed her head. "We are very grateful for your help."

He leaned back in his chair and crossed one long leg over the other.

"Tell me about yer parents, lass."

"My parents?"

He shrugged. "Yer childhood, growing up in Texas. We hear rumors, ye ken, up here in the northeast, about th' wild beasts and th' lawless ways o' th' folk down there. I'd like tae know what it takes tae raise a young woman who can shoot a wolf off a man's back."

The drink had done its work. Ginny was able to breathe. She was warm and reasonably comfortable. The only problem was maneuvering the mug to her lips, balanced between her swollen hands.

She hesitated for a moment longer, then took a breath and did as asked. She found herself describing her school days, and her father's death and her mother's adjustment to the unthinkable. She also found herself telling him about her brother and that led, naturally, to last October.

He listened sympathetically, asking intelligent questions, reserving judgment. When she was finished, he leaned toward her.

"So, tell me, lass, what's Jim done?"

Ginny's eyes had been resting on the Laird's hands. At his question, she looked up quickly. "Nothing. He's done nothing."

"He's no offered ye any violence?"

She shook her head emphatically. "None." She watched the Laird's brow furrow. He regarded her in silence for a moment, then leaned back in his seat.

"There are any number o' ways a man may hurt a woman. He may no even notice. That doesn't make him innocent, just gormless."

Ginny felt a smile twitch at the corner of her mouth. It was a term she hadn't heard in a long time and brought back memories of childhood.

"Why did ye no hit him, instead o' the tree?"

She considered and discarded a dozen possible answers, then chose one she was pretty sure this man would understand. "I don't know him that well."

The Laird looked at her, one eyebrow up. "That is a verry interesting answer. Does he know you?"

She shook her head. "No, and he never will."

"Why is that?"

Ginny shook her head. She'd said enough, more than enough.

"He's disappointed you."

She glanced up, then back down at her drink. No secret there. Her face had given that much away.

Dr. Gordon tapped a finger soundlessly on the table. She watched the motion, waiting. It was mildly interesting to see how regular the movement was, almost like a clock, steady, hypnotic.

An hour later Ginny realized she had told him everything he wanted to know, everything except Charlie's secret. About Jim's tendency to look down on her and her struggle to trust herself and how she had known Jim would be furious, but she'd had to make a choice.

"Ye sacrificed yer happiness fer him."

She nodded.

Gordon's mouth turned up slightly at the edges. "Yer a remarkable woman, Ginny Forbes. I wish ye were one o' mine."

Ginny had nothing to say to that. She would have given

anything to be less remarkable and more loveable.

"What is it, lass?"

She looked up and met his eyes. "I wish I didn't care. I wish I couldn't feel anything. I wish I had never met him."

Dr. Gordon sighed. "Love and life are never easy, but they're worth it."

Ginny found no comfort in that and lifted her mug to her lips only to find it empty and there was no comfort in that either.

"T'would be more restful if we had nae hearts, I know, but then we'd ha'e nae joy."

Joy. No hope of that.

"Ye know what Angus would say, were he here?"

"He'd say, don't give up on my grandson. No yet." She made a point of rolling her 'r's in imitation of her laird's voice.

Dr. Gordon smiled and nodded. "Aye. He'd also say, whatever the cost, each of us has a job tae do. We're born to it. We owe the clan our lives and our allegiance."

Ginny looked at him in silence for a long minute, then nodded. She'd heard Angus say exactly that, many times.

Dr. Gordon leaned toward her, his expression a mix of sympathy and conviction. "No matter how far removed frae Caledonia, we're still Scots. We've a talent for trouble and for surviving. It's in yer blood. Ye'll do what ye must, because ye must, and because ye can."

Ginny felt her shoulders sag. He was right. This journey would end eventually, at which point she could go home. In the meantime, she had a job to do right here. Whether Jim wanted it or not, her responsibility was to help him. Help him get Charlie to Halifax. Help him find his place in the community. Help him decide whether or not he wanted to become the Laird of Loch Lonach.

"I can gi'e ye some tools tae help ye face the task, if ye will.

Something a bit more constructive than broken bones."

She nodded.

"Sleep the nicht. We'll talk agin tomorrow."

Gordon rose, came around the table and pulled Ginny to her feet. "Come. I promised I'd bring ye back afore th' kitchen closed."

* * *

Saturday Evening
Beverwyck Homestead

It was a quarter to seven before the dining room door opened and Ginny stepped through.

Behind her, Jim could see a tall, older man. There was no question who he was. He wore authority as easily as the fisherman's sweater on his back. His mouth was broad and expressive, his eyes a bright blue, even from this distance, and sharp, unfettered by glasses or other signs of human weakness.

Jim had risen to his feet when she appeared. She started towards him and the Laird let her go, but Jim could see his eyes follow her across the room. Jim reached out and pulled her to him, wrapping his good arm around her, his eyes on the other man the whole time.

Mrs. Gordon, too, had risen. She left the table and went to the Laird. Jim saw her speak to him, then they both turned to look at Jim and Ginny. The Laird said something, then looked down at his wife and smiled, then held the door open for her, shutting it behind them as they left.

Jim let out a breath. He looked down at Ginny, seeing the bandages and the remnants of tears.

"What did you do to your hands, Ginny?"

"I punched a tree."

"Why?"

She shrugged, avoiding his eyes.

Jim took a deep breath then turned her toward the door. "Come on."

He took her to his room, discarding his sling and sitting her down under the reading lamp. He removed the dressings Dr. Gordon had applied and took a good look at the torn flesh.

"No broken bones?"

"They haven't been x-rayed, but I don't think so. They don't hurt enough."

"Don't hurt enough." Jim echoed her words, his heart aching. "Haven't you been hurt enough already? You have to smash your hands, too?"

"You're male. You understand that sometimes you have to hit something or explode."

Jim was familiar with the feeling, but couldn't recall ever doing this sort of damage to himself. His hands were his livelihood. He needed them in good working order.

"We'll get them x-rayed, just to be sure."

"I have a prescription to pick up, too."

"What is it?"

"A sleeping pill."

"You told him about the nightmares."

"I didn't have to. He's a very good listener."

Jim pulled her to her feet. "You can tell me the rest when we get back."

Dr. Warner met them at intake. "I've been waiting for you." He smiled at Ginny. When the scans were complete, he went over the results. "No breaks. Just tissue damage. Dressing changes, ice, and rest." He cleaned and bandaged her hands, then prescribed a dose of penicillin, which the duty nurse administered behind closed doors.

Once Ginny had been seen to, Dr. Warner turned to Jim. He

undid the dressing over the wolf bite and inspected the damage. The wounds were still red and the area swollen and hot.

"Hmm. You got the procaine penicillin? And the anti-inflammatories?"

"Yes."

Dr. Warner picked up his computer link and started writing. "I'm going to add an oral antibiotic, one tablet every twelve hours for seven days."

Jim nodded, watching as Dr. Warner re-dressed his arm.

"Here are the sleeping pills for Ginny and here is your antibiotic. You already have the narcotics."

"Enough for three days, yes."

"Don't be afraid to use them." Dr. Warner stood up and stretched. "I'm going to call it a day." He looked at Jim, then lifted an eyebrow. "I suggest you do the same."

* * *

CHAPTER 29

Saturday Evening
Beverwyck Homestead

After dinner, Dr. Gordon settled down in the chair next to Monroe's bed, facing him. The medical staff had cleared out when they saw him coming. They understood patient-doctor confidentiality.

"Hello, Charlie. I'm Dr. Gordon. I'm th' Laird here. I'm also a psychiatrist. I heard about th' wolves. I was wonderin' if ye'd like tae talk about it."

"No, thank you."

Dr. Gordon nodded. He waited for a moment, then started again. "I understand yer wife and daughters were killed by a drunk driver."

"Who told you that?"

"Ginny Forbes told Dr. Warner."

"Oh."

"I hear ye thought o' takin yer own life."

Monroe said nothing, just waited, his eyes on the Laird.

Gordon also waited. He knew the power of silence.

After a while Monroe nodded, slowly.

"I also hear that Ginny talked ye out o' it."

"Yes."

Dr. Gordon nodded. He already had every detail of that

incident at the park. His goal here was to see if he could get Monroe talking.

"Ye saw a psychiatrist after that?"

"They took me to the hospital, put me on some medications."

"Then what?"

"They let me go home."

Dr. Gordon nodded again. "Which medications?"

Monroe shrugged. "I don't know the name. Ginny has the bottle. I gave it back to her."

Dr. Gordon raised an eyebrow. "Ye were no taking them?"

"No."

"Why not?" He was pretty sure he already knew the answer.

"I didn't need them. I just had to work through it on my own."

Dr. Gordon was taking mental notes. Male ego and the illusion of strength in the face of devastating loss. The number of new cases of male depression every day was staggering. Men didn't know how to admit defeat or ask for help. Even when identified, it was hard for them to change the way they coped. Medications were viewed as weaknesses, lifestyle changes—an admission of guilt.

"I hear ye left th' others sleepin' and made yer way off inta th' woods."

"For all the good it did me."

"Why did ye leave yer friends?"

Monroe made eye contact, then looked away. "I was making trouble for them. I thought it would be better if I just left."

An interesting excuse. "What kind o' trouble?"

Monroe shrugged. "I don't know if you've noticed, but they kind of fancy each other."

The corner of Dr. Gordon's mouth twitched. "Aye, I'd noticed. What's it to do wi' ye?"

Monroe's face twisted. "The way they looked at each other, it reminded me of Mandy."

"Mandy. That's yer wife, is it?"

"Yes."

"Tell me about her."

Two hours later Dr. Gordon had what he felt was a pretty clear picture of what must have happened. Monroe had tried to cope by abusing alcohol. His friends had tried to help, but his job had taken a hit and so had his self-esteem. The suicide attempt was probably more of a way to deal with the guilt than a genuine wish to end his life. Men tended to succeed at suicide.

The background seemed pretty clear, but there was still something Monroe wasn't telling him. He'd admitted to hearing his wife's voice, but that hadn't started until after he was deep in the woods and he'd known it was in his head. So he hadn't fled because of the hallucinations.

He'd said he was on his way to stay with distant relatives, but he'd let slip that his brother was in Africa. Even if it was true that he had family somewhere in the eastern United States, the story he'd told was that Jim and Ginny were giving him a ride. If that was so, why would he leave them and set off cross country on foot? A fit of despair, with a self-indulgent temper tantrum thrown in for good measure, might push him to look for a period of solitude, but he'd want to find his way back to them to complete the journey.

Unless he was looking for solitude in which to blow his brains out. But that didn't work, either. He'd stolen a gun, but he hadn't used it. It had taken some careful questioning, but Monroe had told him the pistol was in the pack he'd abandoned in the snow, so it couldn't have been the primary reason for his wanting to be alone. Someone intent on taking his own life deep in the woods wouldn't forget the weapon.

There was something else going on. He was pretty sure none of these three would tell him what it was, but he knew someone who might. He left Monroe in the hands of the medical staff and set off towards his own house.

He let himself in, accepted the single malt his wife had ready, then dropped into his office chair and pulled out the phone.

"Angus, it's Greg."

"Gordon."

"Aye, Gordon, and ye needn't sound sae enthused tae hear from me agin."

"Yer a trouble-maker, Gordon. Ye know that?"

"Aye. Ye've told me often enough."

"Well and wha' is it this time?"

"Were ye aware ye were sending me three patients?"

"I didna send ye any. They were supposed tae be guests. How's th' lass?"

"She'll do. I'm hoping tae get another chance tae talk wi' her afore she leaves us."

Angus Mackenzie sighed down the line. "Take guid care o' her, Greg. We need her."

Gordon nodded. "I know it."

"Wha' aboot th' other twa?"

"Yer grandson has been making an ass o' himself."

"Hrmph. An' ye think ye can fix him, do ye?"

"I think if he's not careful he could lose that lass and that would be a shame."

"I agree, and ye've no need tae tell me what he's been up tae. He told me hisself."

"Guid. Then I dinna ha'e tae insult ye. That leaves the third."

"Monroe."

"Aye, Monroe."

"How's th' leg?"

"He should be on crutches by tomorrow dinner."

"That's guid news."

"Aye, but he's a problem."

"Go on."

"He's no taking his meds."

"Ha'e Ginny give them tae him."

"We can try that, but he also needs tae talk tae someone. He was hallucinatin' his deid wife."

There was a short silence, followed by a sigh. "Weel, I'll see what I can arrange fer him."

"Leave him with me."

"That's no an option."

"Why not?"

"It's just nae possible."

"Angus, tell me wha's going on."

"I canna do that."

"Ye can, ye just won't."

"Trust me on this. Ye dinna want tae know."

Gordon raised an eyebrow. "I canna help him without knowing."

"Gregory Gordon, yer a fine man an' a fine physician, but ye canna save everyone. Let it go."

"What aren't ye tellin' me, Angus? What's th' dirty little secret th' three o' them are carrying on their souls?"

"Greg, listen tae me. 'Tis safer for everyone if ye dinna know."

Gordon frowned, considering the possible reasons for one laird to refuse to level with another. "How can I help, Angus?"

"Get them awa' fra there as soon as may be and ask nae questions."

"Can ye assure me 'tis Homestead business we're talkin'

about here?"

"It is."

"Then ye ha'e my word on it and ye owe me a bottle and a visit."

"Gladly."

"Th' good stuff, mind. Not the raw whisky ye sell tae th' tourists."

There was a laugh on the other end of the line. "I wouldna do that tae ye, Greg. And I thank ye fer yer help."

"Dinna make me regret it, Mackenzie."

"I've a feeling ther'll be regrets soon enough, but I trust this will no be one o' them."

"Let's hope yer right."

Gordon put the phone away and picked up his drink. He hated not knowing what was going on, but he was no fool. If Angus Mackenzie said curiosity could endanger his Homestead, then he would shelve it and do his best for the three young Texans without demanding full disclosure.

* * *

CHAPTER 30

Saturday Night
Beverwyck Homestead

Ginny stood looking at herself in the mirror, wondering how she was going to get out of this mess. She had let Jim remove her shoes and socks, but had retreated to the bathroom to get cleaned up and wiggle into the garment that passed for a nightgown when she was on the road, an oversized tee shirt she had acquired many years before at one of the Highland Games, thoroughly broken in and very soft.

"How are you doing in there?"

"Fine." It had been a long day and she was on the point of collapse, but Jim clearly had something else he wanted to say.

"Let me in."

She took a last look at the mirror, then sighed and unlocked the door.

He wrapped her in a terrycloth robe provided by the Homestead and guided her out into the room, positioning her on one end of the couch and himself on the other, facing her.

"How did this happen, Ginny?" he said. "How did we come to this? After all the things we've been through together, how is it you couldn't face me, couldn't talk to me?"

Ginny met his eyes. "How is it, Jim, that, after all the things we've been through together, you have such a low opinion of me?" She didn't want to fight. All she wanted to do was sleep.

"You misunderstand."

"Do I? You told me to stay out of your way."

"I was protecting you and don't change the subject. You should have confronted me."

Her eyes narrowed. "Do I have to scream at you for you to listen?"

"What you have to do is trust me to make the right decision, for both of us."

Ginny felt her patience snap. She sprang to her feet. "That's it. Get out, Hal! Go and never come back!"

His eyes widened. "Hal?"

Part of Ginny's brain processed the error. This wasn't Hal. She knew that. But it didn't matter. Jim was just as guilty.

"I am *sick* of men condescending to me. Fine! You don't need me, I don't need you!"

He stood up and came toward her, his eyes wide. "Ginny, I didn't mean—"

She interrupted him. "Didn't mean to insult me, again?" She put both of her hands on his chest and shoved, hard enough for him to take a step back, in the direction of the door.

"You think you know everything? That you're always right? Well, I've got news for you, Dr. Mackenzie. *No one* is perfect."

She shoved him again, and again he took a step back.

"Assuming you're not dismissing me simply because I'm a *woman*, either you think my knowledge is irrelevant or my understanding is faulty. But only a fool ignores the lessons learned by others. Are you a fool, Dr. Mackenzie?"

She could see the shock on his face, but she wasn't through. Her voice rose.

"I have skills and experience and wisdom, hard fought, hard won. I know things you don't. I can do things you can't. You owe me respect and, from now on, if you want my help, you will have to ask for it."

She put her hands out again, to shove him again, out the door and out of her hair, but this time he caught her in his arms and closed them around her, holding her, hugging her. He bent down and put his cheek on her head.

"Yes, Ginny. I know."

"You know *nothing*!"

He held on as she struggled. "I know my grandfather sent you on this trip as his representative."

Ginny stopped fighting. "He told you?"

"Yes." Jim steered her over to the sofa, pulling her down beside him. "But he didn't tell me what that means. Will you explain it to me?"

Ginny stared at him. He looked uncomfortable enough for her to believe it was costing him something to ask.

"Tomorrow."

"I won't be able to sleep until I know."

She sighed. "I'm charged with keeping you out of trouble, with teaching you what it means to be a laird, and with staying out of your way as much as I can. And I'm not doing a very good job of it. My emotions keep interfering." She saw his eyes flicker.

"But, emotions or no emotions, you need to realize that I could not stand by and let you be mauled by that wolf. Your ego is not that important, and I will always follow my conscience."

He nodded. "I would expect nothing less."

"Just so we understand one another."

"I have a feeling there's a lot I don't understand yet. Don't give up on me, Ginny. Hit me if you have to, but don't give up on me."

She frowned. "I hope you mean that."

"I do."

"Well, then, today's lesson is, when hunting a man, always take backup with you. If you hadn't been so conceited, I could have shot the wolf *before* he bit you."

"I didn't want you taking unnecessary risks."

"And *you're* the one who gets to decide what's necessary?"

He hesitated. "Well, yes."

"My brain, my knowledge, my experience don't count."

"I didn't say that."

Ginny's head was beginning to ache. "You made it clear you consider me a liability, not an asset. Then you sat me down and told me I needed to let you do your job. Not *our* job. Yours."

"It *is* my job. You were there when Grandfather assigned it to me."

Ginny looked at the expression in his eyes and her heart sank. This wasn't going well.

"Okay, Jim. You do your job, take Charlie to Halifax, and I'll go home, and that will be the end of it." She rose and started for the door.

He caught her before she'd gone two steps.

"Ginny! Ginny, darling, stop! Didn't you just promise not to give up on me?" He drew her into his arms and held her. "Tell me what you want from me."

She shook her head. "You can't give me what I want."

His eyes clouded. "Maybe not today, but I've been told change is inevitable and that human beings are highly adaptable. I can change, Ginny, if I need to. Can you say the same?"

She shook her head again. "I've tried to be normal, Jim. I can't do it. If you don't like me the way I am, there's no hope."

He frowned. "The leopard can't change her spots, I know, but I'm not asking you to change your character, just help me to understand you." He swallowed. "I want you to trust me, the way you do my grandfather."

She pushed herself out of his arms. "Do you really think your grandfather got where he is by demanding others do whatever he says?"

Jim blinked. "He's always telling me what to do."

"He's trying to teach you, but it's proving difficult."

"That's not fair! I've done everything asked of me since I got here."

Ginny looked at him for a long moment, seeing an angry child behind the sophisticated mask of a man.

"Do you know how many times you've insisted on getting your way around me?"

Jim's brow, already heavily furrowed, drew tighter. "Is that what you think of me?"

"It's what I've seen. What's more, Fergus said—"

Jim exploded. "Oh! You'll listen to Fergus will you?"

"Yes! He said you need to share with the woman you intend to marry whatever it was that got you into serious trouble in medical school. You have not done so and I have to conclude that means you don't want *me* as your wife."

His face paled. "Is this a test?"

"No. I'm just pointing out that marriage is a two-way street. Communication—and trust—have to flow both directions."

He stared at her, eyes wide, breathing hard. "All of this because I wanted to keep you out of danger!"

"All of this because you didn't want to think I might be right."

He blinked, then took a breath, several, in fact, then nodded. "Okay. You were right and I was wrong. Does that satisfy you?"

"It's not a contest, Jim. I'm trying to help you."

She watched him struggle, then nod.

"All right. Can we compromise? I'll let you help me, if you'll return the courtesy." Ginny studied his face. He was a good man. She hadn't made that up. They ought to be able to work together. She sighed, then nodded. "Deal."

* * *

Saturday Night
Beverwyck Homestead

Jim swallowed his heart, still sweating. He should have seen this coming. She'd been trying to climb back from the damage inflicted last October, and he'd been encouraging her to trust herself. He should have recognized her need to prove herself to him, to be trusted by him.

"Okay. We're both tired. Let's sleep on it. We can talk again tomorrow."

She nodded. "I think that's a good idea." She ushered him to the door.

Jim stood for a moment, looking down at her. He had no problem with strong, intelligent women in general. There were a lot of them in medicine. It was just this one.

He did respect her, for a lot of reasons, not the least of which was that his grandfather relied on her. But he *needed* to protect her, to take care of her. He needed it as much as he needed to breathe. Tomorrow he would have to try again to explain how critical her safety was to his sanity.

He made his way back to his own room, swallowed his antibiotic and one of the narcotic pain killers, then slid into bed. Ginny wasn't the only one who needed a good night's sleep. With any luck, they would be back on the road tomorrow and this time he needed to stay awake.

* * *

CHAPTER 31

Sunday Morning
Beverwyck Homestead

Jim woke before most of the Homestead was up. He got dressed, then went down to check on Charlie, who was out of traction and in a cast, but still in bed. It was Sunday morning and they were two days behind schedule. Jim tracked down Dr. Warner.

"Is Charlie well enough to travel?"

Dr. Warner's eyebrows rose. "If necessary, yes." They would have to consult Gordon, but he wasn't available yet.

Jim decided he had time to run into town to do a few errands. He grabbed the keys and headed out, his mind on the night before.

She'd called him 'Hal'.

The Laird had put Ginny in counseling after the incident and resisted any attempt on Jim's part to find out what happened in those sessions. Ginny, too, had declined to talk about her relationship with Hal, but yesterday he'd gotten a glimpse of it. A condescending, overbearing, chauvinist.

If she could confuse the two of them, even in the heat of battle, he hadn't been treating her right. She needed a demonstration of his faith in her, his respect for her. And it would cost him, because—whatever he came up with—there would be a risk involved, and there was no way he could protect her from the consequences.

* * *

Sunday Morning
Albany, NY

The dry cleaning attendant pulled the leather jacket off the rack, then opened a drawer and fished out a paper envelope.

"Thought you might want this. We found it in the lining. The hole needs patching and we can do it, but you'll have to leave the jacket here for a week."

Jim opened the envelope and found a .45 slug, which explained why Charlie hadn't been able to find the one from the hijacker's gun. "Thanks! I'll think about it."

He turned his back on the shop, opened the car door, and leaned in, to hang the jacket on the hook. The next thing he knew, he was face down on the asphalt. He got to his feet, looked over, and found the dry cleaner's in flames.

Jim stared at the wreckage, shocked and unsure what had just happened. He closed the door on the SUV, realizing it had deflected part of the blast. The dings in the metal made him wonder if he'd been hit and he explored the backs of his legs. Blood there was, but nothing spurting, and all nerves intact, as near as he could tell. It was hard to examine his own backside.

Jim's brain suddenly kicked into high gear. There had been an explosion. He'd been caught in it. There might be other casualties.

There were workers from the dry cleaners out front, staring up at the structure in dismay. He approached them, asking if everyone had gotten out safely and getting blank stares. Jim looked them over quickly. None seemed in imminent danger.

They would have to be properly triaged, of course. Where were the first responders?

"Has anyone called 9-1-1?"

"They're on their way."

"What happened?"

The worker who had spoken shook his head. Jim asked more questions, but that was all he got. They were clearly in shock. He tried to get them to move back and to wrap up against the cold, but all the warm clothing, their own and everyone else's, was inside the shop. No one had been cold inside so no one was wearing anything warm. The irony was that the shop was putting off so much heat no one was cold.

Jim turned and looked at the structure, watching the flames consume the roof. He knew such places used lots of chemicals. Perhaps one of them had gotten loose and ignited. He glanced around at the employees, wondering if any of them would know, and discovered there were more people in the parking lot than there had been. The newcomers weren't looking at the fire. They were moving away from the area, headed for the street.

Jim moved to intercept the first of these. She had burns down one side of her body, on her arm, her neck and ear, and her hair on that side had been burned off. He looked her over quickly.

"Where did you come from?"

She looked at him, then pointed toward a field behind the shop. Jim sat the woman down, telling her the ambulance was on its way, then headed for the field.

At first glance it looked as if the snow was on fire, but closer examination showed it was actually flaming debris. There were also bodies. Jim looked up and saw the problem.

An elevated mass transit station stood behind the shop. There had been a train in the station. It hung from the platform, cars sliding toward the earth, in flames, or blackened by fires now burning out.

"Dear God!" he whispered.

Jim hurried to the SUV, threw open the back and dug out his medical kit. He tossed his sling onto the seat, pulled on gloves, grabbed dressing supplies and his stethoscope, and headed back into the chaos. He could not help much. He didn't have any airways, for instance, or drugs, and only one tourniquet.

There were burns, penetrating trauma caused by flying shrapnel, impact injuries from falling or being thrown against hard surfaces, and breathing problems associated with inhaling heated gas.

Jim went from victim to victim, trying to identify anything he could do something about. He tore clothing from the victims to make bandages and shanghaied a number of the less wounded to help control bleeding or hold jaws in place so the victim could breathe.

By this time the police, fire department, and ambulances had begun to arrive. Jim kept working. He was kneeling beside a woman, watching the life leave her eyes, unable to do more than hold her hand as she died, when he felt a tap on his shoulder.

"Excuse me. I noticed the stethoscope. Are you a doctor?"

Jim nodded.

"May I speak with you, please?"

Jim nodded again, put the dead woman's hand down, and climbed to his feet. He followed the official across the field.

"This way, please." The man looked back at him to make sure he was following. "We've set up a command center over here." He indicated a large square police truck. As they reached the area, a door swung open and an older man got out. He caught site of Jim and frowned. "Is this the man?"

"Yes, sir."

"How much of that blood is yours?"

Jim blinked, unsure of the question. "What?"

The older man walked toward him, then around behind, then back to stand in front of him. "You're covered in blood. How much of it is yours?"

Jim glanced down and realized he was right. His jeans were soaked through and the oversized white camo parka had large patches of red on the sleeves and front.

"I think the backs of my legs may have been hit. I was bleeding when I picked myself up off the ground."

"You were caught in the blast?"

Jim nodded.

The older man seemed to come to some rapid decisions. "George, take him around back, process him and his clothes. Check him for injuries. Take his statement."

"Yes, sir."

Jim found himself hustled into a popup tent that had been set up in the parking lot. It had a sink, space heaters, tables and chairs, and racks filled with supplies. He was quickly stripped and his outer clothes, including his shoes, placed in plastic bags. They also helped him wash his face and hair, which had suffered splashes of human tissue and body fluids.

When he was reasonably clean, but before he was allowed to get dressed, he found himself face to face with a physician who proceeded to look him over.

"Pin pricks and a bit of a first degree burn on the back of your right leg. Where were you when the blast hit?"

Jim explained about being half in and half out of the car at the time. The physician nodded. "I'm told you're a doctor."

"ER."

The other man raised his eyebrows. "That explains a lot. We got a report there was someone on scene, but no one could tell us who or how he got there so fast." He stripped off the exam gloves and washed his hands. "You know how to keep those wounds clean. I assume you're up on your tetanus. If you suspect contamination, get some prophylactic penicillin onboard."

Jim nodded, thinking he was already on exactly that, thanks to the wolf.

The other man stuck out his hand. "Martin Keller."

Jim shook the offered hand. "Jim Mackenzie."

"Really quickly, 'cause I've got to get back out there and get to work, tell me what you've been doing. Oh, and you can get dressed." He pointed at a table marked 'Red Cross Disaster Relief.'

Jim looked over and found piles of socks, shoes, shirts, pants, and sweaters laid out, already sorted by sizes. He picked through the offerings, then settled down in a chair to put them on. While he was doing that, he told Dr. Keller about the victims, summarizing, because he knew the triage teams were already sorting through the casualties.

"Did you mark the ones you thought could be saved?"

"I didn't have any way to do that, just made sure there was someone with them and told them to yell loudly as soon as an official showed up."

Dr. Keller nodded. "We need to run your fingerprints and get you to write a statement and do a short form victim chart on you, to cover our little visit here. Then we need for you to chart on the people you saw, as much as you can possibly remember. Every detail matters."

Jim nodded. "What can I do to help right now?"

"Paperwork."

Jim made a face. "I've seen trauma before. I can help."

Dr. Keller shook his head. "I'm sure there are people out there whose lives you saved today, but you are officially off the case. You're a victim, not a responder."

"But—"

"No buts. Help me out by doing exactly what I need. I'll send someone in to walk you through it." With that, he turned and left. A woman entered on his heels, wearing the uniform of an Albany police officer. She produced a digital fingerprint scanner and took Jim's prints, then set him up with a small computer. Jim settled down and began to compose his victim statement.

The woman was hovering in the background, which made him a bit nervous, but he told himself it was only to be expected. Once they knew he was a licensed physician, even if a volunteer, they could add his name to the reports.

The woman stepped outside and he could hear her talking to someone. He was done with the statement before she returned.

"Dr. Mackenzie?"

"Yes?"

"Dr. Keller tells me he asked you to write out a complete report on all the people you came into contact with today."

Jim nodded.

"I've been instructed to take you to the station and set you up with a desk."

"Can't I stay here?"

"I'm afraid we need this space. Besides, you'll be a lot more comfortable indoors."

Which was true. There was a cold draft coming in under the edge of the tent. "All right, but I'd like to stop by my car first. I have extra shoes in the trunk."

She hesitated, looking down at his sock-clad feet. "Better let me get them for you. There's debris all over the ground and anything you might pick up could be evidence."

Jim nodded, then handed her the keys and told her where to look for his hiking boots. He'd had no need to take them indoors at any of the homesteads since he'd been wearing his sneakers pretty much continuously. He just wished he'd thought to stuff a pair of wool socks in the toes. The cotton ones the Red Cross had supplied were not very thick.

* * *

CHAPTER 32

Sunday Morning
Dallas, TX

Detective Tran returned from the break room to find an alert on her computer. Someone had run a search on Dr. Mackenzie.

She read the cryptic request with interest. 'Confirm credentials, physician, Texas.' The originating station was Albany, NY. She picked up the phone and dialed the number, identified herself, and asked to speak to the officer in charge.

"Lieutenant Shapiro. What can I do for you?"

"I understand you ran a fingerprint search on Dr. Angus James Mackenzie today."

"Right."

"What are the circumstances of that request, please?"

The voice on the other end of the line sharpened. "What's your interest in him?"

Detective Tran explained she was following up on a homicide and that Dr. Mackenzie was a person of interest who might or might not have information that might or might not help her in her investigation.

"I see. Well, first, can you confirm he's really a doctor?"

Detective Tran's eyebrows rose. "I have no definitive information on that subject, but he is employed in a local emergency room and I have not heard it suggested that he is an imposter."

"Hmm. Guess I need to wait for the official results, then."

"What has happened?"

"You seen the news?"

"Not since last night."

"Well, it might not be on in Texas, but it's getting big coverage here."

"One moment, please." Detective Tran took her phone into the break room and turned on the monitor. A quick scan of the news channels showed her what she wanted. "I see a reference to an explosion."

"We think it was a gas main. The weather has been playing havoc with our infrastructure and it looks as if a pipeline cracked. The levels were way over safety limits in the area."

Detective Tran was watching the images on the screen. "This was a rail station?"

"A light rail, yeah. We think the train set it off, but maybe it was a passenger smoking. Either way, the result was chaos. The death toll's already twenty-three and we ain't through counting yet."

"How does Dr. Mackenzie fit into this?"

"He got caught in the blast, then spent an hour patching up the casualties all by himself. We think he saved at least five of them."

"Indeed?"

"Yeah, but the legal johnnies want to make sure he really is who he says he is, in case any of this comes back to bite us."

"I see." Detective Tran had her eye on the TV screen and could see footage of the disaster, complete with what might have been Dr. Mackenzie working on a patient. The picture wasn't clear enough for her to tell, but if they had his fingerprints, then it was the man himself.

"I can answer half your question for you, Lieutenant. The

fingerprints you ran belong to the man I know as Dr. Mackenzie."

"You had his prints on file?"

"He was the target of an attempted murder three months ago."

"But you don't know if he's really a doctor?"

"There was no reason to check. I visited him in the hospital and heard him addressed by members of the staff as 'doctor,' but that proves nothing."

"True. Well, the medical board will have a photo or something and I appreciate you sharing what you know with me. Is there anything else I can do for you, Detective?"

"Would it be possible to pick him up and detain him while I set up a conference call?"

There was a hesitation on the other end of the line. "Detain him?"

"Not for an arrest, but I would like to speak to him. Can you arrange that?"

Again there was a hesitation. "He's already here."

"In the station, you mean?"

"Yeah. We've got him writing up what he did, for the official file. I'd hate to spoil his day. They're calling him a hero."

"He is not considered a suspect, but he might prove a material witness. It all depends on what he knows."

Detective Tran heard a sigh. "All right. I can hold him, but I'll have to tell him what it's about. And it'll probably take an hour or two to get a clear line, because of the explosion."

"I understand. Thank you."

Detective Tran hung up the phone, satisfied. She could use the intervening time to assemble her thoughts. This might be the only chance she got and she wanted to make the most of it.

* * *

Sunday Morning
Beverwyck Homestead

Ginny sat in the Homestead library, curled up on the sofa. She had risen and breakfasted, then been escorted to this meeting. The Laird sat facing her, an expression of concern on his face.

"We're dealing wi' twa issues here, both o' them serious. Th' first is yer fear and th' second yer ego."

Ginny had her mouth clamped shut, determined to hear him out. She had not been happy with herself yesterday and, if she could, she was willing to learn from this expert.

"Ye want Jim tae acknowledge tha' ye dinna need him, that yer fine by yerself, but it's no true and ye know it. We're human. We need people in our lives." He leaned toward her. "That other man proved ye vulnerable and yer afraid tae make th' same mistake twice."

Ginny nodded.

"Which means yer afraid o' Jim. Afraid o' lettin' him get too close." Gordon sighed. "Tis understandable, but no very healthy."

Ginny wrapped her arms around herself. She'd been trying to trust Jim for months, had succeeded at times, but it was true she still wondered if she would ever feel safe with a man again.

"The other issue is th' reverse o' this one. Ye want tae feel whole, again, and fer tha' ye need Jim's approval and ye feel he's no giving it tae ye."

Ginny took a deep breath and counted to ten, backwards. She wanted to prove she didn't need Jim and she wanted to prove he *did* need her. Put that way, she sounded like a bratty teenager.

What she wanted—what she *thought* she wanted—was for Jim to treat her as an equal, not in everything, but in brains and courage at least.

"How do I get him to respect me?"

"Since he's no here tae speak fer himself, we must focus on you. What he's facing, taking on a Homestead, 'tis a formidable task. If ye wed him, ye wed th' job as well."

Ginny nodded.

"And a laird is just a man wi' all the faults and failings o' such."

Ginny nodded again.

"Ye need tae decide if that's wha' ye want tae do with yer life, devote it tae the Homestead and th' man charged with keepin' it."

"The job doesn't scare me, but being under his thumb every step of the way would drive me crazy."

"Ye want tae be his peer, not his underling."

"Exactly."

Gordon nodded "I can see yer point." He studied her face for a moment. "It won't work, though. There canna be two lairds."

Ginny felt her eyes grow wide. Is that what it sounded like to this man?

Gordon leaned back in his chair, his eyes still on her. "Angus seems tae think ye can be trusted, with his Homestead and with his grandson. Sae it's up tae you, lass. Ye need tae decide. Are ye prepared tae do whatever it takes tae help Jim succeed?"

"He won't *let* me help him. That's the problem. He won't listen to me."

"He will, on one condition."

"What's that?"

"That ye wed him first and teach him second."

Ginny's mouth fell open. "I have to *marry* him before he'll *listen* to me? That sounds like blackmail."

"It is and it isn't," Gordon said. "If ye're his wife, he can trust ye tae keep his secrets and ha'e his back. He can let his hair down with ye and be vulnerable, which will gi'e him a chance tae grow."

Gordon gave her half a smile. "I know 'tis not what ye wanted tae hear. 'Twould be a guid idea, I think, if ye talked with my wife before ye make up yer mind. She's another strong woman. She can tell ye how she copes with me. And I'll ha'e a wee talk with Jim Mackenzie."

* * *

Sunday Morning
Albany Police Station

Jim punched in his grandfather's number and listened as the call went through. Himself picked up on the second ring.

"Grandfather, it's Jim."

"Aye, lad. What's amiss?"

"I'm at the Albany police station. They're setting up a conference call with Detective Tran."

"Auch! Are they noo? Wha' did ye do tae attract th' attention o' th' local police?"

Jim described the explosion and his role as volunteer in the aftermath. "They took my fingerprints to check my credentials. I think that's what caught Detective Tran's attention."

"Are ye all right at the moment?"

"Yes."

"I'll get back tae ye."

"Wait! I think Ginny should take Charlie and disappear, before Tran can send someone out to the Homestead to catch them."

"'Tis a guid thought. I'll see tae it."

"Tell her it's up to her to keep him safe and under the radar.

And don't tell her I said that."

"Why not?"

"Let's just say it will work better if she thinks the idea came from you."

"Ye've no' settled yer wee misunderstand, then?"

"We're working on it."

"Hrumph."

Jim hung up the phone then went back to his paperwork. At least now his grandfather knew what had happened. In the meantime, he needed to decide *exactly* what he could safely tell Detective Tran.

* * *

Sunday Morning
Beverwyck Homestead

Gordon was just pulling his phone out of his pocket to call his wife when it went off in his hand. He glanced at the caller ID, then punched up the connection.

"Aye?"

"Greg? It's Angus."

"I can see that. What can I do for ye?"

"Get Ginny and Charlie awa' fra th' Beverwyck Homestead in th' next hour."

Gordon blinked. "Is there a problem?"

"Aye, and I'll be askin' ye tae rescue Jim as well, but get th'. other twa on th' road first. Then call me back."

Gordon looked over at Ginny Forbes, his eyes narrowing. "Ye want me tae send them off withoot Jim? I'm no' sure that's such a guid idea."

"I agree, but I hae nae choice in th' matter. Can ye do it?"

Ginny's ears had pricked up at his last comment.

"Aye, but I think ye should give Miss Ginny her instructions yerself."

"Is th' lass there? Put her on."

Gordon handed the phone over, then watched as Ginny listened. She made no protest, just nodded, then said, "Aye, Mackenzie," and handed the phone back to Gordon.

"Greg?"

"I'm here."

"She'll be needin' tae borrow a car."

"We can do tha'."

"Ha'e yer people disable th' GPS first."

"Why?"

"Ask me nae questions and I'll tell ye nae lies. I'll wait tae hear from ye."

Gordon closed the connection and rose to his feet. "Let's go, lass."

He placed several calls in rapid succession, instructing the house staff to pack Ginny and Charlie's things, and pull one of the vehicles out of the garage, making sure it was disconnected from the network. His call to his wife included instructions for food for the road. The next was to Dr. Warner, instructing him to bundle Charlie with any necessary medical supplies and deliver them to the front hall. He turned to Ginny.

"I wish I could send someone wi' ye, but I ha'e a feeling Angus wouldna like it."

Her face was pale, but she nodded. "We'll be fine."

He wrote his phone number on a slip of paper and handed it to her. "Let me know when ye get tae the Sunkhaze Homestead."

"Himself told me to stay off the phones until we reach Halifax." She had hers open and was taking the battery out as he watched.

Gordon frowned. What trouble were these three in, to

require security like that? "Wait here."

He strode down the hall and into his office and came back with his spare phone. He thrust it at Ginny. "My backup. If anyone traces it, they'll wind up here. Call if ye need tae."

She nodded.

"All right. Let's get ye going."

The preparations were almost complete. Charlie was in place on the passenger side of the car and Mrs. Gordon was supervising the packing.

Ginny turned on the curb. "Thank you, for everything."

"Yer welcome. Dinna forget tae come back. I'll be wantin' my phone."

She straightened her back, looked him in the eye, then dropped a formal curtsy. "Aye, Gordon."

He watched as she climbed behind the wheel and turned the engine over. She was pulling away from the curb fifty minutes after Angus' call.

Gordon put his arm around his wife.

"Will they be all right?" she asked.

"I hope so." He turned her toward the door. "According tae Angus, we must also rescue the young Mackenzie. Let's go find out wha' that means."

* * *

CHAPTER 33

Ginny pulled out onto I-90 E, headed for Bangor and the Sunkhaze Homestead. They had a full tank of gas and approximately four hours of daylight for a six to seven hour drive.

The safest course of action was to stick to the highways. They would be plowed and lit and would have both food and fuel. That took them south almost into Boston, then up the coast through a highly populated area of the eastern seaboard. Ginny bit her lip. Running. They were running before the law.

Once they were well out of Albany, Charlie broke the silence.

"What happened to Jim?"

"I have no idea."

"What did Himself say?"

She glanced over, trying not to let her anxiety show. "That Jim was at the Albany police station. That I was to take you to Halifax as quickly as I could manage, and that he would send Jim on as soon as possible."

Charlie chewed on his lower lip. "Our gear was in the SUV."

Ginny nodded. All they had was the luggage they had brought inside with them. The good news was that mending and laundry had forced her to bring in the big bags so they were not left with just the overnighters. The bad news was that this did not include the camping gear, Jim's medical supplies, or her pistol, which she had stashed in the SUV.

She bit her lip. "I wish I knew what was going on."

"I'm sure he'll call as soon as he can."

Ginny glanced over at Charlie. "He probably will, but he won't be able to get through. Himself instructed me to turn off all the phones and not turn them back on until we reach Halifax."

Charlie looked over at her. "That sounds ominous."

"It sounds as if someone may be looking for our GPS signals."

"Well, if we have to call anyone, we've got the burner phones. They're not supposed to be traceable."

Ginny shook her head. "Jim has those, too. It might be worth it to buy another, if we can do so without giving our position away. And Gordon gave me his phone to use in case of a real emergency." It, too, was in her pocket, off, with the battery out.

"That might confuse Detective Tran."

"For a little while, yes, but I'd rather not put it to the test." Her mouth settled into a grim line. "We're on our own until further notice. Let's see how fast we can get up the coast and into Maine."

* * *

Sunday Afternoon
Albany Police Station

"Good afternoon, Dr. Mackenzie."

"Good afternoon Detective Tran." Jim smiled at the image

on the screen.

"I apologize for keeping you. I know you have already had a very busy day."

"How may I help you, Detective?" Jim was glad the detective couldn't smell him sweat.

"I have a few questions I would like to ask you." He saw her glance down and assumed she'd made a list.

"First, are you aware that Charles Monroe is missing?"

Jim nodded. "I heard something about a boating accident."

"When was the last time you saw him?"

"Friday night, at the ceilidh."

Jim knew not to volunteer anything, just answer the questions. There were several about Charlie's state of mind before the boating accident and about the custodian who was supposed to be watching him. Jim did his best to answer truthfully, explaining he was neither an expert nor the best source of information.

"Are you aware that Mr. Monroe is wanted for questioning in relation to the body that was found in the Viking longship?"

Jim let his eyebrows rise. "It was my understanding that Monroe was so incapacitated by his alcoholism that he couldn't dress himself. What makes you think he's involved?"

She ignored his question. "What are you doing in Albany?"

Jim was ready for this one. "Ginny wants to do some genealogy and I'm hoping to get in a little skiing."

"Is Mr. Monroe with you?"

Jim was also prepared for this one. He registered surprise. "What? No." Not at the moment, anyway. Jim let his brow furrow. "Can I level with you, Detective?"

"Of course."

Jim licked his lips, shifting in his chair, his eyes darting from side to side. "I'm having trouble persuading Ginny to marry me. I wanted to get her alone so I could work on her."

Detective Tran's mouth edged up very slightly at the corner. "Are you having any luck?"

Jim frowned. "Not so far."

"Has Mr. Monroe contacted Miss Forbes?"

"Not that I know of and I've been with her almost the whole time." True.

"Did Mr. Monroe coerce you into taking him with you?"

Indignation. "No! Haven't I just told you I wanted some private time with Ginny?" Both statements were true.

"Do you know where Mr. Monroe is?"

"No." Also true. He might be in Albany at the moment, or he might be on the road to Maine, or he might be somewhere entirely different, depending on what Angus had decided.

"Would you tell me if you did?"

Solid eye contact. Earnest good citizenship. "Yes." A lie.

Detective Tran studied him through the computer connection. Could she tell? Was the image clear enough for that? She nodded slowly.

"Thank you, Dr. Mackenzie. If I have further questions, I will contact you."

The screen went dark and Jim was tempted to heave a sigh of relief, but he knew they might still be listening in. He was directed to the staff lounge and asked to wait.

Jim found himself pacing. What between the explosion and the video interrogation, it was almost three p.m. He needed to get out of here. God only knew where Ginny was at this point and God only knew what he was supposed to do about it.

The door opened and he turned to find Gordon standing behind a female officer.

"Thank you very much for your help Dr. Mackenzie. You're free to go."

Jim didn't need telling twice. He followed Gordon back to the Homestead, then pulled the SUV up to the front door and jumped out. He was immediately replaced by a crew of three technicians armed with sensors. He watched as they climbed inside and underneath the vehicle, then pronounced the car clean of tracking devices. As if on cue, a second crew appeared, loading Jim's gear into the back and food into the space where Ginny's feet should have gone.

"This is for you." Mrs. Gordon held out a heavy wool coat that Jim suspected had belonged to her husband. The shoulders fit and both the cloth and the cut were well above average. Jim was very pleased to see it.

Dr. Warner and Dr. Gordon had materialized, one on each side of him, Warner armed with a syringe.

"Rabies. It's early, but that shouldn't change its efficacy. Have them draw a titer when you get home." He stabbed Jim's upper arm with gusto and Jim bit back an exclamation. "Couldn't I have taken that with me?" Ginny would have been gentler.

Dr. Warner shook his head. "Needs refrigeration."

Gordon next. "I've given Miss Ginny an extra phone o' mine, in case of emergency, but it'll no' be on otherwise. Here's th' number." He laid his hand on Jim's shoulder, turning him away from the others. "I've a word, I'd say tae ye, about Miss Ginny."

He turned to face Jim, catching his eye and holding it. "Ye canna protect her."

"Huh?"

"Any more than she can protect ye."

"What are you talking about?"

"I ken ye want tae, lad. 'Tis normal for a man tae want tae protect his lass from harm, but ye canna do it. Ye canna protect her from life. Ye shouldna try."

Jim stood there with his jaw dropping, then flushed as he realized what Ginny must have shared with the psychiatrist.

"I wish I ha' more time tae work wi' ye, but ye must go and

smartly." Gordon produced a map to which a bright yellow marker had been applied. "Follow this route. If ye hurry ye can overtake them at Sunkhaze. Good luck, lad."

Jim pulled himself together. "Thank you, sir." He gripped the older man's hand then jumped behind the wheel, threw the car in gear and headed for the gate.

* * *

Sunday Afternoon
I-90, headed east

Ginny drove into the truck stop and up to the pump.

"Rest, gas, food," she announced.

Charlie nodded, opening the door and sliding carefully to the ground. Ginny handed him the crutches.

"I'm right behind you." She filled the tank, pulled into a parking space, and followed him inside.

"What do you want to eat?" He handed her a menu. "Turns out this place has table service."

Ginny selected a chicken salad and coffee and passed her order on to the waitress who had materialized at her side. She saw the girl's eyes linger on Charlie.

Ginny grinned. "I believe you've made a conquest."

Charlie shrugged it off. "She felt sorry for me, because of these." He indicated the crutches. "Put me over here and told me to take my time." He looked at Ginny with a mischievous smile. "I don't think she was happy to see you come in."

Ginny laughed. "Well, it doesn't matter. We won't be here long enough for you to break her heart."

"She'll remember, though. A man on crutches and a girl with long red hair."

Ginny's smile faded. He was right. They needed to stay out

of sight as much as possible.

They ate swiftly, then climbed back into the car. Ginny was driving, of necessity. Dr. Warner had prescribed no weight bearing for Charlie for two weeks. It made transporting him a challenge and how she was going to get him over the border in this condition Ginny had no idea.

The Albany Homestead had given them a front wheel drive hatchback with a surprising amount of leg room. Charlie had scooted the seat back as far as it would go and propped the leg up on the dashboard, to keep the swelling to a minimum.

"Does it hurt?"

He shrugged. "Some."

"You let me know if you have any problems."

He nodded, then sighed. "Stupid move. I'm sorry."

She smiled over at him. "Apology accepted. Now forget it."

"Gonna be kind of hard. I can't exactly drag this leg through the snow. Not on crutches."

"We'll figure it out."

They drove up the coast, watching the light fade on the Atlantic Ocean. Ginny got a glimpse of the water each time the road went over an intersection. It look cold, and the sky continued to be heavy with clouds.

"More snow, do you think?"

Charlie peered out the window. "Hard to tell."

They lapsed into silence, and Ginny found her mind wandering back to Jim. He wasn't exactly left behind, he had the SUV, but Angus had decided she and Charlie should leave Albany immediately. What had precipitated that? And how was Jim involved? Because he was, of that Ginny had no doubt.

"Talk to me, Charlie. I need distracting."

He looked over at her. "What should I say?"

"Anything. Tell me about your life. Have you ever been out of the country before?"

He nodded slowly. "Yep. I have."

He took his sweet time getting started, but, once launched, Ginny found herself breathless at the tales he told. She'd had no idea his military career had been so far-flung.

When he reached the part where he'd come home to settle down with his family, his voice tapered off and Ginny stepped into the breach, offering stories about her own travels. In an effort to cheer him up, she recounted some of the funny things that had happened, the small mistakes that somehow prove no one is immune from foolishness. She had him chuckling, then laughing outright and tucked the sound away in her heart. The hours passed and, sooner than they expected, they found themselves coming into Bangor. Charlie was navigating.

"The Homestead is on the other side. We need to cross the Penobscot River and pick up 178 headed north."

The snow had started again, softening the edges of the road and obscuring traffic signals. They moved carefully through the twisting streets, sinking to almost river level, then rising again on the other side of the bridge. Another half hour found them headed north and into Edington.

"There it is." Charlie pointed out the first of the signs. They turned east, following Hwy 9. Ten minutes later they were at the entrance to the Sunkhaze Homestead.

* * *

CHAPTER 34

Sunday Afternoon
I-90, headed east

Jim steered the SUV through the gates and out onto the access road. The day had gone well enough, in that he wasn't in jail, but they had wasted most of the light. He should have turned his back on that explosion and run. If he had, Tran wouldn't have discovered him. Jim frowned at the thought. He knew it was nonsense. He couldn't change who he was any more that Ginny could.

It was a nuisance not to have the other two as relief drivers. He was facing six hours on the road, five of them in the dark, with his right arm in a sling. If his luck held and he pushed hard, he might make it to Bangor before they closed the gates.

He found himself speeding and deliberately eased off on the pedal. Not only did he *not* want to attract the attention of the police, he also did not want to get into a wreck. He fought with his foot over the next hundred miles, finding his subconscious strong and uncooperative.

He was anxious to get to Maine. He admitted that. He was responsible for the other two and he wanted to catch up to them and resume that role. He eased off on the accelerator again, hearing Gordon's voice in his head.

"Ye canna protect her."

He had promised Ginny's mother he would take care of her. Instead, she was alone with a confessed murderer.

Jim swallowed the lump that formed in his throat. She was safe with Charlie. His leg was broken and she was used to handling patients. And it had been his idea.

She was gone without a chance to say goodbye.

They'd been fighting last night. They'd never had a fight before, not like that. Last night she had raised her voice to him, had told him what she thought of him, had dismissed him. She had also told him what her role was supposed to be on this trip—not his companion, his teacher. It would have been useful to know that sooner.

He replayed the scene in his mind, seeing nuances he'd missed the first time around, thinking of better ways to express himself, wishing he could turn back the clock and try again.

Jim was so caught up in his thoughts that he didn't notice when the sun set and the temperature dropped, nor the steady slowdown of traffic as more and more cars entered the highway. He was approaching Boston, just west of Worcester, MA when he suddenly realized that the traffic was coming to a rapid halt.

Ten minutes into the traffic jam, he turned on the radio and found out what was wrong. The damp roadway had turned into a sheet of black ice. A foolish driver had hit it and skidded. A dozen more had been tailgating and slid into him and each other. This set up a chain reaction that resulted in more than 200 wrecks, some of them deadly and all of them between Jim and his destination. The highway was closed.

* * *

Sunday Evening
Sunkhaze Homestead

Ginny and Charlie sat side by side at the sumptuous feast spread for the guests at the Sunkhaze Homestead. They had arrived just in time to join a sports festival made both challenging and possible by the recent heavy storms.

The air was full of winter recreation. The ski slopes boasted a fresh layer of powder. Hockey teams dominated the rinks. Ice fishing was in full swing on the river. The area also offered snowmobiling, winter hunting, cross-country skiing, snowshoeing, toboggan runs, and dogsledding.

This evening, though, the festivities centered around the dance floor. The fiddling started at eight and Ginny found herself drawn into the sets. She had protested at first, saying she hadn't brought her ghillies, but a pair had materialized and she soon found herself with as many partners as she wanted. Charlie was left on the sidelines, his broken leg resting on a chair, but he, too, found willing partners to sit with him and talk or make teasing comments about the dancers as they sailed past. Ginny kept one eye on the door, but the ceilidh came to an end and the front gates were locked for the night and Jim did not appear.

* * *

Sunday Evening
Boston, MA

Jim looked around. He was trapped in the center lane. The only movement seemed to be on the outer edge. Careful scrutiny revealed some of the less law-abiding drivers heading off the highway and down the grass slope to the feeder road below.

He was willing to do the same, but first he had to maneuver the SUV to the outside lane.

It was another ten minutes before anyone moved, but there must have been other drivers bailing out ahead of his position. Very slowly the cars to his right began to creep forward. Giving in to his worst instincts and heedless of the curses being hurled in his direction, Jim maneuvered to the edge of the highway. Even taking desperate chances, it was twenty minutes before he was in position. The verge was steep and, by now, chewed up and becoming slick. He took a deep breath and went over the edge.

Luck was with him. He didn't roll the SUV. He did slide and was unsure, for a moment, whether he had enough traction to climb out of the mud and up onto the road, but he made it. Then he had to wait until the light changed and the traffic in front of him cleared enough for him to reach the intersection. He used the time to study the map. What he wanted was I-95, headed north. So did everyone else.

It took him two hours to get beyond the obstruction, by which time it was nine p.m. He had no hope of getting to Maine before the Homestead locked up for the night.

He could find a place to sleep or use the overnight hours to close the gap. The drive from Worcester to Bangor was listed as four to five hours. He had until at least six a.m., realistically, before Ginny and Charlie would leave Bangor, and maybe more, which gave him nine hours, total. Surely that would be enough. He paused for gas, food, and a rest stop, loaded up on finger food and caffeine, then set his jaw, put the car in gear, and headed for Bangor.

* * *

Monday, Wee Small Hours
I-95, headed north

At two a.m., Jim pulled the SUV over in Portsmouth. He still had almost 200 miles to go. He'd missed the turn-off to U.S. 95 and ended up in Boston, then had to backtrack, then almost done the same at the Gloucester interchange. Three construction zones that seemed to be doing nothing were next. Then a spot where the crews were putting up a series of electric poles and relays, working by arc lights and with a flagman that stopped traffic every two minutes to let cars in from the other side, only one lane getting through.

Jim cursed the optimism of the GPS mapping system. He didn't dare linger. He topped off the tank and hurried back to the highway, determined to stay awake and stay alert. His margin for error was rapidly shrinking.

His next stop was for another weather-related issue. The storm had washed out a bridge. There was a detour. He followed the slow moving line of big-rig truck traffic around the problem and back up onto the highway. He was grateful for the truckers' company. Not only did they melt the ice on the road, they also gave him plenty of warning if conditions changed.

Just before dawn Jim found himself plunged into thick fog. It had rolled in off the Atlantic and obscured all but a short distance ahead of him. The truckers were used to it. They slowed down, but kept moving. Jim followed his guides through the swirling mists and hoped he'd see the signs when they got to Bangor. The fog scattered the light from the headlamps and the refraction destroyed depth perception. What's more, he found his eyelids drooping. He grabbed another bottle of caffeine and slammed it down.

With the sunrise, the landscape changed. The gray mist thinned, but he had to keep his eyes peeled for cars entering the roadway from hidden drives all up and down the route. Hwy 95 took him straight toward downtown Bangor and he again found himself caught in rush hour traffic, this time the early risers trying to get to work through the numerous traffic signals. Jim debated the wisdom of a rest stop, then decided against it, pushing through the traffic, crossing the river, and picking up the road on the other side.

Half an hour later he turned in at the Sunkhaze Homestead gates. He drove up to the front, pulled to a stop, and climbed out, staggering as his feet hit the pavement.

* * *

CRAPTER 35

Monday Morning
Rte. 9, headed east

Ginny hunched over the steering wheel, peering into the fog. She would rather have waited until it lifted, but, with the threat of police on their tail, she didn't dare take the chance.

She was also still without her talisman. The Bangor and Pittsburgh couriers were at a loss to explain it. They would keep an eye out. Stripped of both its protection and Jim's presence, Ginny felt decidedly vulnerable.

The U.S. terminus, Calais, was a two hour drive from Bangor. The crossing there was called International Avenue and it was open 24/7, year round. She would have no trouble entering Canada (legally). The problem was still Charlie.

Reggie had fitted them all with false papers, including driver's licenses and credit cards and, in an excess of caution, she and Charlie had already donned their new identities. But Charlie's image might be on the police blotters by now and Charlie's DNA had been left behind in Virginia. She couldn't take the chance the guards wouldn't recognize him.

It seemed unlikely he could get himself over the border. He could not use cross-country skis or snowshoes or his crutches. He could probably drive a snowmobile, but that would make a great deal of noise and could not be hidden from the natives.

She had made some careful inquiries at Sunkhaze, but all she'd heard was how this crossing, International Avenue, had been built to handle the increasingly heavy load of vehicular traffic into and out of Canada. There was no suggestion anyone might consider circumventing the facility. On the contrary, her informants had admired the technology that allowed drive-through scanning. They were looking for weapons, drugs, and human trafficking. She would have to come up with something other than throwing a blanket over Charlie and hoping the customs officer would look the other way.

Charlie himself seemed to be thinking along the same lines. They'd both slept well and breakfasted and had a care package in the back with more food in it and third helpings of hot coffee in the cup holders. But he was frowning.

An hour into the drive Ginny started seeing evidence of sunlight. There were patches of white mist appearing among the roiling gray.

The road was in pretty good shape since it was a major east-west artery. It had been plowed and there was a lane open in each direction. Slow going, though. The trucks were taking their time, apparently in no hurry to arrive, and Ginny was getting frustrated at the delays. She couldn't pass any of them until the visibility improved so she tried to compose her soul in patience. She discovered the problem on one of the many curves along the road. They were behind a school bus.

By nine a.m. the bus had delivered its cargo and was off the road. The big rigs picked up their pace. The fog, too, was lifting.

Ginny could now see something of the land through which they were rolling. Most of it was heavily wooded. There were bridges and pull-bys and regularly spaced eateries with gas pumps out front. It was bucolic and serene and Ginny relaxed as the sun rose higher and the fog dissipated, leaving a cloudless blue sky and spectacular winter scenery in its wake.

They were more than halfway to Calais and it had been almost fifteen minutes since Ginny had seen another vehicle on the road. The truckers had pulled away and the few passenger cars seemed to be locals.

"There's something going on ahead of us," Charlie said.

He was right. Ginny could see cars pulled over to the side of the road and people climbing out of them, some with cameras. She slowed down and carefully pulled around the next bend.

"Look out!"

Ginny slammed on the brakes, then fought the car's attempt to fishtail, coming to rest slightly off center and breathing a sigh of relief that she hadn't put it in the ditch. She turned to Charlie in exasperation.

"What is the matter with you?"

He pointed at the roadway. "Look."

Ginny turned back around and saw a black bear in the middle of the road, facing them.

She stared at the obstruction. Black bears were not as large as grizzlies or Kodiaks or polar bears. This one filled only one lane of the roadway, but he was plenty large enough. What's more, he looked unhappy. He had his mouth open and seemed to be considering whether or not he wanted to challenge her right to be in his space.

She sat there in silence for a full minute, then asked, "What do we do now?"

"Is there enough space to drive around him?"

"I don't know. Will he attack the car?"

"Only if he feels threatened, or hungry."

Ginny glanced over at Charlie, but he didn't seem to be joking. She turned the steering wheel and started to ease toward the empty side of the road. The bear rocked from one side to the other and Charlie motioned for her to stop. The bear reared his head and snapped his jaws several times, then rose on its hind legs. Ginny found herself staring up at the animal.

"He's just looking at us," Charlie said. "Just wait."

"Okay." Ginny's voice came out higher than normal and a bit squeaky. She swallowed and tried to lick her lips, but she seemed to be out of saliva.

The animal came down on all fours, put his head down, and started toward them.

"Stay calm." Charlie's voice just barely reached her. "It's a sham, a fake charge. He'll stop." And he did.

Ginny watched the animal backup, then rock from side to side again, then amble across the road and disappear among the trees. She gasped, then dragged a shaking hand across her brow. "That is as close as I ever want to come to a bear outside of a zoo."

Charlie reached over and took her hand. "It's all right, Ginny. We were never in any real danger. He just wanted to let us know this is his territory."

Ginny laughed briefly. "He can have it. Is it safe to drive on?"

"Yes."

Ginny put her hands back on the wheel, pulled into the lane, and started off again.

"Good lookin' animal, that bear."

"I'm glad you liked it." Ginny was still shaking.

"Healthy. It means the population is the right size here. He's getting enough to eat."

"Don't bears hibernate in the winter?"

"Uh huh, but you can wake them up and they'll come out to see what you want. I've done that."

Ginny shook her head. "You're nuts! You know that?"

Charlie grinned at her. "Guess you could say so. I've been hunting my whole life. Ever tasted bear meat?"

"No."

"It's strong and can be tough. Not usually worth the effort to clean and cook it."

Ginny took a deep breath. "I'll stick to chicken, thank you."

"Rattlesnake. How about that? Have you tasted rattlesnake?"

There were no further surprises and the two of them talked Texas until they reached the intersection of State Highway 9 and U.S. 1 where they found a place to pull off and a menu consisting of nothing more exotic than Atlantic salmon.

* * *

Monday Morning
Rte 9, headed east

It took Jim only five minutes to find out Ginny and Charlie had left an hour before he arrived.

"But you must have some breakfast before you go out again. Are you sure you wouldn't like a nap as well?"

Jim shook his head. "Yes, please, to the breakfast, but no, I can't stay longer than that. I have to catch up."

"Well, if you must. Sit. Eat. Have some coffee."

Jim ate with a good appetite and accepted a thermos of hot coffee with gratitude. He took a few minutes to get cleaned up and change clothes, then hit the road again.

Two hours. He was only two hours behind them and on the right road. (There was only the one.) He'd been told which border crossing they were headed for, but there his information ended. As far as he knew, that was all Ginny had, too. What would she do when she reached that crossing? She couldn't simply drive into Canada, not with Charlie in the car.

She would have to wait. She'd find a place to wait, a way to signal him. He watched the morning traffic unwind, then thin, then desert him, leaving him alone with the open highway and a straight shot to Canada.

* * *

Monday Morning
Baileyville, ME

Ginny finished drying her hands, then stretched. What should have been a two hour trip had taken three and her shoulders ached.

She stared at herself in the mirror. She looked thin, tired, pale, and she had no plan. That wasn't like her. Angus had said, "Go!" So she had gone. And now, here she was, facing herself in a truck stop mirror without the slightest idea of what to do next.

She didn't like flying by the seat of her pants. It made her nervous. ICU nurses didn't just wander in off the street and start fiddling with the drip rates. They communicated with the rest of the team. They anticipated problems. They had backup plans for their backup plans.

She frowned at her reflection. The prohibition against using the phones made the danger seem real. Cut off not just from Jim, but from the Homesteads and Angus and her mother, she was on her own to get Charlie to Halifax. She found her breath coming faster and her palms damp.

Her eyes narrowed at the frightened woman looking back at her from the mirror. Was that what Jim was seeing? Was that why he had made such a point of trying to keep her out of danger? If so, she deserved it. That woman didn't look like she could swat a fly without help.

Well, here was a chance to prove her worth to him and to

herself. All she had to do was break a few international laws, evade the domestic and foreign police, and persuade a series of innocent bystanders to collude in her infamy. Assuming she could figure out how to use their innocence to her advantage.

She gave herself a hard stare, then straightened her shoulders. The odds were against her. The law was closing in and time was running out. She needed to get to work.

She located a corner table in the dining area and looked over the menu, waiting for Charlie to reappear. The waitress arrived first. Ginny ordered coffee for two.

"Extra cream. Got it. Be right back."

She was as good as her word, reappearing promptly with the two coffees and her note pad. Ginny ordered a second breakfast, not because she wanted it, but because she thought it would look funny if she didn't, then explained she was very sorry to trouble the waitress, whose name was Gladys, but her companion would have to order for himself when he got out of the restroom.

She nodded, her head cocked to one side. "You here for the Festival?"

"What festival?"

The waitress lifted a flyer from the neighboring table and handed it over.

"International Snowmobile Festival. Joint effort with Canada, but we get people from all over. It's a big deal 'round here." She gestured toward the flyer with her pencil. "Today's the qualifiers. Tomorrow the real fun begins." She smiled. "I'll get started on your order."

Ginny watched her move off, suddenly aware of the other patrons in the fuel stop. Some were obviously truckers, but some sported high-end cold weather gear and expensive sunglasses.

Charlie joined her, setting his crutches on the floor and

easing into his seat.

"Coffee!" He sipped the hot liquid, then added sugar, then sipped again. "What are you thinking, Ginny?"

She looked up to find his eyes on her. "Bonnie," she corrected him.

He nodded. "Bonnie Jean Bowie." He took a sip of his coffee. "Tell ole Laredo Pete what's going through that pretty little head of yours."

She grinned at his affectation of the west Texas drawl. "I'm not sure, yet. What do you think of this?" She shoved the flyer across the table.

He read it between sips, then set it down, his eyes on the other customers. "Looks like we're just two more tourists out for a good time."

Ginny nodded slowly. "I wonder if the snowmobile trails cross into Canada."

Charlie's eyebrows rose. "You thinking of 'borrowing' one?"

"I was just wondering what, exactly, is going on here and whether we can make use of it."

The waitress took Charlie's order, then, after turning it in to the cook, stayed to chat.

Yes, the competition trails crossed back and forth between the two countries. Yes, the participants had to register and were required to produce passports both at the beginning and at the end of the race. They used photo-IDs to authenticate the riders. Had to. Border patrol rules. Lots of cameras. It was televised and went out over the airwaves. And the Internet, of course. Some of the events had money prizes, but most were just for fun. Best trails in three states and two provinces. First aid stations and safety stops along the courses. Well, no, not all the courses. The dogs didn't have safety stops. The trails were too short to need them. Dogs? Dogsleds. They had sleds and snowshoe races and cross-country skiing events, too. Great fun. Entry fees covered the officials, the rest were volunteers, from all over. Too big for the locals to handle it all. Did they want some more coffee?

Charlie's food came with the coffee and he dug in, ending the conversation. Ginny watched him eat, her mind turning over what she had heard.

"The trails cross the border."

Charlie looked up and caught her eye, then resumed his meal. "Security will be tight."

Ginny leaned back in her seat. "My sources tell me that no one cares if Americans cross over into Canada without proper documentation, unless they're smuggling drugs or something. The trouble starts when the American wants to come home."

Charlie looked at her, his fork halfway to his mouth, his expression suddenly cold. "Well, we don't have to worry about that, do we?"

Ginny flinched. She hadn't meant to rub salt in his wounds. "I'm sorry. I just meant, in an event this size, there's no way they can watch everyone."

Charlie relaxed slightly, then nodded. "I'll have to lose the crutches."

"Yes." She chewed her lip for a moment. "But not yet. First, we go check out the races."

* * *

CHAPTER 36

Monday, Noon
Baileyville, ME

Jim pulled into the truck stop and looked around. The place
was busy. Lots of big rigs. Lots of smaller vehicles, many with
ski racks. Trailers, too, with snowmobiles on them. He filled the
tank, located a corner booth in the restaurant where he could
watch the door, ordered coffee, and settled in to think.

His grandfather had been clear on the subject. Neither he
nor Ginny was to use the phones unless it was an emergency.
On the assumption the police were tracking Jim, in the hope he
would lead them to Charlie, that made sense.

He sipped his coffee, watching the big screen TV mounted
above the door. It took him a minute to realize the picture was
a live feed. It was an exterior location, with lots of sunshine
and brightly colored cold weather clothing. There were people
inspecting snowmobiles, tagging them, then moving on to the
next. A man wandered across the frame wearing an armband
with 'Official' printed on it.

Jim picked up a flyer someone had left on his table and read
through it. A snowmobile festival. His eyes narrowed. That
would be a good way to get a man with a broken leg across the
border.

The truck stop made an ideal rendezvous for the three of

them. Too bad he and Ginny hadn't set up a way to find one another. It would be nice if she'd wave at the camera for him.

He finished the first cup of coffee and accepted another. That made what? Twelve in the last seven hours? At what point did you risk caffeine poisoning? He set the second cup down and rubbed his face with his hands, then leaned back into the corner and let his eyes close. He could sit here in comfort for a while, as long as the waitress would let him, and watch that TV and hope Ginny would come to lunch.

She might not be here, of course. She might have decided to go up Hwy 1 and see if she could use any part of their original plan. Or she might have crossed into Canada down here. He knew her well enough to know that, if she'd been handed a golden opportunity to smuggle Charlie across, she'd take it and high-tail it to Halifax so she could use the phone.

Probably she was still here, trying to figure out how to use this festival to cover her tracks. If he could figure out what she would try, he could do the same. That would mean going out on the grounds and looking around. He would do that. In a minute. As soon as he'd finished this cup of coffee. Jim felt his head swim, blackness closing in from both sides. He was familiar with the sensation. He'd suffered through it enough times in the deepest part of the night shift. If he didn't move soon, he'd fall asleep right where he was. Soon. Needed to move. Soon. Open his eyes and move. Soon.

* * *

Monday Afternoon
Baileyville, ME

Ginny made her way to the picnic table where she'd left Charlie. They'd had to swoop in to grab this seat and she saw that he was now sharing it with someone else.

"Bonnie Jean! I'm glad you're back. I want you to meet someone." Charlie gestured across the table. "This is Vincent Wildes. He's here for the dogsled events and he's been telling me about them."

The young man on the other side of the table rose and held his hand out to Ginny. "Hi!" He had a fresh face, a dusting of freckles, and a huge smile. Ginny could just see the fringe of bright red hair under his knitted cap.

"Hello!" Ginny put her warmest smile into the word, shook his hand, then settled down next to Charlie. "This looks like so much fun. I'm glad we decided to stop."

Vincent nodded. "You should stay for the whole week. There's tons of stuff to do. They even let women compete."

"Oh?" Ginny forced her smile to stay put. "Is dogsledding something a woman can do?"

He shrugged. "Sure. It's not as hard as the men's events, of course, and you do need to be able to handle the dogs."

Charlie perked up. "How do you learn to do that?"

Vincent was happy to share. He chatted eagerly about training runs and specialized vocabulary and the details of the sled and track. "I could show you, if you like."

"I would. Can I get there on these?" Charlie indicated his crutches.

Vincent looked dubious. "Naw, we'll need a ride, but I can do that."

"Are the dogs yours?" Ginny asked.

"Yeah. Raised them from pups. They're my babies. Well, mine and Dad's. He owns the team, but I'm the lead trainer."

Ginny expressed appropriate awe at this revelation. "May I come?" She opened her eyes wide and batted her eyelashes, just once, at Vincent. He grinned in response.

"Sure. Let me go get the truck and I'll take you over to the kennels. Be right back." Vincent rose and hurried off, his step exuberant with health and excitement.

Ginny turned to Charlie. "Are you thinking what I'm thinking?"

"If you mean using a dogsled to cross the river, maybe, but I don't see how you're going to get me on a sled. I'm not entered in the race. I don't have the right credentials. And that young man will never give up his chance at glory."

Ginny nodded. "Maybe we can find someone else." She accepted a sip of Charlie's drink, but she wasn't much of a beer drinker so she handed it back, then sat for a few minutes, thinking hard.

"Charlie." She hesitated before broaching the next subject.

He looked at her over the rim of the mug, then set it down and gave her his full attention.

"It might be better if they thought you and I were, well, you know."

"Married?"

Ginny paled. "No. You're wearing a ring. I'm not. But, together anyway. Since we're traveling together."

Charlie nodded. "I know what you mean. They won't bother you if they think you're with me."

Ginny dropped her eyes to the table. "Yes, and I'm sorry to have to suggest it, but it's just until we get you safely over the border."

"Are you ashamed of me, Ginny?"

She looked up, startled. "No! I just don't want to hurt you."

He studied her face. "You're afraid, if we have to pretend to be a couple, it will dredge up painful memories."

She nodded.

His eyes shifted to the beer. "This is the first drink I've had since you stopped me killing myself in the park." He pushed it away. "It doesn't even taste good. It's just camouflage." He looked at her then sat up and took a deep breath. "I owe you my life. I can do whatever it takes."

Ginny blinked back sudden tears and nodded. "Here he comes."

* * *

Monday Afternoon
Baileyville, ME

Jim came back to consciousness with a start. His neck hurt and he was vaguely aware of someone speaking to him.

"You all right?"

Jim nodded, blinking in the afternoon sun. It was coming in the window, almost in his eyes. He sat up and looked at the waitress.

"I must have dozed off."

She nodded. "More coffee?"

"Yes, please."

Jim glanced at his watch, then frowned and looked around for confirmation. There was a clock on the far wall. Sure enough, he'd been asleep for four hours. Four hours! He rubbed his face again, trying to think. She could be anywhere. He pulled out his phone and looked at it. No messages. Could he send her one? If the phone Gordon had lent her was actually off, she wouldn't get it. Maybe she was checking every now and then, though, turning it on, then back off again. She'd want to hear from him, right? To let her know he was all right. Which was what he wanted, to know she was all right, and where she was. Except he was under orders to stay off the phone.

What little Jim knew about phones and the law came from television. He knew the technology allowed GPS location and that properly authorized government agencies could see what numbers a suspect's phone had called. If he called Ginny, they would get Gordon's phone number.

Jim struggled with himself until the fresh coffee had come and been drunk. This was an emergency. He really needed to find her. He picked up the phone and dialed the number to Gordon's loaner. Phone out of service. Of course. What about a text? He tapped out 'where r u?' and sent it, getting another message saying the phone was out of service. She probably had the battery out, taking no chances. She understood the danger.

Jim gathered up his things and headed back to the car. He drove off the lot and headed north, following the highway and going slow, pulling over to let other cars pass and poking his nose into every available parking lot to look over the people and cars. He'd been given a description of the car Gordon had loaned her, right down to the license plates. No luck. He spotted a man on crutches and his heart leaped, but it turned out to be someone with a heavy black beard. Not Charlie. Lots of redheads, too, but not the right one.

He drove through Baileyville, then out the other side and headed up the road, making the Houlton international crossing just before last light, only to find it closed. So she hadn't taken the car across here. He turned around and headed south again.

By the time he got back to Baileyville, it was full dark and the sleepy little town was jumping. Jim spotted at least three taverns, brightly lit and loud. He also saw arc lamps in use along the roadways, and lots of activity, and he could hear motors racing. He pulled into the parking lot of the next pub he came to and went inside.

He fought his way to the bar and ordered coffee, then turned around and looked at the crowd. They were well into their cups. Some were singing, their arms draped across each other's shoulders. Some were arguing about the expected results for tomorrow's race. Some were sitting quietly, watching the emotions heat up and Jim noticed firearms tucked discreetly into side holsters. He drank his coffee and slipped out again.

Back at the truck stop he pulled drinks and snacks off the rack then approached the girl behind the counter.

"Any chance of finding a room for the night?"

Her eyebrows rose. "Yer kiddin', right?"

Jim sighed. "No harm in asking."

She snorted. "No rooms available for twenty miles in any direction. People leave town and let their houses for the week, then live off the income for six months."

"Sounds like a good idea."

"'Cept for the damage. Sometimes it takes weeks to clean up."

"Campgrounds, maybe?"

"Same thing. 'Less yer a trucker, yer out o' luck, but it hardly matters. No one is gonna get much sleep 'til this thing's over. Everything open twenty-four hours a day to make the most of it. I'm working doubles to cover the store."

Jim nodded. "Well, let's just hope they're paying you for it."

She snorted again. "Not enough." She handed him his change with a sour smile. "Have a nice time at the festival."

Jim took his purchases out to the car. No rooms and no peace and quiet, which meant no opportunity to sneak across the border under cover of darkness. They might be sleeping in the car, of course, though without the sleeping bags and blankets, that might prove uncomfortable.

They might have driven along the highway until they found a place to sleep. That seemed more likely. He would do that, too. Get some sleep, then come back and see if he could find a message from her, or a clue, or something. He sighed heavily, his body aching from the cumulative effects of too much caffeine and too little sleep.

Either they were still here, or they were already over the border and halfway to Halifax. In which case, all he had to do was wait for the phone to ring. He got back in the car and headed north.

* * *

Monday Evening
Baileyville, ME

Charlie entered the tavern first, with Vincent holding the door for him. Ginny blinked at the crowd, and the noise. There was nowhere to sit and hardly any room to stand. Vincent brushed past Charlie on his way to the bar, shouting greetings to friends all over the room.

"Vince! Get over here!"

Ginny saw Vincent swerve, then gesture for them to follow. Charlie tapped a shoulder and the man in front of him turned, saw the crutches, then roared with laughter, but made a space for him to move through. It was like that the whole way. The crowd seemed to be sharing some private joke, at Charlie's expense, but with the greatest possible goodwill.

When she and Charlie had managed to gain a bit of floor space in front of the table, she saw a large man in an argyle sweater grinning up at them. It was clear he had been celebrating for some time already.

"What are you doing in that rig tonight? You don't have to suit up until tomorrow!"

Vincent seemed to think this the height of wit. "Joke's on you, Steven. His is real!"

"Real? Really?" The big man rose and peered at Charlie. "Geez! What'd you do?"

Charlie glanced at Vincent.

"He wants to know how you broke your leg."

"Oh!" Charlie's arm came snaking around Ginny's waist, pulling her to him. "A gentleman doesn't kiss and tell!"

This brought down the house. More than a half dozen of the denizens had been eavesdropping. They now turned their full attention on Charlie, grinning and laughing.

"Come on, man! She's too skinny for me to believe that! How'd you really break your leg?"

"Bull riding. Got thrown."

This too, was greeted with cheers and more than a few curious eyes.

"Where are you from?"

"Texas."

The other man, Steven, now made places for them at the table, bullying the previous occupants out of their chairs, and making Ginny and Charlie welcome in his domain.

"You're a long way from home."

Charlie nodded.

"Come for the Festival?"

Charlie shook his head. "Nope. Didn't know it existed." He looked around at the audience. "Looks like y'all are havin' a good time, though."

"The real fun starts tomorrow," Steven said.

"We gotta get him into the race," Vincent said to Steven.

Steven was still eying Charlie. "Well, he's got the handicap. Can you shoot?"

Charlie lifted an eyebrow. "Some."

Ginny smiled to herself. Taciturn Texan. Good move.

"Some." Steven sat back in his chair. "Rifle?"

Charlie nodded. "I hunt."

"Umm." Steven turned to Vincent. "He'll need a sponsor and a gun."

Vincent grinned. "I can do that."

"Excuse me," Ginny interrupted. "What are y'all talkin' about?"

"The Busted Bum Biathlon."

"The *what*?"

Half a dozen excited voices tried to answer her. Steven silenced them. "It's a contest we have here at the festival. Real macho stuff. Cross-country skiing with one leg in a cast and targets the size of quarters."

Ginny felt her mouth stretching into a grin. "How did you come up with that one?"

"One of the regulars broke a leg the day before the race a few years back, but he didn't think it should stop him competing."

Vincent grinned widely. "You showed 'em, Steven! Almost won, too."

"I see!" Ginny smiled at the local hero.

"What d' you want me for?" Charlie asked. "You don't know me."

Steven glanced at Vincent, then back at Charlie. "Tomorrow's the relay. We're one man short." He frowned. "If we can't find a replacement for Zack, we'll have to drop out. So far, no luck."

Charlie nodded slowly. "What would I have to do?"

"Ski seven and a half kilometers, on one leg, shoot straight and hit all five targets, prone and standing. Highest team score wins." Steven leaned forward across the table. "It's not as easy as it sounds. It's all in good fun, but the guys tend to get a bit competitive. You might find yourself tripped along the way."

Charlie smiled. "I can handle myself."

"Even with a broken leg?"

"Yup."

"And you can shoot?"

Charlie looked over at Ginny and their eyes met. She nodded. Whatever risks they were running by registering Charlie in a race would be mitigated by the credit he was building with these men. They might be talked into helping.

"Last time I went out with the boys," Charlie said, "I put every round in the ten at 600 yards. 'Course that was a clear day with no wind and my own rifle."

"Whew!" Steven stuck out his hand. "In that case, welcome to the team, Tex."

There were additional details to sort out and Vincent came and went more than once, but Ginny found herself relaxing for the first time in days. She watched the crowd ebb and flow.

They were a cheerful bunch, laughing and singing and teasing each other. As the evening wore on, they also started competing, boasting of prodigious feats they planned to perform on the morrow. Several of them came up to her and spoke. She smiled and chatted and let nothing of her real life slip into the conversation. If one of them got too chummy, Charlie laid his hand on her shoulder and the interloper would retreat. There were women, too. Charlie collected a small harem of admirers before they left. All in all, a very pleasant evening, topped off by an example of northern hospitality.

"You'll come home with me," Vincent insisted. "Can't have you getting lost tonight. All we've got is sofas, but they're long enough even for you," he looked at Charlie, "and plenty comfortable. I know, I've slept on them more than once."

Ginny was happy to accept. They followed him to a modest house on the outskirts of Baileyville, met his parents and a sister and were quickly settled in the living room with blankets, hot drinks, and the waning embers of the evening's fire.

Ginny was just drifting off when she was hit with a sudden pang of guilt. It had been hours since she'd even thought of Jim. She wished, heartily, that she could call him, but Angus had made it clear. She was to have no contact with anyone Tran could trace until Charlie was safely across the border and delivered to the Halifax Homestead.

Jim was probably here, somewhere. Gordon would have given him the same directions he'd given her, cross at International Avenue. Jim would recognize the potential of the Festival. With so many people on crutches tomorrow, Charlie could hide in plain sight.

He'd be looking for her, for them. Looking, maybe, for a signal from them. She should add that to her To Do list. And she should look for the SUV.

But even if she couldn't find Jim, or he them, she had her assignment and the beginnings of an idea. A lot would depend on just how much testosterone was floating in the air tomorrow. Whatever happened, it promised to be an interesting experience.

* * *

Chapter 37

Tuesday Morning
Baileyville, ME

Jim had managed to find a room in the Danforth area, fifty miles north of Baileyville. Not cheap, but clean and good food. He'd gotten in around nine p.m., gone straight to bed, and slept ten hours. With a hot shower, clean clothes, and a lumberjack breakfast under his belt, he felt better. He also felt encouraged.

The TV in the breakfast area had included a segment from the local Game Warden, explaining the dangers of interacting with the Maine wildlife. To illustrate, he had shown a video clip of tourists on Hwy 9 trying to drive around a black bear that was in possession of the road. Jim watched, fascinated, as the bear charged the vehicle, cameras recording the whole thing. The driver of the hatchback was a redhead.

The clip was too short to be sure, but Jim was convinced the driver was Ginny, the passenger was Charlie, and the hatchback was the one they had borrowed from the Albany Homestead. He drove back to Baileyville, parked in the public lot, got out of the SUV, and looked around.

At first he thought he was hallucinating. With each leg cast he spotted, he jumped. None were Charlie, though. He counted them. More than thirty in the immediate vicinity and more arriving each minute. He made his way to the nearest vendor and ordered coffee.

"What's with all the broken legs?"

The vendor told him.

Jim took his coffee back to the car and climbed behind the wheel. One-legged skiing and sharp shooting. Talk about tough! But what a break! If he knew Ginny, she would be figuring out how to use this to her advantage. She was here, and so was Charlie. Now to find them.

* * *

Tuesday Morning
Dallas, TX

Five days and she was only just now hearing of it. *Five days!* If Detective Tran had been a swearing woman, she would have indulged in language that could have blistered the sun.

She read the transcript again. It was the testimony of an escaped felon, eight pages of it. He described a white van with Texas plates, two men and a woman, one of the men confessing to a murder and disposing of the body in a boat that had been set on fire.

There was no protocol in place for sharing the ravings of a bitter and apparently lunatic convict with other law enforcement agencies, but someone had eventually routed a copy of this to the Texas clearinghouse. The boat had triggered a match alert and the file had been forwarded to her. Not the actual file, of course, a summary, but there could be no mistake. It had to be Monroe.

Which put him in Roanoke, Virginia five days ago.

The other man and the woman could be anybody, but it was most likely they were Miss Forbes and Dr. Mackenzie. The physical descriptions matched.

Detective Tran's eyes narrowed. She had spoken to Dr. Mackenzie on Sunday and he had earnestly told her he had not seen Monroe since they left Dallas.

Her entire case against Charles Monroe was based on circumstantial evidence, and not much of that. What's more, he had a solid alibi for the time of death. She might be convinced he was the killer, but the D.A.'s office would need more.

Well, the first thing to do was pick him up for questioning. If he was on the run, and if Dr. Mackenzie was helping him, she had grounds for warrants.

She pulled up the forms on her computer, a U.S. detain and extradite and a similar process on the Canadian side. It took her the better part of three hours to get all the paperwork done. Now she had to wait. In the meantime, she needed to update her files. She walked over to the whiteboard, pulled out the green marker and got to work.

* * *

Tuesday Afternoon
Baileyville, ME

Ginny watched the final leg of the relay on a screen set up on a picnic table. She was surrounded by the Wildes family and a dozen more Team Steven supporters, all cheering hysterically as the third man approached the handoff point. Vincent was alternating between sitting beside her, his arm around her waist, and leaping to his feet, roaring. The weather was cooperating, with golden sunshine and temperatures hovering just above the freezing mark.

The official start of the race had been at the headquarters

of the Moosehorn Wildlife Refuge. The first leg looped through the woods to a safe zone where each contestant fired from both standing and prone positions.

The second leg started from there and moved toward Old Hwy 1, south of Baring. The firing range this time faced south, away from town. The third leg headed southwest, toward Bearce Lake, the most rugged of the four sections. The last leg circled back and ended here, at the junction, but required the skiers to stay south of the intersection, to avoid collisions with motor traffic.

The teams were being shuttled to and from these points by support crews, all dressed in distinctive colors and all celebrating as hard as they could. They, too, were sporting fake casts (or leg immobilizers for the less committed), making the number of men in casts in the area today something in the neighborhood of three hundred.

The times were hardly Olympian. In a standard biathlon, the skiers averaged two minutes per mile on groomed tracks and with two good legs. The contestants in this race were lucky to finish a mile in half an hour. There had been a lot of falling down and getting back up again and a few disqualifications as competitors shrugged off the temporary disability and went at the race full tilt.

Ginny had been astonished to see how many men were competing. Each team had four members and there were three levels of competition: "Just Kidding", "Mine's Bigger Than Yours", and "Don't Even THINK About It." Team Steven fell into the last category. The beginner class (Just Kidding) had twelve teams; the intermediate, ten; and the advanced, fifteen; for a total of one hundred forty-eight contestants. The officials had been starting the teams in volleys all day long. The premiere event, however, was this one, the last of the day.

Team Steven was in the lead and Charlie had the anchor

spot. They had taken him out early this morning to let him get used to the borrowed rifle and his accuracy had convinced them to put him in last.

Ginny knew he could shoot. She'd even heard him say he could ski. What she didn't know was whether he was physically up to this level of exertion.

There were spotters along the route, watching to make sure no one fell hard enough to need rescuing, and each of these, apparently, had a phone with a video feed. There was no lack of coverage, just discipline. The images bounced and slewed around, making it hard to recognize what she was looking at. Every now and then, though, she could identify the acid green jersey Team Steven had adopted flashing through the trees.

The handoff had happened and all eyes were on Charlie. For a full twenty seconds she had a clear view of him, moving his body from side to side, using the poles as if they were an extension of his skeleton, poised and balanced and tremendously strong.

"Look at that!" someone said.

"He's a natural." There were murmurs of agreement, then the image was lost and the party resumed.

Ginny was biting her nails before the final sprint. Charlie had performed the miracle, ten clean hits, and was headed for the finish line, in front of all the other competitors, but he no longer looked like it was easy.

"Come on! You can do it!" They were cheering for him, for him personally, as well as for the team. He was approaching the finish line. He was over it. He was down.

Ginny felt her heart stop, but it was just the excitement of the team, they had jumped on him, knocked him down. They were picking him up again, pounding him on the back, lifting him above their heads and carrying him to the truck, then heading for the reviewing stand.

Ginny watched the ceremonies with a dry mouth. Here was something else she hadn't counted on, photographic evidence of Laredo Pete Harmon winning the Busted Bum Biathlon for Team Steven. When they finally let him come to her, he moved as if he had nothing left.

"Pete?"

He pushed the cheap plastic trophy at her. "I won, Bonnie." He was grinning like an idiot. "Makes up for that last bull."

She shook her head at him. "You are one tough hombre," she said. "Now what?"

"Now," Vincent said, "we eat and we drink and we celebrate into the night!"

Ginny shook her head. "He needs rest. Look at him."

Vincent turned and studied Charlie, then nodded. "I keep forgetting his leg is really broken."

They loaded Charlie into the truck and took him back to the Wildes house. Ginny settled Charlie on the couch, then waited on him, making sure he ate and got lots of water. The rest of the team had followed and the party surged around them. Ginny found herself pulled into the celebration.

"Bonnie Jean, darlin'," Charlie called, "you behave yourself."

Ginny waved from the arms of the man who was swinging her around the living room. It was time to see if she could put her plan into motion. She maneuvered her way into Vincent's arms. He was happily inebriated and bursting with pride.

"I'm the one who found him! You should be thanking *me*!"

Ginny reached up and took both of his ears in her hands and pulled his face down so he would see her.

"Remember our bet?"

"Yeah!" he grinned. "I remember. He wins, I give him a ride on the dogsled tomorrow. He loses I get to take you to bed tonight." He gave her a lopsided smile. "I don't supposed you'd let me do that anyway?"

"Tell you what, if you're still on your feet when this party ends, I'll let you kiss me goodnight."

"All right!"

Ginny kept a weather eye on Charlie while the party raged on, then spilled out into the night, taking Vincent with it.

"I'll be back for my kiss!"

Past midnight Ginny found herself pulled off the sofa and into Vincent's arms. It turned out he was a good kisser and still both drunk enough and happy enough to let her push him into his own room and return to the couch with only a moderate amount of wrangling. She found Charlie watching her.

"Bonnie Jean Bowie!"

"Yes, Pete?"

"What did you promise that boy?"

Ginny came over, sat down on the edge of the sofa beside Charlie, and lowered her voice.

"I made arrangements for you to ride his dogsled across the river tomorrow. Not the whole race, just a short bit of it. I'll meet you on the other side."

"And what did you promise him in payment?"

"It was a wager." She explained the bet.

Charlie's eyes grew large. "I'm really glad I didn't know that when I was out there today. It would have taken all the fun out of it."

"That's why I didn't tell you."

"I seem to be in your debt again."

She shook her head, smiling. "Not this time. You won. So I don't have to pay up. Vincent does."

Charlie looked at her, the corner of his mouth curving up as he shook his head. "You're a braw lass, Bonnie Jean. I just hope Jim knows how lucky he is."

* * *

Chapter 38

Jim pulled his phone out and looked again for a response from Ginny. Nothing. He hauled his arm back and swung, but stopped short of flinging the thing into the distance. It wasn't the phone's fault. It was just that today had been incredibly frustrating.

It shouldn't have been that hard to find one man in a leg cast, even among all the impersonators. Jim had gone about it systematically, eliminating the women, then any man who had dark coloring, then any man who had a cast on the *right* leg, since Charlie's was on the left.

He'd seen scores of fair haired men, tall enough to be Charlie, who turned out not to be Charlie. He'd also seen more than a dozen redheads that might have been Ginny, but who weren't. There had even been a moment when he'd seen a tall blonde with a redheaded woman. Still not them.

The problem was the shifting, moving mass of humanity. He was pretty sure he'd seen and eliminated the same people over and over again. They wouldn't stay put.

It turned out there were dozens of places where the revelers were congregating. There were the official venues: the reviewing stand, the judges' tent, and so forth. There were vendors' stalls, picnic areas, bars, pubs, restaurants, and any place with a fire or central heating. And there was the rolling stock.

Jim had never been to a truck rally. Had he done so, he wouldn't have been so surprised to see trucks coming and going, at speed, making doughnuts in the fields and buzzing the crowds.

In defiance of the rule that no live thing should ride in the back, each pickup was filled to overflowing with celebrants, each truck louder and more excited than the last. Jim predicted nothing but disaster before the day was out and was glad he wasn't on duty at the First Aid station.

There were snowmobiles, too, though most were upriver, on the trails. The ones down here were conveying revelers from place to place, like the golf carts they used at the Games back home.

Jim had hitched a ride to the National Wildlife Refuge and spent some time walking the biathlon course. He'd come back along the second leg of the relay, then crossed Old Rte 1 into Baring, then walked down to the edge of the St. Croix River. He looked across into Canada, wondering for the umpteenth time if the other two were already over the river and on their way to Halifax.

By that time, the day was waning. The last race had been run and the officials were clearing the track, making sure no one was left behind. Jim accepted a ride back to his car.

He managed to find a pub with an empty chair and wedged himself in, sympathizing in silence with the harassed waitress. It took more than an hour to get his meal, during which time the crowd, arrayed mostly in red rugby shirts, seemed to be grieving a close second place finish in one of the races.

"But did youse see dat guy? He's da real ting," one of the men at the next table said.

"It's 'cause his leg is broke!"

Jeers and catcalls greeted this.

"No, I'm serious. Not faking. Said he was from Texas. Broke it being thrown by a bull."

Jim had choked on the word 'Texas.'

"You wouldn't tink a guy from Texas could ski."

"*He* sure could."

"Took the trophy," a third man said. "We'll never hear the end of it."

Jim finished his meal as rapidly as he could, then moved in on them, buying drinks all around and inserting himself into the conversation. His careful interrogation elicited only the fact that the interloper was tall, blonde, and from Texas. They didn't know which leg was broken.

"What did he say his name was? Mic! I'm talkin' ta youse! Pete, wasn't it? Laredo Pete! That's it."

Laredo Pete. Jim had trouble controlling his expression. Charlie had embellished his fake ID, adding a backstory and a nickname.

"Look! There's his picture." They were pointing to the TV. Jim twisted around in time to see Charlie, outfitted in acid green, posing with three other men. There was too much noise for the voiceover to be heard, but the caption read, "Team Steven wins Busted Bum Biathlon."

"How can I find him?" Jim asked.

His companions shrugged. Look for the acid green jerseys. Ask them. And why do you want him, anyway? You a reporter? We got better stories than that. Now you just take the snowmobile races. Tomorrow and the day after, with the finals on Friday. That's a *real* competition.

Jim extricated himself with a promise to go upriver to the snowmobiling venues tomorrow, then started canvassing the remaining watering holes in town. He found a number of acid green jerseys, but none that could tell him where the hero of the day could be found. Past midnight he finally gave up.

The celebration had been loud and volatile. Under cover of that much alcohol, Ginny might have seen an opportunity to grab Charlie and slip away. Should Jim go prowl the river bank? It had looked too wide and too cold to swim, but maybe he was underestimating Charlie.

One of the things Ginny had added to the packing at the last moment, to Jim's mocking laughter, was a pair of binoculars. He pulled them out now, wishing she'd gone one step further and added night vision. He lifted them to his eyes, scanning the waterside.

There were patrols along the edge, with dogs, on both sides. He watched for several minutes. Was it just here? Because of the crossing? Or because of the festival? Or was this every night, the entire length of the border?

He jumped when a hand fell on his shoulder, turning abruptly to find an officer of the law beside him.

"What are you doing here?"

Jim swallowed his heart. "Looking at the river. There's something going on."

"Why do you want to know about that?"

Jim shook his head. "No reason. I'm still too keyed up from the festival today. Couldn't sleep. Thought I'd take a walk," He nodded toward the water. "Didn't expect to see patrols. Got curious."

"Your ID, please."

Jim handed over his wallet.

"Texas, huh? I heard about the Busted Bum. Was that you?"

"No. A friend. That was some performance."

The patrolman nodded. "So what are you doing out here after midnight with binoculars?"

Jim's mind was racing, right along with his heart. He

shrugged. "I heard some people talking about swimming the river on a dare. Came to see if anyone was really drunk enough to try it. Found the patrols. Thought they might be looking for a body."

"Uh, huh. Turn out your pockets, please."

Jim complied. Ten minutes later, the patrolman seemed satisfied. He handed back the wallet.

"You're an MD?"

"Yes."

"Sorry for the inconvenience. It's the drug runners we're after." He gave Jim a hard look. "I've got nothing to hold you on, but I strongly suggest you stay away from the water. Do I make myself clear?"

Jim nodded. "Yes, officer. Thank you." He turned immediately and went back to the car, put the binoculars away, then drove back to the truck stop.

Jim examined his face in the bathroom mirror. Did he look like a drug runner? Needed a shave, of course. But a fine upstanding citizen such as himself? He lifted an eyebrow. Did his guilt show in his eyes? Maybe that was what law enforcement looked for, a guilty conscience, and he was a rank beginner. It was a miracle he'd gotten away.

The encounter made two things clear. One, Ginny and Charlie were not crossing the river under cover of darkness. Not tonight. Wherever they were, they were still in the U.S. Two, Ginny was going to need help from someone who knew all about the border patrols.

Jim went back into the cafe and searched the tables until he found an abandoned program. It outlined the rules for each of the competitions, explaining to the public what to expect. This included safety and security information, with a plea to cooperate with the officials and a carefully worded precaution against straining Canadian-U.S. relations. He tucked it into his jacket and drove back to the Lodge.

Once in his room, he went to work, studying the trail maps. What they needed was a way to cross the border as part of the fun. He marked each place where the routes crossed either into or back from Canada.

Both snowmobiles and dogsled races were on the docket for tomorrow. Of the two, it seemed more likely Charlie could handle a snowmobile. If Ginny could figure out how to get the hero of the Busted Bum into that race, then he could disappear on the other side.

Jim lay awake for another hour, trying to think of ways for Laredo Pete to enter, then disappear from, a high-profile, heavily monitored international race, and coming up with nothing. Tomorrow there wouldn't be any fake casts. If Charlie got into a race, any race, that cast would mark him. After his triumph today, though, the question was whether anyone would care.

* * *

Chapter 39

Vincent woke with a hangover and it took some effort to persuade him he couldn't just go back to bed. Ginny made sure Mrs. Wildes was warmly thanked for her hospitality, then the trio set off for the truck stop.

From here, Vincent would drive to the dogsled staging area. Ginny and Charlie would meet him at the rendezvous. Ginny put a hand on Vincent's arm. "This is for you." She tucked a hundred dollars into his hand.

He looked at it and tried to protest. "I can't take that."

"For expenses. You'll need more ammo at least."

He hesitated, then smiled. "Thanks."

"And Vincent," Ginny stepped closer. "Thank you, for everything." She put her arms around his neck and kissed him, thoroughly. He blushed, then kissed her back.

"You're welcome!" He gave her a hug, then headed off.

Charlie was grinning as she got into the car.

"Not a word to Jim about that!"

"My lips are sealed!"

She'd had trouble figuring out what to put in the note she was leaving tacked to the bulletin board in the truck stop. It had to look innocent to everyone else, had to explain to Jim. He might not see it, but if he did, she was pretty sure he'd understand.

"You all set there?" she asked.

Charlie looked over at her and nodded. "Let's roll!"

* * *

Wednesday Morning
Maine / New Brunswick Border

Charlie watched the approach of the sled, a combination of excitement and apprehension gnawing at his stomach. He'd had dogs, hunting dogs, his whole life and understood how to talk to them. He'd also had a crash course in sled dog signals. The weather was clear and the trail well marked. Should be okay.

The sled pulled up beside him and Vincent hopped off, letting Charlie take his place on the back.

"The dogs know the way. Just keep them moving." He settled down in the basket.

Charlie climbed aboard, just as he'd been shown, shouted, "Hike!" and they were off.

It took his breath away to see how fast they were going. The dogs made a lot of noise. Happy noises. He'd been told they loved to run, loved to pull the sleds through the snow, loved the attention they got from their handlers. He could believe it. He knew a doggy smile when he saw one.

They turned a corner and Charlie noticed the woods thinning out. They were approaching the river.

"Will the ice hold?" Charlie shouted the question.

"It should." Vincent shouted back over his shoulder.

Charlie hoped he was right. It had been warmer yesterday than the organizers had anticipated.

"Hike," he called to the dogs. They had slowed down, sniffing at the trail, using caution when stepping out onto the frozen surface. Charlie wondered if they knew something he didn't. He could see the other side easily. All he had to do was stay between the markers.

There was no border crossing here. No official one, anyway. The Canadians waited on the other side at the next checkpoint armed, not with guns, but with stopwatches. He would be off the sled by then. He looked up river, noticing the movement of water in several areas. Not truly frozen after all, but as long as he stayed in the groove, they should be fine. The dogs had apparently decided it was safe to cross. They were already approaching the other side.

It was a beautiful day and under other circumstances he would have gotten a big kick out of this, but Charlie was nervous and his casted leg ached with the motion of the sled. He'd be glad to get back into the car.

"Help!"

Charlie jerked his head in the direction of the sound. Had he heard something? Really?

"Help!"

A young voice. Female. Where was it coming from?

"Please, somebody!"

He had it now, over to the right, downriver, about a hundred yards. He could see a head above the edge of the ice.

"There's someone in the water!"

"Where?" Vincent asked.

Charlie pointed. He knew if they stopped he would be putting his escape at risk, but he couldn't just ignore a cry for help. His training, as well as his conscience, wouldn't let him.

He finished the crossing, then brought the team to a halt.

"What are you doing?" Vincent demanded.

"She'll die if we don't get her out." He was already off the sled and running. On his broken leg. Probably not a good idea.

He stepped back out on the ice and moved carefully in the direction of the voice. It was a girl, clinging to the edge of the ice. It had broken under her weight. Hell! If the ice wouldn't hold her weight, it certainly wouldn't hold Charlie's.

He looked around, trying to figure out how to approach her. He'd heard you could use slider boards, skis, sticks of wood, anything to extend your reach, and that you had to lie down flat on your stomach to spread the weight over more ice surface. Vincent had come up behind him. "Jeez!"

"Don't come any closer. Do we have anything she can grab onto?"

"Wait a minute." Vincent ran back to the sled and returned with the tarp that lined the basket. "Here."

Charlie knelt down on the ice, then lay down flat and started to squirm.

"Stay calm. I'm coming." The girl's eyes turned in his direction. Good, she had heard him. Charlie was getting a much clearer view of the girl, her face pale, her lips an amazing shade of blue. How long had she been in the water? Charlie pushed the tarp in front of him.

"I'm coming. Stay very still." He didn't know where that came from, but it couldn't hurt. The girl needed to listen and conserve her strength for the climb out.

"Here, mister!" Her teeth were chattering so hard she had trouble getting the words out.

"I see you."

Charlie pushed the tarp along the ice, moving slowly and listening for cracking sounds. It wouldn't do for both of them to go in.

"Take hold of the tarp."

The girl tried, but her fingers no longer worked.

"Okay. Put the tarp between you and the ice, then grab the

edge and hold on."

Charlie had gotten as close as he dared. He was still about five feet from the edge of the ice, but he could see the spider web of cracks already in place.

He watched as the girl took a good, if clumsy, grip on the tarp.

"I'm going to back up. Don't let go."

The girl nodded.

Very slowly Charlie inched backward. He could feel when the girl's weight crossed the line of ice and began to press down on the edge. The extra weight produced a series of cracking noises and Charlie paused for a moment, to let the ice settle, then slowly began again to pull the tarp, with the girl on it, back toward the woods.

It took him ten minutes of excruciatingly slow squirming to wriggle back to the point where Vincent could help. Between them, they hauled the tarp off the river. The girl lay on it, not moving, just gripping the edges and shivering. Charlie bent down and lifted her to her feet.

"Come on."

They loaded the girl into the sled, Vincent's arms around her, then set off toward the rendezvous point. Luckily, it was close. Five minutes brought them in sight of the hatchback.

Ginny opened the door and climbed out when they pulled up, her smile freezing when she saw what they had brought her.

"Oh, my!" She grabbed the girl and pulled her into the car.

Vincent glanced at his watch. "You got this?"

Charlie nodded, then stuck out his hand. "Thanks!"

Vincent shook it, then jumped on the sled. "Got to go. Good luck!" He set off, as fast as possible.

Ginny drove straight to St. Stephen, followed the highway signs to the hospital, and pulled up in the ambulance bay.

"Let me handle this," she said. She put her arm around the girl and hurried inside. She was back in ten minutes.

"That was fast."

"I told them I needed the ladies room. Let's go and keep your head down!"

She steered out onto New Brunswick Highway 1 and headed for Saint John. Once they were away from St. Stephen, Ginny looked over at him.

"What was that all about?"

Charlie shifted his leg carefully. It was beginning to hurt.

"She fell through the ice. We couldn't just leave her."

"No, of course not." Ginny looked at him, a smile spreading across her face. "Welcome to Canada!"

* * *

CHAPTER 40

Charlie looked out the window. Around them lay his new home. He tasted the idea in his mind. Home.

Home is where the heart is. His heart was with Mandy and the girls. Not here. *Home is where you hang your hat.* Well, he'd need a hat here. His ears hadn't been warm yet. *Home is where, when you have to go there, they have to let you in.* That made the Halifax Homestead home. What was he going to make of his new home?

He took a deep breath. "You know, I didn't think I'd be able to pull this off, that I'd ever feel good enough about myself to start over." He glanced at Ginny. "Guess, underneath it all, I'm still Charlie."

"A Navy SEAL and a Texan and a Loch Lonach Homesteader. Yes. Those things will stay with you." She smiled at him. "I'm very proud of you, Charlie, and I know Mandy is, too."

Charlie's mouth curved up at the thought.

"Ginny, can I talk to you?"

"Of course."

"This has been a hell of a ride and I've heard more than I know you wanted me to."

She glanced over at him, then back at the road.

Charlie chose his words carefully. "You and Jim, you belong together. You need to make it happen."

She didn't take her eyes off the road. "I can't change him."

"Nope. Just yourself. So do it."

She caught her breath. "What do you suggest?"

"First off, he's a man and we're kinda slow catching on. Give him time."

He saw her lips twitch. "Okay. What else?"

He crossed his arms on his chest, his brow furrowed in concentration.

"I've been doing a lot of thinking on this trip. I miss Mandy something awful, but she was a good woman. Thinking about her is like thinking about a sunny day when the fish are jumping." He chewed his lip, looking for the right words.

"What Jim's facing, taking on the Homestead, training to be Laird, is kinda like what I'm facing. He's left his old life behind him and he's taking on one he doesn't know much about. He's gonna need help, just like I will, to start over."

"What if he doesn't want my help?"

Charlie snorted. The problem with women was they didn't understand how simple men were.

"He wants it and he wants to be able to look at himself in the mirror without cringing. Mandy used to manage me and I knew it, but it was a little game we played. She pretended to be helpless and I pretended I could do anything. She'd bat those eyelashes at me and I'd melt right into her hands. I loved every minute of it." Charlie smiled to himself, then looked over at Ginny.

"I'm just saying, you have more power than you know. Hell, women have all the power in a relationship. Men, well, we're at your mercy and I hope you feel kindly towards Jim 'cause he's good people."

He saw Ginny reach up and brush at her cheek.

"So are you, Charlie," she said. "So are you."

* * *

Wednesday Afternoon
Baileyville, ME

Jim pulled the phone out of the packaging and settled down on the back seat of the SUV, feeling like a fool. The damned thing had been in the car all along.

He'd never used a burner phone before and wasn't sure how it worked, but Reggie had set them up and Reggie could do anything, so Jim was not really surprised when the Laird answered.

"Grandfather, it's me."

"Auch! Jim! I dinna recognize th' number."

"This is one of the disposable phones Reggie set up for us."

"Aye. How are ye lad?"

"Fine, but I haven't been able to catch up with Ginny." He summarized the trip from Albany and Charlie's exploits of the day before. "And I had a run-in with the border patrol last night."

"Auch! 'Tis a guid thing yer no in jail! Ye musn't take such chances, lad."

"How closely are they watching me?"

"That convict ye picked up, he's tellin' anyone wha'll listen tha' Charlie is runnin' fra' th' Texas law. He described th' van and gied a partial license plate. Described th' three o' ye as weel. It got back tae Detective Tran."

Jim swore under his breath. He still felt they were safer together, but not if the police could follow him.

"Is Charlie across th' border?" Himself asked.

"I don't know. I think Ginny is planning to use one of the

races. Lots of the trails cross back and forth, but it's all under tight security so I don't see how she can manage it. I'm at the snowmobile venue at the moment. No sign of them here. I was just about to head down to the dogsled races, but, honestly, I don't know."

"Call me agin and let me know what ye find oot."

"I will."

Jim hung up the phone, then dialed Gordon's loaner phone. Out of service still, but this time he left a message.

"Ginny, it's Jim. Call me at this number as soon as you get this message." He duplicated it in the texting system, giving the burner phone number, then put it in his pocket and pulled out his regular phone.

What would Tran think if this phone went dead? Would she assume the worst? Only the guilty would suddenly go dark? Or would she assume he'd forgotten to charge it up? He decided to keep using it until it actually did run out of power. Truth was always safest.

He drove down to the dogsled venue and looked around. No Charlie, no Ginny, and no acid green jerseys. Lunch, though. He bought himself a meal, trying to look innocent, aware that he might be on someone's 'suspicious persons' list.

He hung around the dogsled venue for a couple of hours, asking questions, trying to get a feel for the event. It was another beautiful day, but the forecast was predicting change. Snow coming in this afternoon and another arctic front. The final day of the Festival was going to be a challenge.

When he was sure he couldn't find out anything more, he went back to the truck stop. No sign of the hatchback. He parked and went in, deciding he wanted coffee and maybe something hotter than the tepid meals he'd been getting at the venues. He settled down in the restaurant and ordered stew and coffee.

His eye wandered over the other patrons. Most were obviously either townies or visitors come for the festival. Some were, just as obviously, truckers, commercial long-haulers, moving from Canada to the northeastern U.S. and back again. They had routines and bored faces. Jim watched as one approached a bulletin board. Even from here Jim could see it had job opportunities posted on it. Lots of slips of paper. A way for those looking for work to connect with those who had jobs.

He finished his meal, then gathered up his coat and moved toward the board, casually, not wanting to draw attention to himself. It was an outside chance. She might not even have seen it and, even if she did, what were the odds he would?

He stood reading the notices. Most were printed on white paper. Some had been computer generated. A few had decorations, or colored ink, or something else to make them stand out. One had a Cross of St. Andrew drawn in the corner. He took it down and read it.

"To the Laird of Loch Lonach, Having a wonderful time. Wish you were here." It was signed, "Airsaid," and had a location and a date/time listed at the bottom. Bailey Rips. Today's date. Ten a.m.

Jim felt the adrenaline kick in. It was a message, a rendezvous, and he'd missed it by five hours. Would she still be there? Where was Bailey Rips, anyway? He hadn't seen it on any of the trail maps.

"Is there a computer I can use?" The girl behind the counter pointed across the room.

"The truckers use that one. Just give it your credit card."

Jim hurried over and sat down in front of the device. He pulled out his wallet, then paused. This would leave a paper trail. He carefully extracted the credit card Reggie had set up for his alter ego and offered it to the machine.

Fifteen minutes later he had a printed map and directions

from the truck stop to the Rips. The adrenaline must have helped for Jim had realized, in time, that Ginny would be on the other side of the border. He printed out another map, this one from the truck stop to the point in Canada that did NOT show on the road map. It DID show on the satellite image of the area, an access road to a point just on the other side of the rapids. He closed the account, retrieved his card, picked up a coffee to go, and headed out.

* * *

Wednesday Afternoon
Dallas, TX

The computer on Detective Tran's desk pinged. She had the device set to let her know when a message she was interested in came in from a law enforcement agency, whether her own or another. She got a lot of junk notices and sometimes she had resorted to muting the ping, but this time she was grimly satisfied, both at the speed of the response and the contents of the message.

Charlie Monroe's DNA had been found on the escaped convict's skin and clothing. At some point the convict had come in contact with something Monroe had touched.

She scanned the rest of the report. There were no other matches. So, still no hard evidence of Miss Forbes or Dr. Mackenzie being involved, much less culpable. But of Mr. Monroe, there was a strong suggestion that on last Wednesday he had been alive and halfway to the Canadian border.

* * *

Chapter 41

Wednesday Noon
Saint. John, New Brunswick

Ginny and Charlie drove into Saint John an hour and a half after leaving the Rips. The road took them along the harbor and, to Ginny, the town looked like every other industrial seaport the world over. Charlie seemed to like it, though. He was sitting up straighter and looking around at the water and boats.

"Are you hungry, yet?" she asked

Charlie nodded. "How about there?" He pointed to a modern-looking establishment that offered coffee and sandwiches. Ginny pulled in and parked. They examined the menu, then took their purchases to a table in the corner. Charlie licked the sauce off his fingers.

"Ummm. Good thing I like fish."

There was a large screen TV in each of the corners of the restaurant, so customers could be sure to see it and eventually Ginny did notice. What she saw stopped her in mid-bite.

She couldn't hear the news report, but she could see the picture. It was Charlie. There was a banner that gave his name and the fact that he was wanted in connection with a death in Texas. She poked at Charlie, motioning at the TV screen. He looked up and froze, then finished his sandwich.

"Never did like that picture."

The newscast showed road blocks being set up on the highway they had planned to take out of Saint John and around to Halifax. Then a telephone number and a clear appeal to the populace. If you see this man, phone it in.

Charlie wiped his hands, his eyes still on the TV. "What do we do now?"

Ginny had no idea. They were still four hours from Halifax. She couldn't stick Charlie in the trunk of the hatchback. There was no way the searchers would overlook a man-sized hiding place. He couldn't shuffle through the snow on crutches at each police barricade. The toll booths had cameras. The bridge spanned a quarter mile of open water too cold to swim. If she couldn't find another way to reach Halifax, they were trapped.

* * *

Wednesday Evening
Canada

Jim crossed the bridge into Canada, and followed the official's directions to pull into a parking slot. He handed over his real passport and identification and the border patrolman compared his face to the ID picture. Jim's fake passport was currently hiding in a special sleeve, provided by Reggie, guaranteed to avoid the usual scanning technology employed by law enforcement types.

"Anything to declare, Dr. Mackenzie?"

"Nope." Jim had left the guns in a locker at the Baileyville Truck Stop.

"Purpose of your visit?"

"Genealogical research, in Nova Scotia."

The patrolman nodded. "We get a lot more of that since DNA testing got so popular. Would you exit the car, please?"

Jim stepped out and watched as the officer went through the back of the SUV.

"You look like you're planning to camp out."

"Not up here. Did that back in the States. From here on it's hotels all the way."

The guard nodded. "Smart move. The weather up here can get nasty this time of year."

He made several notes on his tablet, then handed it over. "Sign here, please."

Jim looked over the form, then added his signature.

"Thank you. Have a nice visit."

"Thanks!" Jim got back in the car made his way toward the Canadian side of the St. Croix River.

Following the map, he arrived at the Bailey Rips at about five. The sun was on the horizon and the clouds blocked the last of the light, but it was easy to see there was no one here. He turned around and headed back into St. Stephen.

Where to from here? And when was she going to check her messages? He pulled the burner phone out and turned it on. Still no response. At this point, she was at least six hours ahead of him. She must have driven on into Nova Scotia. That was the only thing that made sense.

It was a five hour drive to Halifax from here and the snow would slow him down even further. He called his grandfather, using his regular phone, and asked him to call ahead and let them know to expect him, then got in the car and set off up NB-1 headed for the Trans-Canada. With any luck at all, she was already there, safe and out of the weather. He wished he could say the same for himself.

Jim drove on, seeing no evidence of the hatchback in Saint John or Moncton or on the road at any of the places she might have pulled off for food or gas or rest stops. He could not avoid the roadblocks, but they didn't seem to be looking for him.

They opened the doors and shone lights in the SUV, then waved him through.

It was past midnight when he arrived at the Halifax Homestead. He pulled into a parking space and got out. They were waiting for him at the door.

"Dr. Mackenzie? I'm Mrs. Robertson."

Jim followed the Matron inside. As soon as the door was shut, he turned and asked the only question that mattered.

"Is she here? Ginny Forbes?"

"No, and we haven't heard from her either. We were hoping you would know what happened."

Jim shook his head.

Mrs. Robertson handed him a battered manila envelope, addressed to Ginny. "I know the mail is supposed to be delivered only to the person it's addressed to, but I thought this might contain a clue."

Jim tore it open and pulled out the talisman, feeling his heart twist. Maybe if she'd had it with her she wouldn't be lost.

"Thank you. I'll see she gets it."

"This way, please."

They escorted him to a bedroom on the second floor, helped with the luggage, and made sure he had all he wanted to eat, then left him for the night. When he was alone, Jim pulled out the burner phone and dialed Texas.

"Grandfather."

"Jim! Are ye all right?"

"I'm fine, but Ginny isn't here."

"Ye passed her on the road, perhaps."

"I don't think so. I was looking carefully."

"Auch, weel, th' lass has probably found a place tae spend the nicht. No need tae worry about her. No just yet."

"You haven't heard anything?"

"Nae."

"She hasn't called her mother?"

"She's under orders not to."

"I know that." Jim was chewing his lip. "She left me a note pinned up on the bulletin board at the Truck Stop today, but I didn't get it in time."

"Did the twa o' them get across th' border?"

"I think so. The note said I was to meet them on the Canadian side."

"All right, then. She's layin' low. Dinna worry, lad. If she needs us, she'll let us know."

And with that Jim had to be content.

He got ready for bed and curled up under the covers, then reached for the TV remote. He was channel surfing, looking for a weather report when he saw Charlie's face suddenly fill the screen. Five minutes later he knew what had happened. She was laying low all right. They both were. They hadn't moved fast enough and the roadblocks had cornered them somewhere in New Brunswick, and what on earth was he going to do about *that*?

* * *

Wednesday Afternoon
Saint John, New Brunswick

Ginny's mind was racing. The gamble on the Busted Bum had paid off, in that Vincent had helped Charlie get across the border, but at the cost of twenty-four hours they could not afford to lose.

There was no way of knowing whether or not the girl Charlie pulled from the river could identify him. There was no reason to believe any law enforcement persons, on either side of the border, had seen Laredo Pete win the biathlon. But either could be true and anyone who saw his photo on the news might recognize him.

She didn't think anyone other than Vincent could connect Charlie to the hatchback, but she couldn't know for sure, and, in spite of her efforts to establish goodwill, she wasn't sure Vincent wouldn't turn them in.

She was staring out the window of the restaurant. On the other side of the highway was yet another dock, looking like all the rest at first, but this one had a sign, 'Nova Scotia,' and an arrow.

Ginny's eyes narrowed. They had originally ruled out the ferry from Portland to Yarmouth because of the border crossing, but they were in Canada now.

She picked up Gordon's phone, ignored the blizzard of incoming signals, and concentrated. Ten minutes later, she knew there was a ferry between Saint John, New Brunswick and Digby, Nova Scotia, that it left Saint John every morning in February at nine a.m., and that the crossing took two hours and fifteen minutes to cover the fifty miles of water in the Bay of Fundy. Another ten minutes gave her the name of a motel near the dock.

She brushed the crumbs off her hands and hustled Charlie out to the car. They managed to get away without any obvious sign that someone had recognized him. She hoped no one had been paying attention.

They drove to the motel and Ginny went to see if they had a vacancy. She found herself blessing Reggie MacDonald yet again. She'd had no trouble putting the room on Bonnie Jean Bowie's credit card once she produced 'her' driver's license and passport.

She returned to the car with the room key.

"One backpack each."

"What are you planning?"

"We have to abandon the car. We can walk onto the ferry, then hire a car on the Nova Scotia side."

"Why do we have to leave the car behind? It's a ferry. It takes cars."

"Because of the bear. Remember all those people taking pictures? If even one of them showed your face in that car, the police will have the description. We can't chance it."

They spread out the gear in the room, deciding what to take and what to leave behind. She pulled out the gemstones and laid them on the table. "Do you want to carry any of these?"

Charlie pushed the sparklers around with his fingertip. "Yes. Let me have the clear ones."

"Why clear?"

"Because they disappear in water. It will be easier to hide them." He pulled a small red bag off his belt and showed it to her. It was about the size of Ginny's hand, made to look like a tiny backpack, faded and worn.

"This is my survival kit." He opened it and pulled out the contents. There was a whisper-weight survival blanket; a tiny glow stick; a whistle with a compass built in; a plastic baggie with tissue inside; and an ancient-looking screw top container, army green and made of rubber. He unscrewed it and dumped the contents on the bed.

"Matches, tinder, emery board, tweezers, fish hook, and line." He took the diamonds and carefully dropped them into the bottom of the container.

"And here's a neat trick." He took a black disc and dropped it into the vial. "That thing just fits the diameter. It creates a false bottom. When I put this stuff back, it will push the disc down further and wedge it in place. That way, someone can tip it up and pour the contents out and the diamonds will stay put." He demonstrated. "But even if the disc gets moved, someone looking down into the vial probably won't see anything, 'cause the diamonds are clear. And if they get wet, you won't be able to see anything at all."

"Nice!" Ginny put the remaining jewels back into the velvet drawstring bag. "I'm going to put the rest here." She showed Charlie the inside pocket in her jacket. "We need some Canadian cash. I'll go find an ATM."

In the end, Ginny brought back foodstuff for dinner; hats and gloves; the equivalent of five hundred dollars U.S., in Canadian bills; two tickets for the morning ferry; and a ticket stub from a car park near the pier. It was unattended and labeled as meant for use with the ferry, so the car should be all right for a day or two, assuming all went well.

Ginny felt a qualm in the pit of her stomach at the thought. Not much had gone right with this trip. Why did she think this would be any different? She handed Charlie the cash.

"I hope that will be enough."

He nodded and stashed the money in his wallet.

"I apologize for making you walk to the ferry, but I didn't want to leave the car in the motel parking lot overnight. Someone might have noticed."

They both took advantage of the bathing facilities, then settled down to try to get some sleep. Not surprisingly, Ginny had trouble. She kept seeing disaster every time she closed her eyes. In the deepest part of the night she sat up suddenly, shivering, and found she had waked Charlie. He climbed into the bed beside her and pulled her into his arms.

"Just pretend I'm Jim and go back to sleep."

Ginny did as told, comforted by the feel of male arms around her, even if not the ones she wanted. She closed her eyes and drifted off again, waking next when the alarm clock sounded time to rise and face the day.

* * *

CHApTER 42

Thursday Morning
Saint John, New Brunswick

Ginny made her way to the street, stepping carefully. Even so, she hit a patch of ice, lost her footing, and almost fell. As she hauled herself upright, she caught a movement out of the corner of her eye. She turned to look and felt her heart leap into her throat.

There was no mistaking it. The Cù-Sìth. A huge, shaggy dog, always depicted in green fur. It stood there now, glowing green in the early morning darkness, looking at her. The Highlanders believed it was a harbinger of death.

Ginny stared, telling herself it was a mirage, but she was wrong. As the traffic light turned from green to red, the dog did, too, and she could see it was an Irish wolfhound, its pale fur translated by a trick of the light, not demonic possession.

It continued to look at her for a moment longer, then turned and loped off. Ginny caught her breath and hurried across the street. It was just a dog. A living, breathing, warm-blooded mammal. Nonetheless, she decided not to mention it to Charlie.

* * *

Thursday Morning
Saint John, New Brunswick

Ginny had done her best to assure Charlie blended in with the other passengers. He already had heavy sweat pants, snow boots large enough to fit over two pairs of socks and the cast, a faded turtleneck, and a pilled sweater. The winter jacket they'd bought in Virginia had suffered from hard use and no longer looked new. She'd added a cap with ears like the natives wore, which would cover his hair and change the shape of his face. He'd also stopped shaving in Albany and now sported a manly stubble.

She'd been worried about Charlie's ability to walk from the motel to the ferry, but it hadn't been too bad. He limped, of course, and should have been on crutches, but she'd substituted a cane and this way maybe it would be mistaken for a chronic condition. People would look away and that could be useful.

Still, she'd bet good money that Jim would want to take that cast off just as soon as they got to the Halifax Homestead. She felt a stab of unease at the thought.

Where was Jim, anyway? He hadn't shown up at the rendezvous. Had he even seen her note? Was he in jail in Albany? Had he been sent back to Texas? Without permission to call him, she would get no news until she reached Halifax.

They were beginning to load. She moved over into the pedestrian queue, and watched the first six cars drive slowly down the ramp and into the belly of the ship. Then the deckhands were opening the gates for the foot traffic.

The ship could handle 700 passengers, but there was nowhere near that number in line this morning. It was off season and only locals and lunatics like herself would be using the ferry today. She ended up several people ahead of Charlie because of his limp, but he looked calm and relaxed. She tried to do the same.

She made her way through security and up onto the viewing deck. As a scenic vista, it was a disappointment. Heavy clouds threatened snow and an icy fog lay on the water. Ginny could see nothing beyond what was immediately around her, and that consisted mostly of huddled passengers waiting for the snack bars to open.

"What's the holdup?"

Ginny looked over at the woman who had spoken. She was addressing a crewman who shrugged. "Don't know, ma'am." He moved off.

"As if we weren't miserable enough, having to wait to get underway." Her male companion nodded without lifting his eyes from his phone. "Yes, dear."

"At last!" The unhappy woman announced the moment of departure. Twenty minutes late.

The cause of the delay soon became apparent. The Canadian version of police officers, three of them, walked past and made their way forward. There was no way for Ginny to know why they were onboard. Perhaps this was routine.

Still, it wouldn't hurt to keep Charlie out of sight. She found him on deck, leaning over the rail. He glanced over at her.

"There's an awful lot of cold weather in Canada."

"It's February. According to the tourist flyers, the summers are great. Wait until July. I bet it won't hit a hundred and ten in the shade up here."

He laughed shortly. "No. I don't suppose it will." His eyes rested on the surface of the Bay where it disappeared into the fog. "I've heard there's good fishing along this coast."

Ginny nodded. "The locals will know where to go and what tackle you'll need." She looked out at the water. "Did you see the policemen?"

"I did."

"If they start searching, duck into the head."

Charlie nodded.

"If we get separated, turn on the beacon and I will find you."

"GPS?"

"Yes and no. It sends a distress signal, but it doesn't use the same frequency as NOAA, so it won't trigger a search and rescue and it requires a tracker so only authorized people can follow you."

"What's the cover story for today, if we need one?"

Ginny turned to face him. "That we met on the boat and fell into conversation." She grinned up at him. "Is it all right if I say I took an instant fancy to you?"

"Sure." He smiled down at her.

Ginny was going to have to leave Charlie behind when they got to Halifax and for the first time she realized she might not want to. She swallowed the lump that was forming in her throat and turned back to the water. "I'm never going to forget this trip." She heard him sigh.

"Me, either."

* * *

Thursday Mid-Morning
Bay of Fundy, Canada

They were more than halfway across and it was beginning to look as if the Canadian police weren't interested in Charlie. As of this moment, one of the three officers hadn't been seen since embarking and the other two were leaning against the rail, watching the water slide by. Ginny sidled closer, trying to overhear their conversation.

"Yeah, he's supposed to have murdered a man."

Ginny caught her breath at the taller officer's words.

"If we find him, we're to ship him back to Texas, at our expense, though the department might get reimbursed, eventually."

"Did you read the report?" the second officer asked. "The dead bloke killed his family."

"Why wasn't it a justified killing, then?"

"They think he stalked the perp for a month before he knifed him."

"Well, there you go. What makes them think he's aboard the ferry?"

"Someone saw him on the dock. Thought they recognized him from the telly. We're supposed to detain him when he tries to get off the boat."

Ginny moved quietly away. She found Charlie on the other side of the vessel. His face lit up when he saw her.

"Look, Ginny! Whales!" He made a place beside him and she slid into it.

"They're looking for you, Charlie," she whispered. "I overheard them talking."

She heard him sigh. "I guess I'm not really surprised."

"No." Ginny leaned on the rail, looking into the fog and trying to see what the rest of the watchers had. "I'm sorry."

"For what?"

"For not having managed this trip better."

He slid his arm around her and gave her a quick hug. "Don't worry. Something will turn up."

"Look!" Someone shouted. Ginny saw a fluke rise out of the water, then slide underneath the wave.

"It's too early for whales."

"Well this one's lost, then."

Another voice. "What kind is it?"

"I don't know. I didn't get a good look at it."

"Maybe you imagined it."

"No, I didn't. See? There it is again."

The crowd gasped as the huge animal's tail rose just yards from the side of the ferry, then came crashing down, spraying the onlookers with what felt like sleet. There were several cries of alarm and many hands grasping the rail in sudden fear.

"What's it doing?"

"There's something caught on its tail."

"Christ! It's a kid!"

Ginny saw they were right. There was a rope around the whale's fluke and attached to the rope, caught in it, was the shape of a young man. He was struggling to get loose, still alive, but in very great danger of being drowned.

Ginny turned to find Charlie climbing the rail, a knife in his hand. She didn't even have time to tell him not to do it before she saw him dive into the frigid water.

She felt her heart stop. As she watched, Charlie reached the whale and caught the trailing rope. She saw him grasp the boy's arm and pull himself up, then vanish beneath the water. The crowd on the rail was gasping, crying out, shrieking for help. "Look!"

The boy surfaced, struggling for breath.

The ferry couldn't stop quickly, but it could turn back and did so now. It pulled around, circling the area where the boy bobbed in the icy water, lowering a rescue boat.

"What about the other, the man who saved him?"

Ginny watched the water, looking for a sign of life, any disturbance. She saw the whale's fluke once more, still trailing the rope, then nothing. Nothing at all. Charlie was gone.

* * *

Thursday Late Morning
Bay of Fundy

Ginny was not a screamer. When she got scared, her throat closed and she could make no noise. She made no noise now.

No one paid her the slightest bit of attention. She was just one more shocked female clinging to the rail, aghast at having seen sudden death up close. She could hear the turmoil around her. Voices, pitched high and shrill. Lower, authoritative, but distressed. One comment pierced her brain like an ice pick.

"I got it all on camera! This stuff's great!"

She turned her head to see a passenger gazing at his phone in ecstasy. Ginny tore her hands off the rail and turned her back on him, heading to the lounge. Her foot caught in something and she looked down to see Charlie's backpack, abandoned on the deck.

She picked it up and took it with her. Would the authorities know he'd had a pack? Would they look for it? Search it for clues? She slipped into the ladies room, locking herself in the handicap stall.

She pulled Charlie's extra clothes out of his bag, running her hands over them. This is what survivors do to the possessions of dead loved ones, she thought. But Mandy was dead, too. They were together now. She should be happy for him.

She swallowed hard and told herself to focus. She went through the pack, looking for anything that would identify him, wondering if it mattered. If the pack was found, they would know he had been here. But he's not here now, she thought. So how could it hurt him?

She pulled out a folding knife and looked at it, blinking in surprise, suddenly realizing what she'd seen. He'd worn his *sgian dubh* this morning. He'd had it in his hand when he went overboard. How had he gotten that past security? The attendant must have missed it somehow.

He had looked like a transient with a bad leg. A strong young man with a bad leg. A veteran. Someone to show compassion for, to pass through without too many questions. It was almost enough to reduce her to tears. She struggled through the rest of the pack, finding nothing incriminating, then stuffed everything back inside and zipped it up.

She let herself out of the ladies room, making sure no one was watching, descended to the lower deck, stashed his backpack in an empty locker, pocketed the key, and walked away.

She sat down on a bench, numb with shock, and waited for the trip to end. Over and over in her mind she could see the Cù-Sìth. It had come for Charlie, not her. If she had said something, would he still be alive?

When her turn came to disembark, the officer looked her over carefully.

"You all right, Miss?"

Ginny pulled herself together. "I saw him die."

The officer nodded sympathetically. "It was a very brave thing to do. Did you know him?"

"No. We fell into conversation this morning, that's all."

The officer handed her driver's license back to her. "Thank you, Miss Bowie."

Ginny nodded, then moved down the gangway and stepped off onto Nova Scotia soil. Halifax was still a three hour drive away. If she found a car and left now she could make it before she lost the light, maybe before the snow started falling again.

She located the car hire and chose a four-wheel drive vehicle that could handle the steep inclines and slick roadways. She took the opportunity to switch back to her true identity, in case the police had somehow connected Bonnie Jean to Charlie through the ferry tickets. This would tell anyone who looked that Ginny Forbes had been in Digby, but what did it matter? Charlie was dead. She couldn't lead the police to him now.

She set off in the general direction of the main highway, her mind numb, her heart aching. On impulse, and because she was sure she wasn't safe to be on the roads, Ginny pulled over into the parking lot of a local pub. She needed time to think, and a place to do it in, and here she could get something hot to drink. Maybe something stronger as well.

* * *

Thursday Morning (CST)
Dallas, TX

"Is it him?"

Detective Tran looked up to see her supervisor in the doorframe.

"Yes."

"You're sure?"

"That is Charles Monroe and *that* is Virginia Forbes." She pointed at the woman in the white parka.

"What did the Mounties say?"

"Harbor police," she corrected him. "A citizen saw him boarding the ferry and reported it. The police confirmed the visual identification. They planned to detain him and send him back with the ship to be escorted across the border into Maine." She gestured at the video, still looping through the various clips of the whale incident. "He may have realized they were closing in and chosen to die instead."

The supervisor frowned. "I've had mixed feelings about this one from the start. Sometimes I wish we could just turn a blind eye."

"The Canadians say they will do their best to recover the

body, but the tides are against them." Detective Tran rose from her chair and faced her supervisor.

"I would like permission to fly to Nova Scotia to close the case."

"What can you do there you can't do here?"

"Speak with Miss Forbes, face to face, while the incident is fresh."

He crossed his arms on his chest, a speculative look on his face. "How badly?"

"I beg your pardon?"

"How badly do you want to go?"

Detective Tran's eyebrows rose. "I am willing to take a vacation day and pay my own expenses. Why?"

"I have a proposition for you." He gestured at her chair, pulling another up for himself and settling down in it. "Let's talk."

* * *

Chapter 43

Thursday Noon
Bay of Fundy

Charlie let go of the rope and headed for the surface. His SCUBA training kicked in, reminding him that, in a rapid ascent from depth, holding his breath could rupture his lungs. He had no idea how deep he'd gone. He might run out of air, but he'd just have to pray it was enough. He started to blow bubbles. They flew towards the surface and he followed them up, breaching a swell, then getting hit in the face by it, gasping, his lungs searing.

He went under with the next wave and came up fighting, this time into darkness. He struck out with his hands and found something solid. Disoriented and beginning to shiver, he grasped what could only be an oarlock, the thing you put an oar through to row a small boat. His head was out of the water in what appeared to be a pocket of air. He ran his hand along the edge and decided he was underneath a capsized dinghy.

Charlie took a deep breath, then put both hands on the wood, one on either side of the oarlock, and heaved. The side of the small boat came out of the water and he was able to see the ferry in the distance. He let go of the dinghy and considered his situation.

He needed to get out of the water. At this temperature, he

wouldn't last long. He couldn't right the boat without help. He had no way of signaling the ferry and even if he did, drawing attention to himself would mean swimming right into the hands of the police. Maybe he could climb on top of the boat.

He took another deep breath, put his hand on the oarlock to make sure he went the right direction and not too far, then dove under the side of the boat, coming up in the clear and turning to look. He was right, it was a small boat, capsized and floating on the surface. No oars in sight, but there was a rudder board. He worked his way around to the back of the boat and gripped the protrusion, hauling himself up onto the hull, shaking with cold and gasping for breath. Once out of the water, he closed his eyes, his teeth chattering so hard he was afraid they might break.

Charlie was pretty sure he was going to die of the cold. He could hardly feel his hands or feet and his nose and ears ached. If this kept up, he'd go into hypothermia and a lethal sleep. Fairly soon, actually. He was sorry to disappoint Ginny, but couldn't see any way to prevent it. Even if he turned on the beacon, assuming he could, how was she to reach him in time? His only consolation was that he'd seen the boy being pulled into the rescue boat. He could feel his heart slowing, giving in to the cold. 'I'm coming, Mandy,' he thought, then closed his eyes and let go.

Voices, or something like, and other noises. The fog made everything seem to be coming from the wrong direction. Then a collision of some sort. Charlie let his consciousness drift off again.

When he came to, he found himself naked, wrapped in a blanket and shivering in the warm air.

"So you're still with us," a voice said.

Charlie looked in that direction and found a very rough-looking man, a bit older than himself standing in the door of the cabin, his sea legs making it no problem to stay upright in spite of the swells.

"What's yer name?"

"Ch-Ch-Charlie."

"Can you drink something?"

Charlie nodded.

The other man came over, pulled out a flask and held it to Charlie's lips.

Charlie took a small sip, feeling the liquor burn all the way down. He was sure it wasn't a good idea, but he drank it anyway.

"Thanks."

The other man nodded. "You were on the ferry."

Charlie nodded then sat up and looked around.

"You pulled me out of the water."

"Off the skiff, actually."

There was a disturbance in the gangway and the man stepped aside to admit a woman with a cup of something steaming in her hands. She gave it to Charlie, meeting his eyes. "Thank you," she said.

Charlie blinked. "What for?'

The other two exchanged glances, then he saw the woman set her mouth in a grim line. "For rescuing my boy from certain death." She turned and looked daggers at the man.

"Shut up, woman. He doesn't need to know that."

"At least Mick's alive."

"He lost the cargo and the police have him."

"And whose fault is that?"

"His, you stupid besom. Get out of here."

Charlie put his eyes on the soup and drank it slowly, careful not to spill any of it.

"Why'd you do it? Go in after him?"

Charlie looked up and met the other man's eyes. "He was

just a boy."

"You could have drowned."

Charlie shrugged. "I owed God a life."

That got an interesting response from the other man. He blinked, then seemed to relax a bit. "Meaning you've killed someone."

Charlie nodded.

"Well, that's all right, then."

Charlie's eyebrows rose. He was beginning to put the pieces together. The man who stood watching him was on the wrong side of the law.

The man settled down on the berth opposite him. "You headed to Nova Scotia?"

Charlie nodded.

"Got a job lined up?"

"Maybe."

"Because courage like that, and the ability to use a knife, I could use a man like that."

Charlie was thinking hard, his brain slowly coming back to life. He looked at his host. "Is he your son?"

"Yeah. A total screw-up, but mine."

Charlie finished the soup. He brushed at his lips, trying to feel his way forward. "I would like to get to Nova Scotia and I would like to do it without the police knowing. Would that be possible?"

The other man raised an eyebrow. "Like that, is it? Yer a Yank."

Charlie nodded.

"Ah. Could be expensive."

"I could make it worth your while."

"Hmm. Got it on you?" He looked over at the pile of sodden clothes.

"No." If so, there was nothing to stop this man from

dropping Charlie back in the drink and helping himself to whatever Charlie owned.

"You could be lying."

"I could be telling the truth." Charlie considered the skipper, for it was clearly his boat. "I hadn't planned to go overboard."

"No. I don't suppose you did. So is it on the ferry?"

"Name your price."

"A thousand, Canadian, and I'll put you ashore in Nova Scotia, as far from the police as we can manage."

"Three hundred."

"Eight."

"Five."

"Seven."

"Six"

"Deal." The bandit's face split into a smile. "We're an hour out. I'll get you some dry clothes."

"Thanks."

Charlie waited until he was alone, then fished out the beacon and activated it. Hopefully Ginny would be able to pick up the signal. He was pretty sure the swim hadn't affected it. It hadn't the first time, but he didn't know the range and he didn't know when Ginny might have the opportunity to turn on her receiver.

His host returned promptly with dry clothes and a cup of hot coffee.

"Here. See how these do."

Charlie tried them on, his host watching.

"Not too bad." He nodded his approval. Charlie agreed.

The shirt was flannel and much warmer than the one he'd been wearing. The coat was heavy, but not as well made as the one he'd lost. He'd had to settle for his own boots, still wet from his swim, but they would dry and the socks were wool which meant they would be warm, wet or dry.

He pulled on the drawstring of the sweat pants, then reached for the beacon.

"What's that?"

"It's a key chain that floats."

"That might come in handy. Maybe I need that."

Charlie eyed his host. He did NOT want to lose the beacon. "I'm pretty sure you could get your own. Everyone has at least one back home. Anyone who fishes, anyway."

"Ah, yes. I like the idea. A souvenir of fishing you out of the Bay."

Charlie shrugged. "If you don't mind the fact that it says 'Texas' on it and someone might ask where you got it."

His host laughed. "I'll just say I found it floating." He held out his hand.

Charlie remained calm. He was entirely dependent on this man's goodwill. What's more, if he seemed to attach too much importance to the keychain, the captain might start wondering why. There was no way to tell if Ginny would try to follow the signal. She might think he was dead. Or the device might not be working. It might be out of range or the police might have Ginny's tracker. Charlie decided to cut his losses and find some other way to reach Ginny.

"And this?"

"My survival kit."

"Any drugs?"

"Aspirin." His prescription painkillers—along with the anti-depressants—were in Ginny's purse.

The captain opened the zips and poked at the contents with his finger, then pulled out the plastic container. He unscrewed the lid and looked inside.

"What'cha got in here?"

"Matches, tinder, fishhook."

"Hmm." He put the lid back on and stuck it back in the

miniature backpack, then tossed it over to Charlie. "You might need that. Snow's predicted for tonight. Here's yer knife. If it had been a gun, I'd've kept it, but that thing's no use to me."

Charlie nodded, tucking the survival kit into a pocket of the sweat pants and the *sgian dubh* into the top of his sock.

"Which brings us to this." The captain held up the thumb drive.

Charlie stared at it, realizing the tape must have come loose, or been pulled off by his rescuer. He felt his mouth go dry. Mandy! He'd almost lost Mandy!

"Pictures of my family."

"You don't mind if I look, do you?"

"Help yourself."

Charlie watched as the other man produced a small computer and plugged in the storage device.

"Pretty girl. These your daughters?"

"Yes."

"You left them behind?"

"They're dead."

The other man looked at him, his brow furrowing. "Something to do with that life you owed, I bet."

Charlie nodded.

"Did you kill them?"

Charlie felt a flash of anger. "No. I killed the man who killed them."

"Ah. So that's why you're here." The captain looked through the rest of the files while Charlie waited, then closed the folder and handed back the thumb drive.

"Sorry mate."

Charlie clipped the thumb drive to the drawstring of his pants and made sure it was secure.

The captain then pulled Charlie's wallet out and opened it, glanced at the fake ID, then at Charlie.

"I thought you said your name was Charlie?"

"That's the name my mother gave me. I won't be using it up here."

The other man nodded then turned to the cash section and removed the folding money. He counted it carefully.

"Here's what we're gonna do." He handed the wallet back to Charlie. "I'm gonna keep this," he put the money away in his own wallet, "and the credit card and your watch, as payment for services rendered, and put you ashore and we're gonna call it even, on account of the fact that you saved my miserable son's life. How's that?"

Charlie nodded.

"You don't know me. I don't know you. The clothes can't be traced so you can keep them or get rid of them. It doesn't matter."

He rose to his feet and Charlie followed him out onto the deck. They were met by a few curious glances, quickly averted, and one genuine smile from the wife, then Charlie found himself going over the side of the vessel.

They climbed down into the dinghy—Charlie was pretty sure it was the same one he'd found capsized, only there were oars in place this time—and settled down in the bottom of the boat. The fog was beginning to lift and there were patches of clear water ahead.

"The tide's coming in."

The other man rowed quietly toward the shore. Charlie had twice felt an urge to ask his name. It seemed only polite, but he'd controlled himself. It was clear that curiosity was not an asset under these circumstances and it was good practice for his new life.

"There aren't many places you can land on this part of the shore and the natives are nosey so I've arranged for a friend to meet you and take you to the crossroads."

The little boat pulled around a ragged wharf and grounded on a rough beach. Charlie clambered out.

"Straight on from here is the Canadian Forces Base. I suggest you steer clear of it. Backroads. That's what you want." The other man held out his hand. "Good luck, mate."

Charlie took his hand. "Thanks. You, too." He watched the other man climb back into the boat and pull away from shore, then disappear into the fog.

Charlie turned and headed up the ramp. It was rough going. The rocks slid out from under him at each step, his feet squelched in the damp boots, and the angle of incline had him panting. Good thing the cast was fiberglass, not plaster.

At the top of the slope stood a small car, a man leaning against the hood. He nodded to Charlie, then opened the passenger side door and gestured for Charlie to get in. They drove for fifteen minutes, Charlie seeing nothing along the way except snow covered fields, then the man pulled to a stop.

He leaned across Charlie and opened the door, indicating they had arrived at their destination. Charlie climbed out, then turned to thank the driver, who nodded, slammed the door closed, made a quick U-turn, and drove off without saying a word.

Charlie looked around. They were indeed at a crossroads, but there was no one on the road. He glanced at the sky, estimating the time from the winter sun, still hiding behind the clouds. Two or three hours of daylight left, maybe a bit more, if the snow held off.

He rubbed his forehead, trying to stimulate his brain. He was stranded in Nova Scotia with no way to contact Ginny or Jim or the Homestead. He didn't know where he was or how to get where he was going. He had lost his money and credit card, though he still had Laredo Pete's passport and driver's license, and the diamonds.

Well, first things first. Since he was still alive, he'd better see what he could do to stay that way. The road went either to the left or straight ahead. Straight ahead lay the military base. He shrugged his shoulders, turned left, and trudged off into the Nova Scotian winter.

* * *

Thursday Noon
Digby, Nova Scotia

Ginny sat huddled in a booth in the back of the pub and tried to think.

There was a TV in the corner of the bar. Not surprisingly, the local news was having a field day. They had gotten hold of eye witnesses and were interviewing them, most of them delighted to tell the lurid tale of sudden death. There was footage of the rescue—the boy being hauled aboard the ferry—and footage of Charlie diving into the water, climbing up on the whale's fluke, cutting the rope, then disappearing under the waves. She tried not to look at it. Tried not to cry when she couldn't help seeing it.

Her head came up as a man sat down in the seat opposite her, putting something down between them. She looked at the kindly, bearded face across the table from her.

"Drink. It will do you good."

Ginny regarded the bartender, for that was who it was, then nodded.

"Thank you." She picked up the drink and took a sip. It was not the best whisky she'd ever had, but it was not bad and it had the desired effect.

"I recognized you from the tube," he said, nodding at the television. "Friend of yours?"

Ginny shook her head. "No. We met on the boat." She took another sip of the Scotch. "It was a shock, seeing him die like that." In a moment of inspiration she added, "I had a brother." She let the lie hang in the air.

The bartender nodded. "Are you hungry?"

Ginny shook her head. "I'm fine, thank you. What do I owe you for the drink?"

"It's on the house and you should eat something. I'll be right back." He slid out before Ginny could protest. He was back in five minutes with an excellent fish stew and hot bread. In spite of herself, Ginny found it was possible to eat and the hollow feeling inside turned out to be partially her empty stomach.

Her host sat across from her, when he wasn't needed to tend the bar, asking questions and telling her about life in Digby. Ginny told him she was here to do some genealogical research and asked about historic sites, libraries, and any local specialties she shouldn't miss. He was well informed and very entertaining. An hour later she took her leave, feeling a good deal better.

She pulled out onto the roadway and headed for Nova Scotia 101, still with no idea what to do. The road ran parallel to the beach, the Bay of Fundy off to her left. Out there, somewhere, was Charlie. Out there, somewhere, was her reason for being here.

Digby was located on the inside of a large cove, sheltered from the wind and water, but most of the western shore of Nova Scotia was open to the Bay. According to the barman, there were lighthouses all along the shore, most of them still in use. Ginny wondered if there was any chance of seeing anything from one of the promontories. She spotted a sign, slowed for the turn, then headed for the coast.

The fog had lifted and she could see the water, though the sky still lowered, heavy with impending snow. She walked the cliffs for a bit, watching the tide rise in the Bay of Fundy.

Just so had women walked and gazed and ached for all the men lost to the sea, for a thousand years. How many men lost? How many women left behind? The tears were warm as they ran down her cheeks, until the wind hit them, then they felt cold as death.

Ginny was trying to be sensible. It had been his choice to save that boy. He died a hero's death. That was something. It was more than something. It was redemption.

She wiped her eyes, then pulled out the tracker. It was a morbid thought, but she should check to see if the beacon was sending. At the bottom of the bay, maybe. Or in the belly of a fish. He could have lost it, of course. It didn't have to be his body she was trying to locate.

Reggie had shown her how to press the edge of the tiny receiver, then touch the screen to activate the search. Nothing. Out of range, perhaps. Or not active. When had he had a chance to turn it on?

She looked up from the device, her eyes scanning the water. Would the body come ashore? Or would it wash out into the Atlantic on the next receding tide? The locals would know. They'd be looking. She swallowed another bout of tears, hunting for a tissue in her pocket, wiping her eyes, not really hearing the first faint response from the beacon.

It wasn't until she tried to brush a loose strand of hair back from her face, bringing the receiver up to her ear, that she heard it. She started, then looked down, then sat down hard on the ground. A blip, faint, and straight ahead of her, in the Bay. In the water.

She started crying again, then gave way to anger. She hadn't seen this coming when she agreed to accompany Jim on this trip. And where the *hell* was Jim anyway? Why wasn't he here, helping her? Why was she sitting all alone on a frozen cliff watching a dead man tumble through the waters of a frigid bay?

Angus had been wrong to trust her with Charlie. She'd managed to get him into Canada, but not to Halifax. Maybe Jim was right. Maybe she really wasn't up to the task.

She covered her face with her hands, rocking back and forth, then pulled herself together, wiped the tears away, and faced the situation.

She looked at the receiver again. The blip was still there, moving slightly. Not surprising. Waters were known to ebb and flow. If it was his body she was watching, she could follow it, find out where it came ashore and retrieve it, maybe, for a proper burial. The waters were still coming in, still rising.

Would the body come toward her? It wouldn't float, not yet, not until the gasses formed, so it wouldn't be on the surface. Nothing to see. Unless the beacon had come loose and was floating around on its own. That might come in. Her eyes were on the water, scanning the surface, hopeless, but looking anyway. That was how she saw it. Not a body, a boat.

Her heart leaped in her chest and she quashed it ruthlessly, but her heart had been right. Thirty minutes of watching convinced her the signal was coming from the boat. The signal was headed for Digby. So was the boat. The tide was still rising in the opposite direction. The signal, whether a body or a man or just a floating keychain, was on that boat.

* * *

Chapter 44

Jim slept through breakfast Thursday morning. He'd been up very late, letting his grandfather know that Ginny and Charlie were trapped in New Brunswick, and trying to come up with a plan.

He slipped past the door to the Great Room and helped himself to the lunch buffet laid out in the dining area. He had the room to himself and that suited him just fine. In his present mood he didn't want to talk to anyone.

He finished his meal, then got another cup of coffee and wandered back to the Great Room. It had a huge TV mounted on one wall with more than a dozen people in front of it. They were making noises Jim classified as 'ghoulish,' the kind onlookers make when watching a horrific scene, usually involving blood and body parts.

He stepped into the room and approached the back of the crowd, his eyes on them, then on the screen. He watched for a moment as the announcer explained what they were seeing.

"In a spectacular feat of bravery today, an unknown man dove off the ferry, swam over to a passing whale, and freed a teenager that had somehow gotten caught in a rope twisted around the animal's tail. The boy was rescued by the ferry. The man has not been found and is presumed dead. The story is even more remarkable because several passengers were filming the whale and caught the whole thing on camera. Here is an exclusive, first-hand look at what happened."

Jim had his coffee to his lips as the picture changed. He stared, then realized what he was looking at.

"Ginny!" He dropped the coffee.

Several people turned to look at him.

"That's Ginny!" He pointed at the image, gone as soon as seen. "Can we get it back?"

Mrs. Robertson had hurried over to deal with the spill.

"Come with me," she said.

Jim found her hand on his arm, pulling him first into the kitchen, then beyond it to an elevator. She took him up three levels, then led him into a room full of electronic equipment.

"Henry, can you pull up the noon news, please?"

"Which channel?"

"Let's start with CBC."

Jim watched as the tech pulled up the Canadian Broadcasting Company feed.

"What are we looking for?" he asked.

"Something about a whale in the Bay of Fundy."

"Oh, that!" The young man spun a few controls and the image of the ferry popped onto the screen. He let it roll.

Jim watched over his shoulder. "There! Freeze that!"

"Can't. We'll need to do a frame by frame to get anything other than copyright image and blur. Watch it again."

He launched the clip again, then two more times. By the end of the third viewing, Jim was sure.

"That's Ginny. She was on that ferry." What's more, the man who had dived off the ferry and saved the boy's life was Charlie.

"Can you get me a copy of that clip? Something I can put on

a computer?"

"Sure. I'll collect the rest of them, too."

Jim turned to the Matron. "I'm going to Digby. I don't know when I'll be back."

"How can we help?"

"Make a copy of that footage and send it to Angus Mackenzie."

Jim grabbed his coat and keys, then flew down the stairs and out the front door, cursing the snow that now lay on the SUV, forcing him to sweep it off before he could drive the vehicle. Even so, he was out the gates and on the road to Digby in twenty minutes. He pulled out the burner phone and called Himself.

"Grandfather!"

"Auch Jim! Ye sound a wee bit flistert."

Jim explained the incident on the ferry, his words tumbling over one another, forcing him to repeat himself to be understood.

"Charlie dove off th' ship?"

"And saved the boy's life. Yes."

"Ginny was wi' him?"

"Yes."

"Where is she noo?"

"I don't know. I'm on my way to Digby to see if I can pick up her trail."

"Let me know, lad, when ye find her."

"I will."

Jim hung up the phone, but left it turned on, cradled beside him in the car. Now, with Charlie no longer in danger from the police, maybe *now* she'd call. He set his jaw and drove as fast as he dared toward Digby and the ferry dock.

* * *

Thursday Afternoon
Nova Scotia 101

Ginny ran to the car, turned it around and headed back toward Digby, the tracker out on the seat beside her. It took her several tries and two hours, but she finally managed to locate the pier where the fishing trawler had pulled in. She found a place to wait and watched as a couple, obviously in the midst of a quarrel, got into a battered truck and headed into the town. The signal was coming from that truck. No Charlie.

Her heart sank again. Still, if that man had the beacon, he could tell her something. How had he gotten it? Could she ask him to give it to her? What would he think? Nothing good, she suspected.

She followed the couple into the city and straight to the police station. Ginny caught her breath. She couldn't follow them in there. She found a parking space and settled down to watch the doors. Sure enough, an hour later they emerged with a boy in tow, *the* boy, the one Charlie had rescued.

Ginny tailed them back across town to a rather grubby neighborhood full of tract housing. She let them unload their unhappy cargo, the man cuffing the boy as the argument continued, showing her which door to approach.

Ginny carefully pulled out the velvet bag with the loose gemstones in it and looked them over. The most impressive was a dark blue topaz. It was larger than the others, being almost the size of her thumbnail, a fine quality, not absolutely flawless, but close, and cut to sparkle in any light at almost any angle.

It was all she had to bargain with and she might not need it, but it was better to be prepared. She tucked the other jewels away and climbed out of the car. The light was fading and she could feel snowflakes settling on her cheeks as she knocked on the door.

It took a moment, but eventually the woman came to answer the knock.

"Yeah?" She looked Ginny up and down.

"I'm looking for the man who saved your son's life."

The woman hesitated for a fraction of a second. "We haven't seen him."

Ginny put on her coldest expression, hoping she was being mistaken for someone with a badge under her coat. "You have either seen him alive or seen him dead, or both."

The woman's eyes flickered. She studied Ginny for a moment, then stepped back to let her in, then closed the door behind her. She looked Ginny in the face. "He was alive when he left the boat."

Ginny nodded. She might be lying, but she might be telling the truth. "You have a keychain you took off of him. I'd like it back."

By this time the man had joined his wife. "What's going on here?"

The woman answered, her eyes still on Ginny. "She wants the keychain."

The man turned to look at her, one eyebrow raised. "How do you know about that?"

"None of your business." Ginny tried to make it sound harsh and true. She crossed her arms on her chest and looked at him, imagining him as the face on her paper target, her gun settling down to make nice little groupings; eyes, nose, forehead. It must have worked for he shifted his weight from one foot to the other, looking uncomfortable.

"It ain't worth nothing."

"Then you won't mind giving it back."

The man had pulled the keychain out of his pocket. "It has sentimental value. But I tell you what." The man looked up.

"You can buy it off of me."

"You want a reward for returning stolen property?"

"I saved his life. That deserves something."

"He saved your son. You're even. Where'd you put him?"

"Ah, well. Information costs extra."

"Did he offer to pay you?"

"Yeah. One thousand Canadian, but all he had on him was five hundred."

She nodded. "I'll make up the difference." She pulled the gemstone out of her pocket, but didn't show it to them, yet. "Where did you put him?"

"Margaretsville, on the ramp. That's the last I saw of him."

Ginny held out her hand for the keychain. When he handed it over, Ginny turned to the woman and took her hand, placing the topaz in the center of it. "This should settle the debt."

The woman gasped. Her husband came over then reached out and touched the jewel with his fingertip.

Ginny seized the momentary distraction and slipped out. She jumped into the car, threw it in gear, and took off. She followed the signs to the 101 and headed for Margaretsville.

It took her an hour to get up the coast to the turn off. Margaretsville was another historic lighthouse. Ginny found herself back on the coast, this time in a snowstorm, with almost zero visibility, and both beacon and receiver in her possession. Nonetheless, she parked the car, got out and started searching, calling Charlie's name and trying to separate the whistle of the wind from the sound a man in trouble might make. She had a flashlight. He would see that, even if he couldn't hear her.

She kept an eye on the time. Charlie was no fool. He wouldn't have stayed on the beach with the weather moving in. He'd have found some sort of shelter. She chewed her lip, trying to think.

That blood-sucking pirate had taken Charlie's money and probably anything else he thought could be converted into cash. Charlie needed a warm place to spend the night and he couldn't go far, not on that broken leg. He was here, somewhere.

Ginny soothed herself with the common sense of this line of thought. Best case scenario, he was in a house or other solid shelter, but, in this storm, she would never know it. Worst case scenario, he was lying in a ditch and she would still never know.

She got back in the car and spent another three hours driving up and down the coast road from Margarestville to Port George, then back again, as far as Harbourville. No bodies in the ditch and no Charlie hobbling out of the snow in response to her call.

When she finally decided she could do no more in the dark, with the snow coming down, she made her way into the nearest town, located a bed and breakfast, and settled in for the night.

Ginny hugged the knowledge to her heart that Charlie had survived the whale, had been picked up by the pirate, and had been deposited on the coast—alive—just hours ago. She frowned at the thought of his spending the night in the snow. She wanted to call in every resource available, to mount a full-scale search and rescue mission, but that could not be hidden from the police.

She wished she'd thought to give Charlie the number to Gordon's spare phone, but she hadn't expected them to be separated, or him to be separated from the beacon.

The Canadian police had known where to look for Charlie, had set a trap for him. She couldn't trust the phones, couldn't trust the natives, couldn't trust anyone but herself. Jim might have done a better job, but Jim wasn't here, and she was. It was up to her to figure out how to find Charlie and get him safely to Halifax.

Ginny was bone tired, but she couldn't sleep. She tossed and turned and dozed, waking frequently, her mind struggling with the problem of her missing menfolk. The night seemed to stretch into eternity, but under such conditions, even eternity passes. The darkness slowly turned to dawn and she rose to begin the search again.

* * *

Chapter 45

Charlie limped along the edge of the road, grateful for the help he'd received, but wishing it had extended to a lift into Halifax. He had located a thick branch to use as a substitute cane, but his leg throbbed and he was tired and hungry and wanted nothing more than a warm bed and twenty-four hours of uninterrupted sleep.

When she knew they would be landing in Digby, Ginny had pulled up a map of Nova Scotia. The two of them had studied it, tracing the road system and calculating the distance they would still have to travel.

It was a sort of peninsula that ran roughly northeast to southwest. The main road to Halifax crossed the landmass halfway up. Charlie pulled out his survival kit and located the compass. The road he was on angled northeast.

On the grounds that he'd seen the ferry south of him when he was in the water, Digby was south of him now. They had stayed in the Bay of Fundy, so he was still on the western shore of Nova Scotia, Halifax being on the eastern shore. What he didn't know was whether the Canadian Forces Base was north or south of the main road. He should have thought to ask that.

He glanced up and down the road, seeing nothing. The

route seemed deserted. There were no lights and no houses and no evidence of civilization, except the pavement under his feet. Just the wind and the cold and the lowering sky. He settled his wool cap more securely, pulled the heavy seaman's coat up around his ears, and set off, counting the steps.

Two thousand steps equaled (roughly) a mile. Charlie had reached one thousand seventy-five before he found a road sign. It didn't help. All he learned was that he was on NS-221 E. No mention of Halifax.

He rested for a moment and tried to get into Ginny's head. They were separated, with no way to communicate. He couldn't even tell her he was alive. What would she think? Probably, that he had drowned.

If she decided he wasn't dead, or she didn't want to accept it, she would follow the beacon, expecting to find him, and find the smuggler instead. Charlie felt his skin crawl at the thought of Ginny in the hands of that man.

If she somehow managed to avoid both mistakes, she still wouldn't know where to look. The only firm point of reference was Halifax. Sooner or later, she would have to go to Halifax.

His best bet was to find the main road and stay on it until she drove by. So, stick to the highway, head for Halifax, and hide unless he saw her. He trudged off.

An hour later he'd changed his mind. The highest priority was no longer trying to get to Halifax, it was finding shelter for the night. Route 221 was clearly rural. He'd seen two farms, but nothing else. The snow had started and the light was going. He scanned the fields around him, selected a likely-looking building and headed off cross-country.

It was a barn and the sounds (and smells) coming from it indicated livestock, which meant heat and drinkable water. He examined the exterior, looking for signs of a security system.

He followed the wall, turned a corner and found a door. No

lock, just a latch. He eased it open, alert to a booby trap, but there was nothing. No lights, no siren, no dogs. He slipped inside and closed the door behind him.

He stood very still for a moment, giving his senses a chance to evaluate the situation. The wind whistled through loose boards and somewhere off to the right a shutter was banging against the wall. There was no artificial light, not even an LED, so no electronics, and it was cold. On the other hand, there was hay.

He waited until his eyes adjusted to the interior, then found he could make out shapes. He identified the main door, and the stalls. He could hear animals moving; slow, contented sounds. To his right were bales of hay. He slipped toward them, feeling his way forward, located a good spot, and sat down.

The great thing about hay is that it puts out heat as it decomposes. He had his back up against one bale and another on his left side, a barrier against the wind and cold. He sat there, eyes closed, for a long time, his thirst keeping him awake. Also, his leg hurt.

Another hour and he'd decided he needed water more than he needed stealth. He pulled out his survival kit and extracted the glowstick. It was small, about the size of his index finger, and wouldn't put out much light, but under these conditions it would seem very bright indeed. He activated it and looked around. Two cows, both ignoring him.

He located a bucket, filled it with snow, and set it on the hay to melt. He scooped a few handfuls of snow into his mouth before he closed up again. With the worst of the thirst partially assuaged, he made his way back to his seat, pulled some loose hay out to make a bed, got his emergency blanket out of his survival kit, and settled down to sleep.

He sent a quick prayer of thanks, by way of Mandy, for the rescue and the hay, then composed his soul for the night.

Tomorrow, whether he could find Ginny or not, he would have to head for Halifax, though how he was going to do that with no money, on a broken leg, and with the police after him, he had yet to figure out.

* * *

Thursday Afternoon
Dallas, TX

At four p.m., Central Standard Time, on the same day Charlie went into the Bay of Fundy, Angus Mackenzie opened his door to Detective Tran. She refused his offer of coffee, but accepted a seat in the living room.

"How may I help ye, Detective?"

She met his gaze. "I would like to visit the Halifax Homestead. I believe you can make that possible."

Himself lifted both eyebrows. The wee detective had managed to figure it out, had she?

"'Tis an inhospitable time o' year fer sightseeing. May I ask wha's behind this request?"

"I wish to see Miss Forbes, who I understand is staying there at present."

Himself frowned. "Oh, aye? And wha' do ye need Miss Ginny for?"

The detective's eyes remained steadily on his, cool and apparently sure of his response. "I am hoping to close the case on Charles Monroe. To do that I must interview the eyewitness."

"Eyewitness?"

Detective Tran gave him a bland expression. "Perhaps you have not yet seen the video footage showing Mr. Monroe sacrificing himself to save a boy from drowning. Miss Forbes shows clearly in the images. Since there is only one Homestead in Nova Scotia, I assume she is there."

Tran leaned forward. "I need her testimony. If I am able to confirm the death, I can close the books on the case, which I think you will find a desirable outcome."

The Laird's eyebrows drew together. "'Tis never desirable tae lose a clansman."

"No. I should think not. Will you arrange it?"

"When do ye wish tae go?"

"Tomorrow. I plan to stay just the one night and fly back on Saturday."

Angus studied the woman's face. She was right. A quick end to this manhunt would be good for everyone involved. "I'll mak' th' arrangements."

He rose and escorted the officer out, watching her get into her car and drive off before closing his door.

A formidable woman. She left him with an uneasy feeling about the fate of his grandson and Ginny. He'd already talked to the lawyers and been assured they were safe, as long as Charlie wasn't found alive. So why did the look in that woman's eye give him the feeling the lawyers were wrong? He picked up the phone and started making calls. No mere guest this one. She would need careful handling.

* * *

Thursday Night
Halifax Homestead

Jim pulled onto the Homestead grounds and found a parking spot near the door. The snow was coming down steadily, had been for hours. He'd been checking with the Homestead at intervals, hoping to hear that Ginny had arrived safely, but no such luck. Still no word from her and still no response to his phone and text messages.

He was tired and frustrated and confused. Why hadn't she shown up?

He'd been able to confirm she got off the ferry and rented a car. A bit of asking around had also located a barman who'd seen her, had recognized her from the TV footage and been kind to her. Jim almost hugged him, but settled for a truly hearty handshake and the purchase of an expensive bottle from behind the bar.

So she was warm and fed and mobile as of one p.m. What had happened after that? Where had she gone? Why hadn't she come on to the Homestead? She should have been here by four at the outside. Instead, she had vanished.

Jim trudged up to the front door and let himself in. He'd given the information on the rental car to Reggie. His other idea he'd taken directly to Himself.

The main road, NS-101, was a standard highway, well-traveled, even in bad weather, and with traffic patrols. If Ginny'd had an accident, someone should have noticed. Himself agreed it was worth a try and promised to follow up, but pointed out that asking those kinds of questions would draw official attention. Why not give her another day? She was probably just waiting out the storm.

Jim had argued, insisting that, since Charlie was dead and Ginny was missing, the delay didn't make sense. Himself had been sympathetic, but firm and Jim had reluctantly agreed to give Reggie a few hours to see what he could do.

But he didn't like it. Especially when the wind managed to cut through his coat, reminding him of the dangers of hypothermia. She might be fine, lying snug in a bed somewhere. Or she might be lying unconscious on the side of the road. How was he to live with himself if she could have been found, could have been saved, if only he'd known where to look? His only comfort was that he hadn't been troubled by the Sight—no feeling that Ginny was in danger. Not that he put any stock in that, of course.

There ought to be some way to reach her, some way the police couldn't use, to find her. Something he knew that no one else did. He fell asleep with the sick feeling he was missing something, overlooking something, something obvious, but he couldn't figure out what it was. It haunted his dreams and when he woke, he felt as if he hadn't slept at all.

* * *

Thursday Night
Dallas, TX

It was approaching midnight and Angus Mackenzie peered over Reggie's shoulder, watching him work.

"You realize," Reggie said, "there will be hell to pay when Jim finds out."

"Aye, but it canna be helped."

"We could tell him where she is."

"We could tell him where th' car is."

"And the beacon."

"Aye, and th' beacon, and th' receiver." Angus sighed. "Is there any way tae tell if 'tis the lass or Charlie or someone else we're seein'?"

Reggie shook his head. "Here's what I can tell you. The beacon was activated at eleven twenty-nine a.m., Atlantic time, which is fifty seven minutes after Charlie went overboard. GPS coordinates put the activation just over twenty-one nautical miles out from Digby, in the Bay of Fundy. The signal then moves up the coastline to a point off Margaretsville. It sits there for about twenty minutes, then heads back to Digby where it stays until six p.m. local when it starts back up the coast, this time on land. It wanders a bit over the next three hours, then finally settles at the coordinates for Middleton, Nova Scotia. One hour later, it goes dark." He took a breath.

"The receiver I gave Ginny went live at two p.m. It follows the beacon back to Digby where the two signals merge. The receiver follows the same route as the beacon, then, five minutes after we lose the beacon, the receiver also goes offline."

"Wha' does it mean?" Angus asked.

Reggie looked up at him. "At a guess, whoever has possession turned them off."

"Th' same person has them both?"

"Yes."

"And tha' person is staying in Middleton."

"It looks like it."

"Wha' aboot th' car?"

"I accessed the third party database that tracks the rental car locations. They collect the GPS coordinates in case someone has a wreck or steals the car. It's supposed to be confidential, but the security is almost non-existent. Using the information Jim gave us about the make, model, and year, I was able to get the Vehicle Identification Number, then locate the file. That car followed the same path as the receiver."

"Which implies it's Ginny wha has possession o' the beacon and th' receiver."

"Now, yes, it does."

"I dinna follow."

Reggie turned his chair around and faced the Laird. "The receiver went live in a location on the Nova Scotia coastline. The beacon went live out in the middle of the Bay of Fundy. If Charlie activated the beacon and it was in his possession when the beacon met the receiver in Digby, then the two of them are together."

"Meanin' Charlie is alive."

"Meaning Charlie *may have been* alive for some period of time after he went into the water. But if they met up in Digby, why didn't they drive straight to Halifax? And why did the two devices and the car spend time going up and down the Nova Scotia coastline?" Reggie lifted an eyebrow. "It's at least possible the person who brought the beacon ashore wasn't Charlie. That person might also have met up with Ginny, conked her on the head and taken possession of both devices and the car."

Angus shook his head. "That doesnae make sense. A stranger wouldna' know about th' beacon and wouldna' care if he did. He might steal th' car, but why go up and doon th' coastline then? I'm thinkin' 'twas Ginny huntin' fer Charlie."

"In which case, Charlie got separated from his beacon and Ginny did not find him when she followed the signal. I wonder what she *did* find."

"And wha' about th' Bed and Breakfast?"

"Someone using Ginny's credit card checked into a B&B in Middleton."

"But she's no answerin' th' phone."

"You told her not to."

Angus sighed. "Aye. I told her tae call only if 'twas an emergency."

Reggie nodded slowly. "Which implies she has a very interesting way of defining 'emergency'." He chewed on his lip. "If we assume it was Ginny in possession of both devices and the car, trolling the coastline for Charlie, then she hasn't found him, but she must think there's a chance she will, or she'd have gone on to Halifax. Which means she either knows or is hoping he's still alive."

"Which means, we must keep th' secret a while longer."

Angus sighed. "I prefer tae believe she's safe, holed up in th' cottage in Middleton, but I see it might not be so." He laid a hand on Reggie's shoulder. "Find a way tae get a message through, Reggie. I need tae know it's her."

* * *

CHAPTER 46

Friday Early Morning
Margaretsville, NS

The cows woke him. It was still dark, but Charlie knew he needed to be gone before the farmer came to milk them. The snow in the bucket had melted from the heat coming off the hay. He drank, then put the bucket back where he found it, packed up his meagre gear, and slipped out.

The snow had stopped, though the sky still hung heavy with clouds. He made his way across the field, hoping no one would notice he was leaving tracks, and hobbled off in the direction of the road. Moving would help keep him warm, but today he would have to find more than just a barn for shelter.

By sun up Charlie had made his way back to the road. It was deserted. So, where was Ginny? Still in Digby? Had she gone on to Halifax? Could he phone the Homestead maybe? Ask them to send a car for him? Charlie frowned at the thought. They wouldn't know his voice and he couldn't be sure he wasn't talking to a policeman.

What he needed was a kind soul who wouldn't turn him in on sight. Not to mention the fact that he was getting rather hungry, having eaten nothing but snow since yesterday noon. The cash was gone, but he had the diamonds. Who would buy a diamond from him? Not a thief. He'd just kill Charlie and take the diamond and everything else he could find. A reputable dealer then. Of diamonds? Here?

Charlie's eyes narrowed. Where there were soldiers, there were pawn shops. According to the sign, North Kingston was two miles further up the road, handy to the Canadian Forces Base. No guarantees, of course. Charlie sighed, squared his shoulders, and set off for town, in the hope of finding food, a pawn shop, and transportation to Halifax.

* * *

Friday Morning
Middleton, NS

Ginny was alone in the breakfast area with the television on. She didn't have to wait long before the station threw a photo of Charlie on the screen. They had decided he was drowned. There had been so many witnesses to his disappearance and no evidence of him being picked up by any of the boats in the area. The skippers had all been interviewed and all said they had not seen him.

Ginny's mouth set in a hard line. She knew of at least one skipper who had seen him.

The boy had been instantly identified by the police as a known drug runner and his father, the owner of a boat suspected of being involved. The boat had been searched and the boy and father questioned carefully, but no evidence of Charlie—or drugs—had been found. So the police had let them go. That explained both the police station and the father's willingness to take money, rather than fame, for rescuing Charlie.

The police were asking for the public's help in locating any evidence of the dead man and directing them to several social media outlets. Ginny grabbed a pen and wrote down the addresses. With that many pairs of eyes, it was possible someone had seen or heard something and she couldn't hope to find every inhabitant of Nova Scotia as unprincipled as the drug runner. They might turn him in before she could reach him.

Ginny finished her breakfast, trying to decide how to tackle the search for Charlie. Assuming he had been alive and in reasonably good health when he was put ashore, then he was somewhere in the area.

Finding him if he was in shelter would be a problem, since she had no idea who it would be safe to ask what of. Finding him if he was outside meant investigating any lump of snow large enough to be human, alive or dead. Was there any way to tell what might be him and what was just a refuse pile coated in snow?

At that moment Ginny experienced something she identified as the fortuitous coming together of the right question and the right useless bit of data buried in her mind. It had happened before. She seized the thread and followed it to its source.

Human beings, live ones, put out heat as a byproduct of cellular metabolism. A human, either alive or recently dead, would register as a heat source among all this snow. What she needed was something that could detect a hot spot in the woods. And she knew just where to find one.

The public Internet in the lobby gave her the address of a hunting and fishing supply store just up the road. She wrote it down, paid her bill, and headed out.

She had to wait a half hour for the store to open, but had no trouble describing what she wanted. She got a few sideways looks, but she smiled and explained it was a present for her boyfriend whose birthday was coming up. She bought extra batteries, made sure the Game Finder worked before she left the store, then turned back toward Digby and the section of Nova Scotia coast just south of Margaretsville.

By lunchtime she was sure he wasn't anywhere in the area. She was both relieved and disappointed. He wasn't hunkered down in a haystack and he wasn't a decaying body in a ditch on the side of the road. He was in shelter somewhere. But where was she to look next?

* * *

Friday Morning
NS-103 W

Jim had eaten breakfast, then hit the roads again as soon as he could get the car rolling. There had been no news during the night, no new clues as to what had happened to Ginny. He hadn't seen anything of her on the main road yesterday, so today he was searching the alternate route, the longer, less traveled way from Digby to Halifax, looking for signs of car trouble, of violence, of something to explain her absence.

He had nothing to do but think. He had to get into her head, to understand what she was doing. Why had she chosen (he grimly clung to the belief that she was still in a condition to choose) not to come straight on to the Halifax Homestead?

She couldn't feel good today. Not if she was human. With Charlie dead, she had failed to complete the task Himself had set for them. Failed spectacularly, on camera, for the whole world to see. What would her conscience demand of her, before she could admit defeat?

She would need to do everything she could think of, before asking for help. She had seen Charlie die. She probably had seen the subsequent news coverage. She would know how little chance there was of finding him, either alive or dead, and how much more likely it was the authorities would get there first, but she would look.

Jim's eyes narrowed. She would look.

He pulled the car over to the side of the road and grabbed his wallet. It was still there. He pulled the half-a-credit-card sized device out of the slot and examined it. He hadn't given it a single thought since Reggie had handed it to him, one to him, one to Ginny, explaining how they worked.

Charlie had the beacon and would have to turn it on. Both receivers could follow that signal, but they, too, had to be turned on and within the fifty mile radius to pick up the signal. Jim closed his eyes and tried to remember exactly what Reggie had said. Unlike the beacon, the receivers used the GPS system, which made them trackable, so the safest thing to do, if you didn't want to attract attention, was to leave them off until needed. He slid his finger along the edge until he found the power button. The device sprang to life.

Jim found his mouth dry. This was what his subconscious had been trying to tell him yesterday. If Ginny was hunting for Charlie—or Charlie's body—she would have her device on. If Charlie's beacon was on, Jim could follow it, too.

But even if the beacon wasn't on, and it was doubtful Charlie had activated it before he jumped overboard, Reggie could still find her, using the GPS in her receiver, and tell Jim where she was, and he could go to her.

Jim pulled the burner phone out and dialed home.

"Aye, Jim?"

"I've thought of something." He explained his theory.

"Auch. 'Tis a good thought. I'll ask Reggie tae look."

"And you'll let me know?"

"Th' minute we find her, aye."

Jim put the phone away, then set the receiver on the

console, the sound turned all the way up and angled so he could glance down at it as he drove. He put the car in gear and pulled back out onto the roadway.

It explained the delay. She had stayed in the area, to see if she could find the beacon, and been caught by the weather.

Jim swallowed hard. If he was right, she was coping with a shattering loss, by herself, handicapped by the need to keep away from the authorities until she was sure there was no hope. When she was certain she could no longer hurt Charlie, she would call.

Jim felt his chest tighten. He could imagine her, alone, in despair, weeping for the loss of Charlie, blaming herself, and unwilling to face the truth. If he could find her, he could take her in his arms and explain it wasn't her fault, that she could not have prevented this tragedy. She knew, she must know, he wouldn't blame her, and, as the hours ticked by, it seemed more and more apparent that she was chasing a ghost. She should come in.

He looked out at the bleak countryside, covered in bleak snow, and thought bleak thoughts about life and death and misery.

* * *

CHAPTER 47

Friday Morning
North Kingston, NS

The pawn shop wasn't open yet. Without so much as a dime in his pocket Charlie could not buy breakfast so he settled down to wait. He found a back corner, sheltered from the wind and heated by the building against which he leaned. It wasn't exactly the Ritz, but it was comfortable enough.

When he woke, it was to the smell of coffee somewhere close by. Boy! What he wouldn't give for a cup of coffee!

He hauled himself to his feet and went back to the Pawn Shop. He pushed on the door and let himself in.

The proprietor's smile faded as he took in Charlie's generally disreputable appearance. "How can I help you?"

Charlie had already pulled the largest of the diamonds out of its hiding place and had it in his hand. "You want the truth?"

"That is usually the best choice."

"I have run away from home, had my cash and credit cards stolen, and need to sell something to get back on the road."

"You don't look as if you have anything I'd be interested in."

Charlie nodded. "I don't blame you for doubting me. I'm sure you have to be careful." He pulled out the fake ID and glibly recited the information on it. Reggie had gone to the trouble of making it look as if the Texas driver's license had been in "Pete's" wallet for at least a year and the immersion in the Bay of Fundy had added to that effect.

Charlie then pulled out the diamond and set it on the counter. He scowled at it. "I should never have bought that thing in the first place."

The proprietor picked up the stone, then pulled a loupe out of his pocket. He examined the gem closely and Charlie saw something that looked like greed in his eye, just for a moment.

"You had this hidden?"

"I did."

"How do I know it's not stolen?"

Charlie was prepared. Ginny had given him particulars on the gemstones, knowing he'd probably have to negotiate with a suspicious buyer. He pointed at the stone.

"*That* is a one carat round, VS1, clarity grade E, cut grade ideal, for which I paid almost five thousand U.S. dollars last November."

"May I ask why you bought it?"

"I was planning on having it set as an engagement ring."

The proprietor looked up from the stone. "And why are you selling it now?"

"Because the woman I bought it for is why I'm not at home right now. I expect I'll get over the mad eventually and go back to Texas, but even then, I won't want that stone. I'd much rather have a motorcycle."

The proprietor's lips twitched. He set the diamond back down on the velvet tray. In the lights of the jewelry counter, it exploded with fire and in that moment Charlie saw why a woman might want a colorless stone. He'd never understood that before.

"We don't deal in loose stones. There's no market for them."

Charlie looked at him, his eyes narrowing. "Ever been

married?"

"No."

"Take my advice. Steer clear of it." He pointed to the diamond again. "When I showed that to her she said it wasn't big enough. That's when I decided she wasn't sweet enough." He sighed. "Look, I get it. You don't trust me. Why should you? But here's the deal. I don't want that stone. I need money and I'm willing to take a loss on it. Can you help me?"

The proprietor looked at him for a long moment.

"One thousand, Canadian."

"Three."

"Fifteen hundred and that's my final offer."

Charlie looked at him, then nodded. "I'll take it and chalk the rest up to experience."

"Very good, sir. I'll start the paperwork."

It took him twenty minutes to fill in all the information necessary to complete the sale, at which point Charlie picked up the money and thanked him.

"If you ever get to Texas, look me up. I'll show you around the spread and you can pet a longhorn."

Charlie let himself out of the shop, thinking that Ginny had been right about how hard it might be to sell the stones, but the plan had produced some badly needed cash so he was happy.

He turned up the street, located a diner and bought himself breakfast. He sat in a booth and watched the TV screen. Sure enough, before he had finished, his face appeared. This time the banner said he was presumed dead and the police were hunting for the body.

So he was dead, was he? That should take some of the heat off. He ran his hand over his chin. Maybe he should keep the face fungus. A beard would make a good disguise.

He finished his meal, threw some money down on the table

and headed out to the motorcycle store. He had no trouble finding it, but there he hit a snag.

Not only were the used machines too expensive (the cheapest costing twice what he had in pocket), but the regulations required documents he didn't have (motorcycle rider's license and insurance). He reluctantly gave up the idea and asked for advice on how to get to Halifax.

He was directed to a car hire service on the other side of the highway. Here he had a bit of luck.

First, the salesman at the motorcycle shop gave him a ride. (They had struck up a friendship over inspecting the machines.) Second, the car hire had a car available and the owner wanted it delivered to the Halifax airport.

The man behind the counter was on the phone. "What do you mean you can't?" There was a pause. "I don't have anyone else! You can be sick later. Suck it up and get over here." Clenched fist and dark scowl. "Don't bother." If it had been a landline, Charlie was sure he would have seen the receiver slammed down. As it was, the owner of the device stabbed at it hard enough to mark the screen.

The proprietor took a deep breath, then turned to Charlie, not yet able to be cordial, but trying to be professional.

"What can I do for you?"

"I'm told I can get a ride from here to Halifax."

The man behind the counter looked at him, his eyes narrowing. "Halifax?"

"Yes."

"Today?"

"Yes. Is that going to be possible?"

"No. My driver is sick."

"Is there a bus station, then?"

The proprietor shook his head. "The buses stopped running years ago. Not enough demand."

"Train, then?"

"You've missed it."

Charlie felt his spirits sag. Was he going to have to walk to Halifax after all?

The man behind the counter looked at him, frowning slightly. "Can you drive a car?"

Charlie looked back. "I can, but I can't rent one. My credit cards were stolen."

The agent's eyes narrowed. "You look like you've been through the wars."

Charlie agreed. "I was mugged and tossed in a snow drift two days ago. But I have friends in Halifax who can help, if I can reach them."

The other man sucked in his cheeks. "Why didn't you call the police?"

"I did. They filed a report and said they couldn't take me all the way to Halifax."

The man eyed him in silence for moment.

"You got any money?"

Charlie nodded.

"What about a license?"

Charlie pulled out Laredo Pete's driver's license and handed it over.

The agent looked at it, then at Charlie, then seemed to make up his mind.

"The company won't let me rent a car without a credit card, but I can hire anyone I want to ferry cars from place to place." He looked down at the driver's license. "Texas. Never met anyone from Texas before."

Charlie smiled. "Well now you have."

The other man nodded. "Normally I'd use a local man, one I know and who lives here so I can track him down if I need to."

Charlie nodded. "Sound policy." He waited for the 'but'.

"But I am between a rock and a hard place." He fell silent, obviously weighing the risks. Charlie waited patiently.

The agent heaved a big sigh, then seemed to warm up to the idea.

"I have a contract to deliver a car to the Halifax airport. It has to be there by three p.m. My driver is sick and I will have to go myself if I can't replace him." He studied Charlie's face for another long moment and Charlie began to be afraid he would make the connection with the news reports.

"Are you willing to drive to the Halifax airport and leave the car there and can you get there before three p.m.?"

Charlie nodded. "I am and I can."

The agent nodded. "All right, then. I'll call my contact at the airport. He'll pay you two hundred, cash, when you deliver the car in good condition and on time."

Charlie stuck out his hand. "Deal."

The other man shook it. "I'll have the GPS tracker on. Don't break the law. I don't want any questions. You're responsible for gas. Make sure the tank is full when you turn it in."

"Yes, sir."

The agent glanced at the clock. "Better get started."

He came around the counter and spotted Charlie's limp.

"Can you drive with your leg like that?"

Charlie nodded. "As long as it's an automatic."

"It is." They went out to the lot and the agent made sure everything was in order, then waved as Charlie drove out of the parking lot.

Charlie found himself wondering just how often human beings were willing to ignore common sense for the sake of profit. He shrugged, then pulled out onto Nova Scotia 101 and headed for Halifax.

* * *

CHAPTER 48

Friday Noon
Middleton, NS

Ginny located a café where she could get lunch and plan where to look next. The limiting factor was his leg.

She spread a map of Nova Scotia out on the table, trying to decide how far and how fast Charlie could go. Considering he was male and young and really pretty strong, it seemed likely he could do about half what an uninjured average human being could do. That meant a walking pace of less than two miles per hour, maybe as little as one, if you factored in the snow.

She took the elastic band off the end of her braid and put her finger in one end of it and set it on the coastline below Margaretsville. Then she set a pencil in the other end of the elastic, pulled it out to measure one mile, and marked the map in a semicircle around his starting point. She did the same for the two mile radius, then looked at her work.

Two hours. He'd been set down at about one p.m. yesterday and the snow had started around three. Which way would he have gone?

Everyone else might think him drowned, but would Charlie think *Ginny* would believe he was dead? Would he expect her to stay and look for him or drive to Halifax and wait for news?

Whatever he might think of *her*, he was a Navy SEAL. He

would do his best to stay alive and, in a relatively civilized location like this, that would mean taking advantage of the available resources.

Ginny located the Middleton town library, found a table, and laid out her materials. With a bit of help from the librarian, she made a list of food, lodging, car hire, fuel, medical clinics, information sources, tech supplies, pawn shops, second hand shops, and churches in the area.

She longed to ask the librarian if anyone else had been requesting similar information, but didn't dare. When done, she gathered up her research and went back to the car.

He needed money. Assuming the pirate hadn't also taken the survival kit, who among that list of resources might be able to change a diamond into cash? There was only one possibility, a pawn shop in North Kingston, up the road a bit, and seven miles from the shore, but still a possibility for a determined man. She would ask there.

Before she left the library, however, there was one more thing she should consider doing. It offered free Wi-Fi and would be a pretty safe way to access the Internet since the IP address would not identify the user. She should consider looking up those social media websites and see if any of them had news of Charlie.

For this task Ginny pulled out her computer. She'd brought it because it had no GPS and she'd been lugging it around unopened, but she had plugged it in last night so it had a full battery charge. She accessed the Internet and steered the browser to the first of the social media addresses. Here she paused.

She had used her own credit card for both the rental car and the night's lodging, to distance herself from those ferry tickets. It would be better, though, if Ginny Forbes didn't appear to be hanging around Middleton, researching Charlie.

She created a series of new accounts, using Bonnie Jean's identity, and had access to all five sites within ten minutes.

She called them up, one by one, and searched the entries. There were numerous 'sightings', but none credible. Of course, none of these people knew what she did about where Charlie had come ashore (assuming the pirate was telling the truth), or about his broken leg. She closed out of those accounts and considered what to do next.

Himself had told her to stay off the phone until Charlie had been delivered safely to the Halifax Homestead. Did that apply to e-mail as well? What if Jim had tried to reach her that way? She did NOT expect to hear from Charlie, even if he'd had access to the Internet. He was 'off the grid' until they could establish his new Canadian identity and no one had anticipated his needing a secure e-mail account before arriving in Halifax. Jim was another matter.

The police would be able to identify the IP address from which she connected to her e-mail account, but only if they knew to look and only if they had a warrant and even then it would take days. Besides, she was supposed to be on a vacation in Nova Scotia. There should be nothing suspicious in checking her e-mail.

She typed in her password and waited while the usual deluge of junk poured off the Internet and onto her laptop. She ignored it, looking for Jim's name. Nothing. Well, that made sense. He would know her e-mail wasn't secure. Neither was his.

There was a note from Reggie, however. Encrypted. Sent this morning. She stared at it for a full minute, wondering what sort of danger opening that e-mail might carry with it.

The FBI had endless resources for cracking e-mail encryption and seemed willing to do so without a court order. They might already know what was in the note. But why should they? Ginny was not a fugitive. Neither was Charlie, yet. He was a 'person of interest', not yet arrested or charged. The authorities seemed to think it worth their while to follow him, to try to catch him, but she was pretty sure they couldn't charge her with a crime until they charged Charlie, and now he was dead. So, was the manhunt over?

Ginny's palms were sweating as she touched the key that would open the file.

"Got word yesterday of the tragic loss of Charlie Monroe in the Bay of Fundy incident. Canadian police assure U.S. counterparts they will do everything possible to confirm the death, but the body will likely not be recovered because of the tides in the area and proximity to Atlantic Ocean. Detective Tran on her way to Halifax for your eyewitness account. Himself would like to know where you are. Reggie."

The e-mail included instructions for replying in encrypted mode. Ginny read them carefully, then sent a reply.

"Thanks for the heads up. Am on the road to Halifax, but delayed by weather. G."

She chewed her lower lip. Tran's presence complicated things. Any further delay in arriving at the Halifax Homestead would look suspicious.

What's more, when she got to Halifax, she would need to convince everyone she believed Charlie was dead. A month ago she would have said that was impossible, that she could not fool Detective Tran with such a huge lie. But now? With Charlie's life and her freedom hanging in the balance?

There were no other e-mails that mattered. She closed the computer, put the car in gear, and headed for the highway.

* * *

Friday Afternoon
Hwy 8, Nova Scotia

Jim's phone rang and he grabbed it off the seat beside him.

"Hello?"

"Jim? Jim! Where are ye, lad?"

"On Nova Scotia Trunk 8, approaching Digby from the south."

"We've heard fra' Ginny!"

"What? Where is she? Is she all right?" Jim steered the car one-handedly onto the shoulder of the road.

"Aye, lad. As near as we can tell. She's on her way tae th' Homestead. Ye need tae get back there as fast as ye can."

"Okay. Why?" Jim was already turning the car around.

"Detective Tran is flyin' in tae talk tae her and I'd rather ye were there when that happens."

"I'm on my way. Did she say when she was going to be there?"

"Tran?"

"No, Ginny."

"Nae, lad, just that she was on the road headed that direction."

Jim nodded into the phone. "Let me know if you hear anything else."

"Aye, lad. Now go!"

* * *

CHAPTER 49

Friday Afternoon
Halifax, NS

Charlie pulled out onto the highway, being sure to notice the speed limit (110 kilometers per hour) and the speedometer (also in kilometers) so he wouldn't attract any unwanted attention. The trip would only take an hour or two, but then he had to find his way to the airport and, after that, to the Homestead.

The weather held off and the traffic was light until he got close to Halifax. He had no trouble following the signs to NS 102, then the airport.

The attendant clearly had his doubts about Charlie's respectability. He went over the car with a fine toothed comb, but Charlie had been careful to leave nothing behind and had filled the tank just outside the airport. He was allowed to walk away with a grudging nod and the promised two hundred dollars, Canadian.

In the airport he picked up a hot meal and bought himself a hat with ear flaps, to replace the one lost in the Bay of Fundy, and a souvenir sweat suit with *Halifax, Nova Scotia* printed on it. He would have preferred something heavier, but the top had a hood and it fit under the coat the smuggler had given him, and the second pair of pants fit over the ones he was currently wearing. As a result, he found himself on the edge of the Homestead paying off the taxi driver, reasonably warm, and with a full belly. He hadn't been able to replace his watch yet, but he'd checked the clock on the taxi before he got out. It was four fifty-five p.m.

"And it's a good thing the snow hasn't started. Are you sure you don't want me to drive you up to the gate? I've never stayed there, but I understand they take in visitors. Should be comfortable enough."

Charlie thanked the driver and waved as he pulled away. As soon as the cab was out of sight, he slipped into the woods and started to reconnoiter. There was still half an hour of daylight and he didn't have winter camo, but the rough coat was a dark brown and his sweats were olive green so he blended in with the winter vegetation.

He'd been astounded to find Nova Scotia covered in evergreens. There were sections of land cleared for farming, but the majority of the island was hills (some of them quite steep), covered in conifers. Very different from the wide open spaces of Texas. Much easier to hide in.

He took his time, making sure he knew exactly where all the other movement in the area was and what it meant. Going slow and being very careful, he made it to within sight of the front doors just as the sky came down, blocking the sunset and bringing the first flakes of snow with it.

Charlie stared at the front of the complex. His sixth sense was on high alert and he wasn't sure why. Was it just that he'd been in hiding for so long? Or was his guilty conscience pricking him? Or was it the fact that he'd misplaced Ginny and didn't have anyone to vouch for him?

He sank to the ground and peered at the lighted windows, wanting to get out of the weather. His leg was beginning to worry him. He was pretty sure it shouldn't be hurting this much.

He watched as a car drove in through the gates, then up to the front door. He couldn't see who was driving and he didn't recognize the car, but then, he wouldn't. They'd left the hatchback in New Brunswick.

The figure that got out was bundled up, which meant he couldn't tell if it was male or female. In the dim light he could see the coat was a light color, but nothing else. It *could* have been Ginny, but he couldn't be sure. If it was her, she'd find a way to let him know.

If he presented himself at the front door and she was there, she could vouch for him. If she was gone already, or hadn't arrived, he would have to explain who he was and, probably, offer some form of proof. They were expecting him, but they wouldn't want to admit an imposter. Would Laredo Pete's ID do?

He stiffened suddenly. Someone was coming out.

He watched the front door open and a uniformed police officer emerge. He turned and shook hands with someone Charlie couldn't see, then trudged off across the parking lot, got into an unmarked car and started it up.

Charlie crouched closer to the earth as the car drove past him and out onto the access road. He watched it turn south, heading for Halifax, then looked back at the Homestead. The front door had closed and there was no further movement on the ground floor, but someone had turned on a light on the second floor. The window overlooked the front drive. As he watched, it opened and a flash of yellow appeared. No, yellow and black. A flag.

Charlie's mouth settled into a grim, straight line. He recognized the flag. The Yellow Jack was a maritime signal used internationally to indicate quarantine. All the SEALS had learned to read ships flags as a matter of course. Clever of her to recognize that. So Ginny was inside and telling him it wasn't safe for him to enter the building.

He glanced at the sky. It wouldn't be a good night to be out in the elements. He slithered off to go find a spot to hole up for the night.

* * *

Friday Afternoon
Halifax Airport

Detective Tran collected her bag from the carousel and glanced at her watch. Three-thirty, local time. She considered a cup of coffee before locating a cab, but decided against it. The sooner she got to the Homestead, the better.

She stood on the edge of the street, waiting for her taxi, her eyes scanning the inhabitants. Remarkable how familiar they seemed. That one could easily be Miss Forbes' grandmother. The man on the bench resembled Mr. Mackenzie, and the tall, scruffy young man in the dark coat and green sweats, the one with the limp, could be any of the dozen or so she had seen in and about the Loch Lonach Homestead, except for the fur cap pulled down over his ears. No one in Texas ever needed that sort of headgear. She glanced at her watch again. No telling what she would find at the Halifax Homestead. She would need to be alert. Maybe she should have opted for that coffee after all.

* * *

CHAPTER 50

Friday Afternoon
Kingston, NS

Ginny drove the fifteen minutes up the road to North Kingston, and located the pawn shop. The proprietor would never believe two strangers with loose gemstones would show up on the same day by accident. And, if he had given Charlie money, he would have no cash for her. So she decided not to try to sell one of the gems. Instead, she would try to buy Charlie's diamond. She opened the door and entered the shop.

The proprietor greeted her and asked if she was looking for anything in particular. Ginny smiled, her eyes ranging the shelves.

"Yes, please. Jewelry."

He nodded, leading her over to a glass case. "What would you like to look at?"

Ginny made 'ooo' and 'ahhh' noises, letting her face indicate delight at the baubles she saw displayed there. In truth, none of them were up to her standard, but she didn't let that stop her. She tried on the rings, admired the earrings and necklaces, and sighed heavily.

"I don't suppose you have what I really need."

"What's that?"

"I've lost a diamond out of a ring and I'm looking for a

replacement. Do you handle loose stones?"

The proprietor hesitated. "Well, we don't see many."

Ginny waited, looking hopeful.

He frowned, then made a small deprecating gesture. "I have a few."

Ginny turned on the charm. "May I see them, please?"

He nodded, then pulled an envelope out of the safe, laying the individual stones out on the velvet tray for her inspection.

"This is what we have for sale at the moment."

Ginny looked them over carefully. No joy. "What's in the other envelope?"

The proprietor opened it and showed her the gem. "It came in this morning. We can't sell it until it's been to the appraiser."

Ginny smiled. She knew that stone. "That's okay. It's too big for my needs." She picked up the smallest stone and set it on the back of her hand. "How much for this one?"

He named a reasonable price and she happily handed over her credit card. She tucked her purchase away in her purse and wondered if there was any way she could find out more.

"How long does it take to get a stone appraised?"

"Usually a week. Are you interested in that big one?"

"I might be. I often pick up loose stones and have pieces made to order with them."

"Funny you should come in today," The proprietor volunteered. "It just goes to show."

"Show what?"

"I was telling the man who brought it in that I probably shouldn't take it, since we get so few calls for loose stones, just readymade jewelry."

She laughed. "And here I show up, looking for a loose diamond! I guess this is my lucky day. Did he say why he was selling?"

"He said he'd decided the woman he bought it for wasn't

worth it and he'd rather have a motorcycle. We had a good laugh over that."

Ginny's smile broadened. "Thank you so much for your help! I hope this one fits my ring, but even if it doesn't I'll make sure it gets a good home. 'Bye!"

A motorcycle! Ginny drove out of sight, then found a spot to pull over and examine her list. Sure enough, there was a purveyor of motorcycles in North Kingston. She hurried over to the lot. When questioned, the salesman clearly recalled Charlie.

This time Ginny said she was looking for a wayward brother who had been talking about buying a motorcycle for months, but hadn't been given permission to do so by his loved ones, an overbearing widowed mother and the mother's choice of a fiancée. This salesman was less gregarious and said only that men ought to be allowed to live their own lives. Ginny apologized for the intrusion, wrung her hands and added, "I don't suppose you know which way he went?"

"No, miss. Not my business."

"No, of course not. It's just that I wanted to give him something before he disappears."

The salesman screwed up his face, clearly not wanting to get embroiled in a family argument. Ginny opened her eyes as wide as they would go and blinked rapidly, then swallowed, then gave him a brave little smile. "Thank you for your help."

The salesman nodded, then, "Halifax, he said."

"Oh! How very kind of you! Can you tell me when he left?"

"I dropped him at the car rental agency at eleven-thirty."

"Thank you! God bless you!" Ginny followed his directions to the rental agency.

"Oh, yes. He left here around noon. We're just waiting to get confirmation that the car arrived safely at the Halifax airport. Are you the friend he's been trying to reach?"

"Yes!"

"Well, you should be able to catch him at the airport. Maybe you can phone ahead and have him paged. Or, I've got an idea! I'll call my agent and have them leave a note for him. How about that?"

Ginny caught her breath. "That would be wonderful!"

"What shall we tell him?"

Ginny thought hard for a moment. What she wanted to say was, 'Stay away from the Homestead, the police are waiting for you', but she couldn't send that message through two innocent parties. "Tell him I'll be home by dinnertime and to call me then and I'll come pick him up."

"Okay. Hang on a minute." The rental agent dialed the phone, spoke to his counterpart in Halifax for a moment, then hung up.

"I'm sorry. We missed him. He's already gone."

They tried paging him as well, but 'Pete Harmon' failed to pick up the white courtesy phone. She thanked the agent, and climbed back in her car. She was too late. He was already in Halifax and walking right into a trap.

* * *

Friday Afternoon
NS 101

Ginny headed out onto the highway. She was almost three hours behind Charlie. Well, she couldn't be unhappy about making sure he wasn't lying in a ditch near the coast. She just wished she'd known sooner.

From this point to Halifax was only an hour. If Charlie had gone straight to the Homestead from the airport, he was already caught.

She wished fervently they had called in time to catch him, to warn him not to simply walk up to the door and ring the bell. Would he do that, though? Really?

In his place, she would have staked out the Homestead and waited to see who showed up. After all, he'd been a wanted man for almost two weeks now. Had he learned sufficient caution, or had the whole thing just blown up in their faces?

Ginny shook her head at the problem. She had slightly over one hour to figure out what she needed to do. Best guess, per Reggie's e-mail, Detective Tran was at the Homestead and would be waiting for her.

What about Jim? Where was he? He hadn't gotten her note to meet them at the Bailey Rips, not in time, at least. He hadn't tried to e-mail her to set up a rendezvous, probably figuring that her account was accessible to the police and therefore too great a risk. What about the phone?

Gordon probably gave him the loaner's number before he left Albany, but Angus would have told Jim the same thing he told Ginny. Stay off the phone until you deliver Charlie. Had Jim seen the news? Did he know Charlie was 'dead'?

If so, he might have tried to call her, figuring he couldn't endanger Charlie anymore and that they, Jim and Ginny, should get their stories straight before facing Tran. That would make sense. And if that was the case, he was probably wondering why she wasn't responding.

Ginny bit her lip. She wanted to know Jim was safe, but she was mad at him, too. What had he done to fall foul of the Albany police? Didn't he have sense enough to stay under the radar? The fastest way to find out was to call Angus, but she couldn't do that until she knew what had happened to Charlie.

Nor could she stay missing without Detective Tran assuming she was guilty of something. They were expecting her, had been for a day. That video clip had been all over the news. She would have to come up with a story that covered the last twenty-four hours.

Ginny's eyes narrowed. The safest thing to do was tell the truth. She had been in shock over Charlie's death and spent time looking for him along the shore, waiting for news of him, then been caught by the snow and forced to take shelter for the night, then back to the coast this morning until reason compelled her to face the fact that he was gone.

Ginny swallowed hard. She would need to look the part and she wasn't much of an actress. She hadn't slept last night. That would help. But everyone could read her face. Was there any way she could put that to use?

It was impossible for her to dissemble, but not impossible to remember. If she could feel again what she felt on the ferry when she thought it was true, and let the grief overwhelm her, would that be enough? She had plenty of mistakes to accuse herself with, plenty of past pain to draw on.

She dredged up her worst fears and put her inner critic to work.

If Charlie was already there she would have to show joy that he was alive. Well, she would be happy about that, and sad that he'd been caught and *they were all going to prison*. That was a depressing thought.

And what about Jim? Would she ever see him again? She had grown quite used to having him around. She kind of liked him, liked being in his arms. *Of course, he might have decided she wasn't worth the trouble. Probably had. Especially since he'd had a chance to see Sarah again and compare the two. After all, he'd made sure she knew how little he really thought of her.*

Angus had been wrong to trust her, to place his faith in her. *Who did she think she was, anyway? She was a nurse, just a nurse and one Hal had used, had been willing to do much, much worse to.*

Why did she think she could help, anyway? She had screwed the whole affair up. *It would have been so much better if she'd just stayed at home, doing her pitiful little job, soothing fevered brows, following orders. Not pretending she could manage anything, much less anything as important as Charlie's life.*

Fifteen minutes into the exercise, Ginny was already weeping. She brushed the tears off her cheeks and focused on what else she needed to do before she arrived. Was there any way to signal Charlie not to approach the Homestead? She went through all the warning signs she could think of. It had to be something a SEAL would recognize. Navy meant ships. Something to do with ships. Lots of ships in the Canadian Maritimes.

She was already approaching Halifax. She could see the skyline and the surroundings were beginning to look urban rather than rural. What she needed was Internet access.

She spotted a coffee shop with free Wi-Fi and pulled in. She opened a browser and looked up Navy signaling and hit pay dirt. Now all she needed was a flag store. One just up the road. She drove on, found the shop open, went in and lucked out again. Both flags were in stock.

The weather had held off, but that was changing. It had started to snow and the wind was rising. She paid for her purchases, hurried back to the car, and stashed them in her backpack. Now for the real work.

In the forty minutes it took her to drive from Halifax to the Homestead Ginny managed to call up every black, despairing thought that had ever occurred to her, to remind herself how stupid she could be, how badly she had mishandled this trip, and how unfair it would be to Jim to saddle him with an emotional cripple. By the time she pulled onto the access road, she could hardly see for the tears streaming down her face. It might have been more convincing to drive off the side of the road into the ditch, but then she'd have to wait for the tow truck. She swiped at her eyes and aimed for the guardhouse instead.

* * *

Chapter 51

Friday Afternoon
Halifax Homestead

Jim pulled into the parking lot and looked around. No sedan that matched the one Ginny had rented, so she wasn't here yet. He was both happy and sad about that. He wanted her safe, but he also wanted to be here to greet her. He let himself in the front door and shook the snow off his boots.

"Dr. Mackenzie, the woman you were expecting—"

"Ginny?"

"No, the other one, the detective from Dallas, asked me to let her know when you arrived."

Jim met the Matron's eyes and saw comprehension in them. The Halifax Homestead had agreed to take Charlie in, but not to bring down the house around their ears. They would be cautious around authority figures.

Jim nodded. "Where is she?"

"In the Great Hall."

"Mrs. Robertson." She had started to turn away, but turned back to face him.

"We don't wish to place you in a position where your kindness is repaid by damage to you or your facility."

She broke into a smile that contained just a hint of mischief, then reached over and patted his arm. "We're in no danger. Let me know if you need anything."

Jim nodded, then headed down the corridor and into the Hall. Tran was seated in one of the wing chairs. Jim walked over and held out his hand.

"Detective Tran. I hope you had a pleasant trip." He pulled up a chair and sat down, angled so he could face her and also see the door.

"May we offer you a drink? Something to eat? Do you need anything?" Jim did his best to imitate his grandfather when entertaining local officials.

"I have been well taken care of, thank you. I lack only Miss Forbes' presence and I am told she is expected shortly."

Jim let his brow furrow. "Yes, I hope so."

"You were traveling together, I believe?"

Jim looked her straight in the eye. He'd been planning what to say all the way back from Digby. "I was delayed in Albany by the explosion so I sent her ahead. We didn't want to waste any of the time she had blocked for her genealogical research."

"Ah. That explains why she was on the ferry, but not why you got here first."

"She found something that interested her in Maine, a snow festival, and spent a day there, then another in New Brunswick doing research, then got caught by the front. She's been holed up waiting for the roads to be passable again."

Tran studied him for a long moment. "She was with Charles Monroe when he went overboard."

Thanks to Angus' excellent spy system, Jim knew exactly what Ginny had told the Canadian police about her relationship with Charlie. He looked puzzled. "What do you mean? Charlie Monroe? Our Charlie Monroe from Dallas? How could he have been on that ferry? Didn't you tell me he drowned in Lake Lavon?"

Detective Tran's expression grew drier. "Apparently not,

since he seems to have drowned in the Bay of Fundy yesterday."

Jim screwed up his face, trying to convey confusion and succeeding fairly well. Just how much did Tran know? And how much was he, Jim, supposed to know?

"You mean that guy Ginny was standing next to on the ferry? That was Charlie? How did that happen?"

"I will be interested to hear her explanation."

Jim nodded. He needed to catch Ginny at the door, to talk to her before she came face to face with Tran. He rose from his chair, excusing himself, and was halfway across the room when a noise at the front entrance caught his attention. It sounded like someone crying. In the next moment he saw who it was.

* * *

Friday Afternoon
Halifax Homestead

Ginny pulled up to the gate and waited for the guard to let her in. He looked at her driver's license, then her face, then picked up a phone and spoke into it. She saw him nod, then hit a switch of some kind. The gates slid open.

"Go right in, miss."

Ginny drove onto the grounds, across the parking lot, and up to the porte-cochere.

The main building was large and impressive and the yellow glow of light from the windows beckoned through the blowing snow. She turned off the engine, pulled her backpack across the seat, then paused before she opened the door.

You don't want to be here, don't want to face what you know lies on the other side of that door. You've failed. Charlie drowned and you failed in your mission to deliver him safely.

Himself told you to take Charlie to Halifax and you failed. He's dead, or, if he isn't, he's in custody and you're all going to prison, and if that's the case all the effort and sacrifices have been in vain. Either way, you've failed.

She climbed out of the car, went up to the front door, and rang the bell. Her chest hurt, and her head, and the cold was making it hard to breathe.

You aren't worthy of any husband, much less Jim. You aren't any good for him. If he gets his way and marries you, you're going to destroy him, make his life miserable, kill his love for you. No one could love anyone as stupid as you are. It's your fault he's in trouble. If you hadn't gone to the Laird, hadn't pleaded for Charlie, Jim wouldn't be involved. He would be safe at home, going to work and keeping his nose clean. If he goes to prison, it will be your fault.

She was shivering, as much from the emotional distress as from the weather. She could feel tears spilling out onto her cheeks and the sudden chill as the wind hit them.

The door opened and Ginny saw a middle aged woman in a fisherman sweater and tartan skirt.

"Miss Forbes?"

Ginny nodded.

"Come in! Please, come in. We're so happy to see you at last." She gestured toward the vestibule and Ginny stepped inside.

"This way, please."

There was a look in her eye that it took Ginny a minute to identify. Sympathy, or pity, perhaps.

Appropriate. She was a pitiful creature, a miserable excuse for a human being.

She brushed at her eyes to keep from tripping over the carpet, but didn't bother to wipe the tears off her cheeks.

If only there was some way to avoid this confrontation,

avoid the censure, the blame. It would be easier to run into the snow, to disappear in it, than to face them.

Her guide led her down the corridor and into a huge room dominated by a massive fireplace. The room seemed full of people.

Facing them hurt. Physically hurt. She didn't know where Charlie was. Didn't know if he was safe. Didn't know what she was going to tell these people who had agreed to help him. And what about Jim? What was he was going to think of her? He was going to be angry, or hurt, or maybe he just didn't care about her anymore. She wished she didn't care.

Ginny took two steps into the room, then stopped. She should act surprised. She wasn't supposed to know Tran would be here. Surprise, dulled by the fact that it didn't matter. Charlie was dead. Tran couldn't hurt him now.

"Detective Tran?"

"Ginny!"

Before she could react, he had her in his arms.

"Ginny! Thank God!"

Ginny turned to him and, as if on cue, lost all control. She put her face down on his chest and started to sob.

He steered her over to the sofa and sat her down, pulling her into his arms. She had no idea how long they let her cry. All she could hear was Jim's voice in her ear, telling her it was all right now.

He was helping her out of her coat. He'd already pulled off her hat and scarf and gloves. They lay in a pile on the floor beside him, gently steaming in the heat from the fire. The warmth felt good on her exposed skin, but what she wanted was the warmth of his arms.

He spoke in her ear, very quietly. "Are you all right?"

It was an intimate question, just between the two of them. She nodded.

Then, just as quietly, "We saw what happened."

There was a TV screen in one corner of the room. Ginny could hear the announcer, still talking about the sensational rescue at sea and the lost man, and a plea for help finding his body.

She sucked in a breath, swallowed hard, and looked up into Jim's face.

"He died a hero." She could feel the tears welling up again.

"Miss Forbes?"

Ginny turned to face the long arm of the law, the woman who had chased them across a continent.

"The man on the video, was it Charles Monroe?"

Ginny nodded, the tears spilling over.

Detective Tran nodded in return. "That closes the case."

Ginny just looked at her, her heart aching at the thought of Charlie, his wife and children gone, his own life tossed into the icy water of the Bay. Dead. All dead.

"I will be flying back to Dallas tomorrow and would like to file your statement at that time. I will need to talk to you."

"But not tonight," Jim said.

"No. Tomorrow will be soon enough." She hesitated. "I am sorry for your loss." Detective Tran looked at her with something that might have been sympathy.

Ginny found herself unable to answer, her throat closing on the unexpected kindness.

Jim came to her rescue, pushing her to her feet, one arm around her waist.

"Come on." He picked up her backpack and steered her out into the hallway.

* * *

Friday Evening
Halifax Homestead

Ginny let Jim take her upstairs to a guest room furnished with thick carpets and heavy curtains. As soon as the door closed behind them, she broke out of his arms, reached over and turned the lock.

She put a finger to her lips, pulled the Yellow Jack out of her bag, and headed for the window. She opened the frame as far as it would go and leaned out. There was no way to tell if Charlie was out there or could see her, but she had to try.

Jim's arm was around her waist already. "Ginny!"

She spread the flag into the wind, then draped it across the bottom edge of the window, lowering the sash until it held the fabric in place, then turned back to face Jim.

"There!"

"What are you doing?" His face was white.

"Playing a long shot." She took him by the hand and led him over to the couch, then sat down facing him. They hadn't been alone together since that last disastrous night in Albany.

She met his eyes. "We have a lot to talk about."

He nodded, then sucked in a breath. "Before you start, I want to say something. Charlie's death was not your fault. No one blames you. There was nothing you could have done to prevent him going overboard to save that boy."

"Charlie's alive."

He froze. She wasn't even sure he was breathing for a moment.

"How do you know?"

"I've been tracking him for the last twelve hours. At least, I think it's him. It's someone who sounds like him; a tall blonde with a limp. He isn't here, is he? He hasn't been arrested already?"

Jim shook his head. "We haven't seen him."

"Thank goodness. Reggie's e-mail said—"

"Reggie?"

Ginny nodded. "Reggie sent an encrypted email telling me Tran would be here. I was afraid Charlie would walk into a trap and I couldn't reach him. He'd already left the airport by the time we called. I had to get here first and persuade Tran to go home, which meant convincing her Charlie was dead. The flag is to tell him not to approach the Homestead until she's gone."

She saw Jim blink.

"Those tears weren't real?"

She sighed. "They were real."

He ran his hand over the back of his head. "I think you'd better tell me what's going on."

It took Ginny almost two hours to tell Jim everything that had happened since Angus had sent her off from Albany. He nodded as she explained about the dogsled crossing, then frowned as she described confronting the pirate and the search for Charlie along the Nova Scotia coastline.

"I left you a dozen messages."

"I didn't get them." Ginny crossed her fingers on the half-truth. She hadn't opened even one of the messages from the unknown number and she hadn't seen any with Jim's number.

He leaned forward, his brow furrowing. "When you thought Charlie was dead, why didn't you call me?"

She looked at him, at his face, then sucked in a breath and told him. "Because I didn't want to talk to you."

He looked startled. "Why not?"

"Because I had lost Charlie and I didn't want to hear you say, 'I-told-you-so.'"

His eyes widened. "Why would you think I'd say that?"

"Because of what you said to me after the wolf, that I should let you make the decisions for both of us." She sighed.

"You were right. Angus shouldn't have sent me off alone."

Jim shook his head. "That was my idea."

"What was?"

"I wanted to show you that I *did* trust you, even with something as important as this. So I asked Grandfather to send you on ahead, and to take Charlie with you." He reached out and took her hands in his. "But I never intended you to have to do the entire trip by yourself. I expected to catch up with you in Maine."

Ginny stared at him. His idea?

He continued. "And I was wrong, that night. You don't need someone telling you what to do." He sucked in a deep breath.

"You didn't fail, Ginny. You got him over the border. I had no idea how I was going to do that, not after he broke his leg. But *you* figured it out. As for that pirate, I'm really glad I wasn't there. He would never have given in to another man. Not without a fight." Ginny's mouth twitched at the thought of Jim taking a swing at the boat captain.

"I wouldn't have thought of the game finder, either. Or known how to sweet-talk the pawn shop owner and the motorcycle guy and the rent car proprietor into giving me the information I needed. If I'd been there, I would have been a liability, and I might not have been able to see that. You didn't fail. You've been amazing."

Ginny studied his face for a long moment. She hadn't expected praise from him. And it had been his idea to send her out alone. She took a slow breath. "When Charlie was lost, I was angry with you, because you weren't there to help me."

He gave her a half smile. "I'm sorry." His smile faded. "It almost killed me, to see your face on that video and know you were alone and I couldn't reach you." He swallowed.

"I don't want to hurt like that again, but I've had to face the fact that what I want isn't always the best thing for either of us." He shook his head. "If I give in to fear, I won't be able to function, not at the hospital, not at the Homestead."

"What are you talking about?"

He reached over and brushed her cheek with his fingertip. "Shall I tell you what my grandfather said to me, about you?"

Ginny nodded.

"He said you were like my mother, a Viking throwback, strong and brave and capable." His gaze turned inward. "But she wasn't strong enough, and I wasn't there to save her."

"Her death wasn't your fault."

"No, I know that. But I don't want *your* death on my conscience either."

Ginny swallowed, then slid over beside him and put her head down on his shoulder. His arms closed around her.

"The one great truth of life," she said, "is that we all die. We can't let that keep us from living."

"I know that. I know I can't protect you from life. All I can do is help you face whatever comes."

Ginny relaxed into his arms and was suddenly overtaken by a jaw-cracking yawn. She'd been running on adrenaline for more than twenty-four hours, but she couldn't sleep yet.

She climbed to her feet, staggering, and went over to lean against the window. Jim followed her, taking up a position behind her and wrapping his arms around her.

"He's still out there somewhere," she said.

"He's a SEAL. He'll find shelter."

Ginny stood looking out the window at the Yellow Jack, now cracking in the wind.

"The storm's getting worse."

* * *

Chapter 52

It was past midnight when Jim came slowly to consciousness. The room glowed with a pearl-colored light. It illuminated the furniture and the walls and the woman in his arms, turning her skin to alabaster. He had persuaded her to stretch out on the bed, to nap, and had lain down beside her, not realizing he, too, was on the point of collapse.

"Did I wake you?" she murmured.

"Yes." He smiled, then rolled up on his side. "Why aren't you asleep?"

"I wanted to look at you."

"Have I changed?"

"I think I'm the one who's changed."

He saw her swallow.

"Did you ever reach for something you wanted, Jim, then pull back because you were afraid touching would destroy it, like touching a soap bubble?"

He nodded.

"That's what I'm afraid of." Her eyes glowed in the colorless light, limpid and liquid and he could see the fear in them. "I'm afraid, if I reach for happiness, it will vanish."

"I'm not a soap bubble, Ginny. I'm not going to disintegrate if you touch me." He took her hand in his. "Flesh and blood, bone and sinew. I won't last, not forever, but my love for you will."

She smiled up into his face. "That sounds like a lovely soap bubble."

"Did you know that a Scot holds the world's record for the longest lasting bubble?"

"Is there such a thing?"

He nodded. "Sir James Dewar. His record is one hundred and eight days. He was studying surface tension."

He smiled. "If anyone can make a soap bubble last a lifetime, we can." He bent down, intending to kiss her, but his stomach chose that moment to remind him he hadn't eaten since lunch.

"Well, that was romantic!"

She giggled.

"Are you hungry? We missed dinner."

"I could eat something." She nodded.

"Okay. Stay warm. I'll be right back."

He kissed her swiftly, then climbed off the bed. He hadn't undressed, so all he had to do was slip his feet into his shoes and he was ready. He let himself out into the hall, closing her door behind him.

There was no way to call the elevator without disturbing the rooms on either side of the shaft, so he composed his soul in patience and hoped no one was awake and watching. Not that he was doing anything wrong. Just a midnight snack and a private conversation with his intended.

He exited the elevator and walked down the hall, passing windows that looked out onto the snow-lit night, trying to remember where he had seen the kitchen. He made two false starts, then found the right corridor.

The kitchen door swung both ways on well-greased hinges

that made almost no noise as he entered the room. He stood for a moment, letting his eyes adjust to the darkness. There was no window in here, but there was something else.

Jim's skin crawled as he realized he could hear someone breathing. He slid his hand along the wall beside the door, hunting for the light switch, then felt himself grabbed from behind.

There was a hand over his mouth and a strong male arm around his chest, pinning one arm down, but the other, the one that had been on the wall, was free. He used his elbow and drove it into the form behind him, hearing a satisfying 'oof' as a result. He broke free and turned rapidly, one hand finding and throwing the light switch, the other coming up, fist ready to continue the fight, and froze.

"Charlie!" he hissed.

"Jim!"

The two of them grinned like idiots, then did the male equivalent of a hug, punching each other on the shoulder and shoving each other off balance.

"Where the hell have you been?" Jim demanded. "How did you get in? *Why* did you come in? Didn't you get Ginny's message? We've got to hide you."

Charlie nodded. "I got the message. Got hungry, and cold, so I decided to slip in, look around, then out again. Those windows need better locks."

"There might have been alarms."

Again Charlie nodded. "I disconnected the wires. Made it look like the ice had done it. Didn't want anyone interrupting my midnight snack."

"That reminds me!" Jim looked around quickly, then grabbed a towel and started loading food into it. He shoved it at Charlie and started on a second load, including a glass of milk for Ginny.

"We can't use the elevators. There are cameras in them."

"This way." Charlie indicated another corridor. "Stairs."

The route was longer, and Jim couldn't help noticing how difficult it was for Charlie to use his left leg, but they managed to get back to Ginny's room without raising an alarm. Jim opened the door cautiously, slipped inside, then motioned for Charlie to follow him in. When Charlie was inside, Jim closed the door behind him and turned the lock. That sound triggered another.

"Good evening, Mr. Monroe."

* * *

Saturday Wee Small Hours
Halifax Homestead

Jim almost dropped the food and he did spill the milk, his hand jerking and the liquid sloshing over the rim of the glass. He turned to face the voice and was not surprised to see a movement in the moonlight, followed by the table lamp being turned on.

If this had been a movie, the woman standing there would have had a gun in her hand and Ginny in a death grip, the muzzle to her temple. As it was, Detective Tran simply waited for the two men to recover.

Charlie did so first. He limped across the room, set the food on the table, pulled up a chair, and sat down.

Jim swallowed hard, then did the same, taking a moment to wipe the milk off his hand, and choosing to join Ginny on the side of the bed. He took her hand in his.

Detective Tran looked at each of them in turn, then sat down on the edge of the couch, her back straight, her ankles crossed, her expression unreadable.

"Would you care to explain?" she asked.

Ginny spoke first. "I thought you believed he was dead."

Detective Tran nodded. "I did, until I heard a noise, looked out my window, and saw the signal. That flag was not there before your arrival. Dr. Mackenzie was inside the complex. The only person you could be signaling was Mr. Monroe."

Ginny nodded, sighing. "It was a calculated risk."

Detective Tran nodded. "That was quite a performance, Miss Forbes. May I ask how you accomplished it?"

Ginny caught Jim's eye. "It turns out a leopard *can* change her spots, if the need is great enough." He gave her hand a squeeze, then looked at Detective Tran.

"How did you know to come to Ginny's room?"

"After I saw the signal and realized what it must mean, I decided to keep watch. I saw Mr. Monroe's unorthodox entry into the building and was following him when you came down the hall. Once you had joined forces, I was pretty sure I knew where you would go." She looked over at Ginny. "I persuaded Miss Forbes of the inevitability of the confrontation and suggested she might want to get it over with."

Charlie sighed. "I'm the one you want. Let them go."

Detective Tran turned her eyes on him. "You are hurt."

He nodded.

"But you went over the side anyway."

He nodded again.

"Why?"

Charlie shrugged. "I couldn't save my own children, but I could try to save that boy."

She nodded slowly. "Why did you run?"

"I'm an outlaw."

Detective Tran's brow furrowed. "You have not been charged with breaking the law."

"I have."

"I do not understand." She looked from Charlie to Ginny.

"You already know," Ginny said, "that the Scots descend in part from the Vikings."

Detective Tran nodded.

"You may also know the Viking justice system gave us the word for 'law', set up a jury of twelve men, and established the first parliament."

"The Althing."

Ginny nodded. "Among the concepts they came up with was a choice of punishments for those convicted of offenses. In the event of a death, as in this case, one could make monetary restitution to the injured party's family. One could engage in a blood feud. Or one could be exiled—outlawed."

Detective Tran looked over at Charlie.

Ginny continued. "The outlaw had to leave behind everything that was his—friends, job, family, all gone. Further, he lived under constant threat of being killed, lawfully, by anyone who went hunting for him. Sort of like the bounty hunter system we have now."

Detective Tran raised an eyebrow. "Mr. Monroe was outlawed by your community."

Ginny nodded. "Charlie was judged and convicted and sentenced under a system of laws that gave rise to the one you've sworn to uphold. He's not escaping justice. He'll suffer every day, for the rest of his life, for what he did."

"And you, and Dr. Mackenzie?"

"We were assigned the task of throwing him out of Loch Lonach."

Detective Tran was silent for a long moment. "You mentioned blood feuds."

"It used to be that the injured party and the offender were allowed to work it out, blood for blood, but we don't permit that any more. It was too easy for it to escalate to whole families, then whole communities. The solution was too costly."

"Why did you chose this archaic system of justice, rather than turn him over to the police?"

Jim felt Ginny's hand tighten within his. She took a deep breath. "It was his choice. The Texas criminal justice system released the man who killed his family onto the streets of Dallas. Had it done its duty, there would have been no reason for him to act. But having acted, we could not let him escape justice."

"Why Canada? Mexico was closer."

"We could not enforce the punishment without the help of the other Homesteads and there are none in Mexico."

Detective Tran turned to Charlie. "Is what Miss Forbes says true?"

Charlie nodded. "All true."

"Do you regret your actions?"

Jim held his breath and was sure Ginny was doing the same.

Charlie sighed. "Yes. I've had some time to think about it and I wish now I hadn't done it. I wasn't thinking clearly. It just hurt so bad. I wanted to make him hurt, too, but I settled for making sure he couldn't kill anyone else." He spread his hands. "I know that's no excuse. I'm sorry for the trouble I've caused and I'm ready to take my punishment."

The room fell silent.

Jim sat waiting for what Detective Tran would do next. She had them dead to rights. She knew, now, that Charlie was guilty of the murder back in Dallas, and that Jim and Ginny had been helping him escape.

She sat quietly watching them, her eyes moving from one to another, then back again, spending the most time on Charlie. Eventually she stood up. The other three followed her lead, Charlie moving slowly and in obvious pain. She looked at him for another long moment then turned to Ginny.

"Please make yourself available immediately after breakfast tomorrow to complete your statement. I must leave for the airport at ten o'clock."

Ginny nodded.

Detective Tran looked at each of them one more time then let herself out, closing the door behind her.

* * *

CHAPTER 53

Saturday Very Early Morning
Halifax Homestead

Ginny stared at the door, her blood curdling, then turned to face the other two. "What do we do now?"

Jim shook his head.

Charlie dropped back into the chair and Ginny crossed the distance in three steps, suddenly furious. Didn't he realize he'd destroyed Jim's career?

"Why did you ignore my signal?"

Charlie looked up at her. "I'm sorry."

"If you'd just waited until she left, we'd all be in the clear. Just a few more hours!" Her heart was pounding, thinking about everything he'd put them through. How could he be so stupid, so selfish? "Maybe we can lower you out the window. You can have my car. Steal it! Run! You can still escape, even if we can't."

He shook his head. "I can't run anymore, Ginny."

"Of course you can. If you don't, Jim and I will have sacrificed everything for nothing."

He reached out and caught her by the wrists. "I'm sorry, Ginny. I can't run anymore."

"*Why not?*" she demanded.

"It's my leg. I think it's infected."

Ginny caught her breath, stopped in mid rant, her mouth hanging open. She dropped to the floor, tearing her eyes from his face and focusing instead on his foot.

"Jim, get the lights, please."

He had beaten her to it, pulling a standing lamp over and turning it on. She was carefully unlacing Charlie's boot. She eased it off his foot, then did the same with the sock.

He was right. There were red streaks running out the bottom of the cast toward his toes and his foot was swollen and hot.

"That cast has to come off," Jim said. "And we need blood cultures and IV antibiotics." Ginny saw him catch Charlie's eye. "You were right to come in. If you'd stayed out in the snow another twenty-four hours it might have killed you."

Charlie nodded. "That's what I was thinking."

Ginny looked at Jim. "Do you have any idea where the clinic is?"

"No."

She got to her feet and headed for her backpack, pulling the now useless 'all clear' flag out and tossing it aside, hunting for Gordon's phone. She found it, reinserted the battery, and turned it on.

"Mom? It's Ginny."

"Ginny? What time is it?"

"The middle of the night. I need your help, please."

"Of course."

"Call Himself. Go over if you have to. Get him out of bed and on the phone."

"To you or to Jim?"

"Either, but fast." She read out the number of Gordon's phone.

"I'll get right on it."

The connection went dead and Ginny hung up. She hoped

this wouldn't take very long. Every minute put Charlie in more danger. She felt horrible about yelling at him. She turned to him and started to apologize. "Charlie, I'm sorry—" The phone went off.

"Ginny?" It was a sleepy Himself.

"I'm sorry to wake you, but we need your help and it won't wait."

"How canna help?"

"Tell me who is safe to talk to up here and how to reach him."

"What do ye need lass?"

"Access to medical care. Now."

"Auch aye. Gi'e me a minute."

Ginny waited impatiently. She turned to find the eyes of both men on her.

"Ian Somerled." Himself read her the number. "Ye'll call back, lass?"

"As soon as I can."

Ginny broke the connection and dialed again. Dr. Somerled answered on the second ring.

"I'm so sorry to get you out of bed, but Angus Mackenzie said we could call on you."

"Yes. How may I help?"

"We have a possible case of blood poisoning post broken bone."

"Where are you?"

"At the Halifax Homestead, in the guest quarters."

"I'll meet you in the Great Hall in fifteen minutes."

"Thank you!"

Ginny hung up the phone and relayed the message.

Jim raised an eyebrow. "Fifteen minutes? He must have not gone to bed yet." He swung toward Charlie. "We need to get you downstairs, and as quietly as possible."

"What's the point?" Charlie asked. "She already knows I'm here."

"Plausible deniability," Ginny said. "She left us alone together. That was on purpose. As long as we're the only ones who know, she can control the situation."

Jim nodded, sliding his arm under Charlie's, and helping him to his feet. "Let's go."

Ginny held the door for them then moved swiftly to follow, grabbing coats, phones, and her backpack. They entered the Great Hall to find Dr. Somerled already there.

* * *

Saturday Wee Small Hours
Halifax Homestead

The fire had burned down. It gave off a red glow that offered not much in the way of light, but quite a lot of heat. Dr. Somerled took a quick look at Charlie's foot then nodded to Jim.

"Let's put him in my car. You can follow me."

The two men maneuvered Charlie into the back seat of a car parked beside Ginny's rental, then she and Jim followed their guide out the front gate, heading northeast, along NS 102.

The evergreens threw moving shadows across the road and they almost missed following Dr. Somerled into a corridor hidden among the trees.

Another five minutes brought them to parking lot fronting a brightly lit building. Someone with a wheelchair threw the door open and came out to help get Charlie out of the car.

Ginny followed the men and the wheelchair inside. The lobby housed the security office, which was standing open and apparently expecting them.

"This way." Dr. Somerled motioned toward the back, then led them through a series of offices to an elevator. "I phoned ahead. The crew should be setting up."

"You keep someone here all the time?" Jim asked.

"We have to. It's too far out of Halifax to ask people to come in quickly. So we take turns. In the summer we hike and fish. In winter we sleep, read, knit."

They piled into the elevator and started down.

"I thought Nova Scotia was nothing but bedrock," Ginny said.

Dr. Somerled nodded. That's mostly true. This started out as a stone quarry, then old Tam Craig discovered gold in the slag."

"Gold?"

He nodded. "It's one of the ways we pay the bills."

"You have your own gold mine!" Jim whistled.

Dr. Somerled laughed. "Yes, but don't tell anyone. When we took the site over, it was being used as a garbage dump."

The doors on the elevator opened to reveal the most impressive facility Ginny had seen yet. Not only did everything sparkle in the overhead lights, but there was evidence of full computer sensor integration. They were being scanned.

They put Charlie in a treatment room and got to work, a half dozen helpers materializing out of nowhere.

Dr. Somerled nodded at one of the women. "My wife, Kathy." She smiled, but did not break stride.

Ginny knew enough to step out of the way and watch. Just as they had done in Albany, the team had Charlie stripped and draped in no time flat. Ginny watched him run his hand over the sleeve of the gown.

"Are you cold?" she asked him.

He grinned. "No. The gown's heated!"

They slid an intravenous catheter into place and drew blood before starting fluids and hanging the first dose of antibiotics.

Dr. Somerled explained as they went.

"We'll begin with broad spectrum coverage, but switch to biologics as soon as the DNA analysis is complete."

"Biologics," Jim said.

Dr. Somerled nodded. "And stem cells, which we'll use to knit his bone. Which leads us to imaging." He pulled a mechanical arm around and over the bed. "Do any of you have metal on you?"

Both Jim and Ginny shook their heads, but Charlie looked puzzled.

"What kind of metal?"

"Any kind. The machine is a very powerful magnet and it will attract metal to it forcefully."

"Then you'd better put this somewhere safe." He pulled the *sgian dubh* out of the top of his sock and handed it to the closest attendant, a pert blonde whose eyes grew big at the sight of the knife.

"Is this the one ye used?" she asked.

Charlie looked at her in surprise. "Used for what?"

"Tae cut that boy free from the whale."

He nodded. "What do you know about that?"

She looked up from the knife. "Auch, man! Do ye not know yer a hero?" She smiled at him, then suddenly blushed and hurried away to put the knife out of reach of the magnet. Charlie's eyes followed her out of the room.

Ginny and Jim waited until Dr. Somerled decided they had caught the infection in time, then headed back to the Homestead to find out what Detective Tran had decided to do with them.

* * *

CHAPTER 54

Saturday Morning
Halifax Homestead

Ginny looked up as Detective Tran entered the room, spotted them, and approached their table. The detective handed her a set of papers. "Read that, please."

No one spoke as Ginny read through the document.

It was her, Ginny's, account of what had happened to Charlie, cleaned up and put in legal form. It started with a summary of how she and Jim had arranged to go on vacation after her shocking discovery of a body in the Viking long ship, how Charlie had arranged to ride along, and how Himself had authorized the two of them to escort Charlie on his trip, since he was still, officially, in the Laird's custody.

It culminated with her testimony that Charles Monroe had gone overboard in the Bay of Fundy to save a young man's life, his actions caught on camera and witnessed by the world.

"Is that statement accurate?" Detective Tran asked her.

Ginny looked Detective Tran in the eye and nodded. "It is." Not complete, but accurate.

"Would you sign it, please?" She held out a pen.

Ginny took the pen and signed her name.

Detective Tran then turned to Jim, handing him a similar sheaf of papers.

Ginny waited in silence while he read it through.

"Is that statement accurate?"

"It is." He picked up the pen and signed where indicated.

"Thank you." Detective Tran gathered up her papers, placed them in a satchel, put the satchel on the table, then folded her hands on it.

Ginny swallowed hard. "What happens now?"

"I am going back to Texas to file these and recommend the case be closed."

Ginny licked dry lips. "Why?"

Detective Tran met her eyes. "Charles Monroe is missing and presumed dead."

Ginny nodded.

"He was never arrested and never charged." The detective's eyebrows drew together. "I have no jurisdiction in Canada. Even if I knew he is alive at this moment and in hiding and where, I could not pursue that lead myself."

Ginny found her stomach churning.

"The evidence against him is thin and circumstantial and he has an alibi. That makes this a 'misdemeanor murder'."

"A what?"

"A situation in which a person is suspected of murder, but there is not enough evidence to convict him in court. Such a person often gets off without punishment, an outcome you have prevented."

Detective Tran was silent for a long moment. "Do you believe in divine retribution, Miss Forbes?"

Ginny nodded.

Detective Tran spoke slowly, her eyes on her folded hands. "In my culture, it is a concept considered without merit since the time of Confucius, and yet, the ancient tales are there. They describe powers greater than man that take punishment for an evil deed into their own hands."

She looked up. "In your culture, too, the ancient gods dispensed vengeance according to their own code of ethics." She tapped the satchel with her forefinger. "Charles Monroe sacrificed his life to save that boy. It is rough justice, but fair."

"And us?"

"According to these sworn statements, you had no knowledge of Mr. Monroe's actions. Nor was he a fleeing felon. Therefore, I have no grounds on which to charge you."

She stood up and gathered her possessions, then looked from one to the other, her eyes settling at last on Ginny. "I was granted leave to come to Canada on the condition that I accept the role of liaison between the Dallas Police Department and the Loch Lonach community. You will be seeing more of me."

* * *

Saturday Morning
Halifax Homestead

Jim drew a shaking hand across his brow, then collected Ginny, and steered her upstairs to his room. When they were inside, he crossed to his luggage, reached in, and pulled out his bottle of single malt.

"Is that the antifreeze?"

"Yes." He poured them both a wee dram and handed one of the glasses to her.

Ginny shivered. "I feel as if she'll be looking over my shoulder for the rest of my life."

Jim nodded. "She certainly has us over a barrel. What do you suppose she has in mind?"

"Not prison. Not at this time, anyway."

Jim sighed. "I guess we have to be thankful for that."

"Does she know where Charlie is?"

"She may suspect, but I think she doesn't want to know. She didn't ask. Which means that—officially—Charlie is dead. So," Jim lifted his glass, "here's to the memory of a very brave man, Charles Monroe. May he rest in peace."

* * *

Saturday Morning
Halifax Homestead

Ginny had gone back to her own room to get cleaned up and changed for the day. Jim had done the same and was now stretched out on his bed, thinking about the trip.

He couldn't help feeling a nervous sort of letdown. Detective Tran owned their souls, but they knew something about her, too. She couldn't turn them in without risking they would report her for her own version of selective record keeping. She, too, was now an accessory after the fact in the death of that drunk driver.

Liaison to the clan! Because of Charlie's act of vengeance. It would be an uneasy alliance at best, on both sides, and what Himself was going to say when he heard about it Jim had no way of knowing.

Something he'd read once floated into his mind. "A noble friend is the best gift and a noble enemy the next best." Tran could go either way, but Jim had to admit that, on the whole, he'd rather have her as a friend. Someone like that could be very useful to the clan. Very useful indeed.

* * *

CHAPTER 55

Saturday Late Morning
Halifax Homestead

Ginny looked down at Jim's sleeping form. His hair was tousled, the curls making him look younger than he really was. She hated to wake him, but she was on a tight timetable. She reached out and brushed a lock of hair away from his eyes.

"Jim?"

He stirred, then stretched, then opened his eyes.

"Hello." He smiled up at her.

"I have to drive into Digby," she said, "to return the rent car, then take the ferry over to New Brunswick and retrieve the hatchback, then drive back to Halifax. If you want to help, you need to come now. The ferry leaves at four."

"Can't we do that tomorrow?"

"I'm already in penalty mode. I was only supposed to drive to Halifax, not search all over Nova Scotia for Charlie." She sighed. "It's all right. I'll find some other way to get back."

He sat up and looked at her. "I don't want to let you out of my sight. The last time I did that, you disappeared."

"Then get your shoes on and let's go."

He rubbed his face. "We have two borrowed cars."

"Three."

He nodded. "I mean, once you return the rented sedan,

we'll still have a car each. The hatchback has to be returned to Albany and the SUV to Charlottesville."

She cocked her head to one side. "Where are you going with this?"

"If we both have to drive, we won't be together for the first two days of the trip home. Also, I want to see Charlie again and you need to do some genealogy here, in Halifax, to satisfy the curious back home."

Ginny nodded. "That's true. I'll need photographic evidence of our vacation."

He stood up and stretched. "I'll bet we can find someone willing to ferry the hatchback to Albany, then fly home, at our expense, of course. Let's get the rent car taken care of today and plan to take the ferry across to St. John tomorrow. We can spend the night there, then head for home the next day."

"Sounds like a plan. If we hurry, we can visit a couple of the local cemeteries before the light fails." Ginny turned to go, but he reached out and caught her hand.

"Wait, I have something for you." He pulled her across to his suitcase, fished out a manila envelope, and handed it to her with a flourish.

Ginny looked inside. *"My talisman!* I was beginning to think I'd never see it again." She slipped it over her head, then found Jim touching it, looking closely at it.

"When you told me about this thing, I didn't believe you." He looked up and caught her eye. "I think I've changed my mind."

* * *

Saturday Late Morning
Halifax Homestead / NS 101

When the sedan had been safely returned and the bill settled, the two of them climbed into the SUV and headed back to Halifax.

Jim looked over at Ginny. She had her eyes on the scenery, dark forest resplendent in white, but no smile on her face.

"Are you all right?"

"Yes." She stirred in her seat. "You haven't told me what happened to you in Albany."

"I didn't have nearly as much fun as you and Charlie did." He described the explosion and the video interview with Detective Tran.

"You were hurt?"

He shrugged. "Not much and not enough to keep me from coming after you. I spent the rest of that day and all of the next trying to catch up, and everything that could go wrong, did."

He described his frustration with that drive in vivid detail, emphasizing his efforts to take shortcuts and the inevitable delays caused by them.

Ginny was laughing. "Oh dear! I wish I'd known."

He reached over and took her hand. "What would you have done, if you had?"

"Turned my phone on."

"In defiance of the Laird's instructions?"

"Sometimes you have to bend the rules."

"I wish I'd known you were coming over on the ferry. I would have been there to meet you."

She sighed. "I wish you had. That was a horrible twenty-four hours."

Jim nodded, his smile fading. "When you said the tears were real, what did you mean?"

She took her hand back, turning again to the scene outside her window. "The reason everyone can read my face is because the emotions are never very far away."

"But you used that, to convince Tran Charlie was dead."

She nodded.

Jim frowned to himself. If he married her, would she pull the same stunt on him?

"Was that fair, to manipulate her that way?"

Ginny sighed before replying. "Manipulate. That word gets a lot of bad press." Her brow wrinkled. "When you set a bone, you manipulate the leg, to achieve the outcome you desire."

"Not the same."

"When you're examining a patient, you manipulate the setting, the pace, the focus of the conversation, all to achieve your goal."

"That's so I can help, and I don't think of it as manipulating another human being."

"When you get me alone and try to talk sense into me, you manipulate the environment and the subject, to make your point."

Jim squirmed. "I use the tools at my disposal, skills I've learned, and good judgment, and I don't use them for evil."

"That's what I told your grandfather."

Jim looked over at her. "What?"

"I told him you didn't need me, that you were perfectly capable of doing whatever had to be done, without my help."

Jim felt his heart constrict. What was she saying? That she was washing her hands of him? Was she letting him down gently, with compliments to ease the pain?

"What if I disagree?"

She looked over at him for a long moment. "Angus usually listens to my opinion."

Jim's breath caught in his throat. The unspoken corollary

was that Jim didn't.

When they set out on this adventure, he'd been under the misapprehension that he was in control. He knew better now. She'd been sent along to keep him out of trouble. And he'd caused her some. By not listening.

She was watching him.

"It's all right, Jim. You don't need to say anything. Charlie's safe. The job is done and we can go home."

* * *

Saturday Evening
Halifax Homestead

The fire crackled cheerfully, just the right size, and a comforting counterpoint to the cold outside. The Halifax Homestead did not make the mistake of overheating its public rooms so Jim was pleasantly aware of the contrast.

The lamps, too, were comforting, casting gold light rather than blue, a throwback to the incandescent bulbs that had been replaced by the cold clarity of light emitting diodes. He gazed into the fire, his feet up on the coffee table. He was wearing borrowed slippers and had been promised the furniture was in no danger. He wasn't so sure about himself.

With Detective Tran's departure, the whole Homestead breathed a sigh of relief, but as the tension eased, reaction set in.

He and Ginny had spent the afternoon photographing tombstones and it had made him uneasy. He wasn't old enough to feel creeping mortality in any personal way, but he couldn't escape an awareness that the clock was ticking.

He pulled Ginny closer. She was curled up beside him, snuggling into his side, her eyelids drooping.

What would happen when they got back to Dallas? Would they part, go their separate ways? In Albany, she had tried to cast him off, and he had known in a heartbeat there was no going back. Not for him. But what of her?

Tomorrow they would say goodbye to Charlie and the Halifax staff, hand over the hostess gift, get in the SUV, and drive to the ferry. Once across the Bay of Fundy, they would retrieve the hatchback, park it in the hotel lot, and hand the keys to the concierge, with instructions to give them to the courier who would drive it to Albany for them.

On their way back, they would retrace their steps, staying at each of the Homesteads and sharing vacation gossip. They would both have to be careful, especially with Dr. Gordon. The success of their mission now depended on everyone believing that Charlie had actually drowned.

Jim was under additional orders to spend time with the lairds at each of the Homesteads, picking their brains and getting to know them. He didn't know what instructions his grandfather had given Ginny. Neither had told him.

He bent down and brushed her hair with his lips. She didn't move. She was asleep, asleep in his arms, and all Jim wanted in the whole wide world was for time to stand still and let him hold this moment, and her, forever.

* * *

ChapTER 56

Sunday Afternoon
The Bay of Fundy

On Sunday afternoon the two of them boarded the ferry. The day was fading and there was another front moving in, tossing the spray into the slanted columns of light, making tiny rainbows that vanished with the wind.

Ginny led the way to the lower deck, retrieved Charlie's pack from its locker, hauled it onto her shoulder, and tried to pretend it didn't hold a dead man's ghost. They would mail his possessions to Mrs. Robertson when they got ashore. That would sever the last of her ties to Charlie.

Unlike her earlier crossing, this time there was no fog and Ginny could see the Nova Scotian shoreline as it slid away. The rising tide surged toward the vessel in increasingly cobalt waves frosted with whitecaps and the taste of salt. No whales, though.

Jim had watched the cars being stowed, then made his way to the rail, taking in the sights, his face betraying nothing of his thoughts.

When the twilight settled over them and the vistas retreated into darkness, they moved inside, to escape the cold. They found a lounge with a movie screen Ginny hadn't noticed last time and settled down in the shadows at the back of the room.

Ginny had one leg tucked up under her, turned half-sideways to Jim. She studied him surreptitiously.

He'd been exceptionally polite today, to everyone, including her, as if suddenly aware how much of the success of their trip he owed to others.

But he'd been distant, too. Every word had sounded strained, every look wary, as if he expected her to lash out at him.

From the first, that first night at Hal's party, there had been laughter and lighthearted play. He'd been fun to be around, when he wasn't being autocratic. Fun, and kind, and gentle. He had wit and education and breeding. And courage, and honor, and—

He turned and looked her full in the face. "May I get you something to eat? Coffee, maybe?"

Ginny nodded. "Coffee, yes, please."

When he returned, he had fixed it exactly the way she liked. He settled back down to the movie, sipping his own cup and Ginny knew exactly how he liked his, as well.

* * *

"We're here." They joined the other passengers headed for the exit.

Ginny shivered as the cold air hit her, then led the way down the gangplank and onto the landing. They had to wait while the cars were unloaded, but eventually they were in the SUV, with the heater on.

Ginny looked around, trying to get her bearings in the glow from the street lamps. Luckily she had a good 'bump of direction'. She managed to guide him to the car park with only a small course correction.

"I hope no one has booted it," she said. "I didn't plan on being gone this long."

They were in luck, though. She had paid the charges using her alter ego's credit card and the machine had simply charged her for the additional two days. She dug out the keys to the hatchback, then climbed behind the wheel, and headed for the hotel, with Charlie's ghost sitting beside her.

"Women have all the power in a relationship."

Maybe so, but was it power she really wanted?

* * *

Sunday Night
Saint John, NB

They found the hotel without difficulty, cleaned out the hatchback, checked in, settled arrangements with the concierge, then retired to their room. Conventioneers had taken over the town for the week and the only room that had been left was the bridal suite. Jim seemed to find the arrangements amusing.

"You didn't want your own room? We could have gone somewhere else."

"Do I need a locked door between us?"

He dropped his bag on the sofa and came over, capturing her, and pulling her into a hug.

"No. You do not." He caught her eye and held it, his face and tone suddenly serious. "I promise you, Ginny, you will never need to put a locked door between us. Not now, not ever."

Ever. As in *happily ever after*. Ginny had her hands on his chest, one of them over his heart. She could feel the pulse through his shirt, could feel the way his muscles moved as he breathed. Flesh and bone and sinew. A living man. Male.

The chasm opened before her.

She broke out of his embrace, backed off two steps, then stopped and stood facing him, rubbing her hands on her pants.

On the other side of the chasm stood her future, if she wanted it. If she wasn't afraid to reach for it.

He grew very still, his eyes on her, then pulled the bottle of Scotch out of his bag, and poured whisky into two glasses. He handed one to her. She lifted the glass to her lips, and took a sip.

"I owe you an apology, Ginny."

She looked up to find his brow creased, his eyes on his drink.

"I haven't been completely honest with you." He drew in a breath, then looked up. "I've done things I'm not proud of, and I've been afraid to tell you. Afraid of what you might think of me."

Ginny waited.

"There was a party and too much alcohol. I passed out cold in a girl's bedroom. I don't even remember being arrested. I came to in a jail cell." He frowned. "She accused me of rape and I didn't know, for a while, whether I was guilty or not. My father put up the bail and enlisted the help of the Laird, who was a lawyer. He expedited the rape kit and it proved I didn't do it. But the incident remains on my record." He sighed. "I learned my lesson. I haven't been drunk since."

He caught her eye and held it. "No one has had cause to accuse me of that again and no one ever will. Not even a wife. Especially not a wife."

He took another sip of his drink, watching her. Waiting.

Ginny nodded, then drew breath.

"You already know the worst of me. I'm too stubborn and too independent to just take orders blindly. And I've been warned it's impossible for a man and a woman to be equal partners in a marriage."

"Is that what you want?"

"I want you to respect me, to listen to me."

He sighed, then dropped into the chair by the window. "I have another confession to make." He took a pull on his drink, then met her eye. "I'm jealous of my grandfather."

"Jealous?" Ginny's eyebrows rose.

Jim nodded. "I'm jealous of the relationship you have with him, the way you listen to him. And I hate being compared to him." He sighed. "But that's just me being childish. I know his worth and I want to be just like him when I grow up."

Ginny felt the tension in the room ease. "Me, too."

He smiled at her. "What else do you want to know?" he asked.

Ginny sucked in a breath. "Why did Sarah turn you down?"

The corner of his mouth curved into a rueful half smile. "She didn't want to move to Texas, to leave her family behind."

"*You* would have been her family."

He screwed up his face. "Well. Sort of. I suppose."

Ginny looked at him. "Sort of?" She saw him squirm.

"I think she was holding out for marriage."

Both of Ginny's eyebrows rose. "You asked her to come to Texas without proposing marriage to her?"

He nodded. "I had commitment issues."

She almost laughed out loud. "No wonder she refused!"

He nodded, then sighed. "I wasn't in love with her, not that way, and I knew it. I thought maybe I could grow into it, but she cut me loose instead."

He took a sip of his drink then set it aside. "I have a question for you, too. Did you love Hal?"

Ginny examined her soul. "There were things about him I loved. He had such a light-hearted outlook on life, and he wasn't afraid of my brain."

"But did you love *him*?"

She met Jim's eyes. "No."

He nodded. "Okay." She saw him lick his lips, then swallow. "Do you love *me*?"

Ginny took a long moment to consider her answer, thinking about all that had been said, all that had happened since the night Hal had introduced them, then nodded, a smile creeping across her face. "Yes."

"Are you sure?" He was studying her intently and she felt herself blush.

"Pretty sure."

His brow furrowed. "Mrs. Gordon asked me something I couldn't answer so I need to ask you." He met her eyes. "What do you want to do with your life, Ginny?"

She pulled in a deep breath, then answered him.

"I want to be absolutely essential to your health and happiness." She saw him smile, and hurried on. "I want to help you with whatever it is you decide you want to do with your life. To be your good right arm, the person you turn to when you need to work something out, the shoulder you cry on, the friend you know will always be there for you."

His smile widened. "I want that, too, for both of us."

Ginny felt a rush of relief and affection. A good man. She had found a *good* man.

"If I end up as Laird," he said, "and you are my wife, you will be the Matron."

She nodded.

He smiled at her. "You have such a talent for organizing. I'm sure you could run a Homestead exceptionally well."

It was Ginny's turn to squirm. "Yes, well. That's another thing we need to talk about. We didn't know who would succeed Himself. He had no family in Texas, no one to train, and I had no father."

She watched as Jim processed the idea, his smile fading.

"If I hadn't shown up, who would have been Laird after my grandfather?"

"I would, probably."

His eyes grew wide. "I thought it had to be a man."

Ginny shook her head. "Some of the Homesteads are run by women." She shrugged. "It wasn't a sure thing."

"But you were being groomed for the position."

She nodded. Ginny watched as his eyebrows rose.

"Grandfather told me you could be useful, but I had no idea he meant this."

"What he meant was, at least for the present, I know more than you do about how to run a Homestead. Can you handle that?"

He looked at her for a long moment, then nodded slowly. "I think I already knew." His brow furrowed suddenly. "Did he talk to you about it, before he called me?"

Ginny shook her head. "He didn't ask anyone, not even the council." She saw concern spread across Jim's face.

"How do you feel about that, Ginny, being supplanted by an outsider?"

She set down her drink and walked over to stand in front of him. She laid her hands on his shoulders and smiled.

"I think he was right. You will make an excellent Laird and if you decide you want the job, you will have my full support." She dimpled at him. "After you learn humility, of course."

He burst out laughing. "Oh, Ginny! Are you sure you want to take me on? It sounds like I'm going to be quite a project!"

"Well, that makes us even. Are you still willing to take *me* on?"

In answer, he rose and led her to a clear patch of carpet, then went down on one knee, took her hands in his, and looked up at her.

"Virginia Ann Forbes, you know I love you. Will you do me the honor of becoming my wife? Please?"

If she accepted him, there would be no going back. Neither a laird nor his lady could divorce.

It was terrifying to think of herself tied indissolubly to him, to his life, his fate. Even more terrifying to face life without him.

He watched her, his eyes alert, watchful. They were lovely eyes. Not laughing at the moment, but hopeful, tender, encouraging.

Courage. Everyone said she had courage. If that was so, why was she trembling? Her father's voice floated up to her, out of a memory. *"Courage is when you're scared out of your mind and you do it anyway."*

She took a shuddering breath then nodded.

"Aye, Mackenzie, I will."

* * *

CHAPTER 57

Dallas, TX

Ginny swirled the dark amber liquid around in her glass. There were three others with her at the Laird's table, Jim, Himself, and her mother.

It had taken them the better part of the day, starting around ten a.m. and culminating in this after-dinner libation. They had undoubtedly forgotten some detail of the trip, but the bulk of it was there.

Himself sighed. "We'll need tae spread th' word tha' Charlie was lost at sea."

Jim nodded. "Caught on video, story at eleven."

Ginny's eyes drifted up to find him winking at her.

She'd wept when she and Charlie parted. In an excess of sentiment, she'd handed over the beacon, with a comment about it helping him to find his way to his new home. He'd closed his fist around it, then thrown his arms around her, hugging her tightly. There was little chance they would meet again, but the Halifax Homestead would keep Angus informed.

"I'll arrange a memorial service. Sinia, will ye make a note, please?"

They'd gotten in late yesterday and been allowed to wait until today to report to the Laird, but she'd slept badly. She'd tossed and turned for hours before she finally identified the problem. No Jim.

"Detective Tran knows th' truth, ye say?"

She heard Jim's answer. "She knows, but she can't do anything about it. She didn't have enough evidence to convict him and now she's guilty of a cover-up. She can't give us away without implicating herself."

"An interestin' situation." There was a short pause. "Ginny, ye look as if ye've something ye want tae add."

They had agreed to wait until the business was finished and Jim had claimed the privilege of making the announcement, but she was sure the elders already knew. Suspected, at least.

"She does," Jim said. He got up from his chair and came around to her side of the table, standing behind her and putting his hands on her shoulders. She leaned back against him, reaching up to slide her hands into his, blushing in the approved manner of brides-to-be.

"I have an announcement to make," he said. "Ginny has agreed to be my wife. We're going to get married."

Her mother responded first, her face full of pleasure. "Oh, I'm so happy for you both!" The Laird was a bit slower, but no less enthusiastic. "Congratulations, lad! I wish ye both joy and long life."

What followed was the usual barrage of questions and speculations. They had decided to marry on Beltane, May the first. It was a lucky day to be wed, but two months off. Two months she would have to do without him. She pulled his hands down so that his face was level with hers, then whispered in his ear.

"Take me home."

He kissed her cheek, then addressed the elders. "It's been a long day. Please forgive us, but I'm going to take Ginny home, then take myself off to bed. We'll see you tomorrow."

Mrs. Forbes rose and held out her arms and Ginny watched

as Jim let himself be embraced and kissed. She found herself being pulled from her chair the next minute.

"God bless ye lass! God bless ye both!" She watched the Laird turn and lay a hand on Jim's arm. "A word, lad, afore ye go."

The two slipped into the kitchen and Ginny found herself wondering what could have put that uneasy expression on the Laird's face. Ten minutes later, Jim emerged with an equally uneasy expression.

He helped her on with her coat, then escorted her into his car and set off in the direction of the loch. Neither said a word as he drove her home. He followed her inside, then up the stairs, and into her bedroom.

She turned to face him. "Don't leave me!"

He pulled her into his arms. "I can't stay. Not until we're married."

"How am I going to survive two months without you?"

He kissed her thoroughly. "We'll be together every day and after that, every night as well."

"You work nights," she reminded him.

"So do you."

"Oh, right!"

She looked up into his face. "What did Himself say to you in the kitchen?"

"He told me why my father left Dallas."

"Oh! Tell me."

"He said my mother had a family problem that forced her to go back to Virginia for a while and rather than let her face it alone, he took me and went with her."

"Is that all?"

"It was enough. Grandfather told him his place was here, with his people and his job, learning how to be Laird. My father told him his place was with his wife."

The corner of Jim's mouth twitched. "He also told me he regrets trying to force his son to stay, that if he hadn't been so mulish, there might not have been a breach in the family. He apologized for being a pig-headed fool and asked me to forgive him." Jim lifted her chin and smiled down into her eyes. "I think he knows, if pushed, I would do the same, follow my heart."

"Oh, Jim!" She buried her face in his shirt, feeling his arms close around her and his lips on her hair.

He held her for a moment, then pushed her out of his arms.

"Put your nightgown on. I'll tuck you in before I leave."

"I don't wear one."

His brow furrowed. "What about that tee shirt I saw you in, the one with the tartan pattern?"

"I only wear that while traveling, in case of fire."

She saw his pupils dilate. "Ginny Forbes, you're making it impossible for me to get any sleep tonight."

She smiled up at him. "Misery loves company."

He swept her up into his arms, took the three steps necessary to cross the room, dropped her on the bed, then bent down and kissed her again.

"Goodnight!"

With that, he was gone. She heard him hurrying down the stairs, then out the front door, exchanging goodnights with her mother as she came through from the back hall.

Mrs. Forbes climbed the stairs, then settled down on the end of the bed.

"Are you pleased?" Ginny asked.

She nodded, smiling. "We'll have fun pulling a wedding together in only two months, but I expect we can do it. Himself will make sure the Hall is available. The food, music, and dancing are already in place. We'll need to reserve the church, order flowers and invitations, arrange places for everyone to stay, and you'll need a gown."

Her mother cocked an eye at her. "I have a question for you. Marrying Jim means you'll be the Lady of Loch Lonach. That's a big responsibility. When Angus dies, you'll have to give up your personal life and devote yourself entirely to the Homestead. Are you sure that's what you really want?"

Ginny nodded. "Yes, but I hope he lives a long time yet. Jim and I have some things we'd like to do first."

"All right then. Sleep well my darling daughter."

Ginny kissed her mother goodnight, then closed the door and prepared for bed. In two months she would no longer be a free woman. The thought should have terrified her. Instead, it exalted her. Jim's wife. His helper. His companion and friend and playmate. And he—*he* would be hers.

She turned off the light and snuggled down under the covers, trying to settle down, but sleep wouldn't come. The trip to Canada had been full of things that went wrong. *Nothing*, she thought, *will be allowed to get in the way of my marrying Jim. Nothing!* But, having faced the possibility, she could see nothing but disaster.

She tossed and turned, imagining horrors and scaring herself wide awake. In the bleakest part of the night, in desperation, she reached for her phone. He answered on the first ring.

"I knew you'd call."

"Did you know I was going to have a nervous breakdown?"

"I knew you were feeling abandoned. Did you have a nightmare?"

"I didn't get that far. I can't fall asleep."

"Have you tried warm milk?"

"No, damn you! I don't want milk! I want you!"

She heard him laughing and felt the warmth seeping into her soul. As long as he could laugh, she could cope. She tucked the phone to her ear, listening to the murmur of his voice, to his soothing words, his assurances that she was safe and he was hers. She closed her eyes, and let herself believe; believe in him, believe in herself, believe in their new life together.

Two months. The time would fly, and drag, and she would sweat every minute of it. Two months. Eight weeks. Sixty two days. One thousand, four hundred, and eighty-eight hours. A lot could happen in two months, but it had just better not try!

THE END

GLOSSARY

Airsaid (pronounced "air-i-sayed") – full length wool, fleece or silk cloak that goes from the neck to the heels.

Ain – own

Bairn(s) – child / children

Bonnie – handsome

Braw – brave

Canna – cannot

Canny – clever, shrewd

Ceilidh – party

Claymore – sword

Cù-Sìth (pronounced "coo-shee") – a mythical, large, shaggy dog that lives in the Scottish Highlands and foreshadows a death

Dinna – did not / do not

Doesnae – does not

Flistert – flustered

Ghillies – flexible, lace-up dancing shoes, akin to ballet slippers

Gied - gave

Gormless – (Old Norse) heedless

Ken – know

Kine – cattle

Nay – no

Nicht – night

No – not

Noo – now

Sgian dubh (pronounced "skeen doo") – black knife

Sunkhaze (pronounced "sunk haze") – concealing outlet

Uisge-beatha – "water of life", aka "whisky"

Wee dram – an indeterminate amount of whisky

FINAL FLING
LOCH LONACH MYSTERIES, BOOK FOUR

You are cordially invited to join Jim and Ginny as they prepare for a not-so-typical wedding in *Final Fling: Loch Lonach Mysteries, Book Four.*

It was Annabelle, a shaggy Hieland Coo, who found the mangled remains of a woman's corpse lying on the edge of the Highland Games athletic field. When the police decide Ginny's Maid of Honor is the prime suspect, Ginny vows to do whatever it takes to clear her friend's name. It's a race against time with Ginny's wedding day—and her life—hanging in the balance.

If you enjoyed reading *Viking Vengeance*, would you **please leave a review** on Goodreads, Amazon, or your favorite book vendor? Thank you!

THE LOCH LONACH COLLECTION

The Loch Lonach Mysteries
- *The Arms of Death:* Loch Lonach Mysteries, Book One
- *The Swick and the Dead:* Loch Lonach Mysteries, Book Two
- *Viking Vengeance:* Loch Lonach Mysteries, Book Three
- *Final Fling*: Loch Lonach Mysteries, Book Four

Loch Lonach Short Stories
- *Dead Easy*
- *Duncan Died Dunkin'*
- *The Aviemore Cabin Boy*
- *Fifteen Minutes*
- *Out on a Limb*

Loch Lonach Histories
- *Loch Lonach, Its History and Inhabitants*

Award winning and addictive, every book is a five-star read!

To find out more about Ginny, Jim, and the Loch Lonach Mystery Series visit www.lochlonach.com

Would you risk losing everything for a chance at something better?

The Beverwyck Homestead inhabitants were used to harsh winter weather. Not so the visitors from Texas. When Jim Mackenzie and Ginny Forbes decide to take a Sunday afternoon stroll in the pristine wonderland outside their windows, they find their nerves and their wits tested. Lovely to look at, nature can't always be trusted and they find themselves literally out on limb, with death only an icy misstep away.

SIGN ME UP!

https://dl.bookfunnel.com/et9yw1y0qw

Click to join the Loch Lonach Community.

Get a **FREE** Short Story and access to insider news, Scottish lore, and entertaining details about life on the Loch Lonach Homestead.

ABOUT THE AUTHOR

MAGGIE FOSTER is a seventh-generation Texan of Scottish descent. In addition to being steeped in Scottish traditions and culture, she has spent a lifetime in healthcare as a nurse, lawyer, educator, and redhead. Her interests include history, genealogy, music, dancing, travel, dark chocolate, good whisky, and men in kilts, not necessarily in that order.

You can contact her at:
maggiesmysteries@gmail.com or
Maggie@maggiesmysteries.com

Website – www.lochlonach.com
GoodReads – www.goodreads.com/maggiefoster
Facebook – www.facebook.com/lochlonach/
Twitter – www.Twitter.com/maggiefoster55
Instagram – www.instagram.com/scottishsleuthsofdallas/
LinkedIn – www.linkedin.com/in/maggie-foster-lochlonach

Six Virtual Ways to Support Your Favorite Author

Buy their books
Write reviews
Recommend on Goodreads
Request at your library
Post pictures holding their books
Sign up for the e-mail list

Made in United States
Orlando, FL
27 July 2022

20256896R00245